The
LAZARUS
GATE

The
LAZARUS
GATE

MARK A. LATHAM

TITAN BOOKS

The Lazarus Gate
Print edition ISBN: 9781783296804
E-book ISBN: 9781783296811

Published by Titan Books
A division of Titan Publishing Group Ltd
144 Southwark Street, London SE1 0UP

First edition: September 2015
10 9 8 7 6 5 4 3 2 1

A CIP catalogue record for this title is available from the British Library.

Printed in the USA.

To Alison, for ensuring every day that I never grow up.

PROLOGUE

13th January 1890, 6.00 a.m.

LONDON, ENGLAND

The sound of the explosion had barely stopped ringing in the sergeant's ears when he snatched a glimpse of the thin man once again, vanishing around the corner. Somewhere nearby, three harsh trills of a police whistle sounded and, shaking his head to clear his senses, Sergeant Clegg snatched up his hat and steeled himself to join the pursuit.

Moments ago, Clegg had been in a daze, dabbing at his bleeding forehead whilst slumped against the portico of a coffee house. Now he was able to take stock of the situation, and was relieved that few people had been injured in the blast. It was early morning, and but for a few street traders laying out their stalls, street sweepers, and some eager clerks trying to get ahead of the day's work, it seemed that casualties would be limited. The same could not be said of his detail; he had counted three officers unconscious, and a further two groaning in agony by the side of the road. Smoke drifted across the street, and charred debris was spilled over the cobbles like coal from a scuttle. Shopfronts were splintered and smashed.

Clegg's shift had been long and wearying, and by rights it should have come to an end over an hour ago. But police work had a way of pressing a man beyond his limits, and Clegg now found himself pursuing these so-called anarchists through the streets of the West End. He was only dimly aware of the chaos unfurling around him, and of his colleagues dashing after him along Bond Street.

Threep-threep-threep! Constable Harris's whistle snapped Clegg from his reverie, and he squinted to clear his vision, in time to see the stocky policeman charging along the road, waving and whistling as he went, heading towards the junction of Oxford Street. Clegg shouted to any officers who were uninjured to follow him, and staggered off in pursuit. Had Harris seen the anarchists? If he had, there'd be hell to pay.

There were four of them now, with Harris in the lead. Constables Gleghorn and Regis seemed only lightly injured, and had picked themselves up after hearing the commotion. The sergeant's mind raced. Why would dynamiters target a near-empty street? What could be the point?

The sky overhead was a deep indigo, and the gaslights still burned, though they struggled to penetrate the remnants of last night's particular and the palls of grey smoke from the explosion. This didn't make any sense. Clegg pushed these thoughts aside, and reached deep inside himself for reserves of energy, redoubling his efforts to catch up with Constable Harris and whomever he was chasing. The policemen had no sooner reached the end of the road when the sound of clattering hooves filled the air, and a Black Maria approached them at speed from the right, skittering out of a side-street that led to Hanover Square. The two horses pulling it sweated and snorted, their exertions clear to see. The police coach slowed to turn onto New Bond Street and join the chase, and the man seated next to the driver shouted instructions to Clegg. It was the detective from Special Branch, the man in black who had sent them on this assignment just hours ago. Clegg had no idea how the man had requisitioned a police coach so quickly, but he was glad to see reinforcements regardless.

'That's it man, keep going!' shouted the detective, in his Irish lilt. 'We almost have them.'

Clegg urged his legs to keep pace with the Maria, but the events of the day were starting to take their toll on the stout sergeant. His lungs felt raw and his chest pounded. The heavy uniform, cape and helmet felt more and more like a suit of armour.

When Clegg rounded the bend at the end of New Bond Street, the rising sun glared at him along the wide open thoroughfare of Oxford Street. His vision blurred, and his fatigue got the better of him. He pulled up sharply and squinted at the road ahead. Gleghorn and Regis overtook him, their youthful enthusiasm and desire for justice outweighing their bodies' requirements for rest. Sergeant Clegg took a deep breath, and pushed onwards, albeit at a slow jog. He could hear one of his men calling back to him, 'Come on, Sarge. There's three of 'em. We've got the bastards!'

The Black Maria was up ahead, stationary now, and there were more policemen at the scene. He could hear shouts and cries, and then a gunshot rang out into the early morning air. The few people who had seen fit to walk along Oxford Street at this hour scattered away from the commotion, and Clegg forgot about his tired legs and dry throat and raced towards the fight. Another gunshot rang out. Clegg reached the Maria, and was just about to rush into the fray when a dazzling flash of light saturated the area, accompanied by a high-pitched humming noise. No sooner had Clegg checked his run than Harris flew past him, like a rag doll, landing in a heap ten feet away on the cobbled stones. The horses at the front of the Black Maria whinnied and reared, and broke free of their driver's control. They bolted, taking the police coach with them, and headed back along Oxford Street as fast as they could go. Clegg was scared now. He took one look at the burly lad on the ground, clenched his teeth, and turned to face the danger. The coach was gone and with it his only cover, but he was still aware of the constables around him, and of the Special Branch man. Ahead of him was the Marble Arch, and the remaining policemen were fanning out, brandishing their truncheons menacingly, whilst the detective pointed a stubby pistol towards the archway. Clegg took his place in the line, in time to see the thin man—the man they'd pursued all over the West End this morning—waving a gun in the direction of his colleagues with menace. The leg of a second fugitive disappeared through the arch, and Sergeant Clegg squinted in puzzlement for an instant. Hadn't the leg of the running anarchist been rather slender? Had he really seen the flash of lace at the stockinged ankle? A woman! Clegg pushed such thoughts aside, for surely his mind was playing tricks on him. In any case there was no way out for them now. The sadistic buggers would take cover in the archway, behind those walls of thick white marble, but they'd have to give it up eventually. They were in the middle of an exposed stone square—a courtyard surrounded by wide roads—and the archway was gated secure. This was their last stand.

There was another flash of light, although not as bright as before, and definitely coming from the arch this time. The thin man winked at them, turned his back and darted into the archway. But the detective had other ideas, and fired his gun again, this time finding his mark. The thin man dropped to the ground, the back of his skull a bloody mess.

'Come on!' shouted the detective, and darted towards the arch. The other officers had surrounded the edifice, but Clegg was afraid—the fugitives were surely armed.

'Hold on, sir!' Clegg cried, and dashed forwards, hoping to reach his superior before he got himself killed. But he need not have worried. When Clegg and the detective reached the archway, there was but one anarchist, the thin man, and he was dead where he'd been shot. Clegg looked around in every direction, and then stared through the archway. On the other side was Regis, looking dumbfounded. There had been three anarchists, he was sure. So where were they?

'Don't just stand there gawping, Sergeant,' the Irish detective snapped. 'Search the body.'

Clegg stepped forward to do as he had been instructed. The thin man was sprawled out on the ground in the shadow of the arch, his brains splattered on the cobbles. The sergeant was about to turn the body over, when he noticed something that made him pause. The anarchist had fallen inside the arch, his right hand outstretched towards the bronze gates of the monument. But there was no sign of the gun that he had been wielding just moments ago. In fact, his right hand was mutilated—the fingers seemingly sliced off cleanly, with no trace of blood. Clegg looked around, confused, and saw the detective looming over him. Clegg didn't need to see his shadowed expression to know that it was as grim as always.

'Search his body,' the man in black repeated.

'But, sir...' Clegg tailed off. He couldn't understand what had just happened; any of it.

Then he noticed that high-pitched humming noise was starting again, only this time it came from the corpse, and was getting louder. The Special Branch man was looking at his pocketwatch.

'Do it now, man!' he hissed at Clegg. 'We don't have much time.'

13th January 1890, 3.00 a.m.

YAMETHIN DISTRICT, BURMA

The manacles around his wrists and ankles curbed his progress, but nothing could stop John Hardwick from walking out of this hellhole. His matted hair was dirty and lice-ridden, and his beard scratched his chest as his head hung low from fatigue, yet his eyes were cold, determined. He felt the rifle butt push against his back once more, a sign that his captor was tired of his woefully slow shuffling.

'*Myan myan lou!*' one of the Burmese guards barked.

John picked up the pace as best he could. His feet were bare, filthy and bleeding. His prison garb was stained and tattered, and he felt so weak it was painful to walk. When he had first emerged from his confinement, he had felt like Jeremiah released, and probably looked not unlike the prophet either. The warm air felt sweeter than anything he had ever known, though he had to squint even at the moonlight, as his eyes were so unaccustomed to light. How long had he been kept in that squalid cell? He wagered months, but it was hard to tell. This was the first time for as long as he could remember he had seen a guard and not been either beaten or force-fed opium, and his thoughts were confused. He tried to clear his head and take stock of his situation, his military training and experience coming back to him now that he was out of that pit of a cell.

He was being marched towards the perimeter wall of the tiny prison complex, along a dry dirt path that sloped down a steep hill. Tall, spindly palm trees lined the track on either side, black against the night sky like spectators on a gallows-walk, perhaps. John could just make out the silhouetted huts and rickety tower that passed for a guardhouse here, and by the moon and starlight he could see that there were half a dozen armed guards beside the tall bamboo gates, and some activity outside them. That such small numbers of rebels had proved sufficient to hold this position in a country that was mostly British-ruled was unnerving. This region had been claimed in the name of Her Majesty almost five years hence, and although the local government paid its taxes to the British governor at Rangoon, the hills were still wild and full of bandits and freedom fighters.

John was flanked by two guards. One set the pace, yanking his chains to hurry him along, the other strolled more nonchalantly. John knew the little bastard only too well, though only as 'Maung'—an honorific name of sorts, which the sadistic and diminutive rebel was entirely undeserving of. A few hours ago, John had been dragged from his cell for more midnight interrogations. Why they persisted in the charade God only knew—if John had known anything of interest, he'd have told them long ago. In fact, after all the drugs and the beatings, he'd probably have told them many times. He couldn't be sure. By now his intelligence must be woefully out of date, and yet the Burmese rebels continued to torture and interrogate him, and the other prisoners, on an almost daily basis. John believed truly that they were merely going through the motions to sate their sadistic desires, and that they hadn't killed him because one day they'd need a British officer to trade. Was this that day? Perhaps, but he was unsure. All he knew was that his torture had ended, for now at least, and he had been brought outside. Outside! This was the first time that he'd breathed the open air for what seemed like an eternity. He refused to let the fact that it was the air of this God-forsaken country sully his pleasure.

Before he knew it, John was bundled into an ox-cart beside a muscular guard, who grunted at him contemptuously. The cart rumbled away from the prison, flanked by two mounted rebels. John looked back to see Maung spit at the ground in his direction, watching his prisoner's departure with enmity in his eyes.

By the time the trade was made, the sun was already high in the sky and the day was hot. They were no longer in the foothills of the Yamethin District. The Burmese guards who accompanied him now were not rebels, but liveried servants of the Crown. His manacles were gone, and he was being half-carried by disciplined soldiers into the shade of a small courtyard. John's head swam. He had passed in and out of consciousness for the whole journey, oblivious to the fact that he must have travelled nearly three hundred miles.

'Welcome back to civilisation, Captain Hardwick. Welcome to Rangoon.' The Englishman who greeted John smiled broadly. That smile was the last thing John saw before he passed out and was caught by the colonial guards.

LONDON, ENGLAND

The Artist daubed the last stroke of oil paint onto his canvas and set down his brush. Smiling to himself, he stepped back to admire his handiwork. Any other man would have struggled to see the painting in the wan light of the apartment, but the Artist appeared pleased.

'Another triumph, my sweet pets. But what does it all mean? Shall we meditate upon it, hmm?' The Artist spoke as if to no one, but turned his head at the sound of movement in the corner of the room, from where his pets looked on.

The Artist pulled a loose robe of Chinese silk over his tattooed nakedness, tying the cord at the waist before tossing his long black hair free of the garment. He strode across the wood-floored room, his slippered feet making barely a sound. The midday sun struggled to find its way into the austere room through two small, grimy windows that overlooked a half-derelict warren of slums and gambling houses in the dark bosom of the Isle of Dogs. The few rays that pushed through were diffused by the constant swirl of opium smoke from the den below. The Artist walked to his bed and sat down upon it, savouring the feel of the thick mattress and satin bedclothes. Reaching to his nightstand he picked up a large glass pipe, lit it and took a draw, sighing as the opiates entered his system. He closed his eyes momentarily, savouring the sensation, before setting down the pipe and taking up instead a silver-tipped cane. Grasping the head of the cane, he rapped its tip hard against the wooden floor. Almost immediately, he could hear footsteps on the stairs below, racing to his door, followed mere moments later by a quiet knocking.

'Come!'

A burly Chinese servant entered the room, bringing with him a billow of smoke from the corridor beyond. He bowed low, his black braided hair almost touching the floor as he did so.

'Master,' he said. 'I am at your service.'

The Artist rose from the bed and stepped forward. Tall and lithe, he towered over the servant who himself was not a small man.

'Hu, I have several errands for you.' The Artist gestured towards a far corner, where six canvases lay wrapped in brown paper beside a lacquered cabinet. 'Deliver those today, and be sure to insist upon the usual price. I am in no mood for bartering.'

Hu bowed again in acknowledgement and waited for further instructions, absent-mindedly fingering the wicked hook that passed for his left hand.

'I would also ask of you to call on Mr. Ruskin again. Tell him that his canvas is ready, but it is too large to move with any degree of secrecy. He must come here—it is in his best interests to view the painting before month's end. And it will be double the usual price. Remember, Hu, that Mr. Ruskin requests the utmost discretion in our dealings. You will be invisible on this errand, understood?'

Hu nodded.

'That is all for now,' the Artist concluded.

Hu moved for the parcels, but hesitated when his eye caught the fresh canvas in the centre of the room.

'What is it, Hu?' asked the Artist, impatience creeping into his tone.

'Will you require a... buyer for your latest work today, master?' Hu asked.

'Ah... no. Not today. This is something altogether more interesting than a mere commission.'

Hu gathered the parcels and bowed again. A bumping and scratching from the closet in the corner caught his attention, and he bowed once more before hurrying backwards in the direction of the door, casting a nervous glance at the corner before heading down the stairs whence he had come. The Artist strode across the room towards the closet, pausing only to take down a jar from a shelf on the wall. When he reached the closet, he reached inside the jar for some strips of dried pork, which he threw down to his pets.

'Yes, yes. You see it too, don't you, my pets; my muses? This is most unexpected. The picture shows us what will come to pass, but how should one interpret such an image? If I am right, then it is all happening rather sooner than expected.' He paused to throw more meat into the closet. Chains rattled as his pets scrabbled for the titbits.

'What am I to do with this information, do you think? Who can I trust?' His ears pricked up as a low murmuring began. He smiled as one of his pets struggled to make a noise—first a gurgling, then a mumble.

'L... L... Lazarussss,' came the weak reply. The Artist's smile broadened with pleasure.

'Yes, my sweet. I rather thought you'd say that. Who's a clever girl?'

PART 1

The world was never made;
It will change, but it will not fade.
So let the wind range;
For even and morn
Ever will be
Through eternity.
Nothing was born;
Nothing will die;
All things will change.

ALFRED, LORD TENNYSON

ONE

FROM THE JOURNAL OF JOHN HARDWICK

3rd January 1891

As I sit here at my desk to write this narrative, outside my window the night draws in all too quickly, and the orange-hued London fog that so characterises winter in this great city has dropped. It is at once enveloping, smothering and yet oddly comforting, comforting because it means that I am home at last. Little less than a year ago I never would have dreamt that it could be so.

The events I am about to record are true insofar as my memory allows. When reading the memoirs and monographs of others, it has often occurred to me that the recorded facts contained within cannot be wholly accurate. The human brain, after all, can only store so much information before it becomes fragmented or distorted. Therefore I have set down in writing every relevant detail as faithfully as I am humanly able, such as my skill with words will allow. I testify to you that this tale is true and in earnest. Though you might well think this story odd, or impolitic, or even unbelievable, it must be told—for who could believe that this document is anything but a work of fiction after reading it? I can scarcely believe it myself, and I wish it were not the truth. For what this 'adventure' has taught me is that there truly are more things in heaven and earth—to misquote the Bard—than one can dream of. And precious few of them are wholesome. I am changed, quite irrevocably, by my experiences. I have learned, this past year, what fear truly is, and I doubt if I shall ever sleep well again knowing it.

This then, is my story; the true and honest testimony of John Hardwick.

28th March 1890

My arrival in London had been unceremonious, but nonetheless long awaited. I had spent forty days at sea with but two brief stops, and no hardship that may have lain in store for me could have dampened my enthusiasm for dry land. Of course, the English weather and the grimy London docks conspired to do just that, but it seemed like paradise to me. I disembarked the Navy steam cutter, HMS *Gannet*, for what I hoped was the final time, finding myself peering through thick swirls of mist on a drear and chilly morning. I closed my eyes to drink in the sounds and smells of London—labourers and ships' captains calling out and barking orders; bells tolling from departing ships across the mist-wreathed Thames; the creaking of ropes and timbers; the clanking of chains, winches and pulleys; the smell of tobacco, coffee, rum and sugar drifting from containers, and mingling with the salty air and smoky London particular. This, then, was home. A home that I had not seen in some six years, yet which still burned brightly in my memories.

My escort awaited me at the gates, and he was not quite what I had been expecting. Not that I'd really known what to expect. Captain James Denny of the Royal Horse Guards was a young, thin-faced man with a surprisingly garrulous nature and easy sense of humour. He and the two soldiers he had brought with him were not in uniform, but presented me with salutes regardless. When I returned the honour, Denny winked and said, 'Oh no, sir. You're a civilian now.' I cracked a smile, albeit a humourless one.

Captain Denny, who insisted I call him Jim, was under instruction to meet me and help me get my bearings. He was at my disposal for a day or two, and whilst I initially felt irked that Horse Guards had sent a nursemaid for a man of my experience, I quickly became at ease in Jim's company and was glad of the companionship. No sooner had we stepped outside the main gateway to the docklands than my head swam. Any sense of relief I felt at the British weather, the cobbled streets and plain architecture was immediately countered by my confusion. I had hoped for a swift return to a more familiar district of the city and, as if reading my mind, Jim showed me to a waiting cab. The soldiers took my few bags—a great relief, for I was still gaunt and weak from my long convalescence—and secured them on the cab's stowage, and in a trice we were away.

My first task, and one of no small importance, was to find somewhere to live. My father had spent so much of his later life on the move that anything resembling a family home had long since been lost to me. After Mother had died my father had grudgingly supported me, but even then I had been unable to lay down roots whilst my studies took up most of my time. What had become of our old properties after Father's death remained a mystery to me.

When I remarked that I had no idea where I would room, Captain Denny became quite animated.

'My dear fellow,' he exclaimed, 'it seems the world is your oyster! You must ride with us to Westminster and seek suitable accommodation.'

I baulked at the idea, and he realised almost before he had finished speaking that lodging in Westminster was beyond my means. Not that I truly understood what my means were, but the bookkeeping would also have to wait for now.

'Of course, if you desire something more, ah, "homely" while you become acclimatised to the city,' he continued, correcting himself as he went along, 'then I can show you some marvellous guesthouses. Let's get you some rooms, courtesy of Her Majesty's armed forces, eh? I know a good place in Bloomsbury if it suits.'

He smiled warmly, and I could detect no real snobbishness. The army looks after its own, and until I had seen the state of my accounts I was rather glad of someone to pick up the bills and organise things for me. I accepted his offer, and he instructed the driver to take us to the north end of Gower Street. I knew the area of Bloomsbury to be an unassuming district, with a reputation for being frequented by intellectuals, artists and dreamy dilettantes, and I was sure it was a place in which I could be anonymous. I craved peace and quiet, at least for a while, without the pressure of keeping up appearances. I felt agoraphobic, like an animal too long in captivity, uncertain of the conditions of its release. I tried to put aside such foolishness but, as we rode, I confided in Denny that there was more to my choice of lodgings than just assets.

'In truth,' I explained, 'I do want somewhere homely, as you put it. I've been away for too long, Jim; experienced more than anyone's fair share out East. I don't mind telling you that I was already feeling stifled when I reached the embassy in Hong Kong—every dinner a formal one, every conversation stuffy and centred on politics. I just want to lay my head on a soft pillow and eat some hearty food that hasn't been prepared by the finest chefs money can buy. A comfortable boarding house sounds far more appealing to me right now than a stuffy hotel or large, empty townhouse. Does that make any kind of sense?'

Jim tipped his head back and laughed. 'Not really, old boy, I'd live in first-rate hotels all my life given half a chance—but I think if I were in your shoes I wouldn't make much sense either.' I couldn't help but laugh with him, and yet I wondered what would happen to him if he were sent out to the front line, far away from the finer things in life to which he was so obviously accustomed. Would he be so ready with a jest if he'd seen all that I had?

The growler rattled its way along cobbled streets, the sound of the horses' hooves almost drowned out by the rhythmic clattering caused by the steel-rimmed wheels of the carriage. I gazed out of the small window as Jim prattled on about all that was current in London; the latest stage shows, museum exhibitions, fashionable writers and society scandals. He was rarely serious, and I wondered how on earth he could command the respect of his men. One soldier rode with us, whilst the other accompanied the driver. The man in our cab was a youthful private, not a day over eighteen I guessed, conspicuous by his silence.

'You know,' said Jim, 'our fathers knew each other. Colonel Denny often talked about Brigadier Hardwick. He was a good soldier, by all accounts.'

'Yes, he was. It was all he knew. And Colonel Denny? Is he…?'

'Oh, he's very much alive, the old goat,' Jim laughed. 'Terrorising the servants, running the old house like a military academy.'

'I know that part,' I said, staring out of the window. 'I often think I should have just given in, and joined up sooner.'

'But you had other dreams. Fathers always want their sons to follow in their footsteps, whether they want to or not. I've seen it before—luckily, when I was a boy, I just wanted to be a cavalryman; and here I am.'

'I wish you more luck than I've had,' I said, earnestly. 'Following in my father's footsteps hasn't been quite what I'd expected.'

'Ah, yes. I heard you had a rough time of it. Wounded? Or captured?' He looked as though he regretted the question as soon as it escaped his lips.

'Captured. Six months, near as damn it.' Jim looked at me,

partly pityingly, partly in wonder.

'I hear conditions out there...' Jim stopped short.

'The Burmese rebels have methods of torture that are alien to an Englishman. Even now the memories are... well, let's just say I don't like to dwell on it. It was only after my release that I discovered how long I had been imprisoned.'

'I don't mean to pry, old boy...' Jim said.

'No, it's fine,' I said, somewhat disingenuously. I wondered if Jim had been ordered to coax answers from me. I had experienced plenty of that recently, but I had no desire to hide anything from the army, no matter how painful the memories.

'Why did the rebels release you? Did you ever find out?' Jim asked.

'No one knows. It was sudden and unexpected—maybe they realised I wasn't going to talk, and decided that they should get some value from me rather than kill me. The rebels contacted the Burmese police only on the morning of my release, and arranged an exchange—six captured rebel fighters for me. Thankfully, a British corporal had been stationed nearby with local forces, and had sanctioned the deal—otherwise I would probably still be languishing in a cell, or dead of malnutrition, or worse. I don't even remember being transferred to their care. In fact, I barely remember anything before I reached Rangoon almost two weeks afterwards. My old commanding officer, Colonel Swinburne, was waiting for me. It took three weeks before I was able to walk without a cane. I remember strolling with him in the grounds of the barracks, smoking cigars and taking a glass of brandy, when he told me that my tour of duty was over; that I was going home. Despite ten years' service, six of those spent overseas, I put up no resistance. Once the colonel decided I was well enough to travel, I donned my uniform for the last time and headed overland to our territory in China.'

'And then in Hong Kong... you were discharged with full honours? Must have been a relief, after everything.'

'I suppose so,' I smiled unconvincingly. 'At Hong Kong I spent a single day and night in the company of a group of British officers at the embassy, and that was the end of my service to the Crown. I took ship the next day as a civilian. I cannot feign disappointment—after everything I had been through I must confess that I'd found it difficult to look to my future career in the army. But now here I am at home, and I have no idea what to do with myself.'

Jim looked at me sympathetically. I avoided his gaze. My honourable discharge from the army had left me reeling. I knew that I would receive a fair pension, and that I had at least a small income from my father's old holdings, though I expected no inheritance from him. But I had known little except a military life, and with no family or property to speak of, I knew it would be hard work to carve a niche for myself back in England. I suppose the prospect was daunting, for I had spent months outside anything resembling normality, and the last few weeks in a sort of dream-like state where my convalescence could happily have taken for ever.

'After all that—you miss it, don't you?' Jim asked.

'It made me sad in a way that I can't really explain. Yes—I miss it. Out there a soldier can make a difference, if only he does his duty. Here... I don't know what a soldier can do here. And I'm not even a soldier any more, am I?'

Jim patted me on the arm. 'This is London, dear boy, seat of the Empire; greatest city in the world. You can do anything you put your mind to. Write your memoirs, make your fortune. You'll soon find your feet, you'll see. And besides, the army looks out for its own. We'll help you find your feet.'

From that point on, Jim seemed determined to talk about other things, and to take my mind off the past. Jim was a bit of a dilettante, perhaps, but he was a cheerful sort, and he helped the journey pass quickly. We followed the great curve of the Thames from the docks at Wapping to the City proper. We passed the yawning, open mouth of London Bridge, which was already busy with traffic even before seven in the morning. Great overladen carts rumbled towards the many docks with their goods, while omnibuses trundled behind, early morning workers stuck behind the trade traffic in their bid to get to their shops and offices on the opposite side of the river.

We entered the quieter streets of Blackfriars and the tree-lined Victoria Embankment, before sweeping northwards past Whitehall and up Tottenham Court Road. The great thoroughfare was like an avenue passing through several towns—so many high streets, each with their own character. On some, the fishmongers were gathered outside with their stalls of fresh fish from the early deliveries. On others, tailors, cobblers and haberdashers were setting up shop, and on others still were costermongers selling fruit, vegetables, salted pork and more. Young boys in flat caps ran back and forth with messages, parcels and bundles of newspapers. It seemed the further up the road we travelled, the livelier and busier London became, as the morning broke.

Just as I thought the traffic up ahead would delay us, the driver veered along a side street and finally out onto our destination, which was not Gower Street as I'd expected, but George Street to the north. I shot a quizzical look at Jim.

'Oh, yes. It's not quite as run-down as you expected, eh? I wouldn't do that to you. It's a top-drawer lodging, but the proximity to Euston makes the rent a snip.' He grinned.

I laughed, and made work of climbing down from the growler. I was about to get my bags, but the two soldiers were there before me.

'Now,' said Jim, 'I must introduce you to your landlady, Mrs. Whitinger. Let me do the talking; if she sees you with that beard at this hour I'm sure she'll think you've come to rob her. You must shave it off at your earliest convenience, by the way—it's simply not the fashion for the younger man.'

I started to understand Jim's character. I imagined that, in his dress uniform, medals, sabre and hat he cut a fine figure at society balls. I didn't fancy his chances in battle, but I also did not hold that against him. Let him make japes and dance, and woo the eligible young ladies while he could, as perhaps I should have done a decade ago.

'Are you sure Mrs. Whitinger will have rooms?' I asked uncertainly.

'Oh, quite sure. She keeps the middle apartment free for officers in need. The last tenant was my friend Daniel, but he got a promotion last month and moved out. Been vacant ever since.' That wink again. 'The flat, that is, not Dan.'

We stepped onto the broad stone steps to the entrance of 11 George Street. It was an unassuming terraced house of dark brick, with large sash windows on each of its three floors. The front door was clean and looked as new, and the window boxes outside the ground-floor windows were tidy, and full of daffodils in bloom, betokening a house-proud occupant. The frosted glass rose above the door glowed with the light from within. Thus seeing that at least one resident was indeed up and about, Jim rapped firmly at the door. We waited less than half a minute before hearing the sound of the bolt being drawn back, and the door opened. Before us stood a small yet stern-looking lady of advancing years, wearing a cornflower-blue dress and a white linen apron. Her silver hair was scraped back into a bun, and her grey eyes looked us over keenly.

'My dear Mrs. Whitinger,' said Jim, 'I hope you are well on this fine morning.'

'Oh, it's you Master James. I wasn't sure you'd be coming, least not yet. Have you brought me a new lodger?'

'I have indeed my good lady. This is Captain John Hardwick, retired.' He announced me with exaggerated grandeur, and as he had intimated to me earlier she eyed me with suspicion.

'Do not worry, Mrs. Whitinger, I can assure you Captain Hardwick is a gentleman born. He has just returned from a tediously long sea voyage after many years abroad, and is in need of comfortable rooms, a good breakfast, and a long-awaited brush and shave.' Jim turned and gave a wink, and looking past him I saw that Mrs. Whitinger's demeanour had softened.

She invited us inside, and bade the two privates take my few bags up to the first-floor landing. She clearly had an affection for Jim, who chastised her with a laugh for calling him Master James. 'I'm a grown man now, Mrs. Whitinger, and a captain of Horse Guards. Really, John,' he said, turning to me, 'I despair. I believe I will always be a fresh-faced ensign to Mrs. Whitinger.'

Mrs. Whitinger showed me up the stairs to my rooms, and Jim followed along. It was almost as I had pictured. There were three rooms—a large lounge ran the length of the house, with a window overlooking the street and a good-sized fireplace in the far wall flanked by two comfortable-looking armchairs. A small Chesterfield sofa, breakfast table and chairs, mahogany sideboard and a tall, half-empty bookcase completed the furnishings. Two rooms led off from that one, a bedroom at the rear of the house away from the hustle and bustle of the main street, and a small study at the front. The apartment overall was of a modest size, light and airy, but with a fussy décor, all flowers, figurines and soft furnishings. It looked homely. I guessed that Mrs. Whitinger had been expecting a new lodger—the bed was freshly made and a small posy of daffodils filled a vase on the windowsill of the lounge. It turned out that she had received a message the previous evening from an administrator at Horse Guards, informing her that an officer might be coming to stay the following day, and to have the apartment ready just in case.

Seeing that I was pleased with my lodgings, Jim began to take his leave.

'The first month's rent shall be paid on the morrow,' he said, and Mrs. Whitinger thanked him. 'I leave you in the good hands of Mrs. Whitinger, John, and shall call on you this evening. I trust you will dine with me?' he asked, although he gave me no time to refuse. 'And don't be too frightened by Mrs. Whitinger; she may look formidable but she's a dear thing really.' Before the old landlady could reply, he was taking off down the stairs, chuckling as he went, leaving Mrs. Whitinger exasperated.

'Really, Captain Hardwick, I don't know what I'm to do with him.'

'I know what you mean,' I replied, with a smile. 'Did you mention breakfast just now?'

'Oh, yes, yes, of course. Please do follow me to the dining room,' she said apologetically, and led the way downstairs again. 'So that you know, sir, I live in the rooms just to the right there, should you need anything.'

Mrs. Whitinger showed me into a small dining room from which the smell of bacon emanated, setting off my rumbling stomach. An English breakfast after months of ship's rations seemed suddenly to be the most important mission of my day. There were two other guests from the upper rooms already tucking into the spread. I introduced myself to my fellow guests, who seemed uninterested in all but the most cursory chit-chat, which was how I liked it.

At last, the others took their leave, and I was able to steal a moment with the newspaper that one of them left behind. One story in particular piqued my interest, and I read it with an inexplicable sense of anxiety.

POLICE DUMBFOUNDED OVER DYNAMITE ATTACKS

LONDON—Scotland Yard has been forced to admit that it is no closer to solving the heinous bomb attacks that have shaken the City in recent months. Speaking at Whitehall yesterday, the Assistant Commissioner, Sir Alexander Carmichael Bruce, admitted that despite hundreds of police hours being spent on the case, the attackers remain at large.

Sir Alexander refused to comment on rumours that one of the perpetrators had been shot at the scene of January's Bond Street bomb last month, on the day when London was rocked by three such explosions. He also could not rule out the possibility that the attacks mark the return of the Irish-American Dynamiters, who have not conducted such activity on a large scale since the Gower Street explosion of '85.

Sir Alexander stressed that London was not under attack and that people should not panic. Anyone who sees suspicious activity that may be linked to Dynamiters should report directly to New Scotland Yard.

It was hard to believe that trouble of this nature could be just around the corner. Having travelled clean across the world from one conflict to another, I had pictured my eventual return to London as utterly serene, as if Britain had never been touched by violence. But of course, there had always been anarchists opposing the status quo, and I presumed that these particular agents of chaos were affiliated with one of the many nations with an axe to grind against England—a list that seemed to be growing rather than shortening during this so-called 'long peace'.

I finished my breakfast and thanked Mrs. Whitinger as she came to clear away the dishes. I took the newspaper up to my room to peruse it more thoroughly, although I fancied a stroll around the locality once I had freshened up somewhat.

There was a large bathroom opposite my apartment, well-appointed with large enamelled tub, washbasin and the first indoor flushing toilet I had ever seen—a luxury that somehow made me feel outside my own time. I unpacked my rather meagre-looking travelling bag and washed, before taking a straight-razor to my matted seaman's beard. The small mirror in the bathroom confirmed my fears—I looked terrible; tired, haggard and unkempt. I had always been tall and somewhat thin, but now I was a shadow of my former self, with barely an ounce of fat on my body and with wiry muscles that resembled taut, knotted cords. My body was a catalogue of pain and suffering, every mark on my flesh providing a reminder of a darker time. I winced as I looked at the scars on my bared torso—burns, cuts, tears, bullet wounds and the tiny round blotches left by hypodermic syringes and vicious torturers' barbs. That was one part of my tale that I had not related to Jim. The countless nights spent wailing at the dark, fighting off night terrors as the opium had left my system. Colonel Swinburne, to his great credit, had never spoken of those episodes, and there was no record of them on my papers. The colonel had seen me cured of my addiction, or so he had thought. Some urges had never left me after I had escaped the rebels' clutches. even as I dwelt on it now, I could smell the mouldy, dirty prison; could hear the screams of the inmates and the sadistic laughter of the guards, until the noise began to deafen me and my head swam. I gripped the sides of the porcelain sink tight, and closed my eyes, willing the nightmare to be gone. As the sounds faded and I regained control of my senses, something darker still stirred within me. I became nauseous and dizzy, and a gnawing hunger tore at my insides until it became a stabbing pain in the pit of my stomach.

I threw my shirt on once more and flung open the bathroom door, heading back to my room in a wild mood. As I did so I crossed paths with Mrs. Whitinger and almost barrelled her over. I think I mumbled something by way of an apology, but did not otherwise look up to meet her eyes. As I closed the door of my rooms behind me, I could hear her calling to me in concern, but I did not answer and she did not press the matter. I was rummaging through my bags with increasing panic, before I laid my hands upon the object of my obsession.

I laid out the small, battered wooden box on the breakfast table. My hands shook as I opened it to reveal the syringe and phial of opium solution within. I stared at it, disgusted by my weakness. In truth, after leaving Rangoon I had indulged my craving only twice, and it was with the weak solution that the phial now contained, given to me by a sympathetic Chinese doctor in Hong Kong. The dose was barely strong enough to quell the symptoms, but I had almost beaten my addiction completely, and the drugs were now there for those times when I could cope no longer. This, I decided, reluctantly, was not such a time. I clenched my fists and squeezed my eyes tight shut until the shaking stopped and the pounding in my head ceased. Until the screams of the prisoners and the shouts of the torturers faded away. Taking several deep breaths to compose myself, I snapped the case lid shut and repaired to my bedroom to dress.

My destination was Covent Garden, although I had not realised that Friday was one of the busy market days in that part of London. I'd hopped onto an omnibus to save my sea-legs from walking, but soon regretted the decision when it slowed to a crawl as we neared the congested streets. The roads were clogged with traffic, largely caused by lumbering ox carts resupplying the market stalls and local traders, and the advertising carts pulling their large billboards slowly around London with scant regard for the inconvenience caused to other drivers. As soon as I spied the towers of St. Paul's looming majestically over the buildings to the south, I hopped down from the back of the 'bus and continued on foot.

After a short walk through the bustling crowds, I turned onto Henrietta Street, counting down the numbers of the shop fronts until I found what I was looking for. An anonymous-looking black door lay just beyond an iron railing, with a small brass plaque next to the doorknocker its only identifying feature.

NAPLEY, FAIRCLOUGH & ASSOC.
SOLICITORS AT LAW

I was admitted to the lawyers' office by an ageing, spindle-fingered clerk with wispy grey hair and a serious face. He extended me every professional courtesy, and I was acutely aware that the clerk was better dressed than me.

It was almost three-quarters of an hour before I was called to see the solicitor, Mr. Fairclough. He was a small, rotund fellow with a serious face that would have looked intimidating were it not for his bulbous nose with small round spectacles balanced precariously on the end.

'Mr *ehm*, Hardwick, is it?' he asked, offering me a seat in a chair facing his overlarge desk.

'That is correct, Mr. Fairclough.' I replied. 'I have not had cause to do business with your firm for many years, as I have been abroad, serving in Her Majesty's Army. But you represented my late father, Brigadier Sir Marcus Hardwick, and now that I have returned I have come to examine the state of the family assets, whatever that may be.'

'Ah, of course. I did not recognise you, sir, but then I believe we met only once or twice and, as you say, it was long ago. I— *ehm*—do remember your father, however, and I'm sure I can be of service. Now, let me see…'

He got up from his tall leather chair and waddled over to a large bookcase, from which he pulled a large ledger. Placing it on his desk, he turned to a filing cabinet by the window and after some searching retrieved several sheaves of paper.

I had not known what to expect. I had fair resigned myself to the fact that most of my father's assets would have long been dissolved or sold off to pay debtors—whether there would be anything left for me to take charge of was questionable. However, I found myself pleasantly surprised. As Mr. Fairclough droned on, I realised that my father had been as shrewd a businessman as I could have imagined. He seemed to have had shares in firms all over London, from haulage and shipping to factories and liveries. Some had gone bankrupt or ceased trading over the years, but many were still solvent, and the dividends had been steadily accumulating during my time abroad. I had inherited a goodly percentage of all my father's assets, and so much of the money, and the shares themselves, were now mine. I was even more surprised to learn that my father had owned properties in various parts of the country—a cottage in Keswick, Cumberland; a small townhouse in York; a flat in Nottingham; an isolated farmstead in Kent; and others too. Whilst inspecting these papers, Mr. Fairclough remarked upon a peculiar irregularity. It appeared some of the properties were still leased or rented, while others had long-standing tenants for whom my father had made provision, and who provided further income. There was more than one estate manager on the books, who dutifully deducted expenses, paid rents into the proper accounts, and looked after the properties and the tenants. My eyes were drawn to one particular paper, listing the deeds to that address near Faversham in Kent, the closest we had come to having a family home. It was there that we had lost my sister, Lily, to pneumonia, an event which had brought to a close perhaps the happiest days of my childhood, and changed the course of my life. I was surprised that it was still 'in the family', and the discovery filled me with a deep longing to return there. Along with all of my father's sundry business dealings that were still active, there was almost too much to take in. The late Brigadier Sir Marcus Hardwick seemed to be running a shrewd and profitable business some ten years after his death.

Mr. Fairclough could see that I was perhaps not best suited to take immediate control of such a web of legality and business endeavour, and so he helped me through the tangle of papers, showing me clearly what was mine and what I was responsible for. There were a few plots of land, derelict properties and even unprofitable agencies that I asked Mr. Fairclough to close down there and then, as with no one to manage them they were leeching off the income; but otherwise I was left with a pile of documents that made me not rich, but certainly comfortable. I arranged for any money that I was owed to be paid into my own bank account, which had lain dormant for some time, and procured what papers I required to prove my identity to the bank manager.

'Congratulations, Mr. Hardwick—or is it still Captain?—it seems you have had a most profitable day. It is always a pleasure to be the bearer of good news; in my line of work it is seldom the case, I am afraid to say.'

* * *

By the time I had reached the bank on The Strand, it was past midday, and I was already starting to feel tired from the morning's activity. I was far from my old self even now. Yet I pressed onwards, meeting with the bank manager and arranging the transfer of funds, bonds and promissory notes. I watched as he jotted down all manner of notes and calculations in his ledger, and breathed a sigh of relief when he presented me with my final account documents. When I had arrived I had feared my father's holdings would be in a terrible state, and that I would have to rely on an army pension to survive until I found gainful employment. As it stood, I need not have worried—I decided to tell Jim that I would pay Mrs. Whitinger's rent on my own after all.

Part of me worried that I might succumb to darker temptations now that I had money in my pocket, but I pushed such thoughts aside. Today, at least, I would enjoy those comforts of home that had so long been denied me. I took my leave of the bank and refreshed myself at a coffee house, before visiting a tailor and ordering four new suits, a new hat, shoes, sturdy walking boots, two neckties, a cravat, half a dozen silk handkerchiefs, a pair of leather gloves and a plain ebony walking cane. I bought a suit off the peg that fitted well enough, and changed into it immediately. The tailor promised to have my new clothes delivered to my lodgings on Monday morning, and even took my old suit away for mending and cleaning. Feeling twice the man I had done earlier that day even in an untailored suit, I headed back towards The Strand. The teeming mass of people on the broad street seemed to part for me, and I filled my lungs with air as if for the first time. Now it felt like home. Now I was truly in London.

That night I dined with Jim at a modest restaurant in Bloomsbury. We talked for some time, naturally, of army life; of promotions and retirements, of battles won and campaigns fought, of the colonies struggling abroad. Jim was good company, and I finally began to feel at ease. I was certainly forced to re-evaluate my earlier opinion of him, for he was not as shallow as he appeared. We talked of my future plans—I knew I had to look into my father's business concerns, I told him, at least to ensure that everything was well; but after that I confessed I had no idea what to do with my time. Jim questioned me on my past, and his face lit up when I explained I had once harboured literary ambitions.

'What I said earlier about writing your memoir—now I'm certain you should!' he exclaimed. 'You have travelled so much, seen so many places and met so many interesting people. It would fly of the shelves, especially if you write it with a little… panache. You have a—how can I put it?—rather unique experience to share with the world.'

I tried not to let thoughts of my imprisonment sour the mood, for I knew Jim meant well.

'I'm afraid the pain of that "unique experience" is still too real in my mind for me to fictionalise it,' I said, somewhat gloomily.

'Who said anything about fiction? Listen old boy, you've been through a lot, probably through more than you've told me, but you've come out of it all right, haven't you? Still got the old moral fibre, faculties all intact? That's a bloody marvel, a triumph! If you wrote up all of your adventures abroad, you could fill a bookshelf with stirring tales, or high-brow memoirs, or penny dreadfuls—your choice, really. But people would lap it up, and it would get your name out there into the literary world. The world is your oyster!'

I smiled. It was the second time he had told me that already, and his enthusiasm was so infectious that I actually considered his plan. He had implanted a thought so deep in my imagination that it threatened to take root—could a long-dreamt ambition be realised? I had the means, and the time, to write my memoirs, and why shouldn't I? However, before the conversation became uncomfortable, and Jim felt compelled to talk more of Burma, I changed the subject, and we resumed a pleasant evening of good wine, rich food and cheerful banter.

* * *

When I returned to my lodgings that night I was in good spirits. As I closed the door of my apartment and lit a paraffin lamp, I noticed a letter pushed under my door. I turned up the lamp and sat at the small table to read it. The envelope was of thick, creamy parchment, and there was no address written on it, just the words 'Cpt. John Hardwick' in an elegant, yet masculine hand. It had been hand-delivered; I made a mental note to ask Mrs. Whitinger about the delivery boy in the morning. Inside the envelope was a short, handwritten missive on crisp white paper:

Captain Hardwick,

   It is with great pleasure that I welcome you back to England. However, there is a matter of business that we must discuss urgently.
   Meet me at my club next Wednesday evening, 2nd April, at six o'clock. The Apollonian, Pall Mall. Show this letter at the door.

                                        Yours, &c.,
                           Sir Toby Fitzwilliam, Bart.

I was puzzled. I had heard of the Apollonian Club, but could think of no reason why I would have any call to conduct business there. It was renowned as a club for the rich and powerful—anyone who was anyone in London sought membership to the Apollonian. I had even heard of Sir Toby Fitzwilliam, whom I seemed to recall was a judge of some repute, though I was certain we had never met.

With a head full of questions, I retired for the night, knowing that I would not sleep. I slept little at that time—without the comfort of knowing that there was a battalion of soldiers outside my door, or that I was safely on board ship in the middle of the ocean, my mind refused to switch off, instead remaining alert to every possible danger, real or imagined. I dozed once, I think, but awoke in a fright, in a cold sweat—a result of fitful dreams in which I relived my worst sessions of cruel torture, and all of my guards and tormentors wore monstrous masks that twisted and writhed as if they were made of melting flesh, and inflicted their brutalities upon me with wicked blades that seemed to grow from their very arms. And then the dragon came, as it always did in the nightmare, and as everyone in the dream was consumed by fire, I woke.

In the small hours, I got out of bed more than once, and more than once passed by the small wooden box that still sat on the breakfast table. Though I was a bag of nerves, and dared not sleep, I would not—could not—allow myself to succumb to those urges; to undo all of my hard work on the road to recovery. I asked myself, as I so often had on such nights of late: What would my father have done?

'Not this time,' I whispered in the darkness, tapping the lid of the box softly. 'Not yet.'

TWO

It was raining as my hansom drove along Pall Mall towards St. James's Square that Wednesday. The heavens had opened and what should have been a balmy spring evening was transformed into a sodden and miserable one. The cab drew to a halt, but a stone's throw from a royal residence, and the war office to boot. I gazed up at the imposing white walls of the Apollonian. A few weak rays of sunlight glinted momentarily from the golden bow brandished by the statue of Apollo above the entrance, before vanishing again, returning the vista to dreary grey gloom. I hopped from the cab, paid the driver and hurried up the stone steps of the classically styled frontage and onto the tiled porch.

The rain dripped from the brim of my hat and ran down my neck. Yet the weather could not dampen my spirits. All those years ago, when I had harboured ambitions of becoming a man of letters, I dreamt of following in the footsteps of those proud members of the Apollonian: Tennyson, Thackeray, Scott—even Dickens was said to have been an occasional visitor. To stand on the threshold that had been trod by such luminaries—and moreover, by invitation—was a singular honour, regardless of what might transpire. As I approached, a servant swung open the doors and greeted me cordially.

I stepped across a vestibule, which opened out into a stately hallway. I presented my letter to the porter, who had already retaken his position behind a lectern-like desk. The servant returned the letter to its envelope, nodded deferentially, and handed it back to me.

'Very good, Captain Hardwick, I am most pleased to make your acquaintance. My name is Holdsworth, the club porter, and I will be happy to assist you in any matter during your visit, no matter how small. If I could take your wet coat? I'll have it dried for you promptly, sir. Now, if you are unfamiliar with the clubhouse, may I direct you to Sir Toby's offices?'

I accepted Holdsworth's offer, and followed him through an archway into the hall. I was instantly glad of my escort, as it quickly became apparent that the clubhouse was larger than it first appeared, and the way was winding. We passed through the great marble hall, up the sweeping stair, to a large and beautiful landing, from which rooms led off in every direction, before passing along a corridor, and up another stair to a more modest level, where the marbled walls gave way to dark wainscoting and heavy flocked paper.

I followed Holdsworth to the end of another corridor, where we entered a small waiting room—a windowless snug, with one other door leading off it. Holdsworth raised an officious finger, which I took to mean that he would be a moment, and knocked on this door. I heard no reply, but Holdsworth opened the door a fraction nonetheless and popped his head inside. After a few muffled words, he opened the door fully, stepped aside, and bade me in, bowing cordially as he did so. I stepped into the office for my fateful meeting, and the door clicked softly closed behind me.

Sir Toby Fitzwilliam, or so I presumed, was standing with his back to me as I entered, staring absently at a small, but rather gloomy oil painting on the office wall, depicting some military scene in a dusty, far away land. Rain pattered on the tall office windows, mirroring the soft *tick-tick-tick* of the large carriage clock on the mantelpiece. When the Lord Justice turned to me, I saw that he was dressed formally in a black suit, gold waistcoat and white tie, presumably for dinner or some function. He was an imposing-looking gentleman, fairly tall and stocky. His face was hard and lined, framed by silver hair and large sideburns flecked with black. His eyes were quick and vivid, like those of a man half his age. He offered me the chair facing his desk, which I accepted. I realised with mild embarrassment that I had been standing smartly to attention, hands behind my back, waiting for him to speak—it was one of many habits nurtured over the last few years that I found hard to shake.

'Captain Hardwick, I am so glad you could make our appointment. Cigar?' Sir Toby spoke in dulcet, refined tones, gravelly from years of smoking and whisky I guessed. He nudged the cigar box on his desk towards me. I refused graciously, and Sir Toby withdrew the box and took one himself.

'I expect you are wondering why I asked you here,' he said.

'I am curious, Sir Toby. I am afraid I haven't the faintest idea how I can be of service.' I remembered my manners. I was out of practice, certainly; though I had complained of the stuffiness of my time in Rangoon, the officers and gentlemen who stationed the furthest bastions of the Empire did not seem to stand on ceremony as much as the gentry back in England. I reminded myself for the fiftieth time that day that this was England, and it was my home.

'Service? An interesting turn of phrase, Captain, for that is exactly why you are here. Tell me, what do you know of the recent dynamite attacks in London?'

'Why, only what I've read in the newspapers. Something about Irish-American anarchists taking up arms against the Crown after a long absence.'

'Irish-American? And what gives you that idea?' He fixed me with a gaze, his expression unmoving. I imagined Sir Toby in court, and fancied his impassive visage beneath a black hanging cap, glaring at a condemned man in the dock.

'I, ahem… again, Sir Toby, it was perhaps only the speculation of the press, but I have no reason to believe otherwise.' I tried to recover my composure, increasingly aware that there was more to this interview than I had expected, and realising that Sir Toby was the kind of man who would set myriad verbal traps for the unwary. 'Of course,' I hastened to add, 'I have only been back in the country these past five days. Mayhap there are intricacies of the story that I have not heard.'

Sir Toby reached into the top drawer of his large, walnut desk, and produced several documents, bound together neatly with string. He untied the parcel and spread the documents out before me.

'This is what we know of the matter. It makes for grim reading, but we have reason to believe that the old Dynamiters have little to do with this case.'

'We? I'm sorry, Sir Toby, I'm not sure I understand.'

'Of course not, my boy,' he said, 'I have yet to explain. By "we", I mean the Apollonian Club.' I must have looked quizzical, because by way of explanation he offered more information. 'Oh, not all of the members, of course. In fact, not many of them at all. But there are those in the club who represent certain branches of the government, and who investigate matters of importance to the Empire. Matters such as these.'

I have always had a knack for seeing connections, and would certainly never describe myself as slow to appraise a situation. Indeed, I believed even then I knew where the conversation was headed. However, I also knew that, when faced with superior intelligence, a military man should always glean as much information as possible before acting—anything else would only result in rash strategy. Therefore I resolved to let Sir Toby get to the point in his own circuitous manner, as it clearly pleased him to hold all the cards. I fanned out the folios in front of me and gave them a cursory once-over. Included were newspaper cuttings, police reports, artist's sketches of bombsites, maps and witness statements. There were accounts of at least half a dozen targets across the city.

'Sir Toby, if I may be so bold… why are you telling me this?'

'Because, Captain Hardwick, I would like you to join this group of investigators. I believe that you could be of far more use to your country here, with us, than you could be either fighting abroad or living out your days in early retirement.'

'Actually, Sir Toby, I was rather looking forward to a peaceful early retirement.'

'Were you indeed?' He looked at me from beneath his bushy eyebrows.

Sir Toby rose from his chair and paced to a side-table which supported a decanter and glasses. He poured two glasses of pale amber whisky and water and passed me one, without asking if I would like it; it was good Scotch. He walked to the window where he had stood when I first entered, and looked out thoughtfully. From where I sat the window was just a black mirror, spotted with raindrops. It had drawn dark all too early. I broke the silence.

'I really do appreciate that you think me suitable for this task, Sir Toby. But I am afraid I am in no fit state to embark on active service so soon, if at all. You see, in Burma…'

'You were tortured and drugged and kept in the dark for six months.' He cut me short, and his words stung. 'I know, John. And that is one of the reasons you are so suitable for the role.' He turned and fixed me with those eyes again. His use of my Christian name was not lost on me. His tone had softened, also.

'Do you have any idea how many men—good men—have fought in Her Majesty's service in Afghanistan, India, China and Burma in the last two decades? And those who come back—how many do you suppose experienced some trauma, some great loss, pain or suffering? And of those, how many do you suppose had it as bad as you? A fair few, Captain Hardwick, and that is a fact. But out of those wretches, how many do you suppose had the mental fortitude to recover their wits, their very humanity? To take ship to London, and in just a few days to have returned to a semblance of respectability, with prospects and resources? Just one, Captain, and that is a fact, too. If you can do those things, then you can help fight a different sort of war. One fought in secret, and one that we must win if the stability of Great Britain and the Empire is to endure.'

He puffed on his cigar, and turned back to the window. I let his words sink in, forcing myself to focus on the details, the nuances. Sir Toby would not be the type of man to say anything without certainty of its effect, and I was not prepared to let him trick or cajole me before I knew what I was letting myself in for.

'I take your point, Sir Toby,' I said. 'But you talk of the Empire as if it is in real danger. From within or without? And even if I were to join your group, whatever that may be, I cannot believe that the fate of our nation rests on the decision. I am—was—a simple soldier. It sounds as if you are speaking of spies; espionage and secrets.'

Sir Toby did not turn around. He swilled his whisky around his glass and took a sip.

'As I intimated previously, our group represents various government agencies, from the constabulary and the judiciary through to other, less public departments. We meet here, and exchange information here, in the closed quarters of the Apollonian. We have resources at this place that our enemies and rivals could only dream of. We are represented by Apollo Lycea, the sigil of our justice, and have been for many years.' He paused to stub out his cigar. 'Did you know that the statue of Apollo at the front of this building was once empty-handed? Now, he holds a bow. The layman knows little of such ancient symbolism, but the golden bow represents our group. In the Lycean Apollo, the god of light, truth and prophecy becomes the god of archery, and a protector against the many evils of this world. Wherever you see the symbol of Apollo Lycea in this city, know that you have found a sanctuary from the wolves that beset the doors of the Empire. We are the Order of Apollo; warriors of an otherwise benign society; the right hand of the Crown.'

He looked at me with a flicker of emotion in his eyes. I thought it a sign of passion, which would ordinarily have been endearing in such an otherwise cold and emotionless man, but in this case I was taken aback by the bombast of his words.

'With all due respect, Sir Toby, I do not understand why you would consider me equal to the task. I am barely fit again after my ordeal, and I am no longer a serviceman.'

'Captain Hardwick,' said Sir Toby, more gently, 'you are of greater use in this matter than you can possibly imagine. Look here.'

Sir Toby took up a dossier from his desk and placed it in front of me. I opened the cover and flipped through the first few sheets of paper, and realised that it contained a comprehensive account of my service history,

'You have dealt with some of the most dangerous rebels in the Empire, helping to secure peace for an entire province of southern Burma. You have fought well on two different continents in three separate campaigns. You have encountered more than one group for whom the sowing of seeds of terror is a viable tactic. More tellingly, Captain, you have been through a trauma that would test the mettle of even the strongest willed soldier, and you have not been found wanting. You are here, and whether or not you are physically recovered, you appear mentally sound, which means you have exactly the fortitude that I require... that your country requires.' He looked at me fixedly.

'Sir Toby, whatever reluctance I may have to resume active duty, I would never knowingly turn my back on my country. But I must know more. What exactly are you asking me to do?'

'I am asking you to investigate, Captain. Investigate and, if necessary, infiltrate this group of anarchists. Unearth as much about them as you can, aid our agents in the capture of these cravens... in short, turn your entire attention to this case, and bring it to a satisfactory close.'

'Infiltrate...' I muttered. My mind wandered at once back

to Burma. Back behind enemy lines, and back to darkness. I pulled my attention to the room once more, eyeing the old man warily. 'I am afraid, Sir Toby, that my initial appraisal of your letter may have been correct. You must have me confused with someone else.'

'I am never confused,' he said flatly.

'Well then, perhaps you misjudged me. Despite your rather flattering appraisal of my service history, I joined the army too late. I never rose past captain; and beyond surviving Burma I do not believe I particularly distinguished myself. Though I miss army life, certainly, I do not seek a return to active duty. I want to go about my business, to write my memoirs, to embrace society, to—'

'To follow in your father's footsteps?' This was the second time he had cut me short, and the second time his words had felt like a slap to the face.

'My father?' was all I could manage to say. Marcus Hardwick had been a man of action, who had served for most of his adult life in India, Egypt, China and Afghanistan. As a boy I had longed for those times when he returned home on leave, thrilling at his stories of adventure in far-off lands and playing for many blissful hours with the strange gifts he brought back for me. Yet later on, in his eyes, I had spent too many years doing too little, struggling with university life and trying to write for a living despite his disapproval, which had been copious.

'He was one of ours, too. A good man, who gave his life for the cause. I understand he has seen you well provided for now that he is gone.'

How could he possibly have known about my father's affairs? He was either telling the truth about my father's affiliation with the Apollonian, or had been spying on me. Even then I suspected both were true.

'My father died in Afghanistan, ignominiously in his bed, the day after the battle of Kandahar,' I said.

'And for thirty years up to that point he was a member of this club; an agent of Apollo Lycea; and my friend. In thirty years, he never shied from his duty, on the field or off it. He breathed not a word of his double life to anyone, least of all his family. I do not believe that your mother, Dora, God rest her soul, ever knew that your father was an agent of the Crown as well as a superb soldier. As I understand it, he pushed you around from pillar to post, never laying down roots, moving to wherever his next assignment took him.'

I looked at Sir Toby in disbelief. He was telling me of my father's double life as what? A spy? And he was doing it as if it were as natural as breathing.

'I am sorry that you never got to know that man as I knew him, John. I am sorry your childhood was not a perfect one. I am especially sorry for the loss of your dear sister, for it must have grieved you as much as it did Marcus. She was a sweet child, and no mistake.'

That, too, struck a nerve. I had been a solitary child; the loss of my one true childhood friend, my sister Lillian—Lily, we called her—had made me an awkward boy, happy to spend hours alone with only books and my imagination for company. The tragedy destroyed our mother, but if her passing had affected my father, he had not shown it. He had provided for me well enough, certainly, but his expectation was always that I would follow him into the army. When I began to show ambition for following a literary path he had dismissed me as a fool and a dreamer. My mother passed away before my twenty-first year, a shadow of her former self. It pains me how cold my father had been towards me at the funeral. We had not spoken after that day, and the next time I heard any word of him at all was when a young ensign had brought me the telegram informing me of his death in Afghanistan. At that time I was already struggling financially and academically, and it had dawned on me that I needed to reconcile my memories of him, to follow in his footsteps and perhaps redeem myself in his eyes. I had written a letter to Horse Guards the next day, and before long I was commissioned a subaltern in the Sixteenth Lancers, the Queen's Own; his regiment, with his reputation to live up to.

'Be under no illusion,' Sir Toby said, seeing the pain writ large across my features, 'your father was a good man; a noble man. He saved countless lives across the globe. He once saved my life, if you can believe an old man like me could ever see any kind of action.'

I could believe it. Sir Toby may have been old, but he still looked formidable.

'As his son,' the old man continued, 'I know there is more to you than meets the eye. In fact, a letter found its way to me last week from Colonel Swinburne in Rangoon. He writes that you showed remarkable fortitude in the face of indescribable hardships; that you survived where lesser men would have perished; and that he is confident that, through it all, you betrayed no secrets of any value to the enemy. That, my boy, is not the description of an officer who has never distinguished himself. It is the description of an exceptional soldier, and a dutiful one at that.'

'This is all rather a lot to take in, Sir Toby,' I said, wavering.

'Indeed it is. And I will tell you all that you need to know in good time—about your father, and the work that he did. But for now, Captain Hardwick, I must have an answer. Are you with us?'

When I next spoke, his eyes fair glittered with triumph. He knew he had me.

'Supposing I take the job. To whom will I report, sir, if I may be so bold?' I addressed him as if he were my senior officer, quite deliberately.

'This is not an orthodox position I am offering you, Captain Hardwick. There will be no headquarters, no barracks, nor even an office. You will have considerable freedom to conduct your enquiries as you see fit, without the need to hand in reports every five minutes. To assist you, all the resources of this club will be at your disposal. If you accept the post you may consider yourself an honorary member and come and go as you please. Your membership will remain active as long as you get results; after all, in order to keep you on the books indefinitely, some other poor so-and-so will be blackballed. We can't sponsor you out of charity.' He paused for a moment, smiling to himself. It is lucky that I took no offence, as he was not about to apologise. 'Some of the other members will be engaged in similar duties to yourself,' he continued, 'and these will make themselves known to you in good time. Such men are of the highest calibre—some even have the ear of the Palace—so you can be sure they can be trusted. Discuss the case with them freely, ask for their aid when necessary, and report to me only when you feel you cannot proceed alone. I shall put my trust in you to do your duty in this matter.'

'Then you presume that I will accept?' I said, trying to maintain all due respect and not a little composure in my tone. Sir Toby had given me very little in the way of explanation as to the nature of this new venture, and yet he turned his head to me, with a flicker of a smile on his lips as if I had said something amusing.

'My dear boy,' he said, 'how could you refuse?'

Sir Toby suggested that I familiarise myself with the club immediately. To that end, Holdsworth introduced me to the club secretary, Albert Carrington, in order to have my honorary membership ratified. Carrington was an officious man in his late middle ages, and such a stickler for procedure as I had never encountered outside the army stores. I was told that I would have to wait at least a week for my papers and business cards, including a certificate of my induction into 'Sir Toby's order'; however, Carrington signed a docket endorsing a temporary membership, allowing me free run of the magnificent building in the meantime.

After regaling me with a list of benefits of membership and club rules, some fascinating, others tedious, Carrington informed me that I was to dine with an established member of 'the order', and that this man would 'show me the ropes'. It was a minor imposition, but I was eager to have answers to some of the many questions that were filling my mind, not to mention the fact that I was famished after a busy day.

My first impression of Ambrose Hanlocke, my dinner companion that evening, was not entirely a favourable one. I had expected a military man, one of Sir Toby's stiff-collared 'warriors' of Apollo, but the man sitting in the formal dining room was anything but. He was no older than me, I guessed, tall and rakish, with oiled black hair and a well-groomed moustache. He was immaculately dressed in fine evening wear, though he appeared a little too debonair for the austere, Regency refinement of the surroundings. From the moment he spoke, I decided that Ambrose Hanlocke was a rogue, albeit a likeable one. It would not be long before I discovered just how right I was.

The dinner was magnificent; fine food prepared by a French chef in four courses, with good wine. It was the best meal I had eaten in many a year, and I think perhaps it showed. Ambrose leaned over to pass comment during the fish course.

'That's the thing about the club,' he said, waving his knife to indicate the surroundings, 'cheap to those who can afford it, off limits to those who can't. I eat like a king in here at least once a week, for no more than the cost of my membership—in other words, John, such luxury is free to the likes of you and me.'

I smiled politely. Ambrose made no real effort to keep his voice down, and I was sure he was being more crude than would be considered acceptable by the clientele.

'Mind you, it wasn't so long ago that the quality of the food in here was rum, to say the least,' he continued. 'Positively rag and famish; may as well have dined at the bloody Reform Club. Still, this new Frenchie knows how to cook. Parisian, you see; bit too much sauce for my tastes, but bloody good all the same.'

'Have you been a member for long?' I asked, hoping to turn Ambrose from his bullish course of conversation.

'Six years,' he replied, before stuffing a forkful of sole into his mouth. 'Or is it seven? I forget—a while, anyhow.' He mumbled his words, his mouth half full of food.

'And you make regular use of the facilities?'

'Too right old chap, and I recommend you do the same!' he remarked. 'The Apollonian is like a palace—in fact, I'll wager it's better than most palaces; all Portland stone, marble, electric chandeliers and plush ottomans. Imagine the cost of running such a home—yet for ten guineas a year we have joint proprietorship of all this. The library, coffee rooms and fine dining… everything. We have footmen in livery, mosaic floors and antique silverware. We can order wine from the stores that would cause the head waiter at the Savoy to question the extravagance. In short, John, everything is of the best, and it costs next to nothing.' He grinned, and finished off his fish with gusto.

'It all seems rather more decadent than I am used to,' I said, 'and, if I'm honest, I would feel that I was taking advantage were I to use these facilities too frequently.'

'Well, it looks as if I've finally found a real gentleman in London,' he laughed. 'I can only assume that you retire of an evening to a palace fit for a Maharaja, surrounded by servants, silk cushions and gilded statues. No? Well, let me tell you this: a man can make his club his home if he is of a mind. I live and lounge luxuriously here as I please. I graze upon the masterworks of the best-equipped private library in the land; I enjoy conversation with some of the most dazzling wits of our time; I often sleep here in the rooms provided. In fact, the only thing I ever need to get through life is a toothbrush. And I've earned it.' His jovial tone dropped to a more serious, conspiratorial whisper—the first sign that he had any sense of decorum whatsoever. 'I have earned it, John, in the same way that you will earn it; because I am a member of Apollo Lycea, the inner sanctum of the club. When I use the order's seal to endorse a report, it would not surprise me if the Queen herself took an interest in its contents. When I investigate a heinous crime, I put my life on the line for the good of the Empire. Do you see?'

I nodded. Ambrose was keen to jest, but he had come to the crux of the matter. There was a momentary pause in the conversation as the waiter came to clear away our plates.

'You are not what I expected,' I said, when the interruption was over. 'Meaning no disrespect, Sir Toby described the order as "warriors".'

'Oh, we are!' Ambrose exclaimed. 'What you really mean is that I am no soldier, unlike you. So you are wondering what exactly it is that I do?'

'I would not have put it so bluntly.'

'Of course not, because of your breeding and military bearing and fine feeling.' There was a twinkle in Ambrose's eye—he was evidently intent on needling me. 'I'll tell you what I do for Queen and country, Captain Hardwick. I listen, I sneak, I skulk and even steal. I whore and I drink. The last two things I do more than I ought. Oh, and they aren't actually part of the job, but you get the gist.'

Ambrose must have registered the look of disapproval on my face. He looked unabashed, and savoured the moment as the waiter placed the main course in front of us, and topped up our iced water and glasses of wine to the sound of distant violins.

'Don't worry, John,' he went on, gulping his wine, 'You won't be expected to do any of the unsavoury stuff. We are all recruited for our own unique talents. I'm an adventurer of the worst kind—I was in all kinds of bother before Sir Toby ever found me, and I might add that he got me out of an awful pickle. You are... well, you're an honest man, which makes you something of a rarity in this nest of vipers. Let me raise a toast. To the last Honest Man in London!'

He raised his voice along with his glass of claret, and I felt myself turning nearly as red as the wine as several sage old heads turned to look at us, frowning. Ambrose beamed. I leaned back in my chair, trying to cover my face with one hand whilst clinking Ambrose's glass. He giggled to himself like a naughty schoolboy and resumed his meal.

I realised that Ambrose must have drunk most of the bottle of wine himself already, and started to understand why he seemed so free of inhibitions. I steered the conversation to more serious matters as best I could while Ambrose devoured his filet mignons, washing them down with more Château Brane-Mouton.

'We should talk about this business with the Dynamiters,' I said eventually. 'I have no real idea of what's been happening, and I suppose I must make a start on the investigation straight away.'

'Indeed,' replied Ambrose. 'Won't do to keep the old bird waiting—he'll be after results. I'm sure he didn't hire you for your wit, charm and God-given grace, abundant as those gifts are.'

'I presume it's not the done thing to admit the likes of me to the Apollonian?' I asked.

'The likes of *us*, you mean?' Ambrose winked. 'No, not done at all. The Apollonian has a reputation to uphold, one of intellectual pursuits, the nurturing of celebrated minds, respectability and episcopacy. There used to be a sixteen-year waiting list for membership. I hear Sir Toby has a daily struggle with the committee about the order; they never seem quite sure who he's granting membership to. In fact, even I don't know how many of us there are. So you're right, old chap, best get results and soon. Tell you what, let's eat pudding and I'll take you to the library and show you the case files.'

I could eat no more, my body still not having adapted to large portions of rich food, so I sipped a cup of strong black coffee as Ambrose wolfed down his fine French dessert, before draining the last dregs of wine from his glass, stifling a hiccup at every pause. When we were finished, he stood abruptly.

'Onwards and upwards, old chap!' he announced. 'No time for sitting around; we have work to do.'

As we wove our way through the elegant dining room, all marble and crystal, and ivory table-linen, I tried to blank out the sound of those sage old clubmen tutting and muttering censoriously. I feared I would have to get used to that.

The library of the Apollonian was every bit as grand as I had hoped, and as well stocked as its reputation suggested. Tens of thousands of volumes, on every subject one could imagine, were lined up on three levels of bookshelves to which wrought-iron spiral stairs granted access. Rare volumes were displayed in locked glass cabinets, and at a glance I spied some philosophical and theological texts that must have been hundreds of years old. A few men sat quietly in the leather armchairs near to the two fireplaces at either end of the room. In fact, the only sound came from the log fires, which crackled softly. The smell of old leather, stale tobacco and musty tomes was pleasant to me, bringing back many memories.

As a boy I had loved books. When my father was away—a frequent occurrence—I had lost myself in tales of adventure, travel and exploration. I had dreamed of owning a good library one day. I started when Ambrose thrust several weighty books and a large rolled map into my arms.

'We might need these. Come along.'

I followed him to a door at the back of the venerable old library, noticing that Ambrose was not carrying any books whilst I struggled with an armful of leather-bound volumes. He fumbled in his jacket pocket, produced a small key and unlocked the door. The outside of the door was decorated with a discreet brass plaque, a cameo of Apollo, with bow in hand. Ambrose stepped into the room and held the door open for me with a foot whilst he lit a pair of paraffin lamps—there were no electric lights in this room. I squeezed between two armchairs and put the books on the desk in the centre of the room while Ambrose locked the door.

'Now, I'm a teeny bit worse for wear, old chap,' said Ambrose, stating the obvious. 'But I have more than enough wherewithal to take you through the case.'

I listened as Ambrose brought me up to speed in his own inimitable style. He unrolled the map—a large-scale street map of London—and pointed out the sites of the most recent dynamite attacks. As he described the events leading up to the attacks, he referred me to the books I had brought in with me. There was a book on the history of Ireland, including the most recent Troubles, a gazetteer of London, and a military handbook of weapons and tactics from around the world. Ambrose remained startlingly lucid, only slurring the occasional word, and I was impressed at his constitution. Finally, he rifled through the files in the office and pulled out several dossiers pertaining to the case.

'Thought as much,' he said. 'Old Toby's had these sent down for you.'

I was surprised to discover that the perpetrators of the Bond Street attack had been pursued across London, and that a gunfight had ensued at Marble Arch. How details of the engagement had gone unreported was beyond me; the sheer number of people who must have borne witness, even in the early hours of the morning, would have made concealing the facts from the press a logistical nightmare. Ambrose assured me that such things were 'par for the course' in Apollo Lycea, and I began to wonder just how many strings Sir Toby was able to pull in the pursuit of the Queen's justice. The other bombings had occurred during the night, only hours apart, first at Kensington and then at Lisson Grove, and these had led to the authorities picking up the trail of the suspects.

'Sir Toby's especially keen to get to the bottom of this case, because these bombings were far too close to the Palace,' said Ambrose. 'Queen Vic may well have heard the explosion from her bedchamber. Worse still, they were even closer to the club. Bloody anarchists are getting too big for their britches.'

'According to this, one of them was a woman,' I said, raising an eyebrow as I scanned the reports.

'Apparently so. Even the bloody anarchists seem to have embraced suffrage these days,' said Ambrose, disdainfully.

'And what happened to these anarchists?' I enquired. The dossier was not forthcoming on the matter, and read as though several pages were missing from the anonymous report.

'They got away,' said Ambrose. 'Although one of them was wounded. We found a few things that he must have dropped during his flight.'

Ambrose handed me a small, battered pocketbook and a scrap of paper, which looked as if it had been torn from a brown envelope. The piece of paper contained a scrawled note—four rows of six barely legible symbols, which looked strangely familiar. The notebook contained some forty-odd pages, each with one or two neatly scribed paragraphs, all of which were rendered in similar symbols to those on the note. This time I did recognise what was written, and I stared at the book dumbfounded.

'You won't get anywhere with that lot,' I was faintly aware of Ambrose saying. 'Some kind of Arabic, maybe, although some of our experts believe it's ancient Chinese or Japanese. Lord knows why the bloody bog-trotters would use that kind of language. We've had our men look at it, but it's all gibberish. We're going through a selection process currently, to find some folk who we can trust to translate it.'

I had been quiet for too long, and Ambrose must have registered my look of bewilderment and, perhaps, horror.

'Are you all right, old chap?' he asked.

'It's not Chinese, Ambrose.' I said, quietly. 'It's Myanmar.'

'My what?'

'Burmese. It's written in Burmese.'

Ambrose had been understandably surprised at my sudden insight. I told him how I had come to serve in Burma, recounting much as was pertinent, but omitting the story of my capture during a routine patrol, and the beginning of my own personal hell. The night drew on as I sat in feverish study of the two artefacts. Ambrose tried to make himself useful, bringing coffee to sustain me whilst I pored over books of linguistics and applied my own knowledge of the language that brought back so many painful memories. In some strange way I hoped that perhaps ardent study of those fearful Burmese characters would go some way to banishing the ghosts of my past. The oil lamp flickered and I became lost to time. Ambrose grew bored, but duty kept him by my side for the most part. He went off to stretch his legs from time to time, but at least tried to look interested. After several hours I had my breakthrough, and my exclamation snapped Ambrose back into wakefulness.

'What is it? Have you cracked it?' he asked.

'I believe I have,' I said. 'It's not simply written in Burmese, which is why it took me so long to work out what I was looking at. Once you translate it into English, it still looks like gibberish—a jumble of words and phrases—that is, until you realise that it is a code.'

'Code? And can you read it?'

'Almost. I believe I can work out a cipher for it, and then we'll crack it.'

I stood and stretched, before re-entering the main library in a search for any books on codes and secret writing. I was invigorated by the breakthrough, despite the lateness of the hour, and I climbed a narrow iron stair to the second tier of books with a spring in my step. Again, the library did not let me down, and I returned to the office clutching five volumes, ranging from the history of the Babington plot against Queen Elizabeth, to a more modern book on military codes. I split the volumes with Ambrose, giving him specific instructions on what to look out for, and within the hour we had the best part of our cipher.

'It is the simplest type of substitution code,' I explained. 'I've encountered their like before. See here.' I indicated the paper I was jotting on. 'The notebook we found contains names and addresses, two per page. These may not be completely accurate, but a good study of this material and the completion of the cipher that we've begun will undoubtedly prove fruitful. The scrap of paper, however, is a little different.'

'In what way?' Ambrose's curiosity was piqued.

'They are not letters, nor even words, but a numerical sequence. In fact, they look to me like map references. Six-digit grid references to be precise.'

'Of where?'

'Well,' I said, 'I should start with Britain and go from there. Do we have any more maps?'

'My dear fellow,' said Ambrose with a smile, 'did you really need to ask?'

We spent our last hour or so at the club ensconced in the map room. That the club had such a room at all was a surprise to me, and a delight. It was the hours spent poring over old maps of the world as a youngster that had led to pangs of wanderlust throughout my boyhood, and which had ultimately inspired me to follow in my father's footsteps. This comfortable, square room was full of maps and atlases from every era and detailing every corner of the Earth. However, for our purposes we began with the Ordnance Survey's map series, which we spread out over the large rectangular tables in the centre of the room.

The club was quiet; it was nearing midnight, and those clubmen who remained on the premises had either retired to their rooms or were enjoying a quiet drink downstairs in the dining room. As we had made to enter the map room, a servant had scurried in before us to turn on the lights and draw the heavy drapes across the tall windows. Only two men occupied the library when we had passed through it, sitting at opposite ends engaged in their own private studies. It filled me with a strange sense of pride that the literary tradition prevailed at the Apollonian even now, and I envisaged the likes of Tennyson and even Wilkie Collins spending many a late night in that very room as they wrought their masterworks.

Our search for the correct map was not straightforward. I'd

learned of the virtues of Ordnance Survey mapping during brief periods serving alongside the Royal Engineers. They often espoused the virtues of good British mapping, whilst cursing the inadequate hand-drawn charts of the East. However, the techniques I had learned in India had not yet reached civilian mapping, and so much improvisation was required. With the coordinates from the pocketbook to hand, and our knowledge of the anarchist's dynamite targets acting as a key to the affair, I was able to draw a more detailed grid onto a map of London, and soon we knew we were on to something. We looked at each other, uncertain of what we had found. Even though I was acting partly on guesswork, the map references I calculated were more than significant.

Kensington Road. Lisson Grove. New Bond Street. And the fourth: Marble Arch.

I circled the four locations with a stubby pencil.

'What does it mean?' asked Ambrose.

'It means that the fracas at Marble Arch was no accident. The anarchists intended to go there all along. Which means they must have had a plan—some means of escape.'

'Then we must investigate the scene again,' said Ambrose, 'and this time with a fine-toothed comb. No stone unturned and all that.'

I nodded sternly.

'But not tonight! It's past twelve already, I haven't had nearly enough to drink, and I'm bloody tired to boot. Let's go home, and strike out for Marble Arch in the morning.'

It was hard to disagree, for it had been a long day. Determined to conduct my investigation by the book, however, I first scribbled a missive to Sir Toby on club notepaper, outlining my discovery and some cursory details of the code, before sealing it, ready to hand to a porter on the way out.

The rain had slowed to but a mist-like drizzle, though we still took shelter on the club portico whilst the night porter went in search of a cab for us. Ambrose's flat was located in Clerkenwell, and we agreed to share a hansom. However, I urged my new colleague to take the cab direct, and have the cabbie drop me near the British Museum. I would hear no protest; I had my overcoat and hat, both of which had been dried by the servants at the club, and I had no desire to return straight to my lodgings without a short constitutional. I had not yet had a restful night in London; perhaps I still had on my sea legs. I coveted the opportunity to take a walk through the quiet gas-lit streets before retiring, to steep myself in old remembrances and, maybe, to persuade myself that it was forgivable—nay, expected of me—to relax after years of wandering and trials.

I disembarked near the British Museum, and Ambrose went on, the carriage clattering on the wide, cobbled thoroughfare and echoing into the night. I stopped for a short time and gazed through the great iron gates at the museum. The sheer familiarity of the place filled me with unimaginable comfort. Presently I checked my pocket watch, and deciding that I'd lingered longer than anticipated, I began to wend my way back to Mrs Whitinger's boarding house.

As I made my way past Russell Square Gardens, I encountered a police constable going about his rounds, shoulders hunched from the chill and rain-cape around his shoulders. We exchanged brief pleasantries, and I moved off down a side-street. I knew better than to loiter near the public gardens at such an hour, and felt somewhat reassured when I saw the street lamps of a main thoroughfare up ahead, knowing that a policeman was to my back. I chastised myself, for I'd had no reason to fear anything in London so far, and yet I felt uneasy despite myself. I turned onto another deserted street, not far from home. I was craving a good fire and a glass of Scotch, but realised that it was too late, and resolved instead to go straight to bed. Then I heard something— the scuff of a boot on cobblestones, from somewhere behind me. It was hard to determine the direction or distance; the streets were so empty that the noise echoed faintly before dying away.

I glanced around but saw nothing, and again coloured myself a fool for my sudden bout of nervousness.

I reached the alleyway that ran across to Gower Street, so close to home, and realised I had done myself no favours—the way ahead was dark, illuminated only by meagre streaks of pale moonlight as it filtered between the gaps in the house roofs, with the low walls of terraces flanking each side of the uneven path. I gripped my cane and pressed on, knowing that I was less than five minutes from the boarding house. That is when I heard again the scuffing sound, this time certainly behind me, and certainly closer. I glanced over my shoulder and again saw nothing, so I quickened my step towards the wan light at the end of the alley. And there they stood.

Two men blocked my way at the end of the alleyway, causing me to check my step. It was hard to discern their silhouettes, but I could not take them for gentlemen. I took a few paces tentatively forward, and they did likewise, confirming that their intentions were not friendly. I turned round, and the sound of footfalls heralded the arrival of another man at the end of the alleyway that I had entered by. If these were footpads then I was trapped. But, strangely, whatever fear I had previously felt began to dissipate with the arrival of these flesh-and-blood foes, for I had faced worse than these overseas. I swallowed my fear and felt better for it, before calling out to the men.

'I say, who is that? I warn you, I mean to come by.'

I did not know why I made a threat, but I surprised myself with the strength of my tone. I sounded like my father, for a moment. The men did not respond, but steadily advanced. I stood stock still, uncertain of a course of action, looking left then right along the dark, narrow passage. The two men ahead of me were closest, and as they drew within a dozen yards or so, I saw an object in the hands of one of them—a cudgel. They meant me harm, and I would not wait for them to come to me. I sprang to action, racing headlong towards the two foes before me, cane gripped tightly in my left hand. The men prepared to receive my charge. The smaller of the two attempted to strike low at me as I bore down on him, and I saw a faint flash of steel in his hand, but I skipped aside and swung my cane at the back of his head, causing him to cry out in pain as it connected with a wet thud. The bigger man—bigger than I had realised—was upon me immediately, reaching for me with one massive arm and brandishing his cudgel in the other. I ducked low and pushed him away with no small effort, before kicking him in the midriff. He staggered a few paces backwards, enough for me to aim a good swing with my cane.

The swing never connected, as someone grabbed my cane from behind, and tried to wrestle it from my grasp. The third man had reached us more quickly than I had anticipated. I twisted around under the cane to face him, and dragged him in close ready to drive my knee into his midriff, but he was spritely and wise to my ploy, using my own force against me as he stepped aside. As I stumbled forwards, I saw his shadowed face, and realised that he was a celestial—at least, I assumed he was one of the many London Chinese. But a niggling voice in the back of my mind questioned whether he was Burmese, and that thought made me sick as the fear returned.

The first man, a scrawny rogue in a flat cap and rough work-clothes, struck out at me again with his knife, and I dispatched him once again with my cane, never once taking my eyes off the celestial. And then the big man came again, the two of them together with their oriental comrade watching. The big man was grappling, trying to take hold of my arms so that the small man could slash at me with his blade, but they did not find it easy. I set my jaw and determined to show the celestial what I had learned back in his lands.

A massive fist clubbed its way towards me, and I drove it aside and into the red-brick wall with a flick of my cane, before lashing out with a kick at the small man's hand. His knife skittered across the flagstones and he had barely time to turn to face me before I drove my forehead into the bridge of his nose, dropping him to the ground like a sack of stones, blood smeared across his face. The big man growled, and glowered at me. The oriental stepped forward, eyeing me menacingly.

'You only make this harder on yourself,' the celestial said, in a strong accent that betrayed him to my trained ear as Chinese.

I pulled off my overcoat and slung it atop the nearest wall, and placed my hat on the ground. Taking up my cane as though it were a sabre, I faced my opponents.

'I've fought bigger, stronger men than you all around the Empire,' I said, with as much bravado as I could muster. 'You will not leave this fight unscathed.'

As soon as the words had left my lips, I doubted their veracity. The Chinaman pulled a long, flat blade from his jacket and grinned. I took a pace backwards despite myself. The assault began; the Chinaman launched himself forwards, more dancing than fighting, twirling and slashing with his wicked knife, and lashing out with foot and fist faster than I could follow. I parried his blows in the style I had learned in the East, with cane and raised shin, and I took heart when I saw the look of surprise on my opponent's face. Unfortunately, my assailant was far more practised than I in his exotic fighting style, and although I fended him off I could not connect with my own blows.

I was slowly but surely forced backward along the alleyway, and I remembered that the policeman I had seen earlier was in that direction. Perhaps he would even be walking back this way on his plodding route. If I could reach the main street relatively unscathed, I could make a dash for it and raise the alarm.

That was when the scrawny man, whom I had foolishly believed out of the fight, recovered his senses. From his prone position on the ground he scrabbled forwards, slashing at me with his small knife, and cutting me on the thigh. As I felt the dart of pain in my leg, I involuntarily shifted my weight and failed to block an incoming kick from the Chinaman, which sent me clattering against the brick wall of the alley. Then the big man was on me. Large, rough hands seized my arms. I threw myself at him in desperation, pounding him against the brick wall, but he was too strong and it was too late—the Chinese thug was kicking at me before I knew what was happening, and I retched and spluttered as a kick to my stomach sent the wind out of me. The big man took a cue from his compatriots and slammed me headfirst into the opposite wall, before throwing me to the ground. I remember the three of them raining blows upon me, as I curled into a defensive position to shield myself from the worst of it. Then the Chinaman's face was level with mine, and he grinned at me with malice.

His knife was raised to my face. I could smell his breath, rank and stale and laced with gin, and his eyes seemed to peer into my very soul. He muttered something to me, but I was in a daze. I had taken several blows to the head, and it is hard now to recall anything beyond that point. Instead of the Chinaman, I could see only Maung. Instead of the claustrophobic London back-alley, I saw the squalid, bare-earth prison cell where I had been long confined in Burma. It was as if it were real; just for a moment, I was back there, and I was terrified that I had never left, and that my sudden release and subsequent return home had been a terrible nightmare—a consequence of a broken and tortured mind. I believe I sobbed at that point, and must have looked a pathetic sight to my tormentor, but all I could think about in those moments was how plausible the theory was. Why would I have been released without warning? Why would I have ever been invited to join the Apollonian? Then my attacker, whom I firmly believed was the bastard Maung, half-laughing at my plight, said to me: 'Are you ready to die, Captain?' And I was. I realised that the Burmese must have gleaned whatever information they required of me in my broken state, or perhaps had simply tired of me, and my time was come. I was half-mad in that moment, I am certain—concussed and unable to think straight, and sure that I was locked in a dungeon with an evil torturer who wished me dead.

My waking nightmare was cut short, not by the fatal slash of a wicked blade, but by the commanding shout of a familiar voice.

'You there! Leave him be, or by God I shall run you through!'

The laughing and taunting of my snarling tormentors stopped, and through blurred vision I saw them turn to face the threat. I heard some indistinct voices, warning the newcomer to back away. I also heard the unmistakeable scrape of a sword being pulled from a scabbard. I tried to lift my head to see what was happening, but all I could make out was a struggle between shadows.

Then one of my would-be killers lurched backwards, clutching his stomach, and staggered past me down the alleyway. Cries of alarm and profanity rose from the other two, and they retreated. The Chinaman fled the fastest, overtaking his wounded companion and leaving him to his fate. The scrawny man was next, and paused long enough to tug at the big man's sleeve, encouraging him to flee, which eventually he managed. It was the big man who had been wounded, run through, I presumed, though by whom? My head was spinning. I slumped back on the damp flagstones, and felt sharp pains shoot through my body. I had no idea how badly I was wounded. Then, another face loomed before mine, but this time it was not one of my assailants, nor was it the face of a Burmese prison guard. It was Ambrose Hanlocke.

'A fine mess, old chap. A fine mess indeed. Still, soon have you fixed up,' he said. I felt a tug at my shirt, and though I tried to move my limbs so that Ambrose would not have to shoulder the burden, I could remain conscious no longer.

THREE

'We are one.'

I said the words without thinking, as I had said them so many times before. Before me stood my father, outside the old thatched-roof farmhouse that we had lived in when I was a boy. He held his arms open as if to offer me an embrace, but I stood firm. I felt nothing in my heart for him then.

He mouthed some words, pleading with me, but no words came forth, only silence. I watched him dispassionately. I was cold, reptilian and calculating. As the old man stepped towards me, a great gout of flame seemed to envelop him, trapping him in a circle of fire. The sky darkened. Where once it had been calm and blue, roiling grey-purple clouds gathered to block out the sun, and my father's pained expression was lit only by the yellow fire that danced around him, throwing its light off the limewashed walls of the house.

Why do you not save him?

The voice came from no discernible source, but seemed to form in my mind. A deep, booming voice. Then I remembered, and I turned to face the dragon.

It was a gargantuan beast, rising up before me like a fiery monument. The dragon's scales flickered green, purple and orange in the light of the flames that danced around its body. Its vast, membranous wings spread out to envelop everything in my vision. Its red eyes glowed like dying embers, and as it lowered its magnificent scaled head to behold me, a plume of black smoke belched forth from its nose and maw, swirling upwards until they became one with the storm clouds.

'I cannot save him,' I shouted above the roar of the fires that blazed everywhere. 'You are the dragon. You are the master of flame, and of the growing storm. His life is in your hands.'

No. We are one.

And as I turned back to look at my father, I realised it was true. My eyes now smouldered like embers. I tasted the sulphur fumes as acrid smoke poured from my mouth and nostrils. I spread my mighty wings that seemed to envelop the entire horizon, and with a great beat of those wings I was soaring into the air.

I encircled the farmhouse, and revelled in anarchy as I lit its thatched roof with a gout of orange fire from my jaws. My father recoiled at the sight, and ran back and forth in his flaming prison cell. I swooped down and beat my wings to drift before him, pricking up my scaly ears to make out what he was saying. It was hard to tell at first, with the fires roaring and the wind whistling around me, but then I heard him.

'A storm is coming. You must come down from there. Do not provoke the tempest!'

I laughed with great mirth, and to my puny father it must have seemed like a ferocious roar, for he stopped in his tracks and looked at me afeared.

'Do not fret for me,' I growled. 'I am the dragon. I fear no storm; I fear nothing!'

My father's expression changed. He no longer looked afraid, or even angry. He looked disappointed. He shook his head slowly and I saw that he was not in awe of me, despite my power. He pitied me. I was a failure in his eyes just as I had always been. In that moment I knew that he did not deserve my mercy, and I breathed deep before spitting out a torrent of flame that smote him where he stood. My rage was so great that I flew around in ever-increasing circles, setting to flame the whole world until all was red ruin.

I woke violently, crying out. I was near certain that I was in my bedroom at Mrs. Whitinger's boarding house, but the room refused to stop spinning long enough for me to tell for sure. Light streamed in at the small sash window, though I had no idea what time it was, nor even what day. The door flew open almost immediately, and Ambrose Hanlocke rushed in, looking concerned. He mouthed some words of comfort to me, but I could not hear him, for my body pained me and my mind was confused. I was in a dreadful fug, and gripped the bedsheets tightly as I tried to compose myself.

'Can you hear me, old chap?' asked Ambrose. 'I said you're home, and you're going to be all right.'

Another man entered the room behind him. He was young but grave-looking, well-dressed and clean-shaven. He carried a Gladstone bag, which he set down on my bedside table and started rifling through.

'This is McGrath, John; from the club,' said Ambrose, although my head swam so much I could barely comprehend him. 'He's a medical man. He's going to give you something for the pain.'

The young man prepared a hypodermic syringe, and something deep in my subconscious must have alerted me to a hidden danger. My fears were confirmed as the man rolled up my sleeve and tapped on my vein.

'Don't worry, Captain Hardwick,' he said. 'Just a bit of morphine.'

I snapped to immediately, and knocked the syringe violently from his hand. Ambrose made a poor job of restraining me as I lurched upright. The glare from the sunlight outside stung my eyes as surely as if pins had been thrust into them. I was vaguely aware of McGrath crying out in alarm.

'Don't put any more of that bloody stuff in me!' I barked, in the tone of a drillmaster.

I slipped my legs out of the bed and tried to stand, and found that I was too dizzy. The morphine fug was still upon me—that they had dosed me while I was unconscious was now certain, and I felt a disconcerting mixture of sickness and delight at the thought of it. Both men helped me return to a seated position before I did myself further injury.

'Captain Hardwick,' the young man said, 'I only wish to help you. If opiates are not to your liking for... ahem... whatever reason, then I can give you something else.'

Ambrose reacted before I did, sensing an embarrassment and seeking to assist, with uncharacteristic gallantry.

'That would be excellent, McGrath. It is no reflection on your bedside manner, I am sure—it's just that the captain had a torrid time in service in the East, a damned torrid time, and it is best to avoid anything that reminds him of that place.'

McGrath nodded. I believe he understood all too well why I railed against the morphine, but said nothing. If he had administered any drugs to me earlier, he must surely have seen the needle-marks from previous injections on my arms, legs or even my belly; although he may have dismissed them along with the myriad other scars that made my skin look like a map of the constellations. Why else he would have pressed ahead and administered the hated drug was beyond me. Inexperience, perhaps? McGrath instead mixed a few potions and powders, which he offered to me, assuring me that there were no opiates present. I drank the tincture gratefully. My head seemed to have stopped spinning, although the throb of a headache plagued me. I knew that if I moved too much I would give myself away with my shaking hands and sluggish perception. My addiction had been fed, and I prayed God I had the strength to resist its call the next time.

* * *

I was instructed to take a hot bath and thence returned to my room to breakfast with Ambrose and his companion, where a small but welcome fire crackled in the hearth. It was almost eleven o'clock in the morning, and Mrs. Whitinger had prepared us a large tray of toast, eggs and black pudding, evidently under duress—when she had knocked on my door, Ambrose had answered, and I had overheard a sharp exchange between them. He had remonstrated with her that I was in no fit state for visitors, but she had still made her point, and requested a word with me as soon as I was well enough. After reminding Ambrose that she was my landlady, not my housekeeper, she had retreated indignantly back to her own rooms, before Ambrose returned to us sheepishly.

'Deuced formidable woman that landlady of yours. I wouldn't want to be in your shoes when you're well enough to wear them.' He nudged McGrath and they both laughed. I think I managed to muster a smile, though I did not feel like it.

The young man, whom I had taken for a doctor, was Archibald McGrath, actually a surgeon recently inducted into the Apollonian. As is the tradition in his profession, he preferred 'Mister' to 'Doctor', and Ambrose jokingly reassured me that McGrath had taken all the relevant examinations, and was no charlatan. I gathered that I was not the first agent to be attended by the young surgeon. As well as working at St Bartholomew's Hospital, his study of the developing field of forensic medicine gave him a unique perspective on club cases. As can be assumed of such a knowledgeable and hard-working young surgeon, Archibald—or Archie—was serious and fastidious. He had a trustworthy manner about him; I learned too that he was a loyal clubman and keen cricketer. Ambrose made one too many wise-cracks at Archie's expense, I thought, as was his way.

Between them, Ambrose and Archie gave me a fairly complete account of what had happened the previous night. I had been assailed by a group of thugs not far from the boarding house, and had been injured as I fought them off. Ambrose had had a change of heart about letting me walk home, especially as I mightn't have been aware of which streets were safe and which were not, and so he had instructed his driver to retrace his path, heading for Mrs. Whitinger's house. When I could not be found along the main route, he became concerned and eventually happened upon my predicament. Once the thugs had been sent packing, I had been brought home and McGrath had been sent for. I had been delirious for some time. Archie had put a few stitches in my leg and had, regrettably, given me laudanum for the pain so that I could sleep. By all accounts I had caused quite a commotion, and Mrs. Whitinger was sore that such an upset had been brought to her door.

'How did you manage to overcome the brutes?' I asked Ambrose. 'I seem to recall a sword being drawn, but I don't remember you being armed last night.'

'I am always armed, dear boy,' Ambrose replied. He took up his walking cane from by the side of his chair and pulled the monogrammed silver knob away a few inches to reveal a tempered steel blade within. 'A nasty surprise for any vagabond, eh? And I have a fair few fencing lessons under my belt, too.'

'And that is not the only type of fencing you practise, by all accounts,' said Archie, taking a sip of his tea to disguise his smug grin.

'Good Lord!' exclaimed Ambrose in mock disbelief. 'John, take a note: on this day Archibald McGrath attempted a witticism. I'm not sure anyone would believe it were I to tell them.' I laughed along with them, but soon I was forced to sober the mood.

'The man you stabbed, Ambrose—do you believe the wound was a mortal one?'

'Gracious no,' Ambrose protested. 'I snagged the tip of my foil in his jacket, and I believe his imagination did the rest. A flesh wound at best. More's the pity, for if he had been seriously wounded he would have been a damned sight easier to trace. Still, the jails are full to bursting with cutpurses and common louts as it is, so I doubt Scotland Yard would thank me overmuch for delivering another such ne'er-do-well to their door.'

'Cutpurses? Louts? So you believe the attack to be a random one?' I queried.

'What else?'

'The Chinaman with the ugly knife,' I said. 'He called me "Captain", just as he was about to slit my throat. He meant for me to die, and he knew me.'

'Are you certain?' asked Archie. 'Good heavens… could this mean the club is compromised? Or perhaps you have enemies from your time in the service?'

'Oh, come now, stop being so melodramatic.' Ambrose threw his hands up. 'You were insensible last night, John. You were raving about the Chinaman being a torturer from Burma—Mung, or Ming or somesuch.'

'Maung,' I said, sullenly.

'Maung, Ming, what's the difference? The fact is, something sent your mind back to that terrible place, and you became confused. Are you sure it was the Chinaman who called you by your rank? Or are you simply confused from the fever?'

'I… I think it was him.' I paused and thought on it for a moment. 'I can't be sure.'

'There you go,' said Ambrose, with a tone of satisfaction. 'Your imagination was running riot, and the celestial reminded you of painful times past. The only other explanation is that someone knew of your involvement with the Apollonian, and that is highly unlikely, especially at this early stage. Did you tell anyone of your membership before leaving there with me last night?'

'No,' I said. I was distracted, trying to go over the events of the previous night, trying to convince myself that I was rational and sane. But Ambrose had made a strong case to the contrary.

'There we are, then. Don't worry about it any longer. Those ruffians will doubtless wash up in the Thames sooner rather than later; their kind always do.'

* * *

It had not been easy to convince Ambrose and Archie to allow me back to work, but I was determined to continue the investigation, and in truth a bath and breakfast had been just the ticket. Ambrose proved himself a valuable ally once again when, realising that I would not be satisfied by further bed rest, he took my side and persuaded McGrath to relent. Archie gave me his card, and made me swear that I would send a messenger to him if I felt any pain or discomfort whatsoever. I could not tell him that my real discomfort was the gnawing hollow inside me, which he himself had caused with his medication; better, I thought, to plunge straight into my work and leave no time for solitary reflection.

Once Archie had taken his leave, I had faced a brief meeting with Mrs. Whitinger, whose formidable demeanour clashed with her obvious concern for my well-being. She stressed that the neighbourhood was a respectable one, and out of earshot of Ambrose told me that she'd never heard of such a thing happening within miles of her door previously. She seemed to bear the burden as though she herself were responsible for my misfortune. I apologised profusely for any upset I may have caused her, and she had accepted my apology graciously, becoming utterly considerate once she realised the extent of my physical injuries. I confess I was touched by her kindness, and determined that I would find some way to repay her as soon as I could.

I was annoyed by the loss of my new suit, which was mostly damaged beyond repair. I asked Mrs. Whitinger to send the jacket to the menders, threw the shirt and trousers away, and wrote an instruction to a messenger boy for my tailor to provide an identical formal suit by the end of the week—goodness knows what the old fellow would think. I produced a sixpence to speed the boy along, before summoning a hansom and heading for Marble Arch with Ambrose in tow once again. I had dressed in a suit of everyday clothes of dark brown linen with a pale grey waistcoat. The clothes were of good quality and well tailored, so I would pass muster were we to pay a visit to the club, but they were austere enough not to attract the attention of more rogues and cutpurses. To my shame, as it was another drizzly day, I was forced to wear my only overcoat again, which still carried moss-stains and pulls from my scrapes the previous night.

'As you said yourself, old chap,' said Ambrose, encouragingly, 'no unwanted attention. And that coat should certainly do the trick.'

Ambrose was apparently never without some degree of finery, and looked dapper as always in his grey fitted suit, silk cravat, top hat and fine ebony cane—an item which I now knew was also a deadly weapon. I made a poor-looking companion for him, I'm sure, with my black eye, bruises and limp, but he kept any further quips to himself.

'This bloody rain is quite intolerable,' said Ambrose, gazing forlornly from the carriage window. 'If it doesn't stop soon I think the Thames might burst its banks.' I glanced up at the pale grey sky, hoping for better fortune today than the weather portended.

At Marble Arch, we found it difficult to inspect the scene of the earlier crime due to the great number of people milling about. Situated as it was at a busy exchange between Oxford Street, Edgware Road and Hyde Park it seemed that every type of street-seller, foreign tourist, pickpocket, cab driver and house servant was going about his or her business at once. The people of London were unperturbed by a bit of drizzle. Street entertainers attracted large crowds, ruddy-faced children raced around like wild creatures, costermongers and newspapermen were lending their voices to a deafening throng, whilst courting couples and their chaperones tried to avoid the commotion to take their strolls through the gardens, harassed every step of the way by flower girls and portrait painters. The press of beggars and street-sellers was such that Ambrose was obliged to find a policeman to help move some of them away from the inner arch itself, using some bogus credentials and garrulous nature to convince the constable to place himself at our service. I ignored Hanlocke's duplicity, assuming it was all in the name of secrecy for our agency. Even then, as I examined the smooth white surface of the arch, we could do nothing to stop folk gawping at us as we searched for clues. Ambrose pulled a small magnifier from his jacket pocket, and handed it to me to assist in my scrutiny, before proceeding to watch me as interestedly as the common crowd.

'They searched the interior rooms at the time, I assume?' I asked Ambrose.

'Of course. Special Branch were there. They may be heavy handed, but they're nothing if not thorough. There were no anarchists hiding upstairs.'

'And the gates were closed?'

'Of course.'

I looked up at the formidable bronze gates. They were not impossible to climb, though it would certainly be arduous, and there was nowhere to go beyond them but to an empty courtyard.

'I am afraid the search may be fruitless. Too many people have walked through here since the anarchists escaped, and the walls appear spotless,' I said, resignedly.

'Should think so too,' said Ambrose. 'National treasure, this. I expect it's been washed down a fair few times since then—mind you, they've made a poor fist of it. Look at that mildew around the base there. Needs a good scrub if you ask me—I should inform the Department of Works.'

Something in Ambrose's tone told me that he would do no such thing. But his remark did cause me to look more closely at the mildewed area, and that is when I made a small discovery.

'Good Lord, Ambrose, I think you're onto something.'

'Eh? Found some incriminating moss, have you?

'You scoff, but perhaps I have.' I drew Ambrose closer, and he knelt on the flagstones with a look of distaste before examining my find. 'See here—there's a discernible line in the mildew, no more than a quarter of an inch wide. And look, see, it occurs on the opposite side too.'

The yellow-green mildew ran just a few inches up the inside

of the arch from the pavement, where it must have escaped the brushes of the street cleaners. At roughly the centre point of the thick inner wall, on either side of the arch, there was a narrow, clean line where the mildew no longer grew. Either side of that line, the growth was pale and yellow for several inches, as though it was dead. It was certainly curious, if not exactly earth-shattering, and Ambrose dismissed the discovery out of hand. However, using the magnifier I followed the mark up the wall, and did my best to trace its path upwards towards the ceiling of the arch, whereupon it soon became too indistinct to see. I squinted at the apex, feeling certain that I could trace the faintest line all the way around the arch's interior curve. To me it looked as though a huge board or pane of glass had once stood in the exact centre of the archway, sitting flush with its smooth marble walls. Ambrose was at a loss.

'I very much doubt this has anything to do with the case,' he said. 'I expected you'd be searching for manhole covers or... well, *something* else.'

'That's already been done, Ambrose,' I replied, patiently. 'We have sworn statements from reliable witnesses, not least a police sergeant, that the area was secure and that the anarchists escaped by unknown means. I am simply exploring every possible avenue.'

'Very well. And what conclusions have you drawn?'

I rapped firmly on the wall of the arch near the marks, and, finding it solid and ignoring Ambrose's suppressed snicker, I got to my feet and looked around at the throng of people going about their business. Those who had stopped to watch us had by now grown bored and wandered off.

'I don't know,' I said. 'I think we should go back to the club and review the case notes, bearing in mind this information. But first, I need to visit one of those booksellers.'

I marched through the crowds, to where I had earlier seen a bookseller with his cart. Ambrose thanked the policeman for his time and followed me. The trader was a middle-aged man with more wrinkles than he had a right to. He instantly went into his sales patter, trying to sell me volumes on everything from French law to river angling, in a cockney drawl that made me doubt he could actually read any more than the titles of his many volumes.

'None of that, my good man. I'm looking for a map of London. A good Ordnance Survey if you have one.'

With only a minor grumble that the sale would be a small one, the bookseller rifled through his cart, with grubby, dextrous fingers that protruded from fingerless woollen gloves. Before long he produced a whole pile of maps, bound together with string, and handed me the one I sought at a cost of threepence.

'We have one of those at the club, if you recall,' said Ambrose.

'Yes. But I intend to deface this one,' I said cheerfully. 'Now come along, we have detective work to attend to.'

'What on earth has come over you?' Ambrose quizzed me as I limped off briskly to cross the road. 'Last night you were all good manners and deference. Now you're like a dog with a bone.'

'Last night,' I said, not slowing my pace as I crossed the street, 'I was at first a fish out of water, then confounded by mysteries, and finally a victim. Today, I am a captain again, and an agent of the Crown, and I intend to carry out my assignment dutifully.'

My companion did not reply, though I am certain he would have been shaking his head in amusement had I turned to look at him. I spoke the truth, but of course there were other, more personal reasons for my change of approach. I could not stop now; to do so would be to invite dark moods and temptation, and probably to wake each evening in some East End opium den rather than my comfortable Bloomsbury bed. Instead, I knew I had to embrace the new-found sense of purpose and heavy motivation that spurred me onwards. Together, Ambrose and I made down Oxford Street to hail another cab, this time headed for Pall Mall and the Apollonian Club.

The club was busier that afternoon than it had been the previous evening. A few clubmen were finishing afternoon tea in the dining room, whilst a large party of visitors were receiving a tour by one of the members. My appearance courted a few sideways glances, but I shrugged them off and allowed Ambrose to lead the way once more to the private office. We were intercepted en route by a formally dressed servant, whom Ambrose addressed as Hollins, and who handed me a letter bearing the seal of Apollo. 'From Sir Toby, sir,' was all Hollins said by way of explanation, before he went about his business. I saved the letter until we were safely inside the office and had turned up the lamps.

Cpt. Hardwick,

It seems that in one evening you have made more progress in our investigation than half a dozen men have made in several weeks. I have passed on your findings to my best clerks. I trust you will find the fruits of their labour with the case files by the time you return to the club.

Keep up the good work.

Yours, &c.,
Sir Toby Fitzwilliam, Bart.

I was somewhat surprised by the praise contained in that short note. Ambrose raised an eyebrow when he read it.

'I always said that Sir Toby was incapable of human kindness,' he quipped. 'If he keeps this up I may have to find new ways to be disrespectful.'

Ignoring him, I spread out the case files on the desk, under the light of the lamps. As intimated in Sir Toby's note, there was a new notebook amongst them, a reporter's pocketbook, which as far as I could tell contained a near-complete deciphering of the coded notebook in a neat hand, along with a few scribbled pencil-notes in the margins. I had no idea who the clerks were, where they were situated, or what hours they kept, but I was startled at the speed and thoroughness with which they had carried out the task. The majority of the entries in the pocketbook represented names and addresses, page after page of them. The margin notes indicated that a goodly proportion of those named were spiritualists, illusionists and so-called fortune-tellers, most of whom were already known to the club. More than a dozen of them were denoted as 'deceased'; three as 'known criminals' and a further three of 'unknown whereabouts'. The names meant nothing to me, although the vast majority of the addresses were in London.

Ambrose scratched at his chin in puzzlement as we went over the clerks' work. And then we flipped past the addresses to a dog-eared page near the back of the book. A brief explanatory note from a clerk explained that every fourth address in the book had contained an erroneous Burmese character, which when collated formed another set of coordinates, like the ones that marked the dynamite targets previously. This was an astonishing find, and both Ambrose and I examined the coordinates excitedly. The margin notes explained that each of the erroneous symbols had been added 'almost certainly' in several different hands, and that there were nine sets of coordinates present. The first three correlated to the scenes of three anarchist attacks the previous year; the fourth was Chelsea Hospital, and of unknown significance. The next four were identical to the ones noted on the scrap of paper, though again not written by the same person. The final coordinate was again of unknown significance, and seemed to point to an area of Commercial Road in Whitechapel. But even from memory, a pattern started to form in my mind.

'I think I have something,' I said.

'Oh?'

'Allow me to demonstrate.' I unfurled my map and made a small cross at each of the coordinates listed in the book. I then drew Ambrose's attention to those sites around the Marble Arch incident. Kensington Road. Lisson Grove. Old Bond Street, and Marble Arch itself. 'I've tried to place my little crosses as close to the actual addresses as I can, given the scale of the map. Now look.' I took the notebook that had been left by the clerks and used the edge of its binding as a makeshift rule, drawing a straight pencil-line between the three detonation sites.

'A triangle?' queried Ambrose, raising an eyebrow.

'Indeed. And if we were to pinpoint the locations, and apply the proper mathematics, I expect that Marble Arch would be in the dead centre of that triangle. Now look at the other coordinates. Battersea Bridge Road and Battersea Park Road on the South Bank, and Sloane Street on the north—what lies in the centre of that triangle?

'Well, it's hard to be exact,' replied Ambrose, 'but it looks like Chelsea Hospital. That bears out the coordinates that we found, but there was no explosion at the hospital.'

'Just as there was no explosion at Marble Arch,' I explained patiently. 'I believe the points of the triangle are prearranged targets for our group of anarchists, and the central coordinate represents their means of escape; perhaps a rendezvous point with others of their group.'

'Your theory seems relatively sound, but why triangles? Why so precise? And how is an exposed archway in the middle of London a suitable means of escape?'

'So many questions, and I confess I cannot answer them,' I admitted. 'Triangles? Who knows. Perhaps it is some cod-symbolic gesture used by the group. Freemasons use geometric shapes in their ritual symbology, do they not?'

Ambrose scoffed. 'Come now, the great and the good of the grand lodges are unlikely to engage in dynamite crime.'

'I never suggested they were,' I said. 'What I meant was that our group may have some occult or symbolic connection, which provides a motivation—or at least a direction—for their crimes. Look at the lists of names and addresses. So many of those people have a spiritualist or occult connection it cannot be coincidence. What we need to learn is whether those people are targets or collaborators, or both.' I saw Ambrose waver, and knew I had started to convince him. I felt perhaps a flicker of triumph.

'Oh, my sainted aunt! From latter-day Fenians to black

magicians in one day,' said Ambrose, looking plaintive. 'I don't fully understand—now that you point it out it almost seems too obvious; too easy—and yet why would one anarchist add to the work of another like this? And why write it down at all?'

'The only reason for committing this information to writing,' I replied, 'would be the importance of precision. The exact locations must be important for some reason. I very much doubt we have all the information we require, but it is a start. Look at the original pocketbook that was recovered from Marble Arch, and the scrap of paper—I should have seen it before. They are not written by the same hand.'

Ambrose examined the items and nodded. 'I think I know what you're getting at,' he said. 'You think that the last coordinate was written by the same person who wrote the other four on that scrap of paper.'

'It will need closer scrutiny, but yes, I believe so.'

'So, the anarchists who carried out the last three attacks were not only targeting specific areas, but were also noting instructions for others in their order. Am I right?'

'That is my train of thought, yes,' I said. 'They carry out atrocities in groups of three, with the fourth coordinate always being their pre-arranged exit point. The group also notes a point of significance in the pocketbook for the next group of anarchists.'

'So, by taking the book,' began Ambrose, 'we have perhaps foiled their next step altogether?'

'I hope so, but we cannot rely on it. What if the targets are all predetermined, and only added to the notebook once the group has surveyed it and gathered intelligence? If that were the case, they may still go ahead with their next attack because they may well believe that we have not cracked their code, and are thus ignorant of their plans. Assuming that's the case, we have only two questions left to ask: When are they planning to strike, and is this new coordinate the starting point for new attacks, or the escape route?'

* * *

Despite my chiding, Ambrose had refused to leave with me for the East End until we had taken tea. 'I'm positively famished, my dear chap,' he had said, before slipping one of the junior stewards a shilling and sending him off to fetch us some cold cuts. We had missed afternoon tea, but the staff at the club were always willing to make special arrangements for members, even rogues like Ambrose Hanlocke.

We found ourselves a corner of the deserted dining room to talk, and Ambrose soon raised the matter of my recent misfortune at the hands of the three cutpurses he had rescued me from. What he was really interested in, however, was my reaction to Archie McGrath's treatment, and I knew that there was no point in hiding the truth, as Ambrose had been there to witness my fear and hatred of opium first hand.

'It's nothing to be ashamed of, old chap,' he said, seeing the colour rush from my cheeks. 'I know that you had a bad time of it in the army, and God knows I doubt I'd have held out half as long as you. But you do have to take it easy; I think Sir Toby has put you back on active duty a bit too soon.'

I bristled at the term 'active duty' quite vigorously, for I did not feel like a soldier, not yet. Though I was gladly serving my country, it was on a voluntary basis, or so I told myself.

'You'd have me go home and pretend that none of this was happening?' I asked.

'Not at all—you've already shown you have an aptitude for all this adventuring business,' Ambrose replied. 'It's just that... well... I've been at this game a long time. You see things—do things—that aren't everyone's cup of tea, if you take my meaning. Maybe those thugs you encountered were a way of telling you to slow down a little, you know? Neither of us are spring chickens, and if you've lost your edge, even a little bit... you don't want to be knee-deep in the mire and find yourself wanting.'

'I've seen plenty of action, and maybe I'm not as sharp as I once was, but I'm certainly wiser. You know the worst thing about my captivity? Knowing that whatever was going on outside, I wasn't a part of it; there was nothing I could do to help my regiment, or my country... Now I'm here, and I have a mission of real importance, I don't intend to turn my back on it and put my feet up. My father was a member of Apollo Lycea, and he wouldn't have shied away from his duty, whatever the cost.'

Ambrose looked thoughtful—almost sad, I thought—and then he said to me: 'I met your father once, you know.' Again, I do not know why such a simple remark affected me so, but I looked at Ambrose with expectation. All he said was: 'Believe me, John, you are not your father's son.'

The words were delivered kindly, but I neither knew how to take them, nor how to respond. I swigged the last dregs of my tea and got to my feet, picked up my hat and coat, and turned to leave. Ambrose, swift as a cat, was standing next to me, placing a hand on my shoulder. I turned to him with a face like stone.

'John... I have spoken out of turn. I'm sorry. I was trying to say that I think you're a good fellow, with a good heart, but I've made a royal hash of it. Can you accept the apology of a blustering cad, and we'll talk no more of it?' He held out his hand. I paused for only a moment before shaking his hand, giving him a half-smile, and leaving the club with him. For better or for worse, Ambrose Hanlocke and I were in it together.

Somewhat delayed in our endeavours, we set off for Commercial Road, in the notorious Whitechapel district. It was past five o'clock by the time we approached our destination. The weather was mercifully mild, and though a chilly breeze blew periodically along the high street and whistled in at the windows of our cab, we would be spared the downpours of the previous day. The route to Whitechapel had been a circuitous one, as our cabbie had been forced to take more than one detour to avoid blocked streets. Many shopkeepers and local markets were packing away for the day, and the number of carts and workmen in the streets made progress by road somewhat laborious. I eyed Ambrose accusingly—were it not for him being a slave to his appetite, we would have made the journey in nearly half the time. Whilst the map coordinates were reasonably accurate, it still gave us more than a quarter of a mile of Commercial Road properties to investigate. Therefore, we had narrowed down our search by trawling through the clerks' list of addresses, and had come up with two in this area. The first was noted as a spiritualist medium, a table-rapper of some small repute, going by the name of Madam Walpole, while the second was a man who was unknown to Apollo Lycea, noted in the book as Mr. F.W. Jeffers.

The district itself lived up to Ambrose's poor assessment of it. Drunkards, both male and female, walked the streets, along with tramps, bawds and luridly dressed 'ladies of the night', who plied their trade even in broad daylight. Litter, grime and detritus covered the thoroughfares, accumulating in alleyways and around the bases of rusting streetlamps like pile of autumn leaves. The unmistakeable smells of rotten vegetables and open drains mingled with the less distasteful odours of hot potatoes and meat pies from nearby handcarts.

We came to Madam Walpole's home first. The terraced house had a pronounced slouch, and no doubt the occupants were glad that it was sandwiched between a funeral parlour and a derelict photography studio, for otherwise the ramshackle home would almost certainly have collapsed. Nonetheless, the dilapidated little house looked out of place, almost squeezed into a gap that should not have been there. Ambrose paused uncomfortably as a prompt that I should pay the cabbie, which I duly did. I also promised him an extra shilling atop his usual rate if he would wait for us for a short time.

We climbed three steep, uneven steps to a front door of dubious prospect, and gave three sharp raps on the iron knocker. It took some time before the door was answered, by a scruffy young woman who, I thought idly, would not be unhandsome were she to brush her hair and don clean clothes.

''Elp you, sirs?' she asked, suspiciously.

Ambrose took the lead before I could say anything, although not in the manner I had expected. He removed his hat and gave a short bow of the head. 'My good lady, we are come to visit Madam Walpole. Is the mistress at home?'

'Mistress, indeed,' replied the young woman, impudently. 'No. She's aht.'

Ambrose gave me the briefest sideways glance, before readdressing the girl. 'I beg your pardon?' he asked.

'I said she's aht,' she repeated. Then, upon seeing Ambrose's pained expression, she adopted the Queen's and said, as if to a simpleton: 'Out! Don't you understand English or somefink?'

'I, erm, that is—' stuttered Ambrose, whose roguish credentials I was now beginning to doubt.

'Look, young lady,' I intervened, more directly, 'we have come to call on Madam Walpole regarding a professional matter. Neither she, nor you, are in any trouble whatsoever, but it is most urgent that we seek her aid. Now, if she is not at home, do you know when she will return?'

'Like I said,' she uttered, with sullen impudence, 'She's...'

'Yes, yes, "aht", I'm sure we understand,' Ambrose snapped. 'Good day to you.' He turned as if to leave, his impatience agitating me greatly. We had not even managed to establish when the elusive Madam Walpole would be returning home. I turned awkwardly, doffing my hat to the cold-eyed girl as I did so, when I heard a sash window scraping open above us. Ambrose and I both looked up to see a small, middle-aged woman with curlers in her hair looking down at us. 'What's going on down there?' she barked. 'Who're you?'

Ambrose once more took the lead, and I groaned inside for fear that he would rankle this woman too. 'My dear lady, we have come in search of the famous Madam Walpole regarding a matter of some import. Are you she?'

'Might be,' she replied, guardedly.

'Then it seems that your, ah, sister here has made some error.

She believed you to be out. Fortunately for all of us, here you are. May we come in and have a word? We will not take much of your time, I assure you.'

'Sister, is it?' she chuckled. 'Well, I s'pose you gentlemen had better come in. Molly!' she snapped to the girl at the door. 'Let 'em in and get some tea on.'

For the most part, the house was as meagre within as it was without. Ambrose and I sat on a worn, floral-patterned sofa opposite Madam Walpole in a shabbily furnished sitting room. There was no fire in the grate, and no coal in the scuttle. As we had entered the small house, Molly had made a point of closing a pair of double doors that led from the sitting room to a parlour at the back of the house. Before the doors had closed, I had spied a room of more pleasant appointment, with a large circular dining table in its centre and deep red drapes around every wall, lending it a dark and somewhat theatrical aspect. It had been a fair assumption that the room was the place where Madam Walpole held her séances, and she said as much whilst Molly ventured to the kitchen to make us tea.

'It's not every day that we get such fine gen'lemen visiting us,' said the medium. 'Not unless it's them philistines from the Society.'

'Society?' I ventured.

'The Society for Psychical Research, I expect,' Ambrose interjected, helpfully. 'They make their living debunking fraudulent mediums who prey on the vulnerable.' He intoned the name of the society with pronounced distaste, and the subtlety was not lost on Madam Walpole. She was a small woman, unduly wrinkled for her age, I thought, and hard-faced. Her skin was dark and leathery, and her eyes were almost black, with long dark lashes that suggested that she may well have been pretty as a girl; I suspected that she was of continental or perhaps even gypsy descent. The girl, Molly, shared some of these characteristics, and I supposed that they were related.

'S'right,' said Madam Walpole haughtily, 'and they've never found me up to no tricks. I run an 'onest house, sirs, and provide a service to them as needs it.' At this point, Molly returned with a tray of tea things. We were honoured with the best china, it seemed, although the willow-patterned Staffordshire set had seen better days. 'Good girl—you run along now and get them candles from Mr. Peake like I told you.' The girl did as she was bid, and with a last flicker of her suspicious dark eyes in Ambrose's direction, she left the room and closed the door behind her. Madam Walpole addressed us once more. 'Would you do the honours, kind sirs? I'm afraid me old hands shake summink awful, and I might spill the tea. Thank you. Now then, I'm afraid I must ask you to get to the point, if I may be so blunt sirs, as I 'ave a meeting here in a couple o' hours and I must prepare.'

We quickly established that Madam Walpole's meetings generally involved the running of séances, and I used a cursory discussion of her clientele to guide the conversation towards my true purpose—the discovery of our anarchists.

'Madam Walpole, have you recently had a visit from any odd fellows?'

'Other than ourselves of course,' Ambrose interjected.

'Anyone who may have struck you as unusual, or perhaps asked you some questions beyond the ordinary?' I continued, ignoring the interruption.

'Other than yourselves, y'say? Can't say as I rightly remember any strangers… Why might you be asking? You with the law?' She squinted at me once more. There was a keenness and strength behind her rheumy eyes.

'Not at all, my good lady,' Ambrose interjected. 'Let me explain our purpose.' I glanced askance at him, uncertain where he was about to take the interview. 'We have reason to believe that a small group of men is attempting to infiltrate the confidences of London's finest mediums. These men are not from the Society for Psychical Research, nor from the constabulary; but they may indeed be something far worse.'

'Oh?' queried the woman, leaning forwards slightly.

'Reporters,' proclaimed Ambrose, with no small degree of disdain. 'And not even the ones from the respectable broadsheets of Fleet Street. I speak, madam, of the gutter press, the penny-a-liners, looking for some sensationalist exposé for their illustrated rags. These men will stop at nothing to glean a story, even so far as to lie and mislead law-abiding members of the public, and hard-working ladies like yourself. They do not seek to portray your profession in an honest light; merely to misrepresent you in order to print some scandalous claptrap in the Sunday papers.'

'Do you mean to tell me that these men may pose as clients in order to trick a poor old woman?' she asked.

'Madam, there are no lows to which they will not stoop,' replied Ambrose. I was impressed—I had thought Ambrose too brusque for this task, but he now seemed a more than adequate foil to my straightforward approach.

'And how would I know these reporters? I get lots o' folk coming to me for readings and such like.'

'Indeed. It is your sterling reputation that led us here today—to entrap a medium of your stature would be a fine prize indeed for these pirates of the free press.' As he ended his reply with gusto, I struggled to restrain my amusement. I wondered if Ambrose had ever dabbled in the dramatic arts for he would surely have made an excellent mummer. 'These fellows would not be from your usual clientele; perhaps their references strike you as dubious, or there would be something about their questions, manners or even appearance that you would perceive as odd. Can you think of any such people who might have visited you recently?'

'Can't say as I'm sure about that, sirs. But I thank you for your concern, and I consider it fair warning. I'll be on me guard from now on.' There was something about Madam Walpole's manner that made me suspect her of holding something back.

'Does that mean you have, or have not, received such visitors?' I asked, perhaps a little impatiently. Her eyes flicked over to me.

'Now sir, I can't rightly recall every Tom, Dick or 'Arry to come through these doors. Seems to me, though, that you've done your duty, and warned me about these wretched reporters. If they've already been 'ere, then what's done is done. If they ain't, then I'll surely be on the lookout. Now, will that be all, gen'lemen?'

'Madam, it is of paramount importance that we find these... crooks,' I said, and even though Ambrose's muted groan was almost palpable I was not deterred from my course. 'If you have any information, I am sure we can come to some arrangement to...'

'Make it worth me while?' She completed my sentence for me. 'I'm very sorry sirs, to have put you to any trouble, but I'm afraid I cannot help you further. Please, I must ask you to leave me to my preparations.' She rose, a little infirmly. I was frustrated at the abrupt end to the interview, but to press her would have been beyond good manners—I could only hope that she would have a change of heart, or that perhaps we could return another time and try to gain her confidence.

Ambrose, however, must have realised that his act had won us little; he stood, thanked our hostess for her hospitality, and was already seeing himself out while I engaged in the farewells. I thanked Madam Walpole for the tea, and followed Ambrose's lead out into the hall, from where I saw him already engaging the driver of the hansom.

'Madam Walpole,' I said, attempting one last gambit so that our time was not completely wasted. 'Do you know of a local man by the name of Jeffers? A Mr F. W. Jeffers?

'I 'ave nothing to do with that man—tapped in the head he is. I s'pose you'll be warning him about these mysterious callers too, will you?'

'So he is in the same line of work as yourself?' I said, trying desperately not to sound clueless.

'Pah! Ee's no respec'able medium, if that's what you mean. Fancies 'isself a fortune-teller, 'ee does; thinks 'ee can see the future. Nobody calls on Frank—not if they want to hear any sense.'

I thanked the woman again, and stepped over the threshold.

However, though our business was concluded, the medium had not finished with me. She placed a hand on my arm and gently bade me stop. I turned to her, and realised that she was concealing herself from Ambrose's view in order to take me into her confidence. There was something odd about her in that moment—her eyes were glassy and unfocused. She leaned forwards and whispered to me in her rasping voice.

'A message for you, for though we have never met I have foreseen your coming.' Her strong accent was softened—the voice sounded unlike her own.

'A message, from whom?' I asked, the merest hint of charlatanry causing me to tire of her elusive nature and mysticism.

'The sins of the father shall be visited upon the son. There is no escape from the house of the dead.'

I stood for a moment dumbfounded, and looked at the woman uncertainly. I was about to say something else, but she was clearly not about to engage me further. Even as I heard Ambrose brusquely calling me to hurry up about my business, the woman was closing her door.

I took my seat in the cab, unnerved despite not truly believing Madam Walpole's theatrics. The hansom rattled away, and I eventually realised that Ambrose was remonstrating with me. He'd had to repeat himself several times before I came to my senses and was able to rebut him in kind.

'Bloody hell, John, are you even listening to me? I'm not sure you're fully recovered—perhaps you should go home and leave the interviews to me. We can't afford to go back empty-handed.'

'You barely got us through the front door,' I argued. 'I feel sure we could have salvaged more from her.

'No, we wouldn't. I thought you had experience with interrogation? The thing with people like her is that you must never let them think that the information they possess is of importance to you. As soon as they think there's something in it for them, or that you're with the authorities, they'll clam up tighter than a muckworm's hatband.' He was right, though I resented his bluntness. I did have experience of interrogation, of course, but the subject was a sore one for me, and I found myself wondering if Ambrose was alluding to the fact that I had been on the receiving end of enemy questioning rather than conducting it myself.

The cab had not far to go before reaching the next address, but I was glad to save on walking with my leg still sore. We crossed the road and approached a tall, red-brick building with a starboard lean, which made it loom quite alarmingly over the alleyway beside it. The pawn shop at its base was boarded up, and it was hard to tell from the cracked and peeling signage whether or not it was still in business. However, our purpose lay with the occupant of the flat on the second floor, and so we pushed open the battered front door and took the stairs to the address in question. The stairwell smelled foul; a confection of urine and liquor, so strong that Ambrose took out his handkerchief and held it over his face as we climbed. The stairs were hard work for me, and my wounded leg ached, but we soon found ourselves outside the door to flat 143c Commercial Road. I rapped on the door, but received no answer. I rapped again; nothing. Ambrose put his ear to the door and listened intently.

'Not a sausage old chap,' he reported. He poked his head over the stair rail and looked first up and then down the stairwell, craning his head to one side as he listened for any movement. He crept back to the door, leaned his cane against the wall, placed his handkerchief on the floor, and knelt down, one knee on the handkerchief. I looked on, bemused, as Ambrose reached into his jacket and pulled out a small roll of leather. He opened it up on the floor, to revealed a set of lockpicks, screwdrivers and skeleton keys.

'Ambrose!' I exclaimed—although even now I wonder that I was surprised at all—and was instantly hushed for my trouble.

'Make yourself useful,' he whispered, 'and keep a listen out. If anyone comes, whistle and act naturally. And by naturally, I mean at ease, soldier.'

Ambrose set to work with his pins and lockpicks, deftly manoeuvring them around the lock and listening for the tell-tale sounds of the mechanism's acquiescence, until before long there was a single, loud click, and Ambrose swung the door open. He looked smug as he waved me inside, and quietly closed the door behind us.

The door led into a dark, cluttered sitting room. The flat itself seemed surprisingly large, but in such an unkempt state that I had to wonder if anyone lived here at all. The curtains were drawn across the two large windows—I opened one pair to let some light into the room, but the last weak rays of the early evening sun found it difficult to pierce the grime-smeared glass. Ambrose looked around the room in disgust, walking silently as a cat whilst poking at piles of books, newspapers and dirty laundry with his cane.

'I suppose we should make a thorough search now we're here,' said Ambrose. 'I'll take a look in here, though I don't know where to start. Call me if you need any help.'

I nodded and moved to the door at the far end of the room. Beyond it was a hallway that reeked of damp and something fouler. Four more doors led off the narrow passage, and the endmost door was ajar, so I went to that one first, listening for any noise within before pushing the door open. I am not sure what I was afraid of; after all, Ambrose and I were working for the Crown. However, I had the strangest feeling of unease being in that horrid, claustrophobic flat, and Ambrose's eagerness to put us on dubious moral ground had not helped my disquiet.

The room I found myself in was a large bedroom. Again, I threw open the curtains to find discoloured, filthy and cracked sash windows in order to shed light on my search. Of course, I had no idea what I was searching for. Other than the name of the occupant, Mr. Jeffers, we had no information to guide us. All we knew was that he was a so-called psychic, though we had only the word of Madam Walpole on that score. I trod carefully around tall stacks of newspapers—almost exclusively old copies of *Sporting Life* as far as I could tell—interspersed with piles of dirty laundry. I was about to start rummaging through a large chest of drawers, when it occurred to me to ensure that the flat really was empty before continuing. I left the bedroom, and could hear Ambrose carelessly rifling through Jeffers' belongings in the living room. With a shake of my head, I checked the other rooms, the execrable smell growing stronger as I moved through the flat. I discovered a quite noisome bathroom, a second, sparsely furnished bedroom, and finally a parlour. The room was light and airy compared to the others, with the drapes wide open. However, when I stepped into the parlour the assault on my senses was most unexpected. First, I saw the clear signs of a struggle; the room had been ransacked, broken crockery and ornaments were strewn around the floor, the table was overturned, and a wooden stool was smashed into pieces. Then the smell hit me—the unmistakeable odour of death and decay. Pressing my handkerchief to my mouth, I moved around the room cautiously, but did not have to look far before I saw the man's body lying on the floor near the window, obscured by a tatty armchair. Flies buzzed around the corpse, which looked many hours old to me, possibly even days. I took my hand away from my mouth just long enough to call to Ambrose, and returned it hastily to stifle a cough.

I looked around for some clue as to what had happened, and was distracted by a red smear on the windowpane. It seemed to have been rubbed across the window by an outstretched hand. The fingermarks in the blood were plain. As I stooped to inspect it, my attention was drawn outwards—the window faced the alleyway outside, and directly across from me was another window from the next building along. There, standing watching me, was a young woman. I had almost not noticed her; I had probably glanced at her before and not realised she was there, for she was clad all in funerary black—black fitted jacket, like a riding coatee over her slender form, high-collared blouse with black ruffs, and dark brown hair fastened back severely beneath a black bonnet. What attracted my attention was her face, a pale, beautiful visage framed against the black of her clothes and the shadows of the room behind her. Her skin was like white marble, shining in the wan evening sunlight, and her large eyes sparkled, almost violet, and yet were utterly impassive. There was something about her manner that was cold and aloof and, although she was pretty, she seemed strangely unfeminine. But, more than that, she was strangely familiar; a figure from a dream half-remembered.

My concentration was broken by a peculiar and incessant vibration, accompanied by a strange noise, a humming sound of ever-increasing pitch. It was faint at first, but was gradually growing louder. How long it had been present, I cannot say, but now it was clear, and getting louder and more shrill by the second.

'Ambrose!' I shouted again, and again there was no reply.

I sensed something new and strange. The air in the room seemed to change—even now I find it difficult to describe, but it seemed to cloy, moving like a vista shimmering in intense heat. The shadows around the corners of the room began to grow thicker, and the entire room appeared to 'bend', as if viewed through aged glass. The hairs on the back of my hands and wrists were on end, and the velvet drapes began to rise gently, as though being pulled by some unseen force. My eyes were drawn towards the far end of the room, to where the curtains were being attracted; there I saw, as if for the first time, a closed door, which I assumed must lead to a closet of some sort. Incredible as it sounds, I cannot be certain that the door was even there before. Around the edge of the door shone a faint, golden light that spilled from every crack. Worse, as the trilling noise ebbed and flowed in horrid, ululating waves, the door appeared to distort and heave, as though it were breathing. My own breath became ragged, and I thought that I must be hallucinating. I rubbed absently at my left arm, feeling almost sympathetically the prick of McGrath's syringe once more into my vein.

I snapped my attention back to the window. The girl was still there, but now she was smiling; a sly, sinister smile that chilled me to the core. And she was not alone. She held my gaze, with an expression of triumph on her face, and blew me a kiss before turning away from the window and disappearing out of sight with two other figures dressed in black. Male or female I could not tell. Whoever she was, she was certainly brazen, but I had no time to dwell on her. The noise grew louder still, and Ambrose had not answered my call. Unsure what to do first, I turned to the body, whoever he was, and a memory jolted me to my senses. The body; the woman in black; the humming noise—I had read of these things before, in the police report at the Apollonian; the testimony of Sergeant Clegg of New Scotland Yard. Panic gripped me; there was a chance that the coordinates we had received were a liaison point for the anarchists, and that they were right now across the alleyway in the adjacent building. There was an equal chance, of course, that this building was the target for the next dynamite attack, and I knew I could not stand around waiting to find out. I needed help, and quickly.

I raced from the room, shouting 'Ambrose! Ambrose! Run for it!' at the top of my lungs, but as I entered the living room and made for the exit, Ambrose was nowhere to be seen. The front door was wide open and I ran through it as if the hounds of hell were on my heels. I pounded down the steps as fast as I was able. By the time I reached the final flight, my blood was thumping in my ears, my chest was on fire from the bruises I had sustained the previous day, and I could feel the stitches in my leg pulling apart. The door to the flats was wide open. I could hear the trilling noise even there, echoing around the stairwell. As I ran out of the front door, my world seemed to fall apart. An explosion ripped through the building above me, deafening me in an instant. The expelled air from the corridor within the building rushed through the door behind me, and the force of the blast propelled me into the road, where I was thrown upon the cobbles amidst flaming rubble and debris from the apartment. Everything seemed to spin as I struggled to hold on to consciousness. A cab—was it my cab?—sped away from the building as the horses bolted. I rolled onto my back and gazed up at the black hole that had opened up in the midst of the building. 143c Commercial Road was now open to the elements, and judging by the flames licking around the blackened rent in the brickwork, there wouldn't be much left of the flat to salvage. I somehow hauled myself up, though I could not walk in a straight line. I looked around helplessly; there were bodies in the street, men and women caught in the blast or hit by rubble. Some were already digging for their friends; others were crawling away in scorched and bloodstained clothes. My head felt light, and I put a hand to it only to pull it away, slick with my own blood. I could make out screams and shouts, and another fearful trilling noise. But this time it was a police whistle, and I staggered in its direction, thankful that help had arrived.

When the policemen arrived on the scene mob-handed, it was not as I expected. The first two officers to reach me began to haul me around roughly, and I was so deaf that I could not hear what they were saying. I could only look at them dumbfounded as they mouthed words at me and shook me by the lapels. I glanced around, and was acutely aware that several people were watching us. Some were pointing at me and gesticulated at other policemen. I was utterly confounded, but found myself being half-marched, half-carried towards a Black Maria. By the time we reached the sturdy carriage, my hearing had begun to return, and I was able to round on the policemen.

'Look here, what is going on? Why are you arresting me?' I demanded. The larger of the two constables eyed me savagely.

'You know very well what's going on, sunshine. I won't be surprised if I don't get me promotion for this collar.'

I was aghast. 'Please, I'm trying to understand; what am I supposed to have done?'

'We were just on our way to find you,' chimed the other policeman, 'cos we've heard reports of a suspicious character hanging around these flats. When we get 'ere, there's been another bomb, and who should be seen fleeing the scene of the crime, but you. And you match the description very well. Isn't that right, Alf?'

'Very well indeed,' said Alf, with menace.

'You don't understand. I was trying to stop the bombings. I work for the Crown.'

'And I'm the King of Italy!' scoffed Alf. 'Look at the state of you!'

'You have it all wrong, officers. I am Captain John Hardwick of Apollo Lycea. Ask Sir Toby Fitzwilliam at the club. He'll vouch for me.' I was finding it hard to string sentences together, and realised that there was too much desperation in my voice. The officers eyed each other in bemusement.

'Sir Toby? The judge? Are you 'aving a laugh? What would 'e be doing at the Lyceum?'

'Not the theatre,' I moaned. 'Lie-kee-ah. The Apollonian Club!' I should not have thrown in the name of the club to these men, but I was fast running out of ideas. The policemen looked at me as if I was a lunatic.

'The Apollonian? You? I don't suppose you've got any proof?'

And I knew I was undone, for I had no identification, and my club cards had not yet been issued. I looked down at myself—I was a bloody and battered mess, old wounds and new bundled up in a scorched overcoat, clothes ripped and dirty. I knew that arguing with these uncompromising oafs would get me nowhere.

'Didn't think so. Get in there, you murdering bastard!'

Alf cuffed me round the ear with a clubbing right hand, and the two policemen heaved me into the Black Maria. Even before it had begun to move I could hear the cries of the mob as they caught wind that the perpetrator had been apprehended. Common folk began to chase after the coach, pounding on the sides and shouting obscenities. I had fancied myself law-bringer, and yet there I was, a villain.

We soon picked up speed and left the scene of devastation behind us. As we jolted across the cobbled roads of the East End I curled up on the floor of a dark, mobile cell with only my agony for company.

FOUR

I woke in a dark Whitechapel police cell, barely able to move for my aches and pains. I touched a hand to my wounds, and discovered bandages there—the police surgeon had at least seen fit to patch me up before I was confined. I swung my legs over the side of my cot, and sat with my head in my hands, listening to the protestations of cockney criminals echoing around the corridors of the police station. The irony was not lost on me. Within a week of returning home from a terrible period of confinement in the Far East, I found myself imprisoned again, for a crime I had not committed, and treated most uncharitably by the very people I was trying to serve. I smiled bitterly. Home sweet home.

Before I could reflect further on my predicament, I was wracked by an intense pain throughout my body, and a gnawing hollowness in my stomach that caused me to retch. As a nigh uncontrollable sweating and shivering overcame me, I recognised at once the symptoms of opium withdrawal. It is a truth long known that no degree of abstinence from that substance can ever truly shake a man's body free from the yoke of its influence. I silently cursed Archie McGrath for administering the drug to me. Now I had to face the consequences of his well-meaning mistake alone. I was feeble as I staggered to the chamber pot in the corner of the cell and expelled the contents of my stomach, coughing like an old man with bronchitis all the while. I do not know how long it took for the unpleasantness to subside, but eventually I was able to return to my cot and sleep once more.

I was awakened by the clunking of my cell door, and rubbed at my eyes in confusion.

'Captain 'Ardwick,' a police constable said flatly. 'You're free to go.'

It was as simple as that; no apology, no explanation. I was led along a dreary grey-brick corridor to a large desk, where a sergeant returned my belongings, before being taken to the front desk and handed over to the care of a smartly dressed man. He identified himself as Neville Proctor, a local solicitor appointed by the club to bail me out of police custody. I shook his hand gratefully, and was dimly aware of his expression of disapproval—an expression that rapidly changed to concern.

'Captain Hardwick... you are injured.' When I did not reply, he turned to the desk sergeant and remonstrated with him harshly. 'My client is a gentleman of standing, and these injuries are clearly deserving of a greater degree of care than your people have administered. You have not heard the last of this.' I was too weary to pass remark, but I appreciated the exaggerated comments on my social standing. My membership of the club perhaps led Proctor to assume that I was someone far above my actual station. I was thankful as the solicitor led me out of the police station with one final, withering glare at the sheepish-looking sergeant as we went.

It was dark outside the station; I hadn't even thought to check my pocket-watch, but now I found that the entire day had almost gone by while I'd been in my cell. Proctor showed me to a cab, where I was surprised to find Ambrose waiting for me. The solicitor said his farewells, and left me in the company of my errant companion.

'Hullo, John,' he said, as if nothing at all was the matter. 'Glad to see you're still in the land of the living, eh? Only, it was a close-run thing back there.'

'Where the devil were you?' I snapped. 'And where have you been until this hour?'

Ambrose adopted a chastened look. 'Look, old chap, I didn't have it easy, and I didn't leave you on purpose. It's all in my report.'

'Your report? You've had time to write a report? And to change for dinner, I see.'

'Thought I might have to wade in with old Proctor. You have to look the part when dealing with the everyday bobby.' Ambrose rapped on the roof of the cab with his cane, and the hansom jolted into motion, sending pain coursing through my very bones. I grunted and held my ribs.

'Good Lord, are you all right?'

'I'll live. You were saying?' I prompted, hoping for some form of explanation.

'In a nutshell, whilst you were poking about in the back room, I heard some kind of commotion outside on the stair. I sneaked out to have a gander, and just caught sight of some black-suited fellow making off out of the building. I know I should have shouted for you, but I assumed you'd be all right, and I didn't want to alert the suspect, so I followed him.' 'As it turns out, I was right to be suspicious. I saw him get into an unmarked growler with some other people, all dressed up like in mourning, and one of them a woman! Well, I remembered that police report about the suspects having a woman with them, so I was suspicious at once. They made off at a right old pace down a side-street, so I hailed a cab and set off after them. We must have been half a mile away when we heard the "boom". Of course I was worried, but there was no turning back, do you see? For Queen and country, and all that.'

'I see,' I said, as calmly as I could. Something didn't add up in my mind, but I tried my best not to betray my suspicions. Would Ambrose really have left the building on instinct to follow a random man, after he himself had gone to great lengths to break into the flat? If he had left when he claimed, then he must have been outside even while the mysterious woman was staring at me from the next building. No sooner had she gone than the bomb detonated. Would they have been able to get so far away in a cab, in so short a time, on those busy streets? I said none of this, instead prompting only with 'and did you find them?'

'Lost them, I'm afraid, somewhere around Brick Lane. Got stuck behind a bloody fire-truck of all things. It was late by the time I got back to Commercial Road, and there was no sign of you. I checked the local hospitals, and even the Whitechapel morgue... I've been worried sick. In the end, I returned to the club to report to Sir Toby—I had no idea you'd been arrested. Why, the very thought of it!'

'It's not the worst cell I've ever been in,' I muttered.

'Ah, quite,' Ambrose said, with a nervous laugh.

'In future, Ambrose, I'd kindly ask that we stick together. These anarchists we're dealing with are organised and ruthless. We're in a battle here, and a soldier does not leave his comrades behind.'

'I'm sorry John, but I only tried—'

'We'll say no more about it. I accept your apology.'

Ambrose blinked twice, incredulous at my tone. Perhaps he was not used to being spoken to in such a manner. More likely he had underestimated my qualities and thought me incapable of taking charge of the situation. Well, I determined in that moment to be the shrinking violet no longer. If I would call myself 'Captain', it was time I acted the part.

'So... what now?' Ambrose asked, hesitantly.

'Now I intend to do what I should have done yesterday. I'm going home Ambrose, for a hot bath and some rest. I trust you will pass on my apologies to Sir Toby, for I doubt I'll be in a fit state even to stand up tomorrow. If you will visit at your earliest convenience, we shall plan our next move.'

'Yes sir!' Ambrose saluted sarcastically. He leaned out of his window and shouted up to the driver. 'George Street, near Tottenham Court Road. And go easy—this man is like to bleed out over the upholstery.'

I tried to smile, but the smallest effort pained me. I was too exhausted even to stay cross with Ambrose, and began to yearn for the comforts of home. We had suffered a severe setback, but tomorrow was a new day.

I barely recall returning to my lodgings, but Archie McGrath was waiting for me to check on my wounds once again. He administered stitches, poultices and painkillers to soothe my many cuts, bruises and aches, and was less than complimentary about the police surgeon who had seen to me after my arrest, for my dressings were poor and he had not attended to my torn stitches. I had been functioning well enough upon leaving the police station, but now there was little conversation. I grew feverish and tired, and when Archie left I fell into a deep sleep. The next time I awoke it was morning again.

The new day's light filtered weakly through the net curtains, yet my eyes still took time adjusting to it. My body ached. My first thought was of the little wooden box and my weak opium solution, but I pushed it from my mind quickly. The room was a blur, but I caught movement from the corner of my eye and forced myself to focus. When I saw a man's silhouette I took it at once for Ambrose, but to my surprise it was Captain James Denny, seated in an armchair by the door. He at once fetched a glass of water to me and helped me drink, and eventually I was able to sit up. Jim sat patiently whilst I struggled to find my voice through a claggy mouth.

'How did you—' I began to croak a question, but Jim interrupted.

'Hear about you? Mrs. Whitinger sent word yesterday. She worries.'

'Yesterday? But I... How long?' Every word was a struggle, and I was thankful that Jim seemed to understand my monosyllabic grunting.

'Two days and a night. It appears that the blow to your head was quite serious. A doctor came to see you, said he was from the club.'

'Did he... give me anything for the pain?' I was hesitant. There was something quite serious about Jim's countenance; this was a different James Denny from the one I had encountered at the docks. He leaned forward and spoke more quietly.

'Nothing too strong. He noticed some marks on your arms and... did not know if you had already received medication.' Jim's pause belied his true meaning. He did not press the matter. 'It's a wonder you got home at all,' he said instead.

'What day is it?' I was groggy, and had no concept whatever of time.

'It is Monday morning. You've missed a miserable weekend, but they say the weather is turning for the better.'

'It's good to see you, Jim,' I said.

'Likewise,' he replied, hesitating as he considered his next words. He seemed to decide that honesty was the best policy. 'I suppose the company you have been keeping lately is quite different from that of the service.'

'I'm sure I don't know what you mean.'

'I am sorry, John,' he continued solemnly, 'I don't wish to burden you with worries when you are recovering yet again, but Mrs. Whitinger is beside herself. She sent for me because she did not know what else to do.'

'Jim, my circumstances are unexpected, indeed, but I would never wish to cause the dear lady any distress. She has been nothing but charitable during my short stay.' I paused, collecting my thoughts—I knew what I had to do to make things right

'As soon as I am recovered, I shall make peace with Mrs. Whitinger, and make other living arrangements, of course. Now that I am of independent means, I must strike out on my own; this episode has merely given me the nudge out of the door that I required.'

Jim reached out a hand and patted my shoulder. He seemed to

approve. 'A fine sentiment, dear boy, but I would not expect you to stand alone so soon—I will help you. And besides,' he added with a smile, 'you've done a deuced bad job of picking your friends so far. I'll have to assist you for your own good.'

I managed to laugh about that at least, before it dawned on me that Jim might know more than he was saying about Apollo Lycea. 'I must ask you, Jim, what exactly have you heard about my circumstances, and the company I have kept?'

'Enough,' he replied enigmatically. 'In particular, Mrs. Whitinger has complained of a popinjay who was most brusque with her when you were recently attacked by ruffians in the street. This is the same man, I presume, with whom you were seen breaking into an East End flat? Yes, the army has its sources too.'

'Then you must know that I am innocent of all charges? That I was acting in the interests of the Crown.'

'Yes. Although to what end, who can know? Honestly, John, within a week of returning to England you have been attacked, turned into a burglar and caught up in some anarchist plot. What surprises me the most is that Scotland Yard hasn't been banging down poor Mrs. Whitinger's door to find out what you know about the other explosions. You must have friends in high places.'

'Other explosions?' I suppose I knew what he was about to tell me before he had even begun. Nonetheless, I struggled to sit up, despite Jim's protestations. I was agitated that the case had moved on without me whilst I had been lying there insensible. Under duress, Jim cursed my stubbornness and helped me to the sitting room. Someone had made up a fire, which was as yet unlit. Jim sat me down in the armchair with a newspaper and scrabbled about for a box of matches as I pored over the front pages. The story of yet another dynamite attack in London was still the main news even days after the fact, and the reports included eyewitness accounts of the latest atrocity, and scathing indictments of Scotland Yard's attempts to apprehend the villains responsible. The first explosion, at Commercial Road, had been unusual due to the time of day. Five people had died in the blast, and a score more were injured; but of course, that had only been the start of the terror that had struck the East End that day. As I'd guessed, with a sinking feeling, there had been two more attacks. One in Shoreditch, which had only narrowly missed the old town hall, and another at St. Dunstan's Hill, audaciously close to the Royal Armouries. The newspapermen were not alone in speculating why those nearby sites of importance had been spared. I had no map to hand, and wanted nothing more than to track one down—I was sure now that I had found the pattern; that I could identify their real target and solve this case.

The fire was blazing soon in the hearth, and Jim called down to Mrs. Whitinger, telling her that I was up and about, and asking for a pot of coffee, before taking a seat opposite me.

'So, are you going to tell me who it is you've been working for?' he asked me directly.

'I am not sure if I can, and that is the honest truth. Nothing has been asked of me except that I serve my country; until I am sure of what is expected of me, I must assume that my work is not to be public knowledge, and that my employers wish it to remain so.'

'I see. I suppose that is understandable, although you have not exactly been acting covertly. As I said before, the army has eyes and ears too.'

'How much do you know?' I was on edge. Although I still trusted Jim and had feelings of loyalty towards the service, I knew I had been careless and naïve in conducting my duties for the Apollonian.

'Don't look so worried. I know what you got up to at Commercial Road. I know that before that you had a meeting at the Apollonian Club, and I also know that your compatriot is named Hanlocke. By all accounts he is a shady character, who lives inexplicably beyond his means and acts like a shameless cad at all times, even when dealing with sensitive old ladies.'

Almost on cue, there was a quiet knock at the door, and Mrs. Whitinger entered carrying a silver tray with a pot of coffee and accoutrements. We exchanged pleasantries, although I could see that I was living under her roof on sufferance. I asked if I had received any other visitors in the past two days, at which I received a cold stare.

'Other than that young doctor and Master James, only one,' she said. 'That rude gentleman, Mr. Hanlocke. He said he'd call back when you were feeling better.' Her tone suggested that she'd rather Ambrose didn't call back ever again. All I could do was thank her graciously; Jim took the coffee things from her and bade Mrs. Whitinger good day.

'Jim, regardless of my association with Mr. Hanlocke, I must stress to you that I believe my work is of utmost importance. I am investigating the most heinous string of anarchist attacks that London has ever seen, and I know I'm getting close.' Jim handed me a cup of coffee, and I paused to sip at it. 'I must return to my employers as soon as I am able. No doubt they will need my report. I am surprised they have not been to see me already.'

Jim glanced towards the mantelpiece, and I instinctively followed his gaze and saw, for the first time, a sealed envelope sitting next to the carriage clock.

'It looks as if they have already summoned you,' said Jim, gravely. I reached for the letter, but stopped as the pain proved too much. Jim stood and made to pass it to me, then paused. 'John, you're a strange sort, I'll admit; I know you've been through a lot, and it's just that...' He tailed off. He was still holding the letter, and I reached out for it.

'What is it, Jim?' I asked, taking the envelope from him. 'Please, speak plainly.'

'I fear you are in no fit state for such exploits.' He was clearly uncomfortable with what he had to say. 'You have been under great strain; Mrs. Whitinger says that you were incoherent after you were attacked on the street last week, as though you believed you were back in Burma. And last night, I came to call on you and you were raving about I-don't-know-what; it was madness and fantasy, really. That's why I stayed the night here, to make sure you were alright. Now you're already talking about going back to work, which sounds to me just as perilous as being back in the army.' He took a gulp of his coffee and set it down on the mantelpiece, looking relieved that he had said his piece.

I stared at the envelope in my hands, somewhat vacantly I suppose, and considered Jim's words. I knew that my actions, my words and even my appearance were not those of a rational, sane man. Perhaps Jim was right; perhaps I was not ready for Apollo Lycea, dynamite attacks, or any of it. I felt Jim's hand on my shoulder, and snapped back to lucidity.

'Look, old fellow,' said Jim, in a kindlier tone. 'I can help you. I can see you aren't going to take doctor's orders and get more rest, so talk to me. Let me share the burden. I don't trust this Hanlocke fellow one bit, so let me look after you. We're comrades, you and I, and as I was sent to look out for you when you returned home, I would consider it neglect of my duties to let you go out of your mind or come to harm.'

'And are they your only orders, Jim?' I asked. 'Or have your superiors told you to question me?'

'Question you?' Jim raised a quizzical eyebrow. 'I think all this cloak-and-dagger stuff has made you paranoid. We serve the same Crown, just through different means. If you're planning to get yourself knifed or blown up at any time in the future, you might do well to remember your friend at Horse Guards.'

Although I did not believe my suspicions entirely misplaced, I saw the sense of Jim's words. And his manner was so candid that I could not believe he wished me any harm, nor would he try to deceive me. He sat down again and refilled his cup, and I turned my attention from him and opened the letter. It was a terse missive, and was as I had expected. Sir Toby wished me a rapid recovery, and requested my presence at the club as soon as I was well enough. He wrote that, given my 'present circumstances', he would understand if 'I chose to renege upon the terms of my membership'. However, he noted that there would be a special meeting on Friday evening after dinner, and if I wished to continue my affiliation with the Apollonian, they would expect to see me in attendance. There was no mention of the dynamite attack, of my arrest, or of Ambrose, and Sir Toby advised discretion regarding the contents of the letter and the timing of the meeting. I slapped the letter down in my lap, somewhat annoyed that I had made the transition from celebrated agent to disposable asset in the space of a few short days.

'Something the matter?' asked Jim.

'It appears that I have been excused duties by my new employers. They make no mention of my findings, nor even if Ambrose passed on what little intelligence we collected.'

'Ah, yes. You said were close to a breakthrough in the case.'

'Jim, I believe that I can trust you. Is that so?'

Captain Denny seemed surprised by the question. 'Of course you can.'

'Then, if you will indulge me, I would like to run some hypotheses by you; some deductions I have made about the case. The things we discuss must not leave this room. I have sworn no oaths, but I firmly believe the fewer people who know of my findings the better—that includes your commanding officer at Horse Guards.'

'You have my word, John. I will help you… as a friend, not as an officer.'

'Good. But is there any chance of breakfast first? I am sick with hunger.'

Jim smiled and got to his feet. 'Capital! That's the first sign of recovery—I shall go and organise a tray.'

Over breakfast I told Jim what I had discovered so far, albeit with a few small details omitted—the identity of my employer, the connection with spiritualists in particular, and the bizarre events that I had experienced in Commercial Road prior to the explosion. With hindsight I have no idea why I spoke so freely at all—perhaps months of isolation had made me more garrulous, or perhaps I was under too much strain and really did need to share the burden. In any case, having someone to discuss the case with was a welcome help; Jim was more attentive than Ambrose, and his contributions refined my theories until I was sure I was in touching distance of the truth. Yet the epiphany that would crack the case remained tantalisingly out of reach.

Jim was fascinated by my 'triangle theory' as he called it, and the precision of the map coordinates. I had no sooner finished my breakfast than he leapt from his seat in excitement and dashed for his coat.

'Where on earth are you going in such a hurry?' I asked him.

'I'm going to get a map!' he declared. 'And a daily paper—I shall be five minutes, and then we will see what these anarchists are up to.'

We spent the afternoon discussing the case, moving in turn moment by moment, from thoughtful debate to excited theorising, the hours flying by. The map was laid out on the floor, weighted at the corners by our coffee cups and sugar bowl, and Jim crawled around marking important locations on it with a pencil as I sat like an invalid in my relocated armchair, pointing directions with my cane in the manner of a great military campaigner.

Eventually, we collected our thoughts and several pages of scrawled notes and drew our conclusions over afternoon tea.

'We have to investigate the central points in each instance before we can come to any firm conclusions,' said Jim. 'Obviously you have already visited Marble Arch, and the strange marks you found are fascinating, but confounding. If we find similar signs at the other two coordinates, then we will be on to something.'

'We?' I asked, with a thin smile.

'Well, I hate to be presumptuous, but you're in no fit state to go investigating alone. And I dare say I'll get you into less trouble than that rake you've been knocking about with.'

'I'm sorry Jim,' I said, with a heavy heart, 'but I cannot take you along. This agency that I serve... I have the distinct impression that I've already said too much. As soon as I'm well I ought to report to Sir Toby.'

'I see,' Jim replied, and took a sip of tea whilst trying to mask his disappointment. He did not put up a fight, which surprised me. Rather than appearing disheartened he seemed sorry for me; as though I had got myself into a mess from which he had hoped to help me escape. 'Well, John, if your mind is set on it, you should certainly visit the hospital,' he continued, 'but if I might make a suggestion, the attacks in that area were carried out late last year, and it is probable that the trail has gone cold by now. I believe the freshest clues will be found at the most recent site, which according to all of our information is here.' He leaned forward and jabbed a finger at the thick pencil mark he had made on the map but ten minutes prior. 'The centre of the triangle is Commercial Street, Spitalfields. And if our suspects are following a pattern of using significant structures to make their getaway, then there are only two possibilities: Christ Church, or the Ten Bells. But you'd best get yourself in rude health before venturing back to the East End.'

'I imagine the Ten Bells is the best place to start,' Jim stated. 'Although you'd best be on your guard in that pit. A few words in the right ears and some persuasion of the monetary kind and you'll surely find out if anyone saw anything.'

I was not so sure about that, as my fruitless conversation with the estimable Madam Walpole had proven. The thought of her made me shudder, and I pulled the woollen blanket that Mrs. Whitinger had left in my rooms up around my legs; the warning the old medium had given me still haunted my thoughts.

'The sins of the father shall be visited upon the son.'

What would my father have done? He had been torn between the army and Apollo Lycea, had he not? Where did his loyalties lie? I wondered, perhaps still half-feverish, who had done more to earn mine.

'Jim... there is more that I ought to tell you.' I did not want to disclose any information about the stranger aspects of the investigation, but I felt that if Jim was set on helping me, I must be honest with him.

I let the information pour out of me, knowing as the words left my lips that it sounded insane. The list of psychics and spiritualists; the medium who had seemed to have a message for me; and, finally, the weird, shifting room at 143c Commercial Road, and the woman in black who I was certain was behind the explosion. Through it all, Jim listened intently, head inclined, interjecting only to clarify certain facts, and seeming not to judge anything that I said. I still was not sure that my state of mind was sufficient for my duties, and it was entirely reasonable that my recent injuries coupled with the morphine administered by McGrath had induced some temporary madness or hysteria that even now affected me. I craved assurance to the contrary.

'So then,' I said when my account was complete, 'do you think me mad?'

'Mad?' Jim looked thoughtful once more. 'No. However, I cannot rule out the possibility that a series of trying events may have taken their toll on you. But, regardless, yours is the only first-hand account that anyone has of an anarchist attack, and so it would be negligent of me not to take your word in earnest, your word as a gentleman.'

'Oh, you have that, most certainly!' I exclaimed, grateful and relieved that he intended to help me still.

'Now, assuming that every detail was as you said,' Jim continued, 'there must be a rational explanation. My first thought is that the use of spiritualists is merely a convenient cover for these criminals. The number of mediums and such like in London grows with each passing week it seems, and from what I read in the dailies most of them are little more than petty swindlers—just the type of people who would aid and abet our culprits. As to one of them knowing something personal about you—it is a well-known fact that these 'mediums' employ confidence tricksters to elicit private information from their victims. It may seem unlikely, but these folk make a career out of knowing all they can about their next target. Do you follow?'

'Yes,' I replied, 'but why on earth would I be targeted at all? How could Madam Walpole have known I would be visiting her?'

Jim seemed to ponder this for a moment, and then nodded with some surety. 'These people you are working for—they do not seem terribly careful in concealing their movements. For a secret organisation, they are a mite clumsy. You and Ambrose were openly investigating this case, using your own names rather than nom de plumes. You could have been followed with no small amount of interest from the moment you left your first meeting with whoever-they-are. Why, for all we know, those thugs who assailed you in the alleyway that night could even have been sent by some foreign agency to deal with you!'

I tried to hide my feelings at this great leap of logic from Jim, for it mirrored my own thinking on the matter, but I did not want to confirm it. 'All the more reason to leave these lodgings,' I said instead. 'I would not like to think I was inviting danger to poor Mrs. Whitinger's door.'

'Nor shall you be, I am certain, but we shall take things one step at a time. I shall have a word with some friends of mine when I leave here today, and make sure that someone keeps an eye on the house until you're ready to move on. If I can't secure an extra bobby on the beat, I'll see if I can't pull a few strings at Horse Guards.' Jim stopped and looked at me with concern. 'You seem tired, and perhaps overly worried—I have taken up too much of your time when you should be resting.'

'No, no—it has been good to talk of work to take my mind off my injuries.' Yet even as I protested, I realised that I was very tired, and my joints seemed to ache.

'Never mind. You have a plan of action, and there is nothing more to do except for you to get better. I would like to help you with the investigation, John, but I fear that my involvement will only get you into trouble. I urge you not to rush back to activity. You have taken several nasty turns, and you need to be right as rain if you're to crack this case.'

I felt guilty that I had rebuffed Jim's offer of assistance; after all, the army was all I'd known for so long. Deep down I felt more loyalty to the army than to the club, and my father had worked for both... hadn't he? 'Jim... I might not be able to investigate the case with you, but that does not mean we cannot work together, for the mutual benefit of the Crown.' I found myself saying it almost without thinking.

'What do you suggest?' Jim asked, looking less put out all of a sudden.

'I'm suggesting that I keep you informed of any major developments, especially such intelligence as might require military intervention. In return, you let me know if you find out any more information at your end... and put a good word in for me at Horse Guards when all of this goes belly up.' We both laughed at that, partly because we both suspected it might come true.

'Send me a message as soon as you think you're able. If the army makes any discoveries, I'll keep you appraised unless I'm expressly ordered otherwise. And remember, I was ordered to look after you; that still stands, John. Whatever mischief you and that Hanlocke fellow get into... whatever you need, you know?'

Jim took up his hat and coat and prepared to leave.

'I'll smooth things over with Mrs. Whitinger for you on the way out,' he reassured me. 'She pretends to be a tough old thing, but she's a sensitive soul beneath it all. I know how to talk her round. I'll have her bring some broth for you later, too; you must try to eat, to stave off a relapse.' I nodded cheerfully and bade him good day. He turned just before stepping out onto the landing, saying, 'Oh, I almost forgot—I brought you some reading material to stop you stagnating. Cheerio!' He nodded towards the side-table, then with a smile and a wave he was off.

Jim's positive nature was infectious, and as he left and his footfall on the stairs faded away, I managed to get out of my chair and walked over to the table, leaning heavily on my cane, to find a pile of *Punch* magazines bundled together with twine. The topmost issue was the latest edition, and the caricature on the front cover was of a policeman, a judge and a politician fumbling around in the dark whilst leering Fenians and foreign-looking dynamiters looked on, and the fuse of a comedic blackpowder bomb burned down. I turned around and stared down at the map and the scattered papers on the floor with a grim determination. Dark forces were at work—of that I was certain—and they had got the better of me twice already. It was time to turn the tables.

I felt rested the next day, and though I wasn't sure I could face adventuring around London, I knew I could not remain cloistered away for ever. I sent a brief missive to Sir Toby, informing him that I was on the mend, and was planning to continue my association with the order, and by extension with the investigation. I penned a second note to Ambrose, informing him that we should resume our duties at his convenience. Afterwards I breakfasted with Mrs. Whitinger, who acted as though nothing was amiss—I could only presume that Jim had had words with her, for she did not seem in the least bit cool towards me, and I was grateful for it. After breakfast I felt fit enough for a morning stroll, but even that proved tiring. I had hoped perhaps to use this unexpected recreational time to visit the British Museum, but just the thought of climbing all of those marble stairs and traversing the great exhibition halls defeated me. So, downhearted, I returned to my rooms and tried to make industrious use of my time.

My father's papers still sat in a large box in my lounge, and I had only sorted half of them so far. This, then, would be my first task. I set about organising them methodically into piles, and writing brief instructions for any outstanding business concerns to my solicitor, Mr. Fairclough. I came once more upon the address near Faversham, which had once been my home, and lingered over it. My late father had taken on an estate manager to look after the house, though I had long thought it sold, and as far as I could tell it was still being maintained thus. I took great pains to balance the books so that my old home could remain in my keeping, and sent instruction to Mr. Fairclough to acquire for me a key to the property, and transfer all of the relevant paperwork to my name and notify the manager of the change, so that I could visit it as soon as my business in London was concluded. *Ah, if only it was so simple*, I remember thinking; the case looked unlikely to be resolved any time soon, and was already absorbing so much of my time that a return to the quiet countryside of my youth seemed a pleasure far beyond my reach.

It was late in the afternoon when Archie McGrath called on me. I took tea with him and he checked on my wounds, encouraging me greatly with his appraisal. I was, it seemed, recovering rapidly, and he changed my dressings, passing comment that perhaps this time I could get some bed-rest and allow my stitches to heal fully. Although he was an earnest fellow, I still felt guarded and suspicious of everyone; my conversation with Jim the previous day had left me feeling slightly paranoid, and I was beginning to long for army life again, for the embrace of the only family I had known for many a long year.

After some awkward small-talk, mercifully interrupted by Mrs. Whitinger's collection of our tea things, Archie made his excuses and left me to my thoughts. I realised after he had gone that I had done little to extend the hand of fellowship to him, even though he really did seem amiable enough. I wondered if perhaps I had become too used to isolation, and forgotten the simple pleasures of good company. I contemplated dressing for dinner and taking a cab to the club, but reminded myself of Jim's warning not to return to duty so soon, and so with a weary head I hobbled off to bed.

When I awoke at the start of yet another day, I felt stronger and full of optimism, and mercifully free from the opium cravings that had marred my recovery. I washed, shaved, and dressed for breakfast. I ate heartily, and even managed cheerful conversation with Mrs. Whitinger, at least partly restoring some of her trust in my good nature.

At nine o'clock sharp there was a rap at the door, and soon after the maid brought in a letter addressed to me. It was a short missive, written on headed club notepaper.

John,

I hope this note finds you in good health. I have today received fresh instructions regarding our investigation. Suggest we meet later today. Please accept my invitation to luncheon at the Mitre on Aldgate. Shall we say midday? I hope to see you shortly.

Your Friend,
A.H.

I felt oddly cross; Ambrose had not deigned to visit these past few days, though of course it was likely that the investigation had taken up all of his time in light of the new attacks. Aldgate seemed an odd choice of venue for a meeting, however—did he somehow know that I wished to revisit the East End, I wondered? Or was it just one of Ambrose's regular haunts? Regardless, I was eager to begin work, and so I scribbled an acceptance note, making brief mention of my intention to return to Whitechapel, and instructing Ambrose to dress down for the occasion. When it came time to depart I took up my cane, which I still needed for support, and placed a notebook and pencil in my breast pocket. As I had mentioned to Ambrose, I was careful to select clothing that would not draw undue attention in the East End, especially in the poorer Spitalfields area. I dressed casually, ready for luncheon at Ambrose's chosen eatery, but carried my battered overcoat over my arm so that I could don it when required to travel *incognito*.

I arrived at the Mitre to find it was not quite the modest dining room I had envisaged. It had clearly once been a tavern, and from the outside might still have passed as one, but the current proprietor had transformed it into a more up-market establishment, no doubt to serve the growing number of senior clerks and bankers that laboured each day in the district. I was shown to Ambrose's table, and I held onto my overcoat, slightly embarrassed to hand the tatty article to the waiter.

Ambrose was already waiting for me, having reserved our table ahead of time, taking care to secure a booth where we might conduct our business privately.

'Ah, there you are, old chap,' Ambrose said as I took my seat. 'You look fit as a fiddle. Mind you, you'll forgive me if I don't embrace you, in case you break.' He laughed and took a sip of wine from a glass that was almost empty.

'Go easy, Ambrose,' I said. 'We'll need clear heads today. Business before pleasure.'

'When have I ever done anything in moderation? Face it, old chap, you really yearn to resume our partnership. Your life must have been tiresome dull these last few days without me.'

'"Tiresome dull"… that's one way of putting it, yes,' I replied. 'And you? I presume you have been busy with club duties?'

'For the most part, although not as much as I'd have liked. Old Toby was keen to keep you in the loop for some reason, hence we are here.'

I expected him to explain why he hadn't visited me on my sickbed, but he merely drained his glass and suppressed a burp. It was all I could do not to smile despite myself. This was the Ambrose I had come to know—unashamed and unabashed. And singularly selfish in his own roguish way. Were we really friends? I felt we were, although for the life of me I couldn't work out why.

We ordered a modest lunch of chops and vegetables, and began to formulate our plan of action, using my map to aid us.

'So, we begin at the Ten Bells,' began Ambrose, 'and question the landlord and some of the locals.'

'I agree, but we must also be on the lookout for anything unusual in the pub,' I added. 'Perhaps I am becoming too untrusting, but I cannot rely on the statements of anyone—who knows how far the influence of the anarchists has spread?'

Ambrose nodded as he sipped his beer. A waiter set down our food, and there was a momentary bustle of activity, before we were once again left alone. I was nervous about the coming day's activity, but at the same time I still felt a determination to further the case and bring the anarchists to justice. I could barely sit still during lunch, instead feeling an agitation to set down knife and fork and begin the investigation immediately.

Ambrose and I determined to find out as much as possible at the Ten Bells, and then if need be move on to Christ Church and speak to the vicar or verger there. We were optimistic of results, but even so we looked at the map and planned a route to Chelsea Hospital, another suspected exit point for the dynamiters, to see if anyone there remembered anything suspicious from the earlier bomb attacks. I thought back to my conversation with Captain Denny; I almost wished I had struck out to the East End with him rather than Ambrose. Regardless of conflicts of interest, I had met no one at the club whom I trusted half as well as James Denny. He reminded me of the men I had served with in the East. How I longed for trusted comrades at my side right now—Sergeant Whittock, Lieutenant Bertrand, Corporal Beechworth... these names flitted at the edges of clouded memory, and God only knew where they were now; those steadfast men whom I had called friends. Now true friendship and trust seemed commodities I could ill afford.

When lunch was done, Ambrose produced a small cloth bag from beside him on his bench. I had not noticed it before, and he slid the bag across the table casually, saying quietly: 'You might need this—best keep it hidden, though, until the paperwork comes through. We might be able to convince the law that you're still in the army, but safest not to let it come down to my bargaining skills.'

As soon as I touched the bag, I knew what it contained. I placed it beside me on my own bench, and peeked inside to confirm the presence of the gun: an old snub-nosed Webley, smaller and lighter than the service revolver I had used overseas, but more than formidable enough for the seedier side of London.

'Checked it out of the armoury last night. I trust it's the type you're familiar with?'

I thanked Ambrose, and was glad of the weapon. When I'd landed back in England after my discharge, I would have resisted the idea of carrying a sidearm and seeking any kind of action, so harrowing were my memories of service. Now, however, I was filled by thoughts of pitting my wits against an elusive, dangerous and determined foe. And, truth be told, of evening the score should the opportunity arise.

Our first destination was Commercial Street, and our route took us past the yawning mouth of Commercial Road, along whose wide street could be seen the havoc wreaked by the recent blast. Though the debris was mostly cleared and traffic now crawled along the thoroughfare, it was a far cry from the crammed and energetic scene that had presented itself to us on our last visit just days ago.

Through the bustle of street life and industry we passed, until the hansom came to a stop near a busy junction, outside the gleaming edifice of Christ Church. As Ambrose paid the driver I stepped towards the church, gazing up at its classical façade and stupendously tall steeple, and feeling almost dizzied by the bizarre, sharp-edged shadows that criss-crossed the frontage, making the unmatched windows and blind arches seem strangely stark and somehow detached, floating ethereally upon a canvas of smooth, white stone. It was majestic; more of a temple than a church, and it seemed so wholly out of place, towering as it did over the small buildings around it.

I felt a tap on my arm. Ambrose indicated the public house across the street from Christ Church.

'Magnificent church,' he stated. 'But we have business over the road first—if in doubt, always take drink before church; it's a rule I swear by. Now, we don't want a repeat of that business with the dreadful Walpole woman, so follow my lead. We do not want to be taken for newspapermen, Scotland Yard, or, worse still, bloody daytrippers.'

'Daytrippers? Here?' I asked, ignoring his assumption that I was some kind of buffoon.

'Oh yes. The spirit of Saucy Jack looms large in the Ten Bells,' said Ambrose. 'Followers of the Autumn of Terror flock here to see where the Ripper's victims used to drink. Puts coin in the tills, but drives the locals to distraction. No, we shall pretend we are former patrons, who have steered clear due to the recent trouble. Let's pretend we've heard some scurrilous rumours in the gutter-press that brings the pub into disrepute. They'll be so angry that they'll tell us all we need.'

'I'm not sure making them angry is the way to go about it. What if it doesn't work?'

'Then we use our fall-back plan.'

'Which is?' I asked.

'You buy them all drinks until they talk.' And with that, he was across the road and through the door with me trailing behind like his shadow.

Ambrose's plan went almost entirely smoothly, which caused me to wonder if, when not playing the dandy, he often caroused with the common working man in backwater establishments. He certainly took to coarse conversation and weak ale like a duck to water.

Upon learning that several fictitious newspapers had named his pub as a notorious haunt of the hated dynamiters, the publican had become most indignant, and his regulars had rallied round him.

'I run an honest establishment!' the landlord had cried. 'If I had cause to believe... why it beggars belief... oh! I should have words with these muck-rakers!' It seemed to me that the press was not well-liked in the East End, doubtless for their endless portrayals of the local colour as gin-addled wastrels and violent thugs in order to amuse the middle-class commuter crowd.

In exchange for several rounds of drinks, the tongues of the regulars were soon loosened and their observations imparted. It was only, however, when I mentioned that the anarchists were sometimes called 'men in black' that we struck upon vital intelligence, which perhaps the police would have overlooked.

'I heard that they always dress in smart black clothes, and sometimes stay near the scene of the crime to witness their handiwork,' I'd said. 'And other times still…' I leaned in and lowered my voice, causing everyone to lean forward also and listen to me carefully, '…they even have women with them, decked out in their afflictions.' There was an audible intake of breath, until finally a small man with a hard, pinched face spoke up.

'I can barely believe my ears, and I swear upon my mother's grave that this is the first time I have heard such thing, but I fear I may have seen something after all!' He seemed nervous and hesitant, but perfectly sincere. He was an old sot named Tom, and it transpired that he had been drinking in the Ten Bells on the evening of the third—as he did most evenings, it seems—and had stepped outside when he heard 'holy hell' breaking loose, which he'd first taken for an earthquake.

'A few of us went outside to see what was happening,' he had explained, 'and there was a terrible commotion. Bobbies whistlin', fire-trucks a-clatterin', and people running all about shoutin' bloody murder. We could see smoke risin' from over the rooftops in three great plumes. Never seen anything like it in all my days. But there was something else. Something that I'd forgotten about until just now.' He had stopped to take a drink, continuing only when he was satisfied that everyone was on tenterhooks waiting for his testimony. 'Across the road we saw two men and a young lady, all dressed in black. Too smart for the time o' day. My mate 'Arold said to me, he says, "Look at them there, in their Sunday best. Didn't know there was a funeral on today." For sure enough, they was heading into the church, and they was in a terrible 'urry;

all flustered and out of puff they were. And 'Arold was right; I hadn't seen a black-coach all day.'

'And what happened? Did you see them again? Where did they go?' I was eager to know more. Perhaps it was that eagerness that stopped him from proceeding, suspecting that I was one of those 'muck-rakers' after all, or perhaps that was all he knew, for all he would say was: 'Dunno sir. I never saw them again, surely, and never paid it no mind until today. And to think, I might have seen them dynamiters with me own eyes!'

At the culmination of Old Tom's tale, it became obvious that our true business was at the church, and we had already attracted too much of a little gathering in the Ten Bells, some of whom were surely suspecting us of being policemen or reporters by that point. We made our excuses and beat a retreat, straight across the road to the Baroque church.

The atmosphere within Christ Church was positively otherworldly. The nave was both spacious and claustrophobic at the same time; Gothic arches, and carved Composite columns seemed to break up every open space, so there was no logical path for the eye to follow into the huge nave until one was actually standing in its centre. The dichotomy of light and shadow was dizzying; streams of pale light poured in through the clerestory, causing shadows of varying intensity to criss-cross the nave before blending into pitch darkness in every far corner. It was as though the architect had attempted to paint a melancholy scene using naught but light. A few large tallow candles were lit here and there, and their smoke mingled with incense from an unseen source to make the very air seem to writhe around us. There was no sound, save for a faint coughing from a solitary worshipper near the altar, and the sound of our heels ringing on the flagged floor as we made for the vestry. There, we met the incumbent rector, Dr. Billing, and his young verger, Michael, who were more than helpful when we explained our business. There was little deception required on our part with staunch men of the cloth, although Ambrose introduced us as Home Office agents nonetheless, leaving me no choice but to play along.

We spent some time taking tea in the vestry with the loquacious rector, with Ambrose at least making a show of professionalism when his mouth wasn't stuffed with cake. Michael spoke little, and after just minutes in the rector's company I doubted that he had much opportunity; the elder clergyman strayed too readily and too often from the matter at hand for my liking, and chattered almost non-stop.

'I do recall,' he said, when eventually he decided to answer my questions directly, 'that on the evening of the third we were disturbed by a loud noise, as though the door had been opened and closed sharply; isn't that right Michael?' Michael was given no chance to reply. 'We were both certain that the door had been locked, so we went out to the nave to investigate.'

It seemed our luck was in, for the two of them had stayed late on the night in question, and had recorded the events in a diary, which the rector fetched to remind himself of the facts.

'We checked the main door, and found the wicket door open,' Dr. Billing continued. 'This was most disconcerting, for I remembered locking it myself, and Michael was certain he remembered me doing so, didn't you Michael? This is not the fairest district of London, and it was near dark outside, so we were concerned that perhaps some disreputable type had entered by force. It was with some trepidation that I poked my head outside and surveyed the scene. There was nothing unusual as far as I could tell. There were a few people scurrying back and forth, still frantic after the dynamite attack, but no one approached our doors or loitered nearby.

'I closed the door once more, and bade Michael watch it whilst I looked around the church. If someone had forced their way in, I did not want to lock the door once more for fear of being trapped inside with the type of individual who would break into a house of God. I fumbled for a match and lit some more of the candles, but just then we were both made to jump out of our skins by another noise, this time from the crypt. Well, I need not explain that we were now in a bit of a funk, for it seemed obvious that someone had entered the church and was rattling about in our crypt. At best, I surmised, it would be a poor unfortunate of the streets, seeking shelter; at worst, a grave robber, though he would find no recent burials down there.

'Though it was tempting to step outside and call for a policeman,' Dr. Billing went on, 'I gathered my wits and decided to investigate. After all, it would be a desperate individual indeed who would knowingly attack a man of the cloth. I crept to the crypt door, with Michael close behind, glancing back towards the front door now and then in case anyone else should enter. As we reached the entrance to the crypt, I am sure I heard a strange whistling sort of noise, which once more threatened to set my nerves jangling. But I steeled myself, and with a muttered prayer I pulled open the door. As I did so, a great and sudden draught blew out my candle, and there came a flash of light—although Michael and I cannot agree on that point entirely. We found ourselves standing in pitch darkness, staring into a dark, silent crypt. There was no longer a whistling noise, or any sign of habitation.

'It took the two of us some time to pluck up the courage to enter the crypt, I can tell you. But when we did, and had lit every wall-sconce and candle, we found nothing. No signs of any disturbance at all. All we could think was that it must have been the wind, and eventually we laughed about it and remarked what sorry souls we would have looked had anyone seen us. With the fright over, we conducted a full search of the building, until we were satisfied that the church was secure. We stayed a full hour after that, but no one came seeking sanctuary or counsel, and so we left for the night.'

The hairs on the back of my neck stood on end, not because the rector's tale was related in the manner of an old ghost story, but because I recognised some parallels with my own experiences, and knew that were close on the trail of our anarchists.

'Is there any other way out of the crypt?' Ambrose asked.

'Technically, yes, but it is not possible that the exit was used.'

'How so?'

'There is a very old passage that leads to the churchyard—an old catacomb, I suppose, which would have been used to bring remains in and out—but it has been blocked up for many years. The doors at either end are chained shut and have not been used in living memory. They were secure when I checked. They also adjoin the vaults, which descend even further beneath the porch, but these have long been emptied and there is no exit from those either.'

At this, Ambrose and I naturally investigated the crypt, finding a doorway at the far end of the vaulted chamber. The rector said that the door had once led to a passageway to the churchyard, but that it had long been filled in and now led only to a brick wall. After a thorough search, we at last made a breakthrough.

Though the signs were faint, they were unmistakeable, and when Ambrose came back to see what so fixated me, he saw them too. Around the stone frame of the door—the door which led to nowhere—was a crisp, pale marking; a thin line of bright, clean stone, perfectly straight, following the curvature of the archway all around its interior. The line was less than half an inch thick, flanked on one side by the commonplace grime of the ages, while on the side closest the door were greyish marks, like soot stains or scorch-marks. These flecked the stones, growing less distinct the further from the linear mark they travelled. It was as though someone had scoured clean the aged stone with meticulous precision, but to what end we could not fathom. It had to be linked to the Marble Arch incident somehow, for the coincidence was too great.

We obfuscated our findings, for we had no idea what to make of them ourselves, and our mission was a covert one. Instead, we assured the good Dr. Billing that nothing was amiss, and that we would eliminate the clergy of Christ Church from our enquiries.

I hailed a cab as soon as we left the church, and we prepared for a lengthy journey as the roads were horribly congested. It was the end of the working day for many, and we had no choice but to join the slow procession of carts, cabs and omnibuses that seemed to characterise this part of the East End. Even the cab was shabby and tired-looking, with bare wooden seats, a grimy floor covered in cigarette butts and an odour of stale smoke.

After three-quarters of an hour we were still in Whitechapel. Ambrose's belly-aching began to grate on my nerves, for, having partaken of too much wine and beer already, and having grown sleepy in the comfortable environs of Billing's vestry, he was now of the opinion that we should repair to the club and continue our investigations the following day. I would have none of it; we had learned much, even if we had yet to unravel the mystery, and I was eager to press on despite my throbbing head and aching bones. We still had not visited Chelsea Hospital, which, if my 'triangle theory' had any credence, would bear similar fruit to Marble Arch and Christ Church.

By the time we reached the hospital it was dark, and the heavens had opened again for good measure. We could find no one at that immense complex who could even recall where they had been on the morning of 15 November 1889, let alone whether or not they saw anyone suspicious. As Jim had forewarned me, the case was too old, and the trail had gone cold.

Ambrose and I made a cursory search of the grounds and principal buildings as the rain intensified. Although there were many large gateways, arches and entrance porticos that could have borne similarities to the sites at Christ Church and Marble Arch, we could find no unusual characteristics or markings on any of them, and after several hours gave up our sleuthing, our spirits as dampened as our rain-drenched clothes.

As our cab plodded and rocked towards home, we talked in hushed tones of the strange markings in the archway of the crypt, and of the mysterious people in black who were plaguing this great city. Who they were, and what their intent was, seemed more obscure than ever, but our progress was tangible. This was a puzzle we had to solve, and time was of the essence.

FIVE

'Jim? I mean, Captain Denny?' I corrected myself as soon as I noticed another man present, a colonel in full uniform, staring thoughtfully out of the library's large sash window at the lashing rain beyond.

Holdsworth, who had shown me in, bowed and backed out of the club library, closing the doors as he went. Jim came and shook me firmly by the hand.

'John, good to see you're well. May I present Colonel Stirling of the Royal Horse Guards.'

The older man turned and nodded. He looked the grim sort, straight-backed and firm-jawed.

'Honoured, sir,' he said. 'Heard a lot about you.' He turned back to the window, as if the drear weather were of infinitely more interest than the company.

'What brings you to the Apollonian, Captain?' I asked Jim. His presence had thrown me off-guard. Sir Toby's 'special meeting' was, I had believed, for members of the order only. As far as I knew, my exchanges with Jim regarding the London Dynamiters case had been confidential, but I could see no other reason why he would be here.

'Looks as if your fellows here are ready to involve the army in… whatever it is you're involved in,' Jim said. 'Colonel Stirling was invited as a representative of Whitehall, and he brought me as his aide. Small world, eh?' It was perhaps my imagination, but I felt Jim looked uncomfortable as he spoke, eyes downcast, feet shifting.

'It's a strange choice for a man of your history to make,' the colonel said, interrupting without moving from his regimented position. 'One might think, if you were fit for active duty, you might have re-enlisted with the Sixteenth. Might I ask why we find you on this side of the line?'

'I wasn't aware of any "line" sir,' I said, suspicious and slightly resentful of the remark. 'In fact, I had never intended to serve again when I returned home. An opportunity presented itself, and I felt duty bound to take it. That is all.'

'Hmm,' was all the reply the Colonel offered, and the room fell at once awkwardly silent.

'Awful weather we're having,' Jim said at last. 'I bet you didn't miss this part of London life.'

'On the contrary,' I said, 'I find it comforting, in a nostalgic sort of way. Absence makes the heart grow fonder, and all that.'

'Hmm,' Colonel Stirling almost growled again, though quietly. I did not know if it was aimed at me or at some internal monologue he was having—his face, as I could see it reflected in the glass of the window, was as stone.

At this, Jim looked at his feet, and then stepped away to the bookshelves, making a play of gazing interestedly at gold-leafed spines. I shuffled the newspapers on the nearest table, but every headline screamed of police incompetence and the dynamiters' reign of terror, and I could not bear to read them. And so I waited in uncomfortable silence, checking my pocket-watch often and wondering why on earth I'd arrived early for Sir Toby's meeting. On my watch-chain was clipped a key, recently acquired, the very sight of which, thankfully, made my mind wander from the rudeness of the colonel.

Early that afternoon I had received a letter from Mr. Fairclough, my solicitor, containing information and sundry legal documents pertaining to the old farmhouse in Kent, along with a key to the property and the name of the estate manager, a certain Mr. Baxter, of Boughton & Sons Estates, Faversham. The key had stirred such emotion within me that I had immediately felt a yearning to see the old place again, though I knew it could not be until my present assignment was complete. In any case, just being able to hold the key in my hands was a rare pleasure, and I had stood in my room clasping it tight, trying to picture a happier time, but the images would not come. I'd had fleeting senses of a childish playfulness, from a carefree summer spent with a loving family, but I could not picture the house, my sister, my mother, or my place in it. Only my father stayed clear in my memories, always a figure of authority, chiding and reproachful. I half wondered if I should return to the house at all, that perhaps nostalgia was playing me false, and that I would find no nurturing, homely old place in which to live out my days when my duty was done. But I clung to hope, and had clipped the iron key to my chain, feeling some small comfort for having it with me.

I was still squeezing the key tightly in my hand when, to my considerable relief, Holdsworth returned to the library. The straight-backed porter cleared his throat before addressing us.

'Sirs—the guests are assembled and your presence is required in the committee room. If you would care to follow me.'

We took Holdsworth's lead to the upper storey, along the dark-panelled corridor, to a long, narrow room, bathed in the warm light of gas jets and a crackling fire. As we entered we saw before us a long, oval table of polished mahogany, around which were a dozen or so high-backed chairs. A projection box was positioned on a side-table at one end of the room, shining its yellowish light onto a white screen that had been placed against the opposite wall.

Holdsworth announced us to the gentlemen who were already seated and deep in discussion, save for Ambrose Hanlocke, who alone was disengaged from the conversation. I was more than a little surprised to find Ambrose arrived ahead of me. Sir Toby rose from his seat at the head of the table, dismissed Holdsworth, and showed the three of us to our seats. He introduced each of the other guests in turn: Sir Arthur Furnival, William Melville of Scotland Yard's Special Branch, and a Mr William James. Ambrose Hanlocke, of course, I already knew, though when he stood and shook hands with the two military men beside me, I could not help but feel a frostiness between him and Jim, and Jim took a seat as far from Ambrose as was possible. As William James extended a greeting to us, I realised from his accent not only that he was an American, but also exactly who he was.

'Mr. James, I did not recognise you; you are the brother of—'

'Of Henry? Yes, Captain, I am. My brother takes all the plaudits while I do all the thinking.' He seemed serious, and for a moment I feared I had caused offence by comparing him to his more famous brother, but his thickly bearded face creased into a warm smile, and he laughed and shook my hand firmly. 'Don't look so frightened, sir. My brother has been here so long that it's a natural reaction whenever I meet an Englishman.'

Of the other members of the group, Sir Toby was his usual stern self; Sir Arthur was a rake-thin man of perhaps forty, with a pale complexion and nervous disposition. Finally there was Melville, whom I knew only by his somewhat fearsome reputation. Though he had built a career on being an uncompromising opponent to terrorists and assassins the world over, protecting London from Fenian plots and even foiling an assassination attempt on the Queen herself, I found him to be a soft-spoken, thoughtful man with a gentle Irish lilt to his voice. Yet there was something in the way he carried himself and the steel of his pale eyes that betokened an inner strength. In all, this was a coalition of powerful men, into which I, Jim and Ambrose did not seem to fit.

We quickly settled into our places, with Sir Toby at the head of the table. It was only then that I became aware of another man, sitting in the shadows behind Sir Toby; a man who had not been introduced, and in fact was being ignored by all. I discounted him at once as a servant of the order.

'Gentlemen,' Sir Toby began, 'now that the formalities are done, I would like to get straight to business. For those of you who are not aware, everyone seated at this table is an agent of Apollo Lycea, and what you are about to hear is beyond state secrets. Outside of the Royal administration, the Prime Minister, and this room, there are few men who have even the slightest inkling of what we are about to discuss, and it must remain so. No one else in the country merits further disclosure at this time.' Sir Toby's eyes met mine fixedly, and his intent was clear. *He knows about my meetings with Jim*, I thought. I knew full well that I should not have confided in anyone outside of the club, but I had been caught in the moment, my thirst for knowledge and adventure clouding my judgement.

'There are also those present who are fairly new to the order,' Sir Toby continued, 'or who have no prior knowledge of the wider implications of this case: the case of the "London Dynamiters" as it has become known. However, everyone here has investigated this matter in one capacity or another, and the time has come for full and frank disclosure of all the facts that we have gathered. Our intelligence has ever been shared on a "need to know" basis—well, gentlemen, everyone around this table needs to know this.' He paused to pour himself a glass of water. My mind turned back to the 'servant' seated behind Sir Toby. I squinted against the darkness; was it my imagination, or was the man dressed as a gentleman, and too old to be a porter or valet?

'What you are about to hear will stretch your credulity to the very limit, and perhaps beyond,' said Sir Toby. 'But the very survival of our way of life depends upon your faith; because that is what it will boil down to: faith. You have my word that, regardless of how unbelievable it will sound, Mr. James is about to reveal to you the truth of the matter, and the gravity of our situation is beyond comparison. To explain further,

Mr. James is recently arrived in London, and comes to us bearing extraordinary news. He is here, gentlemen, because he understands the dynamiters better than anyone alive. I give you William James.'

I sat more upright. That anyone could have made greater progress on the case than even Ambrose and me was of singular interest, and from across the Atlantic?

The American bowed his head and thanked Sir Toby. He was not a large man, but he had a serious and imposing look about him, perhaps enhanced by his bushy black beard, flecked with grey, and a wrinkled, permanently furrowed brow.

'Let me begin by saying that "truth", as Sir Toby puts it, is in the eye of the beholder.' His colonial accent was noticeable, though not strong. 'As a philosopher, I always say that truth is whatever version of events has the most cash value. I guess the story I'm about to tell you is of such import that it has real currency; whether you believe it or not is up to you. What you can believe is that many thousands of lives will depend upon us all acting upon it. Most of you will want to hear "hard facts". I confess I do not have many of those. What I am asking of you is to set aside your intellectual loyalty to hard facts for a moment, for what we are facing is not easily explained away— it is embedded in the unseen and, if I dare even say it, the metaphysical. I am asking you to believe.' At this point I was lost, and I noticed that a frown had found its way onto the features of Melville in particular.

'You are all familiar, I expect, with the ideas of spiritualism, and the widespread practice of the mystical and theosophical arts? These ideas have grown steadily in strength and popularity for the last four decades or so, and it is hard to find a district in London or New York without a whole community of believers, mediums and fortune-tellers. Before you start to question my ideas and beliefs, and thus my words, let me point out that I am not a spiritualist, but a rationalist. I have studied the spiritualist movement for many years—both the confidence tricksters and the inexplicably gifted. In my quest to learn more about the power and nature of the soul, I was led on a path of discovery, a quest to uncover measurable, quintessential truths. But what I found was not what I had expected to find.

'Throughout the ages, religion has taught us that the universe is morally ambiguous—at best ambivalent, at worst indifferent. Good and evil exist simultaneously, and we learn from the Bible that we cannot have one without the other. The world that we know is shaped by the actions of men, and those actions are informed by their beliefs, their morality. What spiritualism teaches is that a man's choices and actions do not cease when he goes to his grave, but rather live on. But where do they live on? If a spiritualist can contact the spirits of the dead, then where do those spirits reside?

'I believe that there may be more to the spirit than is visible, that some obfuscating veil must exist between this world and some other, unseen world. The universe that we know and in which we believe is a mere surface-show for not one, but myriad other states of being. Somewhere, intangible, and tantalisingly out of reach, is a multiverse—an infinite number of places where ideas, beliefs and morality take form. Imagine that, running parallel to our world right now, passing through us like light through water, are other existences; veridical planes inhabited by people just like us—people who are us, but who have made very different choices in life. Some planes may be inhabited by the dead, or by creatures that our most celebrated authors could only dream of, or ghosts, or devils, or angels... my point is that we are not alone. We merely sit behind a recondite, invisible wall and think ourselves safe from forces beyond our control.'

'Mr. James,' said Melville, 'with all due respect, you are talking of heaven and hell, and you do so without due regard to the teachings of God. Nor do you consider the considerable views of the scientific community.'

'Mr. Melville, I understand your concerns fully,' James responded. 'The Church has long held special meaning for many people throughout history, and still does. But the Church represents religion, or one religion in any case, which in itself is a supernatural concept. Religion attempts to explain that there is everlasting life, in a world unseen, which stretches beyond our mundane experiences.'

'I am a God-fearing man,' Melville barked, 'and you will not convince me that there is more than one afterlife!'

'I do not say otherwise. But I theorise that there is more than one life—an infinite number of you, an infinite number of me; physical counterparts of every living soul, all living and breathing beyond the veil.'

'This is nonsense,' Melville scoffed, his accent sounding more Irish the more flustered he became. 'Surely you must at least accept that the greatest scientists in the Empire can find no evidence to support your claims.'

'Science, sir, is a fleeting, new art in the great and long history of the human race. We have discovered a great many things through scientific investigation over the last thousand years, but to think that we know it all is the greatest arrogance. I am sure the next thousand years of science will prove just as fruitful, and will probably even discredit much of our current thinking. Our modern science surely can represent no more than the merest glimpse of the universe's true nature. Science is but a drop of clear water in a sea of clouded ignorance.'

Melville bristled. At no point did James raise his voice or become even slightly antagonistic, but somehow his calmness and thoughtfulness made his words even more pointed.

'Consider this,' James continued. 'The soul is eternal, and so why shouldn't hopes and dreams and the power of thought be just as eternal? Maybe they are part of the soul after all. If I were to die in this world, or even if I merely ceased to believe in something important to me, what would that do to the other "me" in another, unseen world? Science teaches us, after all, that energy can never be destroyed, only transformed—does that apply beyond the veil also? Have you ever been possessed of a notion, or a feeling, and not understood why? Or been compelled to action against your better judgement? Have you never felt that sensation of having been somewhere before when you know that you never have; what the French call déjà vu? The multiverse theory goes some way to explaining these things, or rather these things have no explanation but that of the multiverse.'

'Mr James...' and before I even knew it, I was speaking up. Even in such company as this I somehow felt compelled to voice my concerns, and given James's last words the irony was not lost on me, for I would sooner have held my tongue.

'Yes, Captain?'

'I... that is,' I took a breath and composed my thoughts. 'The idea is a fascinating one, but I am a simple man. I have been a soldier for ten years, and now I am returned to England I find the capital imperilled by an unknown enemy. I do not fully understand your meaning so far, I confess, but with the greatest respect I must ask you this: what has any of this to do with our dynamiters? Are you suggesting that they are driven by unseen forces? Or perhaps you believe that they are come from one of these invisible universes to terrorise us?' I stopped speaking, realising that all eyes were upon me.

'My dear boy,' James said, 'though you will not and cannot believe it, you have arrived at the pinch of the game—you are more than a simple soldier, that much is clear.'

'If soldiers are held in such high regard in Apollo Lycea,' I was surprised to hear Colonel Stirling interject, 'then perhaps your neighbours at the War Office should have been brought into your confidence earlier.'

'Hear, hear,' came a voice from the shadows—the mysterious man whom I had earlier taken for a servant. As far as I could tell, only Sir Toby acknowledged his contribution at all, and even then with but a look of agitation.

'Sir, might I remind you that I am not a member of the order, nor am I a servant of your Crown,' William James replied to the colonel. 'I stand before you offering my assistance in what small way I can; kindly leave me out of any politicking.'

'Hmm,' muttered the colonel.

James swiftly picked up where he had left off, becoming more animated, addressing the entire group once again. 'Captain Hardwick has grasped the nettle. He wants to know where his target lies, and how he can destroy it. The problem is, of course, that finding our unseen assailants is hardly so simple. Three people in this room have set eyes upon the so-called dynamiters—the good Captain, Mr. Hanlocke and Mr. Melville—but in each instance they managed to elude us, and are undoubtedly now returned to their own side of the veil.'

'I must protest.' This time it was Melville who spoke out. 'I listened to some of your hypotheses before the meeting began, but I cannot believe this... this bunkum! What I have seen with my own eyes beggars belief, I agree—but this cannot be the truth of it. It just... cannot be!'

'And what did Sir Toby say at the start of this meeting? He said we needed faith; to believe. If you have any hope of apprehending these villains, then believe you must! What if I were to tell you that these attacks boil down to religion, superstition and belief? That the power of faith itself has made transportation between two universes possible?'

'I would say that you were a madman.' Melville was seething, and it was easy to see how he came by such an uncompromising reputation. His eyes were like dark voids, piercing and inquisitorial, and his voice as calm as still water, yet fierce at the same time. To his credit, William James was unflinching—his cracked-leather face and thick beard were like impassive armour that no amount of insult could penetrate.

'Then you may say that, but please do me the courtesy of hearing me out first, sir. For it is not conjecture that has led me to these conclusions, but reason, collateral facts, and the burden of proof. '

'Gentlemen,' Sir Toby interjected, 'it appears that the

discussion is becoming somewhat heated. I have the advantage of having heard Mr. James speak on this matter before, and have read his papers on the topic, which have been verified by the Society for Psychical Research. I will make available the dossiers with all of Mr. James' theories and notes after this meeting, for you to digest at your leisure. For now, I would respectfully ask Mr. James to keep to the useful facts, to give us the information that will allow our agents, and Mr. Melville's agency, to combat the threat to the Empire in very real terms. Mr. Melville, pray grant us a little more time to put forth all of the evidence to your satisfaction. For now I am afraid I must ask you to set aside your disbelief and assume that what we are dealing with here are agents from another world—people just like us; who may even be us, from a world unseen.' It was clear that Melville was in no way impressed by this request, nor did he believe what he was being told in the slightest, but he acquiesced at Sir Toby's insistence. 'And Mr. James, may I ask you to explain precisely what we are dealing with, in clear terms, so that Captain Hardwick and Mr. Hanlocke may proceed with their duties?'

William James stood, and nodded to both Sir Toby and to Melville.

'Sirs, I am at your service, and will endeavour to stay on topic.' He turned to the rest of us. 'Gentlemen, may I ask that you dim the lights further, because I need to show you some photographic slides.'

He walked to the other end of the table to stand behind the projection box as the room went dark. With a soft clunk the first image flicked onto the white screen. The grainy photograph was instantly recognisable as Marble Arch, and the scene was populated by policemen, while a group of gentlemen gathered around a body, lying prone before the archway.

'This picture was taken by a police photographer at the scene of the Marble Arch shooting. The gentleman in black in the centre of this photograph is our own Mr. Melville. The body he is inspecting is one of the anarchists.'

I was stunned—had one of the suspects really been killed at the scene? Hadn't Ambrose told me that all of the suspects had escaped? The second slide flicked into view.

'And this is the same scene, less than three minutes later.' The image was similar to the first—the police officers who were kneeling by the body were in much the same position as before, others had moved around. But there was a very important omission—the body was gone! A murmur went around the small company.

'It is my firmest belief,' James continued, 'that each of the anarchists—these "Othersiders"—carries with them some device that transports them back to their own world in the event of their death. Whether they activate this device themselves, or if it functions of its own accord once their heart stops, we have no way of knowing, for we have yet to recover a device for study. Mr. Melville managed to gather some small items from the body before it vanished into thin air, but that is all.'

'You know my feelings on the matter, Mr. James,' seethed Melville.

'Oh yes. You see, gentlemen, Mr. Melville would rather believe that some cabal of brilliant scientists is behind the whole plot. Perhaps they are stage magicians? Perhaps they used a powerful acid-spraying device to dissolve the body in an instant, or even some kind of advanced molecular transportory system that one might expect to find in the works of Jules Verne. Anything, in fact, other than the notion that these invaders come from another universe in a multiverse created by human thought and faith.'

I was sure that Melville was not the kind of man to read science fiction, and the Irishman's face supported this idea. I too found the whole thing hard to swallow, and I could see similar opinions writ plainly on the faces of everyone around the table, except perhaps Sir Arthur, who frowned in concentration and nodded sagely.

'Tell them how the other anarchists got away. Let's see how your theory holds up then,' Melville prompted.

'Oh, it's really quite simple. Only I wouldn't call it a theory—this much I'm quite sure of. Thanks to the work of Captain Hardwick here, I have been able to piece together more parts of the puzzle. You see, he first recognised that the so-called dynamite attacks could be plotted on a map of London to form a near-perfect triangle. I believe that the Otherside agents detonate their bombs at a carefully arranged time and place in order to create psychic dissonance—not just an explosion, but a wave of invisible energy—that coincides precisely with the destruction of the exact same corresponding points on their side. The coordinates are meticulously recorded, and the timings are exact, so that the violence of the explosion reaches out across universes, and is felt on both sides. The point in the dead centre of the triangle, which usually takes the form of a door, archway or other portal, then springs to life as a gateway to the other side—for a limited period, that is. The Othersiders prepare their version of the gate with their strange devices, and when it springs to life, powered by the psychic shockwave caused by the explosions, the portal opens on our side too; a literal door between universes.'

'This is too much...' muttered Ambrose.

'But... but...' I stammered.

'Yes, Captain?'

'That is, what I don't understand,' I continued, 'is why they would need such a doorway. If they have the power to activate devices which transport corpses back to another universe, then why go to such lengths to open a doorway?'

'My point exactly!' snorted Melville in agreement.

'There we have two questions in one. The first requires a further leap of logic, I am afraid, and that is: why the doorways? Thankfully, Sir Arthur has helped me with this very issue.'

Sir Arthur Furnival, who had remained silent up to this point, now leaned forward in his chair. As he spoke, William James advanced the slides, to show the crypt door in the vaults of Christ Church, and the wrought-iron front gates of Chelsea Hospital, where Ambrose and I had found nothing.

'Doors, windows, arches and gates are more than just physical portals from one point to another,' he said. 'Over time they collect a psychic resonance—an imprint, if you like—from the countless people who pass through them, because they are perceived by the human mind as gateways to other places. Every time one uses a door a portion of one's own psychical power is transferred to it, rather like a cat leaving a scent trail on table legs. The more a doorway is used, the stronger the resonance—I believe that, if Mr. James is right about the means of transportation between one universe and the next, then a large, old gateway is vital to the creation of the Othersiders' portals. It is more than just a way of physically containing the energies involved. The crypt door in Christ Church was used for many years for funeral processions—imagine the solemnity and grief concentrated on that site over time. The gates of Chelsea Hospital are old, and have seen many comings and goings and, notably, intense emotion from patients and loved ones. These doorways are singled out, I believe, because they are fixed points, that stand in both universes, and have a resonance that can transcend physical existence. Given the age and importance of some of these locations, I imagine their use is obvious to the agents of the other universe. Other points may require certain special abilities to pinpoint. Those gifted individuals of a psychic persuasion are doubtless invaluable in this task.'

There was silence when he finished speaking. I do not believe anyone but James wholeheartedly believed what he had said. Melville could not openly ridicule a man of Sir Arthur Furnival's standing, but the look he gave him said it all—he fancied the baronet a lunatic or an imbecile.

When the silence became uncomfortable, I broke it. 'You said I had asked two questions, Mr. James?'

'Oh, yes indeed,' said James. 'Why use gateways at all when they have the power to go back home without them? I can only deduce that when one crosses between worlds, a portal provides only one-way travel. While living matter cannot return through a single gate without something unpredictable happening, dead matter can come and go—once the Othersiders die, their bodies are transported back home, probably to hide the evidence of their visit. If they were to use their devices whilst they were still alive, I expect they would be killed—smashed to atoms or somesuch.'

'You sound very certain.' This time it was Ambrose who questioned the philosopher.

'I am confident in my deductions, and have certain… intelligence to support my theories. The energy, effort and coordination required to create a new portal from our side—they would not risk such ventures if they could simply return home with a click of their fingers. Why, Mr. Melville saw with his own eyes a group of anarchists escape through Marble Arch, with nowhere to go. And yet he denies the truth of his own experience.'

'That is because I have to believe there is another answer. What you speak of is… is… ungodly!' Melville had come to the end of his tether.

'I bring you evidence of the greatest wonder in God's creation, and you call it ungodly? Why? Because it challenges your understanding of creation? You say ungodly, I say miraculous—but it is all truth, nonetheless. Our suspects are not bloody-minded throwbacks to the Fenian movement, nor are they Prussians or Austrians or any other power that we can name; they are soldiers—agents—from another reality. And, by God, we must start dealing with them as such, or they will surely accomplish their infernal mission!'

William James had snapped, and his outburst caused a general clamour. Melville leapt to his feet, pounding his fist on the table as he retorted. Ambrose threw up his hands in exasperation, decrying it all as 'balderdash and piffle'; Sir Arthur jumped to the defence of the American, whilst Jim and the colonel talked amongst themselves, looking most grave, though I could not hear what they were saying. In the end, Sir Toby called for a recess, and invited us all to take refreshments downstairs. All except Melville and William James, that is—the Irishman and the American followed Sir Toby to his private office for further talks. The mysterious man in the shadows, however, was already gone.

With everyone gone their separate ways, Ambrose and I found a table in a corner of the members' bar and summoned a waiter. I was determined to keep my head clear for the evening's business, so I ordered coffee. Ambrose, true to form, was on the sherry.

'Steady on,' I said. 'No doubt you'll be expected to concentrate on more of Mr. James' theories when we are called back in. What do you make of it all? Are we really under threat from these… "Othersiders", as James put it?'

'Balderdash!'

'Yes, I believe you said that at the time.'

'Have you ever heard the like?' Ambrose snorted rhetorically, a little too loudly. I'd gathered that the Apollonian was unused to having its quiet dignity challenged so. I motioned a finger to my lips to hush Ambrose, and he giggled like a schoolboy, before continuing in a softer tone. 'But really; who could believe such drivel? I find it hard enough to swallow Melville's suggestions about scientists and acid explosions, or whatever he said. It's just beyond the pale.'

'Did you see that fellow hiding in the shadows at the back of the room?' I asked, changing the subject in the hope that Ambrose would lower his voice just a little. 'No introductions… I half wondered if it wasn't someone from the palace.'

Ambrose snorted. 'He certainly acts as if he is. Honestly, you really are green as duckweed at times, old chap.'

I looked at him expectantly, ignoring the slight.

'That was Lord Cherleten. You'll never see him unless he wants you to, and he's rarely about in daylight hours; a regular Varney the bloody vampire. Runs the armoury, and sits at Sir Toby's right hand in the order—under sufferance, if rumours are to be believed. He'll be in charge when Sir Toby retires—thinks he's in charge now, by all accounts.'

'Why would Sir Toby stand for that?' I asked. The baronet didn't seem the type to put up with dissent, even from noted peers.

Ambrose shrugged. 'Friends in high places, I expect. Word is that he goes shooting with Ponsonby of a weekend—when you've got the ear of the Queen's secretary, you might as well have the ear of the Queen. He's making a power play all right, and likes to undermine the old man whenever he can.'

'Undermine how?' I asked. I was annoyed on Sir Toby's part, though I had never even heard of Lord Cherleten.

'For a start, who do you think invited your friend Denny along tonight? Sir Toby does not share information with the War Office, the Admiralty, or any other agency until he's certain of his facts—oh, God… speak of the devil…'

Ambrose took a gulp of sherry, and I looked up to see Jim approaching our table, mercifully without the surly Colonel Stirling at his side.

'I apologise for imposing,' said Jim, 'but the Colonel's been called in with the top brass, and I don't really know anyone else at the Apollonian.'

'That's because it's an exclusive club,' said Ambrose. 'Drink?'

'No, thank you,' Jim replied. He looked at Ambrose somewhat warily. 'So, John, what do you think about Mr. James' theories? I confess I am in two minds.'

'What does Lord Cherleten think?' Ambrose interrupted. Jim responded with a glare.

'I'm sure I don't know what the honourable gentleman thinks. I'm here under orders. I thought we all were.'

'But whose orders? That's the nub, eh.'

'Ambrose,' I said, 'the representatives of the War Office are honoured guests. We must extend every courtesy, must we not?' This drew a shrug from Ambrose, and Jim sat a little more at ease. 'To answer your question, Jim,' I said, 'I think the story is so fantastical that I need to see some real evidence with my own eyes. It is true that Mr. Hanlocke and I have made little sense of the strange things we have found so far, but that does not mean that we have to embrace every theory that comes along, especially ones as improbable as this.'

'You say improbable,' replied Jim, 'not impossible? You have an open mind, and if what Mr. James is saying is true, you'll need it! And what about you, Mr. Hanlocke—will Mr. James make a believer of you this night?'

'I very much doubt it,' Ambrose retorted. 'In fact, the longer we dally here, the more bombs those dynamiters are planting out there, I'll wager. Real bombs, not figments of an overactive imagination.'

'That's strange; you don't strike me as a man of action,' Jim baited.

'Appearances can be deceptive, as your uniform proves. No, I'm sure our superiors know best, but if I were in charge I'd be dragging every stage magician across the land in for questioning. Mr. Maskelyne has a show on this very week. Disappearing ladies are his specialty, I'm told.'

It was clear that Jim and Ambrose were not going to get along. But before the irascible Mr. Hanlocke could launch into further wild speculation, Holdsworth appeared, summoning us once more to the boardroom. Relieved that I would not be called upon for further peacemaking, I followed Holdsworth from the room, eager to hear what William James would have to say next.

When we reconvened, the mood between the three senior figures was somewhat changed. Melville sat next to James, both to the right of Sir Toby, and although the tension in the room was palpable, it was equally clear that they had reached an accord. The mysterious Lord Cherleten was nowhere to be seen. Melville, that notoriously tough, inquisitorial Irishman, seemed strangely subdued. Perhaps I had imagined it, but I felt that he gave me the queerest look as I took my seat.

'Gentlemen,' Sir Toby said, 'I apologise for our short break, but I felt that Mr. James and I had done Mr. Melville a great injustice by not disclosing certain sensitive information to him ahead of time. I have now rectified that mistake, and Mr. Melville has graciously given his agreement for the meeting to proceed.'

'May I then ask, sirs,' I ventured, 'whether we are to assume that Mr. James' earlier assertions are all correct? That we are indeed dealing with some foreign agency from... another universe?' I could hardly conceal my incredulous tone, but at the same time I was filled with a boyish excitement. Deep down, I was hoping for Sir Toby to answer in the affirmative; I wanted to believe this incredible story, and be a part of it.

'That is correct, Captain Hardwick. Forewarned is fore-armed, so to speak, and we must begin the task of gathering intelligence on our internal counterparts immediately.'

'We keep hearing that word, "infernal", gentlemen.' It was Ambrose speaking now, and I feared what he might say after his impromptu sherry. 'But does anyone really know their motives? If they are from some other universe, then how are we to interpret them as good or evil?'

'How can we judge any man so?' replied William James. 'All men are capable of savagery for some cause or another. The difference between a good man and a bad one is the choice of the cause.'

'Do you not consider their callous actions a greater indicator of their character?' I asked. 'These "soldiers" conduct themselves like villains, killing innocents and destroying swathes of our great city.'

'Unfortunately, Captain, if they truly are soldiers fighting for a cause, then these things are surely considered collateral damage. You have seen a great deal of action abroad, I believe—none of us are so naïve as to think that you have never seen an atrocity or injustice. But all for the greater good, yes?'

I paled, and held my tongue.

'What Mr. James is trying to say,' Sir Toby intervened, 'is that any man—soldier or no—can commit a barbarous act for his cause. However, we know that the cause of our opponents is a grim one, which can only be born of malice.'

'And how could you know that?' asked Ambrose, forgetting his place.

'Because,' William James replied, matter-of-factly, 'I have been to their world, and talked to them myself.'

James had managed to stun the group for a second time that night, and the rest of the meeting continued with him telling his extraordinary tale. Supported by more of his photographic slides, William James explained how he had travelled to Alaska many years ago to view the northern lights, initially to assist in his study of magnetism.

Living in virtual isolation, James chanced upon a strange, natural phenomenon near his cabin, which he at first had thought to be some ghostly manifestation. He saw in the cold night air a hazy window open up, through which he could see people eating, drinking and talking, as real as though they were standing on the other side of a pane of glass. When it had closed, James resolved to return to the same spot and observe the phenomenon again, which he did the very next night. Sure enough, at the same time almost every night, the window opened and James was able to see into the other world. He described how, as time progressed, the images became clearer, more expansive, until he felt as if he was a part of that world. And then, one day, quite simply, he was.

'To this day I do not know how it happened,' James said. 'On the night when the aurora borealis reached their crescendo, I left the small party of locals whom I had befriended and went to my place in the woods. When the window opened, it was not a hazy, clouded image in the air, but rather a portal, surrounded by a corona of golden light. I stepped forward dumbfounded, and as I did so, the people on the other side—the people I had almost come to know—seemed to look right at me. They saw me. In the next instant I was amongst them, in their world. The gateway closed behind me and there was no way back.

'Gentlemen, can you imagine the horror of that realisation? The utter fear that gripped me was maddening. For aught I knew I had travelled to the spirit world that the new theosophy schools were teaching of. Though the people on the other side tried to calm me, their confusion and excitement only added to my own, and I think I spent days in a kind of fugue state, inconsolable at the thought that I would never see my family, or my own people, again.

'At length the madness passed—although there are some amongst you who would surely disagree. The people on the other side were scientists, sent to study the phenomenon that had been discovered in their world long before I had chanced upon my "window". Their early attempts to pass objects—and even animals—through the portal had proved disastrous. They believed it to be a window onto another universe, as I now do, but could not traverse it. My arrival had been like a bolt from the blue, and had confounded their greatest hypotheses. And they knew me! In their world, William James is a great scientist, and "his" sudden appearance in their midst was a doubly great shock to them. But, gentlemen, there is a price to pay for dabbling with the laws of nature.

'They told me that there were small portals such as these opening up across the world, and that they were somehow linked to the rise of spiritualism. I could see no connection, but in their world the practice of magic and mysticism is not a supernatural art, but more of a science. They believed that spiritualists and theosophists had somehow roused energies that man was never meant to dabble with, and strange phenomena were occurring all across the globe as a result. They showed me to their lab, where several supposed psychic mediums were wired to incredible electrical machines, being tested for who-knows-what. These psychics appeared fairly well treated, but it was obvious that they were prisoners, and not volunteers. Isolated in the far north, we were apparently beyond the worst of the psychic phenomena, and thus the experiments were comparatively safe to conduct; but the scientists told me that elsewhere, in the cities and towns where human beings dwelt en masse, the very laws of physics were being upset. I began to read their notes, even assisting with their experiments where possible. They said they would help me return home if they could, but our camaraderie and spirit of cooperation was altered soon after, when a telegram arrived from Washington.

'My arrival seemed to have changed everything. For the first time, a human being, with a soul and a conscious mind, had crossed between two universes. All of the terrible things that the Othersiders feared were lurking beyond the veil—and they were not afraid to use the word "demons", gentlemen—were starting to break through. Scientists across the globe were struggling to prevent an upswell in ghostly manifestations and violent explosions of pure chaos, and it all coincided with the time of my journey through the portal. Some members of their expedition sought to turn me over to the authorities in the United States. They mentioned that I would be taken thence to London for "study". It seems that on the other side, the reach of the British Empire is long indeed. The greatest nations have come together in the common interest, ruled by a shadowy cabal who use any means to preserve the world as they know it. It is led by an Englishman known only as Lazarus—an enigmatic dictator, it seemed to me, sworn to lead his people to salvation from the growing esoteric threat. The scientists explained to me that the people needed to believe that God is on their side, and judging by how much this Lazarus fellow is both feared and respected, I'd say he likes to play God more than a little.

'Thankfully, there were others who spoke for me, and determined that they could set things right, if only they could find a way to send me back rather than turn me over to Lazarus. In the end, it was this latter group who won out, and for that I am thankful.

'They subjected me to some unpleasant study, which I will not delve into. Some of it was of the type that our best scientists would mock, but in their world, with their incredible scientific apparatus, they were able to achieve astounding results. They used magnetism—the very thing that I was studying as a philosophical pursuit—as a genuine science and found some method to use my own innate biological energy to create a limited portal. They were incredibly excited by the breakthrough, as I am sure you can imagine. A life's work, come to fruition in a few days—they believed they could now create a device that could, by using vibrations, magnetism and high-frequency sound, pull a person or object back through the veil and into their own world. They would not use it upon me, however, for they did not think it possible for a being to survive the process. This device is, I believe, what the Otherside agents now use to retrieve their dead.'

James paused to take a sip of water, and I took the opportunity to ask a question.

'If I may ask, Mr. James, if you did not return by those means, then how did you find your way back home?'

'The same way I got there,' he said. 'They used their new discoveries to make a good many adjustments to their old equipment. They had been monitoring the window for a decade or more, to no avail, and I had provided them with a test subject for experimentation. Through the use of some marvellous sonic and electrical equipment, and the concentration of the psychic subjects' powers, they were able to harness the rift between worlds, to create a portal big enough for me to pass through. Whereas previously they had been unable to create a stable portal in thin air, we had hit upon the theory of gateways to contain the energy of their strange devices, focusing the power from their machines as a glass may transform the diffuse light of the sun into a tiny point of heat. The psychics conducted some form of meditative séance, entering a trance-like state while wires conducted electrical impulses from their brains. As the portal opened, the demons that the Othersiders spoke of were clearly visible to me, probing for ingress into the real world—as real as their world is to us, at least. When I stepped into the portal I had no idea what would happen.

Even the scientists themselves were not certain—they knew that our two universes were linked somehow, but if there were other universes out there, which one could slip into accidentally... well, if that had happened, I would not be standing before you now. Remember also that the apparatus we used was experimental. They believed they could only open the gateway for a few seconds at most, and warned me not to stop moving until I was back in my own world—and under no circumstances to turn back and attempt to cross through or even touch the portal. I cannot explain what I saw as I crossed over; it was like an hallucinatory dream, but when I finally re-emerged into the Alaskan winter, I saw the portal fizzing and glowing behind me for mere seconds before vanishing. It worked, of course, and here I am.'

'And this... portal? Can it be reopened? Can they still use it?' The question came from Melville.

'The natural portal that I used to cross over in the first place is now closed—I could not find it again upon my return, and many others have tried and failed to do so. There is a detail of soldiers posted to the very site of that phenomenon, standing watch in case it reappears, and anyone—or anything—should pass through it. The Otherside scientists said something about the amount of power required to maintain a portal for any length of time being almost impossible to generate. Before I left, the scientist in charge, a certain Dr. Leiber, told me that it would be theoretically possible to create larger portals for longer periods of time, but that even these would be limited in their application. Most notably, as I have described, a body could perhaps only travel in one direction, and never back and forth as one might wish.'

'Convenient,' sniped Colonel Stirling, barely loud enough for us to hear.

'Mr. James, you mentioned earlier that the Othersiders were here on some dark business, and mean us ill. Yet the men you describe sound rather beneficent. Perhaps you can explain?' This was Sir Toby, asking a question to which he evidently knew the answer already.

'Certainly, Sir Toby, although what I know has been pieced together from various intelligence, and owes much to my own speculation. I believe that the other world is in dire peril, from the predations of supernatural entities. I was told as much, and saw evidence for it with my own eyes. I fear that my crossing over may have accelerated the process. Their agents are finding ways in and out of our world, and whilst here they are assassinating psychics and mediums, and doing Lord knows what else. And it can only be for one purpose, gentlemen. They have decided to abandon their world, and take ours for their own.'

This caused much disquiet amongst the party once more.

'But why kill these "psychics"?' asked Jim, speaking up for the first time. 'Do they fear them for the harm they did to their own world?'

'Perhaps. I have oft wondered if the Othersiders wish to eliminate all such folk from our side, so that there is no similar threat to them if their plan to take over our world succeeds. The death toll so far would certainly suggest so. Captain Hardwick and Mr. Hanlocke can attest to the fate of one unfortunate Mr. Jeffers, a noted medium of the East End. Perhaps the Othersiders fear that our psychics could be used as weapons against them. As Sir Arthur intimated earlier, psychic abilities come in rather handy for detecting them portals between worlds, or at least for identifying potential sites for infiltration and escape. I am certain they are also used for creating them, at no small human cost. I believe that by eliminating psychics—and by that I mean any spiritualist, clairvoyant, gypsy fortune-teller or ceremonial magician who displays inexplicable mastery of their art—the Othersiders are removing opposition to their plans.'

'So when their plan is complete, will they turn on their own psychics to avoid a repeat of all this chaos?' asked Jim.

'Perhaps not. What they gleaned from me during my short stay is that no violent supernatural phenomena had occurred in our world, even though spiritualism had been on the rise for the same length of time. Their dabbling in the supernatural has had quite terrifying consequences, whereas ours has not. Perhaps our two worlds operate under different scientific laws or, simply, maybe their world lies in closer proximity to some incorporeal realm than ours.'

'Closer to hell, more like,' muttered Ambrose.

'But they would slaughter us all to achieve this end?' I asked.

'Yes. I believe so. Gentlemen, you must understand, the Othersiders may have brought this on themselves with nothing more harmful than table-rapping séances, and yet they must surely have convinced themselves that we started this conflict. If I had known what strife I would cause by exploring that damned portal, I never would have done it. I am somehow responsible for firing the first shot, and, make no mistake, we are at war.'

The hour drew late, and there were few more questions before Sir Toby brought proceedings to a halt. We were all sworn to secrecy once more, and told that instructions would be forthcoming so that we might further the investigation.

As we filed out of the room, both Jim and Ambrose made a bee-line for me, but my mind was full of questions that I had not felt it right to ask in the meeting. I asked forgiveness from my friends, and instead walked briskly along the corridor to catch up with a lone figure with whom I wished to speak privately.

Sir Arthur Furnival was an unusual man. I was vaguely aware of his being wealthy and hailing from a powerful family, but his bearing conveyed none of the formidable aspects of his peers, those such as Sir Toby. He sat opposite me in the library, which was now empty of clubmen, and swilled black Turkish coffee around in his cup, staring wistfully into the liquid as though it might bear secrets yet to be foreseen. In the background, silently, Sir Arthur's man, Jenkins, stood motionless. I had been given leave by the gentleman to speak freely in front of his valet, and I wondered just how many of his master's—indeed, the nation's—secrets Jenkins was privy to.

'So, you say that you have some sense of what will come to pass? Like a medium?' I asked. I had pressed Sir Arthur on exactly what insight he had into the plans of the 'Othersiders'—a word that I still struggled to use seriously—in the hope that he could aid my ongoing enquiries. He had informed me, quite matter-of-factly, that he was himself of possessed of some small psychic talent, which was how he had come to assist Sir Toby. I at once regretted talking to him, but etiquette demanded I see through the meeting.

'Not quite a medium,' he said, his voice low and soft, 'although I do have some experience in the spiritualist arts. No; my gift is altogether more... unpredictable. It comes to me in flashes, which at times are difficult to interpret. Jenkins calls it "the Sight".' He smiled at that, but rather sadly.

'And through this... sight... you have seen the anarchists?'

'In a manner of speaking. It is more that I have felt their presence, and more keenly still the presence of their gates. If William James is to be believed, on the other side, people like me are used like laboratory animals, to tear holes in the very fabric of reality. One man's seer is another's weapon.' There was a bitterness now to his tone. 'Perhaps what I feel is not the intrusion of the anarchist agents into our world, but the pain of the poor souls who help them cross the veil. To many psychic vessels such as myself, suffering calls to us far more readily than love.' He winced as he said it. If he was a charlatan, he was deeply entrenched in his own delusion; for my part, I believed that whatever pain he himself was feeling, it was genuine.

'You said during the meeting that I was right about Chelsea Hospital,' I said. 'But when I went back there, I found nothing.'

'I cannot explain that,' Sir Arthur said. 'I visited the site, and found it steeped in psychical energy, which was evidence enough for me. Too much time had elapsed, maybe. Perhaps the physical traces left behind by the gateways fade over time, as the veil between worlds is restored and reality reasserts itself. The same can be said of the Othersiders themselves, of course. We are dealing with an enemy who, over time, appears never to have existed. The perfect spies, wouldn't you agree?' He sipped his coffee.

'If only we could all vanish into thin air at will,' I said. At that, Sir Arthur seemed to scrutinise me, with a look not unlike that which Melville had given me earlier that night. I saw for a moment some of the authority and calculating wits that usually came with a position such as his; and realised that Sir Arthur should not be treated lightly due to his subdued and gentle manner. He was as like to be as astute—and perhaps even as dangerous—as Sir Toby, if need be.

'Sir Arthur,' I said, 'I thank you for granting an audience, though perhaps we should talk more another time. The hour grows late and you will want to get away, I'm sure.'

'You are right, Captain. If I may be of any assistance in the future, you may contact me through Sir Toby. I am only too happy to help.'

We both stood, and Sir Arthur extended a hand, which I shook. And then something most strange occurred.

Upon touching my hand, Sir Arthur twitched as though he had received some electrical shock. His hand squeezed mine tightly, and his eyes became momentarily glassy. He gasped, like a drowning man emerging from the water, and before I knew it Jenkins was at his master's side, prising his hand from mine and steadying the baronet. Sir Arthur recovered quickly, and waved Jenkins away before taking a breath to compose himself.

'Sir Arthur, are you all right?' I asked.

'My dear Captain, it is not my condition that should concern you. You are in grave danger.'

'What?' I forgot my manners, such was Sir Arthur's imploring tone.

'A dark fate hangs around you like a pall, sir. You will be betrayed, more than once, I fear, and will be led to a house of the dead. From there, your future is... uncertain.'

There is no escape from the house of the dead.

I was rattled, but before I could speak, Sir Arthur's legs buckled, and Jenkins was back to help his master into the library chair. Sir Arthur had turned a ghastly shade, and put a hand to his head gingerly.

'Please, Sir Arthur, I must—'

'The master is unwell,' Jenkins said, standing between me and the baronet. The valet, I noticed for the first time, was a broad-shouldered man, straight-backed and square-jawed. A soldier if ever I knew one. I cast a glance around him at Sir Arthur, nodded, and made my way to the door.

'Captain Hardwick,' Sir Arthur said, weakly. I turned. 'This is the curse I have had to bear for the longest time now. If what Mr. James says is true, my kind have brought upon the other universe a great calamity. It has occurred to me that, if they weaken our universe with their gates—with their very, unnatural, presence here—then the same thing could happen to us. The Othersiders seek to wipe us out—spiritualists, psychics, and such like, I mean. And perhaps they are right to do so. They are living proof of the dangers presented by people with... certain gifts. Be wary, Captain Hardwick—you will meet others like me before the end, and you would be wise not to dabble in these forces. You, at least, have a choice.'

With that, the baronet slumped in his chair as if he was sickening, and Jenkins—with a hard look back at me to ensure I was leaving—attended to his master.

Outside the library, I was surprised to find Holdsworth. The man always seemed to pop up whenever he was needed, and often when he wasn't.

'Captain Hardwick,' he said, 'Sir Toby apologises for the late hour, but requests that you take supper with him in his office. If you will follow me, sir.'

Clearly there was no refusing the request, and so, confused, tired, and beginning to feel my aches and pains again after a long day, I followed the porter to see what new surprise awaited me.

SIX

We ate an informal supper in a room just off Sir Toby's office. It was a small but comfortable study that smelt of old books and polished wood.

We went over some of the more fantastical points of the evening meeting, and Sir Toby listened patiently as I expressed in equal parts excitement and incredulity about what lay ahead. He explained some of the details to me again, and I found myself believing every word. Sir Toby Fitzwilliam was one of the most respected, sober judges in England, and if ever there was a man not prone to flights of fancy, it was he.

'John, I said before that I had an assignment for you. I am sure that you are anxious to get to business,' Sir Toby said at last. I nodded in response. 'There is a man, here in London, who we believe to have knowledge of the Otherside agents and their movements. He may well have intelligence that could prevent future attacks, or enable us to apprehend agents who are already amongst us.'

'How can this be? Why have we not brought this man in for questioning already?'

'It is not quite so simple. He is certainly a criminal, yes, but he lives outside the law. Let us say that his knowledge is vast, his webs of intelligence myriad, and his cunning infinite. He has secured immunity from prosecution by the brokering of intelligence, and now he has secured such a position of power that he sells information to Her Majesty's government as and when it suits him.'

'That is outrageous,' I said. My sense of right and wrong was affronted by the thought of a known criminal being allowed such liberties. 'If he knows of this threat then surely the ends justify the means. I will be happy to bring him in for questioning if that is your wish.'

'If only it were so simple.' Sir Toby washed down the last of his meal with water, and poured a glass of brandy from a decanter. 'Our man is based on the Isle of Dogs, in a small Chinese quarter. The area is mostly dockland, but what community lives there is poor indeed, and this fellow rules the roost. You would be hard pressed to find many police officers willing to go there to arrest him, for fear of their lives.'

'Can this be? In our own city?'

'I am afraid so. What I am in need of is not a policeman—why, Melville is champing at the bit to go there himself and put a bullet in our man—but no. I need an honest man who will enter the web of the spider and parley with him. Use your skills in negotiating with the enemy. Bribe him if necessary. Arrest him if you have no other option; kill him if you must; but find out what he knows of these Othersiders first of all.'

I took a glass from Sir Toby, swirled the cognac around for a moment, and took a sip. Despite my misgivings, I found myself nodding an acceptance.

'Good. And are you... physically up to the task? How soon can you take on the assignment?'

'I am feeling much better, thank you Sir Toby. If I may be afforded some assistance then I will go as soon as possible.'

'Oh, you will have men, do not worry about that. I will assign you some experienced officers—Melville will be only too keen to assist in that regard.'

'I am honoured, Sir Toby. Does that mean that Agent Hanlocke will not be involved?'

'I am afraid not,' replied Sir Toby. 'One of Mr. Hanlocke's more recent assignments involved extensive undercover work with a circle of international criminals. Many of the men he brought to justice were Chinese, and some of those were in the employ of your target. Were Ambrose Hanlocke to return to the Chinese quarter, I fear it would be on pain of death.'

That was the first I'd really heard of Ambrose's previous exploits as an agent, and the fact that he had done more for the order than simply pick locks and blackmail dignitaries came as a surprise to me. I passed no comment, preferring to stick to the matter at hand. 'May I ask more about the target? Who is he? How will I find him?'

Sir Toby reached to a nearby shelf and took down a dossier.

'Take this with you tonight. It contains all that we know of the target. He is known as the Artist, because of his reputation as a painter; he's quite good, by all accounts. Unfortunately he is also a gangster, drug trafficker and embezzler. He is probably a spy for the Chinese, though we can prove nothing of course. You will find him at the House of Zhengming, the largest opium den on the Isle of Dogs, and a veritable fortress. There is no point approaching by stealth—his men are everywhere. I doubt you could set foot within a mile of that drug den without his knowledge.'

I barely heard those last words. When Sir Toby mentioned the opium den, a mild panic overcame me. It took all my strength to stay focused on the matter at hand, and to maintain a veneer of calm.

'When you get there, remain vigilant. Every detail you can gather about his headquarters may be of help to us in the future. No agent has ever had an audience with the Artist before, and you will have a unique opportunity to glean insights into his operation.'

'Will he grant me an audience?' I asked.

'He will have no choice. We will offer you every advantage—I will not go into the particulars now, but before you go I will send more detailed instructions. Oh, and it almost slipped my mind; you will need this too,' Sir Toby added. He handed me a large envelope. I opened it and found inside several papers, and a small, silver-plated card case. 'This is your identification—I apologise that we did not provide this earlier; it may have helped to avoid that unpleasantness at Commercial Road. There is some paperwork that I would ask you to sign before you leave, confirming your honorary membership of the club.'

I took one of the cards from the case. Printed upon it in neat copperplate were the words:

CPT. JOHN HARDWICK
The Apollonian Club
Pall Mall, London

I scanned the topmost document in the sheaf, and realised that it was signed not only by Commissioner Monro of Scotland Yard, but also by Sir Henry Ponsonby, the Queen's private secretary. It was almost too much to take in, as even a cursory glance led me to understand that I now held some sway over the Metropolitan Police, and that they would recognise me as an agent of the Crown.

'You will also find some documentation from Horse Guards,' said Sir Toby.

I found the papers almost as he mentioned them, and glanced up at him quizzically.

'In effect,' he continued, "you are made full captain again, and returned to active duty. You are employed by Apollo Lycea, but your status in Her Majesty's Army is retained indefinitely. We felt that you would be more effective with your rank behind you… Do go to Horse Guards at your convenience and collect your new uniform. You are entitled to wear it, if only for formal occasions and such.'

Perhaps I should have been dismayed that my military life had not been left behind as I had thought, but in fact I glowed with pride. The letterhead bore the familiar arms of the Sixteenth Lancers, a regiment that had been my family for so long.

'Thank you,' I said, trying not to show how overwhelmed I was.

'Don't mention it, Captain. Though you may yet find that it is not such a favour, depending on the rigours of your future assignments. I would, of course, remind you that, despite our newfound spirit of cooperation with Her Majesty's Army, you must keep your own counsel on the details of any assignments you receive.'

'Does this have anything to do with Colonel Stirling and Captain Denny?' I asked, reluctant to bring up Jim's name. I was sure I saw a flicker of disapproval in the old man's eyes before he spoke.

'In part. There are… some… within the order who feel closer ties with the War Office will be essential in the future, and now more than ever. Today is our first step on that road.'

'Some within the order… if I may be so bold, Sir Toby, do you refer to Lord Cherleten?'

That drew a glower, and I at once regretted pursuing the topic.

'I see Ambrose Hanlocke has been his usual soul of discretion. Were it not for his undeniable talents I'd have him locked up until the end of his days,' Sir Toby grumbled, though not without humour. I was still unsure exactly what talents had made Ambrose so indispensable, beyond his incredible capacity for drink, but it certainly didn't seem the time to ask. 'Yes, I suppose it is no great secret that Lord Cherleten and I do not always agree on the direction of the order, but have no doubt that we both have the best interests of the Empire at heart. I will warn you, though, John—as I am your patron, as I vouch for you and protect you from the secret meetings and tangled webs of intrigue that plagued your father before you, Lord Cherleten does likewise for other agents within the order. If the time ever comes for you to choose where your loyalties lie, I trust I may depend on you to choose wisely. Do we understand each other?'

'Perfectly,' I said, although in truth I had no idea what import any such choice on my part could have to such men as Sir Toby and Lord Cherleten.

The rest of our discussion was of less consequence. Each of us was tired and, I think, determined to end the night on a less grave note. As the hour was late we concluded our business quickly. There was only one final thing for me to see to before I went back to my lodgings: Sir Toby advised me to go with Holdsworth to the basement office and sign the paperwork affirming my membership of the club.

The basement was very much like the upper floor, characterised by narrow, dimly lit corridors with numerous doors. Holdsworth explained that on one side lay private rooms for members, whilst on the other side were stores, accessible from the kitchens via servants' stairs. But our business was not on that level. Holdsworth opened a small door at the end of a corridor, revealing a set of narrow stairs leading down another floor. At the foot of the stairs was a tiny office, in which a large and officious-looking night watchman sat. I wondered if there was always a man stationed here, and thought what a lonely role that must be. Holdsworth greeted the man, addressing him as Perry, and the guard took up a large bunch of keys and unlocked another heavy door that led to the lower basement proper. This second cellar was as large as the first, but colder and less comfortable. The floors were flagged rather than carpeted, and the walls were whitewashed plaster rather than wainscoted.

We stopped at a small, unmanned reception desk, where Holdsworth saw to my paperwork. To my surprise, I was also given a small key and a card containing a safe combination. Seeing my confusion, Holdsworth led me to a remote cellar room, which was attended by another stout watchman, and showed me a wall of safety deposit boxes.

'The combination is for your strong-box, sir,' he explained. 'Any materials that you acquire during the course of your investigations, which are not considered vital evidence, may be stored here. The key, sir, is for the armoury. If you would follow me.'

Now I was intrigued. The basements of the club were vast, and improbably so. Not only that, but the fact that it had an armoury at all confirmed the status of Apollo Lycea in my mind as a serious agency of the Crown, rather than a firm of clandestine consulting detectives. As we walked the corridors, I observed door after door, some unmarked, and made of studded black iron, but many of polished wood and adorned with small engraved plaques featuring the names of, I presumed, agents of the order. One in particular piqued my interest—it bore the name of A. G. C., Lord Cherleten. I noted it, and moved on.

When we reached one particular metalled door at the end of a corridor, Holdsworth invited me to use my own key to open it. We entered, and the steward turned on the electric lights to illuminate a small room, with half a dozen neat wooden gun racks standing within. There was a large selection of firearms, from shotguns and sporting rifles to heavy pistols and tiny single-shot ladies' guns.

'All agents of the order have access to one or more of the weapons lockers,' Holdsworth explained. 'If at any time you require assistance, please speak to me. All weapons must be signed for, although you are, of course, free to come and go as you please. Will sir be requiring a weapon today?' he asked expectantly. 'I have the necessary dockets.'

I confess that I coveted the guns on display. They were all fine weapons, some brand-new factory models that I had never seen even during my time in the army. All were clean as the day they were bought and obviously well maintained, and I ran my hand along the stock of an American repeating rifle like a boy ogling a bicycle in a toyshop. I had always been a Jack-of-all-trades in the army, and perhaps my lack of specialist expertise had stunted my advancement through the ranks, but if there was one area that I could have excelled in, it was marksmanship.

'No, Holdsworth,' I said, with no small measure of self-control.

'I appreciate you taking the time to show me the armoury, but I will return when my assignment begins.'

'As you wish, sir. Allow me to escort you upstairs, and perhaps find you a cab?'

We made our way back along the corridor, and I was already longing for a fire and a small brandy. However, we had passed no further than a few yards beyond Lord Cherleten's office when I heard the door open and close, and a familiar voice call to me.

'John? Wait up, old boy, I'd like to talk to you.'

I had not expected to see Jim Denny again that night, at so late an hour, and certainly not leaving the office of a man whom I now viewed somewhat unfavourably. In any case, as Jim fell into stride with me and we made our way up the stairs to the lobby, I excused Holdsworth so that we could talk privately.

'The colonel not with you?' I asked.

'No, he went home after the meeting. Lord Cherleten asked to see me. He's an odd sort, isn't he?'

'Never met him.'

'Really? He speaks quite highly of you.'

I stopped at the top of the stairs, and Jim looked at me quizzically. 'What?' he asked.

'Jim... you and I should never have discussed the case. And I'd really rather you hadn't told anyone about it.'

'I didn't mean to get you into any trouble, John. But I was asked directly, and was duty bound. You understand.'

'Of course. But it was unfortunate; now I fear our friendship is being used for political manoeuvring higher up the ladder, so to speak. I don't know much about Lord Cherleten, but I've heard enough to make me doubt his intentions.'

'Heard from who?' Jim asked. 'Hanlocke?'

'It's neither here nor there,' I replied. 'Just be on your guard, lest you become a pawn in whatever game he's playing.'

'The game, old fellow, is that I'm now like you.' He drew a small, silver case from his jacket pocket, and presented to me a card from within. What I saw made me tense up.

'Oh, Jim; forgive me, but I don't like this one bit.'

'What? That I'm finally in on the secret? Seems to me that you're never happy, John. We could work together on this, you and I. And that rogue Hanlocke can take his opinion of me and—'

'No, Jim. We have our own assignments, I'm sure. Unless otherwise informed, we must exercise discretion. I'm sorry... I was wrong to involve you in all this.' I remembered Sir Toby's words all too clearly. I couldn't risk Jim reporting back to Horse Guards, or to Cherleten, until I was sure myself whom I could trust. As Jim's face hardened, I realised that I wouldn't have to risk any such thing.

'I see,' he said, coldly. He pushed open the doors to the grand hall and went on ahead.

'Jim—there's no need to fall out. I just think it's best that we operate in secrecy for the time being.'

'I'm sure you're right, John. I'm sure we'll see each other presently, in the members bar, perhaps. I'll bid you goodnight.'

With that, he was off, leaving me alone in the dimly lit hall as the last vestiges of the membership, faces red from overdoing the liquor, shuffled their way outside to their carriages.

As I made my way back to Mrs. Whitinger's lodging house, the drizzle lightly pattering on the canvas roof of the cab, I was filled with a sense of anticipation, and a strange dread. I was about to embark on the most extraordinary adventure of my life—and to follow in the footsteps of my estimable father—but to do so I would come face to face with my greatest fear. And I would have to do it alone, without the aid of my new friends, it seemed. This would be a great test of my abilities. I prayed I would prove equal to the task, and a worthy successor to the Hardwick name.

SEVEN

On Saturday, shortly before dinner, my orders finally arrived from Sir Toby. They were brief and to the point, providing only the essential information, along with the names of my fellow agents and the meeting time and place: tomorrow at Scotland Yard.

There was scant time to prepare myself, which was probably a blessing, as a lack of preconception could only benefit me when negotiating with a man of such fell reputation as this 'Artist'. My orders were clear—go to the House of Zhengming, speak to the Artist about his alleged involvement with the Othersiders, and extract all the information possible from him, by whatever means necessary. I was to outline in no uncertain terms that the Artist would be expected to conform to Her Majesty's wishes on a matter of grave importance to the Empire. After what Sir Toby had told me the previous evening, I hoped that such a veiled threat would prove sufficient to loosen the Artist's tongue, and persuade him that he was no longer immune to prosecution, regardless of what secrets he knew and what hold he had over certain high-up officials.

I had already begun to devour any information I could about the Isle of Dogs. Everything from maps, London guides and newspaper articles held at the British Library, to dockyard records and police reports. Through all my research, I had found no mention of the Artist, or even of the House of Zhengming, although there were plenty of newspaper column inches devoted to the discussion of organised Chinese criminal gangs in and around London's docklands. The more I read, the more I understood that the Isle of Dogs was a dangerous place. To stray beyond the docks into the heart of that area was to take one's life into one's own hands. Even the police could not be guaranteed safety in such a place. And yet it was into that moral sump that I would have to venture if I were ever to find answers to the greatest mystery of our time.

It was nine o'clock when a knock came at my door, and Mrs. Whitinger announced that I had a visitor. Given her somewhat disapproving impression, I needed not be told that it was Ambrose Hanlocke. Despite the low opinion formed of Ambrose by my landlady, his visit was a welcome one, for I was beginning to feel very lonely indeed on the eve of a dangerous rendezvous. Ambrose himself, when he entered, looked very grave, which was so unlike him that I was at once set on edge.

'Drink?' I offered, automatically picking up a bottle of cognac.

'No, not tonight,' he replied.

At this I knew something was amiss, and so I offered Ambrose a seat and took the chair opposite.

'I found out about your assignment,' Ambrose said.

'Oh?'

'Not all the agents of the order are as tight-lipped as you and I,' he replied, forcing a grin. 'News travels, especially regarding... him.'

'The Artist?'

Ambrose nodded. 'Look, John, I had to come and see you. I feel wretched that I can't come with you tomorrow, but I suppose Sir Toby might have explained?'

'That a gang of Chinese gangsters would like to see you dead?'

'Quite. Ordinarily that wouldn't stop me—lots of people would like to see me dead, I'm sure, and that's just for my extraordinary good luck at cards. But these fellows are something else entirely. The Artist is dangerous, and not to be trusted. I once had to pose as a go-between for his men, and I know that he commands utter devotion from them. Every man in the Artist's employ lives in constant fear for his life. The Artist believes himself above the law; if he thinks for a moment that he can get away with killing you, he will.'

'Good Lord, Ambrose, don't lay it on so thick, will you?'

'You need to hear it straight, John, from someone who knows.' Ambrose stood and started to pace in front of the fire. 'Sir Toby... well, the old man has your best interests at heart I'm sure, but he'll only ever tell you just enough so you don't do anything stupid. Beyond that, he likes to keep a few cards up his sleeve, you know? Trust me when I tell you that there's hardly anyone—anyone at all—left in Whitehall who hasn't had some dealing with the Artist. And that means you never know just who has a vested interest in your success, or your failure.'

'You're telling me to trust no one.'

'I'm telling you, John, not to go.'

I looked at my erstwhile companion in disbelief. 'Not to go? Disobey orders? And then what?'

'Go to the country. Run away and join the circus. Find a nice young lady to lose yourself in. I don't know, John, but believe me, if you go to the Isle of Dogs tomorrow, there's a chance you won't come back.'

Ambrose was so unlike his usual self that I sat up in my chair and for once took him very seriously indeed.

'I can't do that, Ambrose. I don't believe Sir Toby would send me to my death, so there must be more to it. And besides, I'll have good men with me. The best Melville can spare, apparently. I have to do my duty.'

Ambrose sighed. 'Your father's son...'

'Steady on!'

'Look, I didn't think I'd change your mind, so instead I'll say this: do not think that a few policemen or soldiers will stay the Artist's hand. Whatever you do, don't hold yourself above the man, and don't antagonise him. Use all your cunning and diplomacy, John, for the Artist is wily and slippery, and utterly beyond redemption.'

I had never seen Ambrose in so earnest a mood, and I could only nod that I understood him. 'Can you not come along?' I said, perhaps sounding feeble. 'Wear a disguise… or hide in the shadows. Do some of that skulking you say you're so good at.'

He laughed ruefully. 'I wish it were so easy, John. No, I'm afraid they've thought of that—I've been given new orders already. I'm leaving the city for a few days, first thing in the morning. You'll just have to be extra careful without me there to save your skin.'

I tried not to laugh at that, given my sore memory of Ambrose's disappearing act on Commercial Road.

'So… is this the end of our partnership? Has Sir Toby decided I no longer need your guidance?

'I bloody hope not,' Ambrose smiled. 'If you make it back alive from the Isle of Dogs you'll be dead within a month without me looking out for you. Oh, bugger it. Pour us one drink—I should at least toast the condemned man.'

I was not overly happy about Ambrose's sudden nihilism, but he remained in high spirits for the remainder of the evening, and would not be drawn on the details of his new assignment—nor mine, for that matter. I wondered whether Sir Toby had extended his lecture about discretion to Ambrose, and probably not before time. And so we tried to make light of the situation before Ambrose set to leave, saying that he had to pack for his journey.

'Stay alive, John. Remember, you're the last honest man in London—when this is all over, we'll need men like you to rebuild.'

I frowned quizzically, and Ambrose simply shook my hand, took his hat from the stand and left, whistling as he went down the stairs.

I returned to the fireside with mixed feelings. Whatever we had been through, I had come to associate my official assignments with the shameless gentleman thief; that I would have to brave the Isle of Dogs with strangers by my side, even if they were under my command, was discomfiting. Given Ambrose's dire warnings, I became gripped by the idea that the mission would be even more dangerous than I had first thought, and so I started to set down on paper all of my knowledge about the case up to that point, so that if anything should happen to me there would be a body of work waiting for my successor. It was a rather morbid task, and when I had finished I had a folio of handwritten notes, police reports, photographs, maps and the tattered pocketbook written in Myanmar. I wrapped the documents up into a parcel and was about to address it to Sir Toby, when I had the most inexplicable feeling; almost a premonition, I suppose. Acting on impulse, I instead made out the address to Captain James Denny of Horse Guards. I was sure that action was tantamount to treason, but I felt that if the order should fail, then perhaps the army should be given its chance. I scribbled a hasty note to Jim to that effect, hoping that Jim's first loyalty was still to the army rather than Apollo Lycea, and gave the whole bundle to Mrs Whitinger to post should I not return the next day. A prospect I was starting to think was a wholly probable one.

'...So I slipped old Betsy from up me sleeve, and slit his throat before he knew what was happening. Well, seeing me chive that giant put a different slant on things. Moses and Cranky Bill legged it like their lives depended on it – which I suppose they did, on account of my sore 'ead and black disposition. I took out me throwing knife and cracked Moses in the back o' the neck first time – never miss, even in the dark. Cranky Bill was out of sight, shrieking "Mercy, mercy!" like a little vestal virgin. I pulled me chiv out of Moses and shouted, "I'll be back for you, Bill, mark me words." And I was an' all, very next day in fact, with five of London's finest. We went knockin' for him, and smugged him sharpish. He was in the quod by week's end.'

At the culmination of Constable Ecclestone's colourful tale, most of which I hadn't understood, all of us in the Black Maria burst into laughter. All except one. Constable Clegg, who uttered a half-hearted murmur and forced a smile.

'What's the matter, Clegg?' asked Boggis. 'Don't you applaud Constable Ecclestone's heroism in the face of insurmountable odds?'

Clegg cleared his throat. 'Of course; it was, ahem... commendable work.'

'Aw, leave him be Sarge. He's just not used to knife-work yet,' said Ecclestone, sincerely. 'He might learn a thing or two 'fore the night is out.'

'That you will, Clegg,' said Boggis, fixing the former police sergeant with a cold hard stare. 'The criminals you'll face out here are not the usual trash—we don't send Special Branch in to collect unpaid rent, you know. We go where others fear to tread, and bring to justice desperate villains who'd sooner blow your brains out as look twice at you. It's kill or be killed, Clegg. Make sure you're up to the task.'

Clegg looked suitably chastened, and Ecclestone at once lightened the mood with a cheerful, ribald song about a certain— presumably fictional—Mrs. Prigg.

It was the evening of Sunday 13th April—a poor choice of day for ungodly work. I sat upon a hard wooden bench in the back of the coach with three other men around me, and I knew again the exhilaration of riding to battle just as sure as if I were back in the Far East.

I glanced around at the men who accompanied me on this potentially dangerous mission. To my left was Constable Reginald Clegg, a former police sergeant promoted, I gathered, to Special Branch, and the only one of my new comrades to have direct experience with the Othersiders, having served alongside Melville at Marble Arch. He was a large man, perhaps a little podgy around the midriff, but he had a bear-like presence and the no-nonsense look of a veteran bobby. On the bench opposite me sat Sergeant Sam Boggis, a long-serving Special Branch sergeant and a man hand-picked by Melville. He was a specialist in royal security, having served as a bodyguard to none less than the Prince of Wales. This surprised me, for Boggis was a scrawny man, fair of hair and shifty of expression, and I could barely imagine him as an officer of the law, let alone a seasoned and dependable bodyguard. Still, on this night he was to protect me, and I was thankful that such an experienced fellow had been assigned to the task. The final officer was Constable Larry Ecclestone, who had plodded the streets of the East End as a regular copper for some six years before being recruited by the Special Irish Branch, as once was, under the tutelage of Melville's best officers. I was told that his local knowledge would be invaluable, and that he had spent so long on undercover duties over the years, infiltrating illegal brothels, gangster hideouts and opium dens, that he had developed almost a sixth sense for danger in such environments. While we had been preparing for our journey, I had seen Larry stow two sets of brass knuckles, a small leather cosh and a flick-knife about his person, and yet refuse the offer of a pistol from Clegg. I was uncertain whether to be wary or impressed.

We had prepared ourselves quickly and efficiently, with only the most cursory of briefings from Melville and Sir Toby. At seven o'clock our Black Maria departed New Scotland Yard at Westminster, and carried us east along the Embankment, following the curve of the Thames. There had been little traffic, and our police driver had brusquely waved aside what coaches and wagons crossed our path, or else trilled his whistle. Thus unimpeded, our somewhat uncomfortable coach bumped and trundled its way eastwards, past elegant public buildings, wide open thoroughfares, and vast market-buildings, where the air was scented with salt and fish. I peered out of the small, barred viewport as we passed Tower Hill, the last marker of the City of

London, and knew that we were not far from our destination.

'So tell me,' I said, in an attempt to make conversation, 'other than Larry here, have any of you men actually met this "Artist" fellow?' My question was met with a mixture of amusement and surprise.

'Met 'im?' said Larry, half laughing. 'Oh no, sir, none of us. Even I ain't met 'im! As far as the like of us are concerned, he might as well not exist.'

I frowned. 'But I was led to believe that you had inside knowledge, Constable. Is that not the case?'

'Oh aye,' he said. 'I know the area, and I know the Artist's den sure enough. I even had a run-in with some o' his celestials once. But I ain't never laid eyes on the man 'imself. No one has, s'far as I know.'

'What Constable Ecclestone is saying,' interjected Boggis, 'is that you will be the first agent of the Crown ever to set eyes on the most notorious gangster in London. A singular honour, don't you think?'

I was unsure what to make of Boggis' tone, so I simply nodded and sat back on my bench, leaving the men to talk of past 'collars', drunken exploits and loose women.

The Maria veered north along Butcher Row, and Clegg leaned over, disturbing my reverie.

'I'm not sure this is the quickest way to the docks, sir,' he said, over the drone of Larry's singing. Boggis overheard and offered a reply.

'Too right! This way avoids the narrows—if we go down there we'll either get clobbered or else that Chinaman's spies'll spot us. Element of surprise, my lad, that's what we need.'

The cab slowed as we passed the far end of Commercial Road, which was busy even for the time of day, and then finally we were heading southwards once more, picking up the pace as we neared West India Dock.

'Nearly there, lads,' Boggis proclaimed. 'Stow that din, Ecclestone.' Larry fell silent, and feigned an injured look. 'The driver's taking us the long way round, past Canary Wharf. It's the busiest dock around, and we'll be in no danger there. But once we're past the docks I want everyone on their guard.'

The time was almost at hand, and I felt such anticipation that I wondered how I had gone so long without seeing—or even desiring—action for my country. My hand squeezed at the grip of the pistol in my overcoat pocket, the cold metal offering some small reassurance, reminding me that our business at the Artist's lair was born of duty to Queen and country. I pushed aside the thoughts of the darkened nooks filled with heady opium smoke that I would doubtless find at journey's end.

I peered out of the coach one more time, but the darkness was drawing in about us and street lights were few and far between. I could not imagine there would be many lampmen willing to walk the streets of the Isle of Dogs even if the gaslights were there. All the same, I could hear the sounds of the busy docks echoing from somewhere on the opposite side of the Black Maria. All I could see through the vision slit, however, was a rag-tag outline of commercial buildings interspersed with dilapidated houses and flats, many of which were boarded up and derelict.

I felt the coach turn a sharp bend, and when I peered out I knew at once that we were almost at our destination. We were in a poor residential neighbourhood, and my senses were assaulted by the scent of raw filth, stale beer, smoke and discarded rubbish. By the wan light from the windows of poorly constructed tenements I saw piles of rotting boxes and waste stacked in the streets, and beside some of them were people—vagrants or drunkards, I supposed—swaddled up in rags and lying on the dirt-encrusted pavement. Or perhaps they were dead. In any case, we had left behind the heart of industry only a dozen yards prior, and now we were in the worst slum I had ever seen. I doubted there was a collection of more squalid, dingy buildings crammed together in such a fashion anywhere else in the world, and yet there they were, slouching haphazardly within London, the jewel of the Empire.

The Black Maria struggled to wend its way along a pitted street. The sound of its wheels caused a few dull, expressionless faces to peer down at us from upstairs windows. Urchins huddled in doorways, gawping at us with large, dark eyes, like pits of despair. I hoped that we would keep going, but to my dismay the police carriage began to slow, and I realised that the House of Zhengming was a short distance ahead. For a place with a reputation so sinister, situated in so hopeless an environ, I could only shudder at what we were to find there.

Larry stepped menacingly towards a beery-breathed thug whose curiosity had got the better of him. The man took one look at Ecclestone and continued on his way with a muttered expletive. Boggis passed on instructions to the driver, who nodded before flicking the reins and taking the Maria away. With a growing sense of dread, I watched it leave.

'Told 'im to keep moving,' Boggis explained. 'Even the coppers ain't safe round here. He'll check back now and then. Told 'im if we ain't done in an hour, he should send for assistance.'

We stood before the House of Zhengming, which held the appearance of a run-down former tavern, situated on a street corner with a few terraced houses adjoining it. The opium den had, it seemed, grown along with the Artist's influence, consuming many of the neighbouring tenements, for now every window was shielded by thick red drapes within. The walls of the structure were uneven, and the building did not so much stand on the street corner as loom out from it, as though threatening to devour all who flocked to its doors; in a way, I supposed, that was exactly what it did. It exuded foreboding—and of course, I had my own reasons to fear such a place. More than that, a paper lantern glowed green above the front door, illuminating a sign written in both English and Chinese. My knowledge of that tongue was cursory, but I recognised many of the characters when I saw them. And the sign did not say 'Zhengming' at all, but rather 'Zhi Ming', which meant something like 'the time of one's death', or 'fatal hour', if memory served. We were standing outside the 'house of the dead', and my blood ran cold.

'Right then, lads,' said Boggis, addressing Clegg and Ecclestone, 'we go in together, and make sure the way is clear for the Captain. I want you two keeping an eye on our exit at all times. I'll stick to Captain Hardwick like glue. And remember,' he added in a more hushed tone, 'you might get asked to surrender your weapons. We should cooperate as far as can be seen, if you get my meaning.' Boggis added a wink to underline his intent. Larry patted his breast pocket and grinned in response, revealing an incomplete row of uneven teeth as he did so.

Suitably forewarned, Larry led the way, closely followed by Boggis, with Clegg behind me. We entered the House of Zhengming through a heavy door, and pushed through a bead curtain into a dark vestibule. The air seemed thick, and the shadows almost cloying. Faint sounds of chatter and soft laughter droned from somewhere beyond the veil of gloom, but there was no immediate sign of life within. Larry took a few steps towards the end of the short corridor, and our complacence was shattered by an ear-piercing screech that caused us all to flinch, and Clegg to cry out, startled. To the left of the vestibule was a tall cage, set back into the wall in what was doubtless once an old store-cupboard. From the pitch black, half a dozen screeching monkeys were making enough noise to wake the dead, throwing themselves at the mesh of their prison and baring their teeth at us. Boggis was the first to react, lashing out at the cage with a clenched fist and frightening the tiny brutes back into the darkness, whence they continued to chatter at us from a safe distance.

'Well,' said Boggis, 'I suppose we've lost the element of surprise.'

We pressed on, pushing through a heavy velvet curtain into a large room that I supposed was once a bar, now a waiting room for clients. Red drapes covered every wall, and even the windows. Six or seven green Chinese lanterns hung from the ceiling, casting a flickering light across the room. We were greeted curtly by a short woman in a brocade dress, who stood behind an old lectern that had been pressed into service as a desk. Two burly Chinese guards flanked a large double doorway across from us, eying us disapprovingly.

'We're here to see the boss,' glowered Boggis.

'The master is not to be disturbed,' replied the woman, in stilted English.

'He'll be bloody disturbed, love, whether he likes it or not.'

The woman glanced over towards the guards, who responded by straightening themselves up and looking lively. I stepped to the lectern and drew my card.

'My good woman,' I said, 'we are here on urgent business for the Crown. "The master" is doubtless expecting us. If you would be so kind as to alert him to our presence, I am sure it will be in his best interest to grant us an interview and avoid any... unpleasantness... that may upset your clients.'

She considered this for a moment. 'We rely on happy clients. We do not wish unpleasantness... I will send a message to the master, but if he say no, you will leave.'

'Send the message then,' I said, ignoring the last part of her statement. 'We will wait here for his reply.'

She took my card and left the room, leaving us in the company of the guards, who said not a word, even when Larry attempted to engage them in conversation. I hoped they did not speak much English, because Larry could not have failed to offend them in some capacity. In any case, they simply looked upon us impassively until the woman returned.

'The master, he say he will see you, Captain John Hardwick, but you alone,' she said. 'Your friends will wait here.'

'Bugger that. Where he goes, we go,' snarled Boggis. He stepped towards the woman as he spoke, prompting motion from the two guards for the first time. They reached to their belts in unison, undoubtedly to take up some weapon, and paused to see if their show of aggression would be enough to stay Boggis' ire. The sergeant stepped back a pace. Larry Ecclestone stepped forwards, reaching into his coat and fixing the largest of the guards with a glare that would turn a charging bull.

'The master was very clear,' said the Chinese woman, as nervous as I that the situation had escalated so quickly. 'Captain Hardwick only.'

'All right, wait,' said Boggis, his arms outstretched in a show of peacemaking. 'A compromise then. How about you let me in—just me—and the others all wait out here. Under guard, if you like.' The woman looked suspicious. Boggis tried to explain, speaking slowly so there could be no misunderstanding. 'Let us two in the den. These men wait here. Get it?'

She weighed up his words for a moment. 'Very well, you come in. The other two stay here, and do not cause trouble.' Only once we had all reluctantly agreed, and Boggis had exchanged muttered words with the other policemen, did the woman beckon us towards the door. An unintelligible barked command bade the guards stand aside, and we stepped through the door into the lion's den.

We were led through a short corridor, pushed our way through a set of heavy, black drapes, and found ourselves in a true den of iniquity. The room was large, and dimly lit by paper lanterns. The air was thick with smoke from the opium, incense and lanterns—it was as though a London fog was on the rise in the very room. I had seen places like these before, of course, and yet I could not become inured to the sight. Two dozen men, of all ages, lay virtually incapacitated, the wealthier clients on chaises or mattresses, and the poorer ones on simple wooden benches or even just a rug on the floor. Each was attended by a little girl or boy, who held the pipes for the customers and refilled them upon request. I knew that the men who chased the dragon believed themselves in the lap of luxury, in some far-away dream-world, blissfully unaware that their physical bodies languished in a filthy backstreet tavern that crawled with cockroaches and mice. And yet, a part of me would have gladly joined the dreamers still.

A girl fished around in the pockets of a young man, whose head was lolling back on a moth-eaten velvet pillow as the opium draw hit him. The child produced two shiny shillings, and ran dutifully to an older woman who was watching from a corner of the room. The woman took the coins and nodded assent, at which the girl dashed off to refill the man's pipe. That was the way of it—those who dreamt too long would find themselves in for a rude awakening when the money ran out. This one would probably wake up on the cobbles some distance from here, ravenously hungry, dehydrated, with little knowledge of how he had lost all of his coin.

We followed our diminutive host closely. Little niches and corridors ran off haphazardly from the main room, disappearing into the gloom to who-knows-where. I felt disorientated from the very start, for I could not gauge the size of the place. My attempt to gain my bearings was interrupted when we reached a door at the far end of the room, whereupon the woman stopped and gave Boggis a fierce look before opening the door.

'No trouble!' she warned, and we stepped inside, passing through a beaded curtain into a softly lit room.

Stepping across the threshold was like moving between night and day. Coloured Chinese lanterns hung from every inch of the low ceiling, casting flickering light around the room in amber, red and green. The smell of the opium was replaced by the smoke of incense, and around us windchimes tinkled musically, disturbed by a breeze from an unknown source. It took me a moment to gather my wits and adjust my eyes to the dreamy setting. The room was small, but decadently furnished, with tapestries and silks covering the walls, and velvet cushions across the floor. In the centre of the room, sitting cross-legged behind a low table, was a man dressed in an opulent robe of Chinese silk. His black hair fell about his shoulders long and loose. He was blind, I presumed, with a silk scarf tied around his head, covering his eyes. And yet not for a moment did I feel that he could not see me. He looked gaunt and frail, and sipped at a cup of tea before awkwardly setting it down on the table. Two guards—both broad of chest and blank of expression—stood flanking the blind man, who I knew must be the mysterious Artist.

'Ah, my guests have arrived,' said the man, in a thin voice. 'Won't you please be seated? Make yourselves comfortable.'

I sensed that Boggis was about to protest, but I laid a hand on his arm and nodded towards the plump cushions opposite the blind man. He looked irked but sat down with me on the floor.

'Won't you have some tea?' asked the Artist, and began to pour it without waiting for our answer. Boggis eyed the greenish liquid suspiciously. 'Captain Hardwick, is it?' our host asked.

The door closed softly behind us. I sized up the two guards in case the meeting turned out to be an elaborate trap.

'You have me at a disadvantage, sir; you are the Artist?' I asked, though I already knew the answer.

'I am. Though you may call me Tsun Pen.' His answer threw me—I had lingered under the impression that the Artist never gave his true name to outsiders.

'Your coming was foretold,' said Tsun Pen, 'though you have found your way to me sooner than expected. That is to your credit. It shows that you are a tenacious and inquisitive man.'

'I am sorry, sir, but I do not understand. How is it that you know me? And what do you know of my business here?' It was not lost on me that he was ignoring Boggis entirely.

Tsun Pen smiled, like a crocodile. 'Your intentions, Captain, are quite transparent. And you have spent your short time in England blundering around the city getting into all sorts of mischief, have you not? You leave a trail that even a lesser broker of intelligence could follow. As to how I know you... well, surely your employers have confided in you the nature of my relationship with them?'

'There is no "relationship" between you and the Crown,' said Boggis, irked.

'Oh, come now, officer,' cooed the Artist, 'I would wager that whatever agency you work for has at some point received assistance from me.'

'Then you have contact with the authorities?' I asked, agitated both with the Artist's coyness and Boggis' interruption. 'Are you some kind of agent too?'

'Oh, good heavens no! I am a broker of information, Captain Hardwick, and as such it is my business to know all, before anyone else. Nothing happens in this city without my knowledge. Nothing can happen without my having foreseen it.'

'Do you claim that your web of intelligence is akin to some kind of psychic intuition?' I knew as I was speaking that I was being led from my original goal, and that I was in danger of breaching etiquette by allowing my annoyance with the man to get the better of me, but something in his manner brought out the worst in me.

'Call it what you will, Captain—the result is the same. Can you imagine what someone in government would pay to learn the location of enemy spies or troop movements abroad? Or the cipher for a particular code? Better yet, what would it be worth to them to learn of the indiscretions of their key rivals? Do you have any idea how many secrets lurk behind every single front door in this city of corruption? And I, Captain Hardwick, see all.' There was something musical about his softly accented voice, and coupled with the subdued lights and frowsty incense, the effect was almost entrancing. It was difficult to concentrate, but I forced myself to alertness.

'I see,' I said. 'You ply information for profit, and you also take money to keep information secret. In some circles, that would be called blackmail.'

'I do not doubt. Some of what I do may even be called treason, which in a way is why you are here, Captain, and why you bristle so in my presence. You have come to learn secrets, to which only I am privy. Perhaps, by selling you information of such import, I can redeem myself in your eyes? Or perhaps, by paying the piper, you become more like me.'

'You realise that I am here on a mission of utmost importance to the security of England, and to the Empire? To withhold information pertinent to my investigation would be... unwise.' I channelled the very tone that Tsun Pen had thus far taken with me, to make it clear that there would be repercussions if he did not comply. He looked unflustered.

'Captain, there is no need for this dance of words. I have willingly helped every servant of the Crown ever to pass through my doors... oh yes, you are not the first, despite what you may have heard.' Had he somehow sensed my surprise? 'Look around you, Captain Hardwick. These are not the trappings of a man of unimaginable wealth, luxuriating in comfort provided by the British government. These are adequate lodgings for a man of... modest means. I ask a fair price for my talents, and I resist permanent employment by your superiors because I am... unwell, and wish to be left alone. I keep my own counsel, and if my intelligence is to be believed, you would be wise to do the same when you and I part company.'

'What do you mean?' I asked.

'Only that, for a man on the trail of a secret organisation, you seem terribly trusting of everyone you meet. Have you stopped to think about the number of agencies already involved in your investigation? Have you stopped to truly consider who you can trust?'

'This man is notorious for his lies, sir,' Boggis whispered to me, not quietly enough.

'Indeed?' asked the Artist. 'When you return to your club, Captain Hardwick, I urge you to look at the list of members. Why not ask Mr. Ruskin about his dealings with me, and how much I have spoken the truth—truth that has assisted your order in many affairs. If I am so untrustworthy, why do the authorities not only allow my presence in the city, but facilitate business transactions between myself and certain notable figures in society? What if I were to tell you that I am paid well by the likes of Lord

Hartington, Henry Irving, and even Gladstone, for information that has proven time and again invaluable to them? What if—'

But the Artist was cut short. Before I knew what was happening, Boggis had leapt to his feet and launched himself across the table. There was something gleaming in his hand—a pocket pistol. He must have had up his sleeve one of those contraptions so beloved of sneak thieves and roguish gamblers, and the tiny gun had been propelled into his hand by means of a spring-loaded mechanism. Boggis had planned for this moment, and he was going for the Artist with murder in his heart. In that dream-like room, everything seemed to happen too slowly. I called out, but Boggis paid no heed. I saw one of the bodyguards fling himself in Boggis' path as the teapot and cups flew across the floor. The other guard hauled the Artist backwards whilst the first wrestled with the policeman. The pistol went off, fired into the air. There could be no more than two bullets in such a concealed weapon, but Boggis quickly sank the celestial who grappled with him with a low blow, and took aim at the Artist.

I have no idea how I came to be on my feet. I do not remember standing, nor leaping at Boggis. I do not know why I knocked his arm aside as he pulled the trigger, or why I dealt the man a blow across the face that sent him reeling backwards. None of those actions seemed my own; I was driven by instinct, and I prayed that my instinct was right.

The Artist was cowering in the corner of the room, cushions scattered around him. The guard who had been with him at once joined the other one, and the pair of them restrained Boggis. Even as they did so, the door was thrown open and Larry Ecclestone tumbled through it, two more guards holding onto his arms and doing a poor job of restraining him.

'Gerroff me!' he roared. 'I'll bloody do for the lot of yer!'

'Larry, stop!' I shouted. 'Boggis has tried to kill the Artist, and unless you want to be up for treason too, you'd better stand down.' I commanded him as I would have done a member of my company back East, and it seemed to do the trick.

Larry looked around the room and took stock of the situation, then straightened up and shrugged off the attentions of the guards. I saw Clegg peering through the door behind them, indecisively.

'Did you have any part of this, Larry?' I asked. He shook his head, and gawped at the Artist. I realised that to Larry, Tsun Pen was a ghost—a fable of the East End streets, and a terrible thing to behold.

'Tsun Pen,' I said, turning to the man who was trying to compose himself after the shock of the attack, 'I must beg your forgiveness. Neither I nor my other companions had any idea of Sergeant Boggis' intentions. I promise you there will be a full inquest into the matter, but we must conclude our business today. Lives depend on it.' It wasn't much of a persuasive argument, but it was all I could think of in the moment.

Another guard went over to Tsun Pen, and helped him to his feet. I stepped backwards involuntarily when the Artist stood, for he no longer seemed the frail, small man he had previously appeared. The low ceiling perhaps flattered my host, but the Artist now appeared a giant of a man. He moved awkwardly, and I presumed that he suffered from an ailment of the joints that so often afflicts those of prodigious height.

'Captain Hardwick, I have been a gracious host, have I not? I always try to extend the hospitality that my forebears pride themselves upon, and yet I fear that this is not the first attempt on my life. Remember that I told you to be careful whom you trust. There are agencies who would stop at nothing to learn the things that I know, or to silence me once and for all. Some of those agencies are in allegiance with your own. Others are not entirely... *on our side.*'

He stressed those words, and I shuddered. He knew.

'This man... this "Boggis"; I know not whom he works for, but I can hazard several guesses. Perhaps my old friend William Melville has sent his compliments this day; or perhaps this man is one of them.'

My heart sank. What a fool I'd been—if these Othersiders could infiltrate our world with relative ease, then how much had I confided in the wrong people? I thought of Ambrose, of Jim Denny, Arthur Furnival… even Sir Toby himself. I had embraced these people who were virtual strangers to me, latched onto them because I felt like a stranger in my own country. My naivety mighthave cost me dear. I looked at Boggis with disappointment in my eyes, but he had only venom in his.

'I'm no traitor,' he snarled. 'Captain, if you trust this man you're a bigger fool than I took you for. He's a viper, and we'll all be dead before the night's through if you let them take me away.'

'Nonsense,' said the Artist, and he sounded sincere. 'Captain Hardwick, despite this interruption I will conclude our business. But I must insist that your men are placed under guard while we talk. When our business is concluded, you will all leave the House of Zhengming. I never break a contract.'

I nodded. Boggis' head dropped. I turned to Larry.

'Constable, I need you to do as these men say. And keep an eye on Boggis—no funny business, you understand? We have to complete these negotiations. Nothing else matters.' Larry nodded, and stepped aside as the Artist left the room. He had acquired a silver-tipped cane from somewhere, and leaned heavily upon it as he walked.

The small woman appeared again, and Tsun Pen said only: 'Make arrangements for our guests, and bring the Captain to my rooms.'

Once I was satisfied that Boggis, Ecclestone and Clegg were not going to cause more trouble, I turned to the woman, and she led the way through another door. Tsun Pen was nowhere to be seen. Before us stretched a longer corridor, lit by green-glassed lanterns. At the end was a steep stair, shrouded in darkness. I had taken no more than two steps forward when I realised that to my right was not a solid wall, as I had thought, but an old vaulted arch. I hazarded a look into the gloomy opening, and was horrified to see that the cellar had been converted into an extension of the opium den. At the foot of a half-dozen broad steps was a cold, flag-stoned room, with niches in the walls like those in a mausoleum. An old, milky-eyed Chinaman sat cross-legged in the centre of the room. In most of the niches lay a patron. At first glance they would have been mistaken for corpses—so ghastly was their appearance and so immobile their bodies—but they were not dead. This was the underworld equivalent of a theatre cheap-seat; these poor sops had been here for God knows how long, their bodies wasting away faster than their purses had emptied. They were forgotten to the world; forgotten to all except the crippled, shrivelled celestial who watched over them.

That could have been my fate, I thought. I clenched my fists tight. The shakes had returned, so thick with drug-smoke was the air in this place. The woman pushed past me, and urged me to follow.

'You come now. Quick, quick,' she said.

I took one glance back down into the cellar before I followed. I could have sworn that the old man was grinning, and staring at me with his sightless eyes.

I had been made to wait for an interminable time in a draughty upstairs corridor, but was eventually admitted to an attic office, the pitched ceiling sloping towards a small dormer window, through which I could see little but an inky blackness and beads of drizzle.

The Artist stood before us, hunched over his cane, his head almost touching the beams that ran across the ceiling.

'Captain Hardwick, do come in,' he said. 'I apologise for the humble surroundings, but I feel more at home here, and safer, too. Please, be seated.'

A hook-handed guard locked the door behind us. A second guard stood near the Artist, blocking another door, which was the only other exit from the room. I took a seat on the chair behind me. I was not comfortable in the company of these dangerous men, and wanted nothing more than to be on my feet, ready for anything. The guards slouched against the doors, arms folded, and the Artist, Tsun Pen, sat opposite me.

'My dear Captain, let me speak plainly. The events of the evening have left me somewhat shaken, and I am afraid I must risk cutting our new-found friendship short for the sake of my nerves. I have what you need, and I have no intention of withholding any information from you—as long as the proper price is paid. And I know that you bear the fee, do you not?'

His manner had changed, and I felt it was more than nerves. There was something unsettling about his sudden transformation from timid invalid to imposing intelligence-broker.

'I shall pay the price. And you will answer my questions.'

The Artist grinned. He held out a hand, and I reached into my breast pocket for the envelope I had carried with me all the way from Scotland Yard. It contained four hundred pounds, a small fortune. The two guards stood bolt upright, watching my hand for any glimpse of a weapon. When I produced the envelope from my jacket, they relaxed, and the burly Chinese guard took it from me with his good hand, and passed it to his master.

'Thank you, Hu,' said Tsun Pen to the guard. He placed the envelope on his desk, unopened. 'I trust it is all here,' he said. 'And so, you will want to hear all I know of the mysterious agents from the other side.'

His glee was evident; Tsun Pen had confirmed that he knew about the nature of the Othersiders. So there were those outside the club who believed the incredible tale of invaders from another world, and yet still I felt complicit in some maddening lie, some fable with which to scare children in the darkness. Beyond all of that, regardless of my incredulity on the matter, I was on my guard; if even half of what I knew about the Artist was true, then he was a master of lies, and would say anything to turn a profit.

'We will talk in my studio, Captain Hardwick, for I will best be able to show you what you are dealing with there.'

With a nod, the guard opened the door and we followed the Artist into a large, austere room. It seemed to be both art studio and bedroom—the far end of the chamber was a mass of canvases on stretchers and easels, some covered in dust sheets, some half-finished, and others wrapped in brown paper as if ready to be posted. Indeed three of them bore address labels on them, and I tried my best to take a surreptitious look at the recipients; I recognised only one of the names: that of a senior figure at Whitehall. The paintings ranged in size from small studies to huge scenes taller than a man. It was difficult to make out any details, as most of the room was shrouded in gloomy half-light. I could see another door that presumably led to a servants' stair, while a small closet door led off the far corner of the room. I note these observations because, even at the time, I found it a trifle strange—I was certain that the upper floor should not have been so spacious, and wondered if the opium smoke had disorientated me.

I was given some freedom to move about the room, and I took the opportunity to look more closely at the uncovered paintings. I could not discern the subject matter clearly, but determined that the pieces varied greatly in style and scale. Indeed, if Tsun Pen was the creator of those works, I would have considered him either a master of many artistic disciplines, or else suffering from some form of conversion disorder, the product of a fractured mind. Not least of my worries was how a blind man could have produced such works at all.

I was about to lift the sheet that covered the largest canvas in the room, so as to glean a better look in the wan lantern light, when I was distracted by a loud scratching and the jangling of chains coming from the closet door. The Artist was too quick to interject, almost as if he had seen my reaction.

'Worry not, Captain; it is merely my pets, my muses—I have not fed them this evening, and they grow restless. I will tend to them when our business is concluded. For now, pray take a seat, and perhaps I can offer you some refreshment?' The Artist offered me a seat on a chaise, and he sat on the edge of the bed, a four-poster draped in fine silk sheets. I accepted the Artist's hospitality, taking a small sherry from the guard as it was offered. 'I hope you will find that, despite these modest surroundings, we are not uncivilised.' At this, Tsun Pen raised his own glass to me, and drank. I sipped my sherry to be polite.

'The paintings... are they all yours?' I asked.

'Why of course. They do not call me the Artist for nothing. You think it strange that a blind man can paint?'

'I confess I do, though I have often heard of men doing remarkable things when they have lost one or more of the senses.'

'Oh?' he prompted. I was on unsteady ground now—I did not wish to offend my host further by discussing his disability, but I had to proceed. I was eager to get on with business, for I had already spent longer than I would have liked in that place.

'Indeed, sir. I knew several men in India who lost limbs, and were rehabilitated with startling rapidity. Most remarkable of all, a comrade lost his right hand to the surgeon's knife, and yet was writing and sketching with his left within a fortnight, when formerly that hand had been clumsy.' I glanced at the hook-handed guard, cursing yet another *faux pas,* but he did not bat an eyelid.

'Ah, would that I had lost a hand, that I may know such courage,' said the Artist, and I understood not his remark. 'Tell me, Captain, you did not serve just in India did you? I detect something in your manner that speaks of the Far East; my father's homeland perhaps?'

'That's right,' I said, puzzled. 'I served briefly in China, and ended my tour in Burma.'

'Burma is a hard country, Captain. One that I have visited, and where I am in fact known well. I do not think I would be welcome there now, of course, given my... shall we say... affiliation with the British.'

'You spied for us?'

'I detest the word "spy", Captain Hardwick. I prefer "entrepreneur".'

So, he had been paid for his efforts in Burma. Of course, I hardly needed him to say as much. I was fast coming to the conclusion that, though he was blindfolded like Lady Justice, he was the very image of duplicity.

'Is it really so obvious that I spent time in the East?' I asked. I was being drawn into his banal chatter. My head was fuzzy, I guessed from the opium smoke, and I struggled to get back to the business that I had come for.

'Oh, to one such as me, yes. But I confess, I have heard all about you, Captain. I have heard how you found yourself in an altercation recently with some ruffians. Near your own home, too; how disrespectful of them. I heard also that you fought them quite bravely.' Tsun Pen sipped his drink, before his smile returned.

'How could you know this? Do you know who was responsible?'

'Perhaps, Captain. But that is not the matter you are here to discuss, is it? I only grant one wish for one fee. Additional answers come at a price, and I fear that price will be too rich for your blood.'

Now he really was being mercenary. I could have throttled the man, but could not find the reason in it. And so I pushed such thoughts from my mind, and set about instilling some urgency into proceedings.

'To business, then. You clearly have knowledge of the agents who are attacking our city, and I need to know everything that you know about them. Who are they? What is their goal? Most important of all, where will they strike next?'

'Captain, I warned you to consider your questions carefully. However, since you are unaccustomed to our ways, and since you have been such good company, I shall help you. I am a man of my word, and I always honour a bargain once it has been struck. First of all, you already know who these agents are, and what they want. William James has surely shared as much with you, yes?'

'He has shared a theory, nothing more.'

'Then let us assume his theory is correct,' Tsun Pen said, finishing his sherry and handing his glass to the nearest guard. 'They want your world, Captain, and you will risk much if you wish to stop them. If you are not prepared, you will be consumed. You have felt it, yes?' The Artist rose, leaning on his cane, and shuffled past me towards his paintings. I turned in my chair, and began to feel more light-headed. The subdued light, the sherry, the smoke—especially the smoke—they must have been taking a toll. I tried to push the thought from my mind, squeezing a fist tightly to stop from trembling. I could not afford to betray any weakness in front of this man.

Tsun Pen pulled back the sheets from a pair of three-foot canvases, revealing surreal, brooding scenes of tumultuous storms in the sky over the city. There was something vaguely familiar about the style of the paintings, though I could not remember where I had seen it before.

'Come, Captain, take a closer look,' the Artist cooed, and I got to my feet slowly and stepped towards the paintings.

There was more to the work than first met the eye, and I was astonished by the depth of detail that seemed to reveal itself in the very layers of the paint the more one looked. The first painting was mostly of a storm, with the East End silhouetted against a backdrop of red and purple clouds. A streak of lightning illuminated a distressing scene in the bottom left corner: an enormous spider, as big as a house, spun its webs outwards across the city. Its eight green eyes were fixed on a man, standing in its shadow and seemingly holding it at bay with fire; a flaming torch perhaps? At the man's feet were three other figures, crudely rendered but certainly representing dead men. In the shadows towards the lower right-hand corner was a group of black-clad people, poised as if hiding. Behind them, standing tall, was a similar figure, but with a monstrous, reptilian head like a crocodile or maybe... a dragon. Yes, a dragon. That realisation made my heart beat harder.

The Artist motioned to the second painting. The scene was similar, but the spider was gone. Now the people in black stood in the centre of the piece, on a riverbank. I realised that it was the Thames, for a surreal skewed perspective forced the eye to the vague outline of London Bridge through a haze of rain and fog. The far bank of the river was obscured by night, and the five famous arches of the bridge were indistinct, as though there were more of them, spanning some infinite gulf into a realm of shadow. I noticed then that the figures in the painting were all looking down at the river, and the dragon-man was pointing into the river itself. It was the man from the previous painting, the one who had been fighting the spider—he was pale and bleeding, and drowned in the Thames. I am not sure that any form of comprehension dawned on me then, but an inexplicable cold creep began to trickle up my spine.

'I am sorry, truly, for the part I am to play, Captain. But you see, I am as much a pawn in the great game as anyone. What I paint in these scenes always comes to pass. Always. Even if I myself am depicted, I understand that it is no use to defy destiny. Instead, I use the art as my guide. I do what I must.'

I looked at his blindfolded face, confused. And then I realised that the jangling of chains and scraping from over in the far corner had been growing progressively louder for some time— the Artist's pets were causing some commotion. I could not think straight. I put a hand to my temple.

'Are you saying, sir, that these paintings somehow answer my questions? Am I supposed to understand them? Is it some kind of code?'

'Of sorts... it is the future, as certain as the sun will rise tomorrow. These paintings are my life; my insurance. I have sold such works to the greatest men of government, of the arts and the clergy. Even the military have need of my talents; why, I once sold a painting to a certain Brigadier Sir Marcus Hardwick... a relative perhaps?'

That stung me, and the blind man knew he had struck a

chord. More than that, I remembered now where I had seen the Artist's distinctive hand before—in a small painting hanging in the office of Sir Toby Fitzwilliam. In that moment, I felt a keen sense of betrayal; was Sir Toby in the Artist's pocket? But why go to such lengths to involve me—or, of course, to get rid of me?

'This is… balderdash,' I said at last, echoing Ambrose Hanlocke's sentiments about the whole affair. 'Sir, if you cannot or will not give me a straight answer, then I will have to take my leave and report your unwillingness to cooperate to my superiors.' I spoke as firmly as I could, but the words felt laboured. There was something very wrong with me, and it went beyond mere opium-smoke.

'Ah, you are indignant and strong-willed,' he said. 'So very much like the Brigadier. Like father, like son, they say. Suffice it to say, Captain, that I dwelt long on your coming here, and this is what I painted, and I am so very sorry for what is about to pass.'

'Really, Mr. Tsun, I'm trying very hard to understand,' I said. The room was starting to swim, the noises were getting louder, and the Artist was talking in riddles.

'It is simple, Captain. The paintings show what is to pass. I paint the future.'

I was about to shout a protestation, for he was clearly insane, when I lost control of my legs. My knees buckled and I staggered a couple of paces backwards. I backed into the hook-handed guard, who took me roughly by the arms and sat me back on the chaise.

'W…What's going on?' I asked, weakly.

'Listen to me very carefully, Captain Hardwick. Agents from another universe are among us. That is a fact. They seek to live among us and perhaps completely usurp our world, for their own is being torn apart by something quite unspeakable. I do not doubt that they will succeed, for they have knowledge and weapons that we do not, and the absolute determination that stems from desperation. You must at least suspect the truth of it by now, Captain. And with that truth comes the utter hopelessness of your cause.'

'Wh… what? I demand you let me out of here this instant.'

'Indeed, you have what you came for, I suppose. Why don't you go? There is the door.'

I did not believe that he would seriously let me leave. I believed right then that my men were dead, or soon would be. Those corpses in the painting—they were Boggis, Clegg and Ecclestone. So the corpse in the Thames…

There is no escape from the house of the dead.

It was all the effort I could muster to stagger to my feet. The sherry had been drugged, that much was certain. My vision blurred, and everything in the room distorted before my eyes, as though viewed through old glass. The leering faces of the guards loomed at me like nightmare visions, and I followed the pointing finger of the Artist, his laughter echoing in my ears. My hand clasped the doorknob, and I steadied myself for but a moment before twisting it and opening the door. But beyond the door was not freedom, but a small room, which I had taken earlier for a closet. The slavering pets of the Artist bundled forwards, knocking me from my feet. Through skewed vision I saw them, and Good Christ! I wish I could unsee them. They were not animals, but people—of a kind—with such severe deformities that they were barely human in appearance. But human they were. Two women—flabby, fleshy masses, their skin moist and foul-smelling, like rotting meat. In places their flesh seemed to give way, as if their organs were protruding outside their bodies. Their faces were covered in great weals and fleshy protrusions, which obscured their eyes, causing them to scrabble around in search of me as if using scent rather than sight. I realised, finally, that their chains prevented them from reaching me, and so they whimpered, frustrated, like dogs.

I moved away from them as fast as I could, scrambling across the wooden floor, sending several small easels crashing to the ground. I heard then the laughter of the Artist and his men. I tried to clamber to my feet again, but it was no good. My legs were like jelly, and all I could do was crawl, pathetically, towards them, until I was hauled up and thrown into the chaise once again. Looking up, I was confronted by the true terror of my predicament.

Tsun Pen stood before me, his robe unfurled to reveal a long, serpentine torso, lean and misshapen. Beneath his normal arms was another pair, scrawny and vestigial, tipped with long, bony fingers. These secondary appendages stretched outwards like chelicerae, their confinement beneath his robe having cramped them. Silhouetted by the light of flickering lanterns, he resembled nothing less than a gigantic spider, tugging at the strands of the metaphorical web in which I was now trapped.

My mind was fractured, both by the drugs and by the horror of what I had seen. My brain was on fire, and I could feel blood trickling from my nostrils, as though the sheer stress placed upon my mind was rupturing my skull.

'Captain, you will understand now why I play both sides. You will understand that I care not for this world and its fate, for I am born of both worlds. I am the perfect fusion of two counterparts in two universes. I see the future. I am the future!' The Artist sneered and snarled—he was quite mad, though I was little better off.

'I... I can't understand. What? How?' I murmured these things and more. Tsun Pen only laughed as he revelled in my obvious distress.

'All in good time, Captain; for there is a little more time for you... just a little. I will do you the honour of showing you the truth. It is the least I can do before you die.'

EIGHT

I must have passed out. When I awoke I was no longer in the Artist's studio, but in a dark room, lit only by a single candle. I was upright, suspended from a beam by my wrists, which ached as the thick ropes tied around them chafed. It took some time to take stock of my predicament, groggy as I was, and longer still for my senses to adjust. And I realised I was not alone.

Two hunched, animalistic figures lay in one corner. They were but black shapes in the gloom, but I knew what they were, and I turned my head away instinctively so as not to look upon those noisome creatures. That is when I saw Tsun Pen, standing close, silent and unmoving as a statue. He was robed once again, and he hid his deformity masterfully; I could almost have believed that I had imagined the whole thing. He offered me water from a tin cup, which I gulped all too readily, only afterwards gaping at him stupidly as I realised that it could have been poisoned.

'Do not worry, Captain,' said the Artist, seeing my dismay. 'The water is quite harmless. Drink.'

I accepted another cup, and my parched throat was partially soothed. I blocked the sound of the grunting and rustling in the corner from my mind as best I could, and tried to focus on my predicament. My eyes were beginning to adjust to the gloom, and I could make out a door behind the Artist, light shining dimly through the gaps. Near to the door stood the hook-handed guard, who seemed never far from his master's side.

'What do you intend to do with me?' I asked the Artist.

'Me? Oh, nothing at all, Captain. Unfortunately for you, however, my present client has plans for you, and we do not have much time. I promised you the truth, and I meant it—your agency has provided me moneys to give you any information I have pertaining to the Othersiders. I am a man of my word, so ask of me what you will.'

This was beyond the pale. Tsun Pen was playing the part of a devilish genie, granting a wish at a terrible price. But still, I had to cling to hope that I could yet secure my freedom, and perhaps anything I could learn would still be of use to the Apollonian.

'What... are you?'

My words seemed to sting him, and that surprised me; this monster, this Thing that had been so conniving and cruel up to now had seemed beyond mere injurious remarks.

'You wish to know how I became so monstrous that even a soldier like yourself recoils at my sight? It is a long story, Captain, and as I said we have little time. I will tell you the short version of the tale, so that you will understand what you are dealing with; what we are all dealing with.

'I was not born this way. I was made, by the sheer will and power of those beyond the veil. My ability, however, has always been manifest. I was blessed—or perhaps cursed—with the ability to paint the future, to visualise events that had not yet come to pass. Imagine the difficulty of being different as a boy, when one is already half-Chinese in a city of intolerance. Even in the pits of a Burmese prison cell, I do not think you could have been as alone as I was as a child.'

'You'd be surprised,' I retorted.

'Perhaps; perhaps not. In any case, I escaped my predicament as soon as I was physically able, and travelled the world, learning much of the ways of intrigue.'

'You said you would keep it short,' I croaked. I found his

company loathsome and wanted him to cut to the chase. I also realised that if he could be rattled, then perhaps I could force some circumstance that would lead to my liberation. I had no plan beyond that, but it was something.

My interruption did the trick, for the Artist stopped and the smile faded from his lips.

'I did indeed, and I always keep my promises. I shall move my tale on a few years, to Burma, where I met some powerful men who would change the course of my life. I was working for the British at the time; but the men I met were not representatives of any government on our earth. No, eventually I discovered they were Othersiders, as you call them, and that they had need of my talents.

'My mind railed, because my abilities allowed me to see the truth of their claims. I had foreseen their coming for so long, but had been unable to interpret my own visions, so unbelievable had they seemed, even to me. Finally, all became clear; a truth I recognised at once, a fundamental truth about the nature of the universe and my place within it. They told me of my other self, who seemed very much like me, including his uncanny abilities. These abilities were unique, I was told, for my counterpart was called by them a "Majestic", one of the few psychics in their universe able to use his abilities while fending off the attentions of malefic energies, which themselves threatened to engulf the entire globe. With his precognitive powers, they had managed to keep hope alive for all of their kind. And yet, in order to enact their master plan to subsume this universe, they had need of me—those self-same abilities on both sides of the veil would pave the way for the forthcoming invasion, and I was able to name my price.'

'And so for profit you sold out your own people? Are you mad?'

'My people?' he snarled, with sudden venom. 'I plotted and bargained for everything I ever had; and why? Because I had to, Captain. Nobody ever gave me anything. I was lowborn, a freak of nature—hated and derided first for my creed, and then for my powers. And these Othersiders—look at what they could offer! Their infernal weapons and devices of destruction are beyond compare, and their success is inevitable. I merely greased the wheels of progress in exchange for a loftier position. I bettered myself, to spite all those who had said that I could not do it. You would do the same, for the right price.' He stopped, and visibly composed himself.

'But they have psychics already, James said they were wired to machines in order to harness their power,' I said, buying into the fantasy more fully with each passing second.

'Not like me. Yes, their psychics are unlike anything we have on this side of the veil, and indeed they are often incarcerated and experimented on like laboratory monkeys, unless they display the aptitude to become Majestics. But none of them have a direct counterpart on our side with equal power. None but Tsun Pen.'

'So you helped the Othersiders. You somehow predicted events in the future that would be of use to them. You saw their successes and failures perhaps. And their… gateways, their portals? You created them?'

'Not quite; not alone. There is far more to it than simple mediumship, or magic, if you like. But you're learning quickly, Captain Hardwick.'

'So why did they do this to you, their prized asset? I assume it was them?

'Even now, Captain, you are very astute,' said Tsun Pen, with a degree of bitterness in his voice. 'It was hubris that brought me low. I succumbed to greed, like so many others in my line of business. You see, the more the Othersiders came to rely upon me, the higher my price became, and they could not refuse me. Then it occurred to me that my counterpart might be in a similar situation, and that perhaps meeting him would be beneficial to the both of us. In fact, it was not so much an idea as a vision, of the two of us embracing as brothers. How terrible a thing it is, Captain, to have a gift such as mine—a gift that is unfailing, but which requires always a careful interpretation. On that occasion, my vision was not, as I had believed, a revelation that would lead to greater riches, but a dire warning!

'I began by sending coded messages to the other side. It was difficult, but even the Othersiders are not incorruptible, and eventually I managed to persuade one of their agents to carry them for me, and to bring back replies from my counterpart.

'The code that we used was a masterstroke. It was an old language that was no longer used on their side, because the course of history had not run smoothly for its land of origin. You know it, of course.'

'Myanmar,' I said. As I did, I saw that the guard was not looking directly at me, and I looked up at my bonds as surreptitiously as I could, to see if there was a way of loosening them. It appeared not, at least not yet.

'Once my counterpart had the cipher,' Tsun Pen continued, 'it was an easy matter to exchange ideas. We raised our prices, and gave each other ammunition to use in our dealings with the agents. Some of our ideas were positively seditious, however, and we ran a great risk. Eventually I asked my employers if it would be possible to visit the other side, to meet perhaps with my counterpart, but I was refused. Little did I know that they had suspected something was amiss for some time, and my request prompted them to investigate. They are clever, these people, more so than I had realised, and they soon discovered what the two Tsuns had been plotting.

'They came to me, full of reproaches, full of bravado and demands. But I am not a man to be refused, and certainly not one to be bullied. Words turned to threats. Threats turned to violence, and my men leapt to my defence. The agents attempted to escape, using some unseen signal to instruct their comrades in the city to detonate their bombs and open a portal. But of course, I knew where they were going. My visions had revealed to me all of their escape routes, and so it was a simple matter to intercept them. There was a firefight, and they came off badly.

Yet they opened their portal and passed through it.

'I knew that I was in a precarious position. If they escaped me and I had nothing to barter with, then they could return at any time, and I would be their enemy. And so I ordered them followed and recaptured before the portal could close. My best man, Hu, was fastest to react. He reached into the portal as the last of them passed through, and grabbed the agent—one of two women in their group—and dragged her bodily into our realm. As he did so, something astonishing happened. The woman was sundered by the journey, almost turning inside out as the very fabric of the universe rejected her presence. Poor Hu! His hand suffered the same fate. But the woman lived; it was a miracle, and one that I give thanks for every day.' He turned to face the corner behind me. 'Isn't that right, my precious muses? You are so very dear to me.' His words were answered by a guttural moan and the scratching of nails on a hard floor. I shuddered.

'So that... they... are people.' I remembered William James' warning about dabbling with the portals, but I could barely comprehend the terrible thing that Tsun Pen had wrought on these women. Though I was still afraid of those repugnant forms, my heart was full of pity for them. 'And what of the other? There are two.'

'Ah, yes. Two of my men passed fully through the portal to claim another prize, unaware of their fate should they return. One of them did not make it, for he was killed or captured by the Othersiders. The second did return, in a manner of speaking. He heaved his prisoner through the portal, and must have seen her change before he realised that he was even then undergoing the same process. Before he could comprehend his situation, the portal blinked out of existence. It closed, Captain, cutting what was left of my man in twain like a hot knife through butter. I think it was better for him that way.'

That last remark was the first thing the Artist had said to me that made any sense. There was a pained whimper behind me, as if the two creatures understood the story he had just related.

I winced, hoping to God that they did not understand, that they were not still rational and lucid human beings behind those grotesque, corpulent forms.

'Why did they not kill you for what you did?' I asked. Already my own anger at this madman was festering, lending me strength—I knew I would kill him given half the chance, and I could not fathom why the Othersiders had not done the same.

'I was too valuable to them. I still am. But they decided to punish me – you must have realised that much. I am not sure if they knew I would survive the experience, and I doubt that they cared overmuch, but they must have been grateful afterwards, for we have since resumed our business relationship. No, they exacted their revenge in a most unexpected way. I thought I knew of all of their technological marvels, but I was ill-prepared for this vengeance. It was beautiful really—quite biblical in a sense.

'They utilised the same devices that open their portals, and activated them on the Isle of Dogs. Rather than focus their attentions on a small point in order to create a gateway, they targeted the House of Zhengming in its entirety. At the same time, agents on this side opened a portal within my home. A small, weak one—for the conditions are not right to perform this miraculous process just anywhere—but enough to establish the link between worlds in a very tangible and violent way.

'I was in my studio, painting, when I heard the sound of distant explosions. The next thing I knew, the room was filled with a whining noise that grew to fever pitch. The whole building shook, and then my vision became blurred—yes, Captain, I could see back then. I realised that the very building was twisting, contorting before my eyes. It appeared as though the high-pitched cacophony was vibrating the two realities together as one. Then I was wracked by pain, the likes of which no man has ever experienced. My counterpart appeared as if from nowhere, standing directly before me, but partly conjoined to me. We were locked in an embrace, and I imagine I looked as terrified as he did. As the vibrations intensified, we drew closer, until we were one… until we were almost one. Our screams became one scream, and that is all I remember before Hu woke me. I was blind, of course, and hideous to behold, but my loyal servant never left my side.'

Tsun Pen turned from me, and unwrapped the silk scarf from around his head. I knew he was about to show me what the Othersiders had wrought, and I did not want to see, but he turned back to me all the same. I remember recoiling from his hideous face. Bulging sockets, filled with too many eyes, completed the arachnoid appearance of the 'man' before me.

'I frighten you? But of course, what was I thinking?' chuckled the Artist. 'Although what do you expect when four eyes are pushed into the physical space of two? I suppose I am lucky, for although my eyes do not work in the literal sense, I can see so much more than before.' Tsun Pen seemed to look upon me regardless, before—apparently satisfied—he tied the blindfold back around his hideous, sightless eyes. 'This is the power that the Othersiders wield,' he continued, 'and you would be wise to pray for a quick death at their hand, lest you meet a similar fate.

'That is my story, Captain. A cautionary tale, I'm sure you'll agree. Of course, the leader of the Othersiders was quite relieved when he discovered that I lived—though his anger had prompted such drastic measures, he still needed my abilities to complete his invasion of this universe. In fact, it turned out rather nicely for him—my powers are amplified, my knowledge of both worlds consummate, and my counterpart is no longer on their side of the veil; any risk posed to their world by such a powerful psychic has thus been nullified. There were even some benefits for me. My humble opium den, though unchanged from an outside perspective, has increased in size considerably. Some of the rooms, however, are quite inaccessible, due to the unstable effect of sharing space and time with another universe entirely, but that is a small price to pay for real estate, you understand. And so we have an uneasy alliance, the Othersiders and I. They dare not take my pets from me, for fear of further bloodshed, and truth be told I do not believe they really want them back, not in their present condition. But I want them, Captain. They inspire me to greater artistic endeavours. Without them, I would be… half the man.' He smiled, pleased with his jest.

'I understand,' I said. My words stuck in my throat—I felt as though I had swallowed a pint of sand. The Artist offered up more water, which I accepted. I could feel blood trickling down my arm as the bonds bit into my wrists. 'I must know the identity of the… dynamiters. The Othersiders who wreak havoc on London,' I said at last. 'Who is the leader that you spoke of? And how many of them live among us?'

'Oh, my dear boy,' said the Artist, with as much condescension as he could muster, 'you still trust to hope? You still believe, after all I have told you, that such information will be of any use to you whatever? You are single-minded, I'll grant you that.'

'You promised to answer my questions,' I said firmly. 'I must know.'

'Very well,' he replied. 'I will tell you, but the answer will offer you no comfort in your final hours. Their ultimate leader is a man named Lazarus—a government agent, quite senior, I believe. He serves King Albert directly, and is the most uncompromising man I have ever encountered. Next to myself, of course.' He chuckled. I did not ask about Albert—I was already coming to the conclusion that everything on the other side was the same and yet somehow different, and that to interrupt the Artist with irrelevant questions would only lead to more of his endless diatribe. He plainly liked the sound of his own voice a little too much.

'Lazarus,' I muttered. 'Who is he, really?'

'Oh, that is his name now, I believe; who he was is of little consequence to those on the other side. They say he died and came back; they say he will lead his cursed people to liberty, in a world that has not been assailed by the legions of hell. Your world. This rhetoric has made him a saviour in the eyes of his people, and a maniac in yours. You know him, of course. And there are others in his group with whom you have rubbed shoulders.

'Who?'

'Ah, you wish to know the identities of the infiltrators here in London, of course. Captain Hardwick, they are everywhere; dozens of them. You've probably met them and don't even know it. They infiltrate positions of power just as easily as they pose as municipal workers and vagrants. They do what they must, and they do it with ease, because they are us. They are exactly like us in appearance and character. Of course, some unforeseen circumstance may get in the way of their plans; an agent's counterpart may be dead already on our side, or perhaps never have been born due to some quirk in the strands of fate. Without a double, they are of limited use as spies—but on the whole, they walk among us unnoticed.'

'But there cannot be two identical people walking about London at the same time,' I interjected. 'Especially not well-known or important people. What do they do with their counterpart from our side?' I realised as I was speaking that I had become true believer of the multiverse theory as proposed by William James. It crossed my mind that, after all I had seen and heard in the last few days, I had gone mad, and was indulging in the same lunatic fantasy as James, Sir Arthur Furnival and even Sir Toby.

'Usually they are assassinated to pave the way for their doppelgänger. Sometimes they will be captured and tortured for information; anything to make the agent taking their place more believable in the role. Oftentimes even their closest friends could not tell that they have been replaced by an imposter.'

'And how long do they maintain these charades?' I asked, uncomfortable now I realised that even members of Apollo Lycea could have been compromised.

'As long as it takes, Captain Hardwick; weeks, months... even years. They have been crossing over for a long time, gathering intelligence. As their situation worsened, so they became more fixated on our world. Lazarus is a military man, and when he was put in charge of the operation, it stopped being a reconnaissance mission and became an invasion. Their field agents come through from the other side and pass messages to their fellows who have been living here all along. At the allotted hour they do what they need to do—steal some plans, assassinate some key target, whatever their mission is, and then plant the bombs that generate their escape route. They can keep their entryways open indefinitely, provided they can generate enough power, and they have to do so if they wish to stay for any length of time, otherwise the universe itself will push them back to where they came from. Still, it's complicated—they need one way in, and one way out. It's a feat that we on this side cannot replicate, but one that they perform with alarming regularity. But of course, even with all their resources, they do not yet have the means to stay here for ever—for that they'll need a rather large portal, open all the time, I suppose.'

'All the time? Why?' I asked.

'I do not pretend to know the science of it. All I know is that the portal by which they enter must remain open until the agent leaves, at great expense. If the entrance portal is closed early, then the strange device that the agents carry within their bodies will pull them back to the other side. Likewise if the agent is killed. I considered, for a time, operating on my pets, to inspect the devices within them for myself. After all, the accident must have rendered them inert, otherwise my darling muses would have been snatched from me by now. But I couldn't bring myself to harm them… further.'

'If the Othersiders mean to launch a full-scale invasion then they'll need this portal that you spoke of? This large portal… Can it be done?'

'Oh yes, and soon,' the Artist said. 'I hear Lazarus has found a brilliant young scientist who has all but completed his work on a new kind of doorway between worlds. They are imprisoning mediums every day, using hundreds of them to thin the veil, heedless of the inherent danger, and creating electrical machines to generate vast quantities of energy. This new portal will supposedly be free of the limitations of the others, allowing passage freely to and fro, and in great numbers. The people of the other side are lauding the great Lazarus as their saviour. They call his portal the "Lazarus Gate" in his honour, and once it is active… well, I suppose I don't have to explain to you what that will mean.' He smiled, but it was rueful.

'One more… question,' I said, through a fit of coughing. 'Where will they strike next?'

'Ah, that is clever, Captain, for it is really several questions in one, is it not? Do you mean to ask where they plan to enter our universe? Or where will they detonate their bombs? Or where will their agents attempt to complete some other nefarious assignment? A pity you do not have the time—nor the necessary funds—to view my paintings, for the answers you seek are there, if you had eyes to see. You'll be pleased to know that you've at least set the Othersiders back, just a little—it is clear that you have deciphered their coded instructions, which they adopted from my own system. I am sure they are working to overcome this irritation as we speak.'

The guard, Hu, cleared his throat—the first sound he had made since we had met—and Tsun Pen took this as some kind of signal.

'I am afraid the time for questions is over, Captain. Much as it pains me, it seems we have visitors, and it would be rude to keep them waiting. Your fate will soon become clear, but for now I will leave you my pets for company. They are really quite affectionate.'

My skin crawled at the suggestion, and the muculent sound of the two creatures drew nearer. As Hu opened the door and let in some light, I set eyes on them properly for the first time as they lurched towards their master and his manservant on lethargic, bloated limbs. I realised that their chains were no longer anchored, and that they now had freedom to roam the cell, a thought which filled me with disgust. They clambered bodily up the two men, groping and probing with flabby fingers, tongues lolling out of their mouths, acting for all the world like a pair of languid hounds. Hu looked at Tsun Pen imploringly, and the Artist shooed the creatures away, cooing with affection. I could not bear the thought of them touching me, and became terrified of being abandoned in the darkness. But that is what happened—the door closed, and I was alone with the monsters.

I do not know how much time elapsed, but evidently I had passed out at some point from the after-effects of the drugs in my system, and the horror of my situation. I felt more alert than I had earlier, and quickly oriented myself. The room was the same, and my position was the same. I heard the muffled movement in the corner once more, and I felt sick at the sound. There were voices outside now, too, beyond the door, and I strained to hear what was being said. I recognised the sound of Tsun Pen's voice, but he was agitated, though I could not make out the words. Presently the door was opened, and three people stepped inside.

The light stung my eyes, but I took in as many details as I could of my captors before the door was closed and we were all plunged into darkness. Tsun Pen and Hu were present again, but the third inquisitor was a surprise indeed. It was a woman, probably in her late twenties. Her face was pale and pretty, but emotionless. Her hair was pinned back tightly, and her garb was entirely black. Her clothes were strangely out of style, close-fitting and trimmed with lace. Her skirts stopped scandalously at the knee, revealing dark stockings and high boots. Even in the dark that followed, her eyes seemed almost to gleam, so that they were all I could see for a time. There was something strangely familiar about her, though I felt sure she was no ordinary Englishwoman; I knew at once that she was one of Them.

'I know you,' I said, without thinking.

'We have not actually met, Captain Hardwick,' she said, icily.

'Though I had hoped when I saw you on Commercial Road that you would be out of our way for good. And yet here we are.'

Commercial Road—the woman in the window! It all became clear, and yet I still felt an uncanny connection to this woman. There was something else... something oddly familiar about her bearing, but I could not place it.

'Captain,' said Tsun Pen, his unctuous tones fair slithering in my ears, 'this good woman is here to question you.'

'I will answer no questions. I consider myself a prisoner of war, and will not betray my country... no matter the price.'

'Brave words, Captain,' said Tsun Pen, 'but you will not find resistance so easy. We have our ways.'

I laughed in his face. I think he was shocked. The woman displayed no emotion of any kind.

'You know, I was once put to torture,' she said, running the back of her gloved hand across my cheek. 'The experience was the making of me. I fear, however, it will be the breaking of you.'

'This isn't my first time,' I growled, defiantly.

'Oh, of course... Burma, wasn't it? What a delicious coincidence; that you should break Lazarus' code as a result of your suffering. I suppose you felt that it was all worth it? That it had all been for some greater purpose? But sadly no—you simply traded one hell for another, and this time there will be no salvation.'

I narrowed my eyes and prepared myself. 'I have been interrogated by worse than you,' I said. 'Do your worst.'

It began as it always begins. Quiet, persuasive. The questions seeming innocuous at first, then becoming more pointed. The woman wanted to know the names of influential men in Rangoon and Hong Kong, and, of course, in London—in Apollo Lycea specifically. She wanted to know how many people had read my notes on the Othersiders' secret codes, and who my chief accomplices were. Strangely, she interspersed these questions with further queries about my own life, military service and even childhood. This line of irrelevant questioning was doubtless designed to throw me, to break my concentration; but it did not work.

Then it started in earnest. The clubbing blows from Hu's hook hand, the whip, the burns, the cutting. More drugs. I was spun round and round, lights shining in my eyes. Hu used a little pen knife in the shape of a silver fish with an inch-long blade—such an understated weapon, the kind of thing that a child might have, and yet it was razor sharp and when it was slid beneath the flesh, or under a thumbnail, it had the required effect.

Through it all, I stayed true, I answered only thus: 'Hardwick, John. Captain, Sixteenth Lancers.' I said it as the blood ran. I screamed it as the poker seared my flesh. And, by God, I sobbed it when they took my eye. It was Hu, the guard-turned-torturer, who did the deed. On a nod from the Artist he blinded my left eye with the knife and tossed the orb to his master. I screamed obscenities until I became insensible, and could feel nothing, no pain, but for the hot blood running down my face. When the pain became at least tolerable, and I came to terms with what they had done, I knew then that I had been wrong. The bastards in Burma were not as evil as those who confronted me now. It was this—this rage that had always burned within me, deep down—that kept me from turning. I clung to some small sense of duty, not out of bravery, but out of hate.

'A city of corruption, a world of reprobates,' the woman wailed, 'and I have to find the last honest man in London. For the love of God, make him talk!'

Those words struck a chord with me, for had Ambrose not said the same when first we had met? In fact, hadn't Sir Toby himself lauded my honesty before sending me off to the Artist's lair? Perhaps my suspicions earlier in the investigation had not been due to misplaced paranoia after all. The thought that I could have been betrayed steeled me for what was to come.

When the loss of an eye did not break me, they brought out

the needles again, and dosed me with opium, expertly bringing me from the depths of indulgent agony to the heights of ecstasy, and then back to fleeting moments of lucidity. The white-eyed old man from the den below was there, I'm sure, a hideous smile etched onto his gummy mouth as he administered the milky fluid to my veins. In the nightmare that followed, I do not know what I said. I think I must have remained defiant, at least to a point, though I will never be sure. I remember seeing more clearly under the effects of the drug, even with one eye. The Artist was a spider—a gigantic arachnid that almost filled the room. The same venom that dripped from its fangs seemed also to drip from the puncture marks in my arm. Hu was an ugly hobgoblin, a squat, brutish figure grunting obeisance at the spider's every chattered command. The two malformed creatures in the corner were hideous no more. I saw them whole again, huddled together in the corner, half-naked and frightened. In the opium fug, I suppose, I was surprised to see a sort of halo around them—a warm golden light about their heads that marked them as innocents. At one point I remember the women crying and pawing at Hu, begging him to stop the torture. Perhaps I imagined it, for I am sure that these agents of the other universe owed me no kindness. The unnamed woman, strangely, wore that self-same corona of light, though she looked anything but innocent.

I think eventually the pain began to sober me, and I started to understand words, and commit them to memory. The Artist and the woman were engaged in conversation, believing me to be delirious still.

Finally, she glowered at me, and held up a hand as if to dismiss the Artist, a motion that appeared to rankle him more than anything I could ever have done.

'Leave us alone,' she said. 'I would have words with this wretch before he dies.'

'My understanding was—' Tsun Pen began.

'I care not,' the woman snapped. 'All of you, get out! Now.'

Tsun Pen ushered his people from the room. Other than the pets huddled in the corner, I was alone with her. She came close to me, peeled off a glove, and placed her hand on my face. Her fingers were cold as ice, and hard. She turned my head to the light, this way and that, and when she pulled her hand away it was blood-slick.

'You know, it's uncanny. I have seen doubles many times, of course—our work here depends upon it. But when it is someone so... close to home. Well, that is a different matter altogether.'

I grunted something, I think, but had not the strength to speak.

'We need to ascertain whether our plans are threatened, John. We need you to tell us all that you know. But have no doubt, that is not the sole reason for your suffering. No... that is all my doing, I'm afraid. Because I hate you, John. I hate you with every fibre of my being, and I want you to taste just an ounce of the pain that I have felt, before you die. Can you understand that?'

'I...' The words struggled to escape my lips, but with a great effort they came. 'I can... now. I'll... kill you.'

She laughed. Her laughter was musical, beautiful, the antithesis of Tsun Pen's sneer; but there was nothing behind it. No joy, no mirth, nor even sarcasm. Just coldness, like the seductive sound made by inhuman creatures in fairy stories, shortly before their beguiling form is stripped away to reveal the monster beneath.

'Until you have lived to see the death of your own world, of all that you ever loved or held dear, I'm not sure you can understand.'

'It's... not our fault...' I said.

'Perhaps. We know, of course, that the true blame lies with the accursed spiritualists. From the moment those American table-rappers began to contact the dead, the world was damned. When all this is over, every one of them, on our side and yours, will be put to the torch. A fitting tribute, the burning of witches at the stake as in days of old. Then we'll be free... But some ghosts will always haunt us, John. You are one of them. Which is why I need you to die. So I can be free too.'

I had no idea what she was talking about. The fug was truly upon me, and she sounded just as mad as everyone else caught up in this sorry affair; we were all mad, I was certain of it then. And yet, I sought understanding. I needed a reason.

'What have I... ever done to you?' I croaked.

'Beyond opposing us, you mean? Oh, John, you really can't see it, can you? I suppose the loss of an eye hasn't helped in that regard. Look at me!' She jerked my head up close to hers again, and this time bathed her own face in the light. A face like a porcelain doll, unblemished, pale, eyes glassy and sparkling. The scent of strong perfume and strange chemicals assailed my nostrils, mingling with the copper tang of my own blood. I saw something in her hateful features, something familiar again, and I searched my memory for what it could mean.

'I... do not know you,' I said.

'You did. But in this world, I died long ago. I died in my father's arms, a little girl brought low by exposure. And that tragic event has made my role on this side of the veil somewhat more... specialised.'

She pulled her hand away once more, but this time my head did not drop. This time I fixed her with my one good eye, and studied her face. My breathing grew more ragged, my heart beat faster.

'No...'

'Ah, now you have it. When your double was killed in action, he died a hero. But it tore the heart from me. It took the last of my humanity from me. My brother was the only thing that kept me on the side of the angels; he was my only friend. And when I look into your eyes and see him... no. That will not do at all. You are nothing to him, a pale imitation of a great man. I had hoped to find something more here, but you... you disgust me.' She turned away. Tears began to sting my cheek.

'You... are not... Lillian.'

'Those of us who have well-placed doubles in your world kill them, you know. A rite of passage, almost. My brother was meant to kill you if you ever returned to British soil. You were never meant to be released from Burma... and he was never meant to die in this accursed land. All we can do now is mourn the loss of those who have died fighting for our survival. And honour their sacrifice by taking this universe for our own. Know this, John,' she said, no longer looking at me. 'Lazarus is coming, at the head of a fleet so mighty that England will fall in a single night. And then the whole world will follow suit. There is nothing the Order of Apollo can do about it. There is nothing you can do about it... brother.'

'You are not Lillian,' was all I could say. 'You are not Lillian!' I mustered a shout, and did so again, though she ignored me.

Her cruel work complete, Agent Lillian Hardwick stepped away from me and banged on the door, at which the Artist re-entered, with a face like thunder.

'He is of no further use to us,' Lillian said. 'I want him dead, and I want this mess tidied up.'

'Why is this any of my concern?' Tsun Pen replied angrily. 'His people will be coming for him, and I am implicated. This mess is yours.'

'You know the price, Tsun Pen. You'll find a way to save yourself, as you always do. But he dies tonight. Make it look like an accident, and trust to your patrons to save you from the noose. Do I make myself clear?'

'Pefectly.' Tsun Pen's voice was acidic. Lillian left the room, and Hu went with her, leaving the door ajar, so that a pale light crept in from outside. The Artist faced me, again appearing to stare straight at me despite his lack of sight.

'So, the task of killing you falls to Tsun Pen,' he said, softly. 'A pity. You know, John, that your efforts have been for nought. Your nightmares are set to be realised. Soon, the Othersiders will flood through the Lazarus Gate—a fleet of destruction carrying armies untold will take this world for their own. London will fall, the Empire will fall, and the whole world shall follow. You will be spared this hell on earth, but countless millions of others will be slaughtered like cattle to make way for the refugees from beyond the veil. And I—I shall endure. It is foreseen.'

He held up a hand, and through my addled stupor I saw that he had my eye, grasped betwixt forefinger and thumb. 'I told you, Captain, that I would answer further questions only when you had the means to pay me. I think this token is more than enough for one more revelation, especially for the condemned man.'

Tsun Pen moved towards me, so close that I could smell his cologne. I was too exhausted even to recoil. Such was his height, that even though I was suspended a foot off the ground, he leaned in closer. 'There is one more secret, Captain Hardwick. A secret meant just for you. This is why you were chosen, and this is why you will die.'

And he whispered into my ear such secrets, that my heart near broke.

NINE

Slowly but surely I began to come round from the exertions of my torture. My body was almost broken, yet I had somehow managed to remain lucid. There was a tattered cloth tied around my head, covering my empty eye socket, though I do not remember how it got there. The opium fug had already begun to wear off, perhaps due to my tolerance to the hated drug, or perhaps to the indeterminate length of time I had spent there; in its place, the deep, aching pain of my lost eye and the thousand keen cuts on my body conspired to bring to me to my senses.

The Artist was gone, and there was not even a crack of light from beneath the door, if I was indeed in the same room at all. I was alone in a Stygian blackness, hanging limply in a dark void, with the pain from my bound wrists the only indicator that I was not already dead, and drifting in some yawning chasm of Purgatory. I listened hard, and heard the muffled grunts of the pitiable female 'agents' near to me—were it not so horrifying it would have been a relief, for at least I knew then that I was very much alive, and most probably still within the House of Zhengming. I felt one of them brush against my legs, causing me to swing slightly, but I felt no revulsion this time. My own state was so poor, and my mind so overpowered by trauma, that I had no room for further terrors. Instead, I took some small comfort that I was not alone in my suffering.

Then I felt a podgy hand paw at my leg. I tried to ignore it, but it seemed to persist, until it had a hold of my trouser linen. I felt the ropes strain at my wrists—the creature was using me to pull itself upright, and I could barely take the strain. I hissed at it to leave me alone, not wanting to raise my voice for fear of alerting my captors, but it was no use. My one eye adjusted to the gloom, and I saw the dark shapes around my feet. One of the slothful creatures seemed to lie down to support my weight, so that I might rest a second, and it gave me such relief not to have the rope cutting at my flesh even for a moment. Then the second creature began to climb once more, and now I did start to feel the fear and loathing creeping back into my heart, for that noisome remnant of a woman climbed higher and higher, its clammy, misshapen hands gaining purchase on my shirt breast, then my collar. Somehow, laboriously, and with an effort that made it grunt and wheeze, it pulled itself upright so that it was almost facing me, and I felt its hand scrabbling towards my own. I squeezed my eyelids tight, hoping that the nightmare would end, but it did not. Not immediately.

When the proximity of the creature had become truly unbearable, and I thought I would go mad, I felt something in my hand. The creature had pressed something cool and smooth into my right hand, and I needed no time at all to recognise it simply by its shape. It was Hu's pocket knife, the one that had blinded me. The creatures were helping me!

Sure enough, even as I exclaimed my relief, and as the creature who had brought me the knife collapsed to the floor in an exhausted heap, the other one strained to bear my weight. I found reserves of energy somewhere deep inside myself, and set about the bonds with the razor-sharp knife. Two or more times I almost fumbled and dropped the blade, but I clung to it and steadied myself before continuing, for I knew that the creatures would be too weak to repeat their magnificent feat of bravery were I to fail.

I do not know how long I worked, but eventually the rope

gave, and I tumbled to the floor, half-falling on one of the pitiful things. At first I could not get to my feet, so numb were my legs, but inexorably the desire for freedom overwhelmed the frailty of my body, and I stood at last. I cut away the last of the ropes and threw aside the bonds, before beginning a thorough search of the room in near pitch-dark.

With the help of the two creatures, I found a box of matches and the stub of a candle, which I risked to light so that I might better find a means of escape. By weak candlelight I saw that the only furniture in the room was a small table, on which sat a pitcher of water. Again, I took a risk and drank the water down, because I was dehydrated and still heady from the opium. There were only two ways out of the room: the door and a small window, which was covered by a blind. The door was locked, and there was no key in the keyhole, so escape by that route seemed impossible. I considered trying to pick the lock with the penknife, but I was no expert in such matters and feared alerting any guards that might be posted nearby. The window it was, then.

I carefully drew back the blind, making sure the candle was away from the window, and peered out into the darkness through the filthy glass. I guessed it was the early hours of the morning, but could not be sure. There was a new moon, and so little light to see by, but I could make out a tiny yard below. I was in an attic room, it seemed, and I would have to climb along the roof to see if there was a way of getting to the ground. There was a lot to do, but it was far less daunting a prospect than staying in that room and awaiting my executioner. With that thought spurring me on, I opened the sash window as quietly as possible, and looked out onto the roof. It was not raining, although the slates were still damp. I was considering the best course of action when I heard a sound behind me that chilled me.

'P…p…please,' came the voice. I froze, the hairs on the back of my neck standing on end. I turned to see the two creatures staring up at me with pleading eyes. One of them stretched out a clammy hand and tugged piteously at my trouser leg.

'P…p…please,' it said again, in a croaking voice that was far from human. 'K…k…kill us!'

I could have cried at their plight in that instant. The other creature let out a low keening sound, in the way that dogs whine when they are despairing. I held my head in my hands. What was I to do? Was there any hope whatsoever for these creatures? And I remembered that they were still people, beneath all of their deformities. How ignominious their lives, to be treated as pets by the very man who made them so. What dignity would they ever be afforded? Anger filled me. I swore to myself I would kill Tsun Pen for all of his ills, if only I could survive this night.

'Kill… us,' they said. Their pleas were now in unison, and I knew in my heart I could not leave them there in that state. Taking each in turn, I cradled their lolling heads, slowly choking the breath from them. I had not the strength to finish the task in this manner, and once they were asleep and peaceful, breathing with difficulty, I opened their throats with my knife. Even in their last moments they did not struggle, for it was what they wanted. The now-familiar high-pitched whistling sound began to drone in my ears almost immediately. Now they were dead, they would be returned home, in one form or another. But the unexpected noise lent urgency to my actions. I turned again to the window, with tears from my good eye trickling down my cheek.

The scramble across the rooftop was precarious, but somehow I made it to the edge, where I used a small pediment to reach a drainpipe, and climbed down onto a flat roof that jutted from the back of the House of Zhengming. The yard was only eight feet below me, though I had to be careful to avoid being seen. In the yard, next to a small brick outhouse, a wiry man chugged on a cigarette. I instantly took him for one of Tsun Pen's guards, perhaps taking a break after a night of unlawful work. In any case, I would have to get past him if I were to escape, because there was no other way out of the grounds of the Artist's shady establishment.

I dropped almost noiselessly from the low roof, and crept towards the outhouse. As I went, I saw a log store nearby. Praising my good fortune, I slipped the penknife into my trouser pocket and instead picked up a stout log, which I brandished, ready to dash the man's brains in.

I was within striking distance when the alarm went up.

'There he is! Stop him, you idiot!'

It was Tsun Pen's voice. The man flinched into life, and looked about himself, uncertain whether his master was shouting at him or someone else. When he clapped eyes on me, he had scant moments to react, and he was not fast enough. I bashed him over the head with the wood so hard that the impact jarred it from my hands, then I raced forwards to the gate and rattled open the latch. I turned back for a second to see a flurry of movement behind every window, and Tsun Pen staring down at me from the window of the attic room. He leaned forward over the sash, his long black hair scraping the roof tiles, his face contorted into an impotent snarl. He needed no eyes to see me, and I knew that the loss of his beloved pets would stoke the fires of hatred within him. I opened the gate and, with that, I was away.

The cold night air washed over my face in a euphoric wave, giving strength to my leaden legs, and helping me focus on my escape. The House of Zhengming was behind me in a trice. The shouts of men and baying of hounds faded, until all I could hear was the rush of blood in my ears, and my heart pounding in my chest like an echo of my heavy footfalls on the pavement. I slowed only momentarily to catch my breath, and when I did I realised that the danger had not passed, for already there was another clamour rising up from somewhere behind me, and I could hear the barked cries of a party of thugs taking to the streets after me. How many men the Artist could rouse to action at such short notice I did not know, and did not wish to find out.

I ran. I don't know for how long, or how my legs managed to carry me, but I ran. Using the moon and stars as a guide as I had learned aboard ship, I headed as directly west as I could, hoping to reach a dockyard that might still perhaps be open for business. My only chance was to find some civilised people to aid me, or at least hide me—there was no chance of finding a policeman in this part of London, and if I did, the Artist's men would have little regard for their authority, or their lives. So I drove myself ever onwards, keeping to the shadows, using narrow alleyways where I could, darting behind shacks and outhouses when I thought my pursuers were close. But they gained on me with every step; I was tiring fast.

I turned down a dark alley, no more than three feet wide, and raced along it only to find my way blocked by a wiry hoodlum in a flat cap. They must have had men searching for me in every direction, for they could not have got ahead of me except by chance. I perhaps surprised him as much as he had me, because it was all he could do to grapple with me as I barrelled into him from the pitch-dark tunnel. He was strong—or else I was weak—and he wrenched my head back and swore at me, and pressed me up against the wall. Then I realised that I was still clutching the little fish-shaped penknife, and I thrust it up into the wretch's armpit, burying an inch-and-a-half of steel into his flesh. He screamed as if the devil himself had seized hold of him, and I rolled across his prone figure and out into fresh air once more, still holding the knife in a blood-slicked hand.

I was disorientated for a moment, but I knew the villain's cries would alert the Artist's men, and so I powered onwards. I scrambled over a high wooden fence, dropping unceremoniously into a dirty yard on the other side, and scrabbled backwards quickly as a mastiff's jaws snapped at my face. Its muscular neck bulged as its collar cut into its rolled flesh, and the rope that secured it to the wall of the house strained and creaked. I edged around the perimeter fence, keeping an eye on the foaming jaws that threatened me, and let myself out of a gate on the other side. Could I enter one of those houses? Would anyone there offer me sanctuary? I could not have risked it, for the Artist ruled the Isle of Dogs with an iron fist, and I was too close to the centre of his little empire.

I continued my flight over garden walls where possible, through an old brickyard, and eventually to a pump-house near the edge of the river. The sounds of howling dogs and the bloodthirsty calls of the mob subsided momentarily, and were replaced by the lapping of water, the gentle tolling of buoy-bells and the far-off thrumming of foghorns. My heart lurched as I realised that a party of men was drawing near—there would be no respite, it seemed. I flung myself into a foul-smelling forest of huge cast-iron and lead pipes, crouching in the mud to avoid detection as the men hurried past, carrying lanterns and makeshift weapons. One of them stayed behind, waving the others on—he had obviously had enough hunting for the time being. I cursed my misfortune as he set his lantern down on the ground just six feet from my hiding place. He rested against a bollard, and lit a cigarette.

I'd had enough. Something inside me changed in that instant, and I knew that I was tired of running, tired of hiding—tired of everything. Even before I was fully aware of what I was doing, I was standing up and stepping out of the shadows, walking up to the man, who had his back to me. I heard my own voice say aloud, 'Hey there! You. Are you looking for me?' My tone was steady, confident, and threatening. The man turned slowly, his eyes widening and his cigarette hanging limp from his bottom lip. We regarded each other for a moment, and then he came at me with a lump of timber that I had not noticed resting by his side.

I avoided the first swing, and somehow parried a second with the palms of my hands. The circumstances favoured my adversary, but something primal urged me on, and I gave in to the rage that had festered since Burma, but had not been given leave to surface.

I drew the man in close, and spun past another swing of his club, lashing out with the tiny knife as I did so and catching him across the side of the face. He stumbled forwards and cursed, and I kicked hard at his arm, making him drop the lump of wood, before booting him backwards away from his weapon.

He composed himself quickly, and came at me again, swinging his arms in great arcing strikes. I was tired and clumsy, and in my efforts to guard against his attack I dropped the knife, and it was my turn to curse as a big left hand connected with my temple. I staggered, seeing stars, and then the brute grabbed me by the collar and thrust me against the pump-house wall, his face like thunder. I went limp in the thug's arms, acting as though I were knocked senseless. He afforded himself a wry smile, believing himself victorious. In an instant the smile was gone, for my ruse had worked as well for me as it had for Larry. I drove my forehead into the man's face with all the force I could muster, and I felt his nose crunch beneath the impact. He stepped backwards, waving his arms before him like a blind man who had lost his stick. Now I advanced. I jabbed with my left hand at his Adam's apple to silence him, drove the heel of my right hand into his broken nose, then delivered a sharp punch to his kidneys, before skipping back and delivering a swift toe-kick to his groin. As he staggered forwards, I spun around and punched him in the back of his head, with the last of my strength, dropping to my knees with the exertion, but sending him face-first into the mud, insensible.

Doubtless that last blow had not been required, but my blood was up, and I wanted revenge. In that moment, I felt powerful; as though I could walk back into the House of Zhengming and take on the Artist myself. But then I baulked at the thought of confronting… him. That sickening, grotesque image flashed through my mind—Tsun Pen, with his hideous, bulging eyes and flailing, vestigial arms—and I instinctively touched the filthy rag that covered my empty eye socket. No, I could not face him yet. But his time would come.

With no time to lose, I took my assailant's lantern and scrabbled around for the knife, then headed for the docks. Following a perimeter fence of one of the dockyards to the edge of the water, I traversed a set of stone steps to a jetty, where I stopped for a moment to get my bearings. It seemed that the

West India Docks were much further along the riverbank, and I was unsure if I would make it. However, the compound outside which I now found myself seemed to have some business going on within, judging by the lights coming from several small huts on the water's edge just five hundred yards away. I looked across the river at the flickering gaslights of Rotherhithe, that glittered like stars.

I stayed low, moving across the jetties wherever I could, skirting around the edge of the docks. Finally, I reached the steps up to the small dockyard. There were two river ferries moored beneath me, and a few huts ahead of me. I was in a far-flung corner of a larger dock, with rusting steam-ferries and upturned rowing boats collected in a maritime graveyard. In one of the huts, however, a light burned at the window, and smoke poured from a stovepipe in the tin roof, and so I made for it, keeping close to the ruined boats in case anyone should look across the dockyard in their search for me.

I glanced in at the window of the hut to see an old, bearded man stretched out in a battered armchair by a little stove fire. A small terrier lay by his side, and it looked up as soon as I peered in, and let out a high bark. I had no choice then but to announce myself, and so I rapped on the door.

The waterman—for that is what he was—was most alarmed when he saw the state that I was in, and most suspicious when I refused to let him fetch help. I related to him such parts of the story as I deemed pertinent, without giving away who it was that pursued me—for all I knew, this man could be in the pay of the Artist too. I warmed myself by his fire, and accepted a cup of strong tea and a chunk of rather dry bread from him gratefully, before impressing upon him the importance of my reaching the City unmolested.

'I know it is hard to believe right now,' I said, 'but I am an officer in Her Majesty's Army, and I implore you to take me on your ferry, as close to Whitehall as possible. I will see that you are reimbursed for your efforts.'

The waterman, who said his name was Grimes, checked his watch. 'It's damnable early, sir, and I'm only minding the place, like. I'm not really supposed to leave me post.' He stroked his scruffy, greying beard thoughtfully before continuing. 'Look, sir, it's clear you're in a bad way, and I'll help you. I can't be away for long, in case anyone checks up, like, or some o' them riff-raff come in and make free with me stores. I'll take you as far as the Embankment, and see that you find a cabbie or a policeman, whichever comes along first. Will that suit?'

That 'suited' just fine; I could have hugged the man. We made our way to his little ferry-boat, his terrier following close at our heels. He begrudgingly agreed to stay low with me so as not to be seen, and in this manner we reached the boat without being detected, as far as I could tell. Within minutes we were away, the small launch rocking to and fro on the dark waters of the river. It was cloudy overhead, and there was little by way of starlight above us, but the crusty old waterman needed no navigation but the man-made lights along the north bank. A light breeze came across the Thames, and I closed my eyes and breathed in the air of freedom. I felt cold and weak, but it did not matter a jot, because before the night was through I would be at Whitehall amongst officers and gentlemen.

We stopped at the Embankment by one of the old watermen's causeways. Grimes explained that 'Tide's lowest in the early mornin', so we'll have to get off 'ere rather than the stair'. I looked about and saw the stairs that he was talking about, too high up to be of use in the small hours of the morning. So I clambered out of the boat onto the causeway, getting my feet wet in the process, and walking slowly, shivering as I went to the embankment jetty. Grimes moored the ferry and went ahead of me to find a constable. True to his word, he came back to meet me with help in tow. I reached the top of the slope with a relieved smile on my lips, already explaining who I was and where I needed to go, when the man spoke, and I realised it was not a policeman at all, but a more familiar figure entirely.

'John... bloody hell, what's happened to you?'

I couldn't believe it. For a moment I was giddy, and I grabbed hold of my rescuer, laughing like an idiot.

'Ambrose! Dear Ambrose! How did you find me? When did you come back?'

Ambrose did not reply. Instead he tugged at my wrists until, he had extricated himself from me, and stepped away, causing me to gawp at him in confusion.

'I'm sorry, John. I never expected this. I had no idea that they'd... I'm sorry.'

'Ambrose? What are you talking about?' My smile faded, to be replaced by the doubts that had crept into my thoughts during the interrogation; doubts about the loyalty of those closest to me.

'Ambrose,' I said again, more out of hope than good sense, 'stop playing silly beggars. We have to get out of here.'

'I'm sorry,' he said again, 'but you're supposed to be dead.'

He was one of them. I looked at Grimes, who backed away, disengaging himself from the whole business, his dog whimpering. I fumbled for the knife in my pocket and eyed my former friend warily. I was not sure I could manage another fight, but I had come too far to give up. He took a step towards me, and I backed down the causeway. I pulled out the blade.

'Get back, or I swear I'll kill you,' I warned.

There was a scuff of boots on stone somewhere behind Ambrose. Then a voice rang out of the darkness—a gruff, authoritarian voice that I knew at once, and yet didn't want to acknowledge as real.

'Getting quite used to killing, aren't you, John? But this time, I'm afraid the "show is over", as they say in the theatre.'

An older man was walking down the causeway, dressed all in black. He was accompanied by the woman who I could still not bear to think of as Lillian Hardwick.

'You've been most troublesome, John. Perhaps I misjudged you,' she said. 'Be sure that I won't make that mistake again.'

I backed away further along the declivity, until I felt the cold water lapping around my ankles. The brick walls of the Embankment hemmed me in on either side. I glanced back at the river to see Grimes already a hundred yards away, and making his getaway as quickly as he could. I looked at the two new arrivals with despair—I could not believe the twist of circumstance. Lazarus, the man himself, drew a pistol and aimed it at me.

'Captain John Hardwick,' said the Othersider through a triumphant sneer. 'It seems as though you have been blessed with the nine lives of a cat.' The man's silver-grey hair was all I could make out of him, shrouded in darkness as he was. And yet that voice—it cut me with every uttered syllable.

'This… this isn't possible,' I heard myself say the words, rather stupidly.

'Think of it this way: you have been on a journey which is given to so few men to make. But I am afraid your particular voyage of discovery ends here.'

I looked first at Lazarus, and then at Lillian. 'Why?' I asked, though it was not the question I wanted to ask. My mouth became dry, and my voice seemed to my own ears little more than a hoarse whisper.

'You are the fly in the ointment, and I should have dealt with you sooner,' said Lazarus. 'My judgement was perhaps… clouded. It was a mistake to let you live this long, and I never make the same mistake twice.' He took one further step forward, bringing his face from the shadows into the light, and there was no longer any denying it. I saw the man, and knew him; the Artist had whispered to me the truth.

'A pity,' added Lillian. 'In another life, this could have been a sweet reunion. Goodbye, John.'

I was struck dumb. My mouth worked soundlessly, the words stuck in my throat. Ambrose looked sick, shamefaced even, and turned away from me, and Lazarus raised the pistol. Lillian smiled. There was a flash of light, and time itself seemed to slow down. The last thing I saw before I was sucked into the inky water of the Thames was Lazarus' face—my father's face—devoid of compassion, and my long-dead sister beside him, slipping away into the night.

The sins of the father shall be visited upon the son. There is no escape from the house of the dead.

PART 2

He clasps the crag with crooked hands;
Close to the sun in lonely lands,
Ringed with the azure world, he stands.

The wrinkled sea beneath him crawls;
He watches from his mountain walls,
And like a thunderbolt he falls.

ALFRED, LORD TENNYSON

TEN

Lily stood at the door to the garden, amidst the ivy, listening intently, though to what I know not. She was eight years old, and the happiest child I had ever known, and for her to be so still was peculiar.

'What are you doing?' I asked.

'Listen, John. Don't you hear it?'

I inclined my head and listened, but all I could hear was the song of a lark, and a faint breeze whistling through the bushes.

'This is when it always comes,' she said. 'The same time, every day.'

Lily had always been a fanciful girl, but clever beyond her years. I thought this must be one of her games. After all, the old walled garden was her favourite place to play—she believed that there was something magical behind that blue-painted door, as if it led to another world, full of her imaginary friends, of fairy folk and mythical creatures. Lily was nearly two years my junior, but had an infectious enthusiasm and boundless imagination.

'There's nothing, Lily,' I said. 'Come back inside; Mother is calling.'

And then it came—a peal of thunder, so close that I almost jumped out of my skin.

'I told you!' Lillian squealed, delighted. 'You must have heard it that time. He's here, he's here!'

She jumped for joy and then reached for the door handle. I became very afraid, as if there was something terrible on the other side of the wall, and I seemed to know what it was but could not quite place it. I reached out for my sister, but I might as well have clutched at air, for my limbs were leaden and I could not move close enough to stop her—it was as though she was a sprite of yore, skipping out of my reach. In an instant she was beyond my sight, and I stared at an inexplicable pitch darkness that lay beyond the door.

The sun was at my back. My mother's voice faded on a balmy summer breeze. The bees buzzed quietly in the honeysuckle. And yet, beyond the door was a scene of cold night, with rumbling thunder and intermittent cracks of lightning that pierced the gloom. I was afraid, and had my sister not already entered the fearful twilight realm ahead of me, I would have returned to the bosom of my family in the pretty white house behind me. Lily had always been bolder than me. Not to be outdone, I urged my legs onwards, and stepped over the threshold.

I stood on the wooden deck of an immense, four-masted ship. Water lashed over the deck as the vessel was tossed about on gigantic waves, causing sailors in sou'westers to scurry about like worker ants, desperately battening down hatches and tying off wayward rigging. Lightning flickered all around and rain hammered the beleaguered crew, whose shouts were lost on the wind.

I tried to steady myself, but I was only a boy of ten, and found the footing on the sea-slicked deck treacherous. I fell down more than once, grazing my knees, and shivered as I realised that my clothes were wet through. I looked around desperately for Lillian, but she was nowhere to be seen. I was dreadfully confused – I knew not how I had come to be on this ship, nor why. Perhaps I had stowed away, in a bid to escape my overbearing father. Or perhaps I was sailing abroad to find him. Yes, that was it!

We were heading to India to find Brigadier Hardwick, only the going was heavy. But this ship, the *Helen B. Jackson*, out of the United States, was as doughty as the crew who served upon her. I forgot about my sister, as if she had never even existed.

I tried in vain to speak to the sailors around me, but they ignored me and went about their business. And then, amidst the peals of thunder, I heard another sound, a bestial roar that chilled my blood. And the sailors turned to face this new threat, and made all haste to the leeward side of the ship, to the great howitzers that lined the deck. And as the ship heeled and the lee side rose, the source of all my night terrors since the day of my birth hove into view. It was the dragon, and it arced through the air towards us, lighting the sky with orange fire. The rain that drove into the beast condensed to steam, creating clouds of vapour that coalesced around its body, before dissipating in an instant at the beat of those gigantic, leathery wings.

The dragon roared again, and I froze in terror. This thing was all evil personified, and its bellow seemed to shake me from within just as surely as it deafened me without.

The roar of the beast and the rumble of thunder were now a hellish concerto, punctuated by the thumping percussion of the howitzers. The sky was set afire by bursts of shrapnel, and the dragon wheeled and dived, as if swimming through a sea of flame.

It shrugged off the worst the seamen could throw at it, and swooped betwixt our foremost masts, spewing a gout of flame towards the fo'castle, incinerating a dozen men and turning the foremast to kindling. I felt the heat on my face, heard the screams of the men caught in the conflagration, and turned to flee the monster. Yet all I did was run into someone – a woman, dressed all in black. I looked up at her, bewildered, and recognised my sister, all grown up. Good Christ! How had I forgotten about her? She was the reason I had come to this place, and I had almost failed her. Yet she was not really Lillian at all – the more I beheld the woman, the more I sensed something… different about her. She took my hand, and spoke to me in a tone that was soothing, yet somehow dispassionate.

'Come with me, John. Do not be afraid.'

She led me to the starboard edge of the ship. A wave pelted the bulwarks nearest us, sending a man crashing to the deck, yet it seemed to subside before us, and we walked unhindered to the deck rails as the water soused our feet. The dragon was turning back towards the ship for another pass. I was still afraid, but no longer petrified by my fear; not while Lillian held my hand. As the monster drew near, something changed in my sister. Before I knew what was happening, she had lifted me up onto the gunwale, and as the dragon drew steadily nearer, I turned to her in a panic.

'Do not worry, brother!' she shouted, her voice almost lost against the thunder and the monstrous roars from the raging skies. 'This is your destiny. You must face your fears!'

'I can't!' I cried. 'I'm frightened.'

'There is nothing to fear, John,' she shouted back. 'How can it kill you if you're already dead?'

And with those words, I looked down at myself. I was a boy still, but I knew that I was really a man. My little sister was full-grown, but I was not. I put a hand to my face, and my skin was cold and lifeless.

'A storm is coming, John,' spoke Lillian, 'and you must be ready for it, in this life or the next!'

Then she let go of my cold, dead hand—such a small hand, I thought—and I slipped on the waxy netting of the gunwale, and fell back towards the sea. My sister's face grew smaller and smaller as I fell into blackness. I turned my eyes to the heavens, and saw the flames spout forth from the dragon's maw once again, enveloping the entire ship and reducing all on board to cinders.

The inky water enfolded me like swaddling clothes, and for a moment I was content to drift slowly, peacefully to the bottom of the ocean. I closed my eyes, and took a breath, so as better to fill my lungs with saltwater and continue my journey downwards, downwards in the briny deep.

ELEVEN

I will never forget the moment that I awoke from that nightmare, nor the perfect vision of the woman who was there to greet me as I roused.

How many times have I heard wounded men in the service tell of the pretty nurse who sat with them when they woke from their fever? How many of them compared their nurse to an 'angel'? I heard more such tales than I could count, and always thought them charming in their own way, but likened the men in question to overly sentimental schoolboys. How the shoe was on the other foot now!

She leaned over me, mopping my brow with a cool cloth. Her eyes were large, her complexion dark, and her sable hair fell in a loose mane about her shoulders. A more comely girl I do not think I had ever seen, and I fear that my first conscious meeting with her may have begun with a blush as she drew so close to me that I could feel her soft breath against my cheek and smell the scent of her lavender perfume. At this she smiled broadly, and I forgot all of my troubles, all questions and uncertainty; my heart fair sang.

'Where am I?' I asked hoarsely, my throat as dry as desert sand.

'He speaks,' she said with a smile. Her voice was heavily

accented, possibly Balkan. 'You've had a bad time, but you are safe now.'

'Safe where?' I persisted. My question drew a pout from her.

'Away from harm. The country. The weather is fine, there are hills and forests for miles around, and all your worries are behind you. Drink this, and try to rest.' She supported my head and gave me water from a ladle, and it tasted sweeter than the finest wine. I glanced about me, but my vision was blurred. I saw only a soft, diffused light, as of early morning sunlight filtering through a forest grove, and I could smell a sweet scent upon the air, like a confection of incense and rosewater.

I was about to speak again, when I realised that she had been somewhat evasive, and I had the queerest feeling that all was not well. I was 'away from harm', but where? Only then did I remember, in pieces at first, my memory like a shattered porcelain vase being carefully glued together. I recalled with sudden violence the dark, cold night; the flight from the House of Zhengming; the journey along the Thames. I remembered, too, the confrontation with the ghosts of my past, and the dreadful moment when my father—no, when Lazarus—had pulled the trigger and sent me plunging into the murky river. I felt the bullet strike, and flinched bodily. As I did so a tremendous pain shot through my shoulder where the wound had laid me low. The woman placed her hand softly on my chest to steady me.

'Be rested now. There, there, my brave soldier. Be at peace.'

A figure of speech, or did she know me for a soldier? How was that possible? And why would she not tell me where I was? A dark seed of thought took root in my mind, and grew along with my panic. Was I dead? Or was I on the other side of the veil, in the nightmare world of my adversaries? Perversely, I felt that the latter was the worse scenario of the two, for I held in my mind's eye a concoction of what the other side might be like—a hell on earth, full of suffering and fire, where every dark corner held an enemy waiting to strike. I struggled against the woman as these thoughts entered my head, but her hand, pressed gently as it was against me, was like a leaden weight. She must be strong, I thought, and then realised that it was I who was weak as a kitten.

'Please,' I petitioned the woman, 'I must know where I am. How long have I been here? Who are you?' She looked at me, resignedly.

'So many questions,' she sighed. 'I will answer you, but you must promise to rest after.' Only when I nodded agreement did she take her hand away. 'I am Rosanna, and I have been nursing you since you came to us. My friends found you half-dead in London, and pulled you from the river. Someone has hurt you, and we thought you were dead. You were very sick for a time, but you are getting better now.'

'How long was I sick for?' I asked, somewhat relieved that I was not in the afterlife.

'You have been here for almost a week now, delirious and with a fever. You look better today, but you still need rest.'

'A week... and where exactly is "here"?' I asked, still uncertain as to which of James' multiverses I was in.

'The countryside; away from London, away from harm,' she said. She placed a finger to my lips before I could speak further. 'Please, my brave Captain, rest. You are safe with us we are Romani, and whoever is seeking to do you harm will not find you here. Even we do not know where we are half the time.'

'Captain?' I asked. 'So you know me. How?'

She sighed theatrically, and picked a tattered card from a side -table. My card, albeit a begrimed one. 'There was more than one of these on your person,' she said. 'I guessed they were yours— and I guessed correctly. Don't worry, Captain John Hardwick, I did not see your name in my crystal ball.' With that she laughed musically and smiled at me, which made all of my fears and questions ebb away. She was older than I had first thought—I reckoned she was in her middle twenties at least—and her voice held some quality that made her quite impossible to contradict.

'We found a few things in your pockets. Your cards, a few

coins. There were scraps of paper, letters perhaps, but they were ruined by the river-water. The men who found you took you to an apothecary to remove the bullet—they were not sure if you would want to be taken to a hospital, in case you had... run afoul of the law.'

I doubted that these gypsies would understand the full significance of the information on my calling card, but I was still somewhat nervous that my identity was known. I had no idea if I could trust these people, or if they were who they said they were. I had only the word of this pretty gypsy girl, and even though for all I knew the agents in black could have been descending on that place at that very moment, I somehow trusted her. I glanced around once more, my vision becoming clearer. I was in a tent of some sort—the soft light that I had observed earlier was diffused by the pale canvas walls. For the first time, I noticed the sounds of men talking outside, of wood being chopped, of birdsong. A fire crackled somewhere near the tent. Everything seemed so pastoral and serene, I was quite overcome. I remembered suddenly the things that had befallen me, visions of torture and betrayal flooding violently into my mind. With a start I put a hand to my left eye, and was wracked with self-pity when I felt an eye-patch. For a fleeting second I had hoped that some of my memories had been just nightmares induced by fever, but I knew then that no nightmare could match the horror that I had lived through at the hands of the Artist.

'Shh,' Rosanna hushed me. 'Someone has done something terrible to you, it is true, but you are safe and well. We do not care who you are or what you have done, only that you need help. When you are strong again, you can travel with us or go on your way, as you wish. But please, get some sleep, and we will talk later. Be happy, John Hardwick, for your fever has broken and you are on the mend.'

I tried to speak, but my voice stuck in my claggy throat. Rosanna offered me more water, which I gulped, and nodded my thanks. I had little choice but to follow her instructions and sleep, for my body was exhausted even if my brain was not. Indeed, the hallucinations I had been experiencing were beyond mere nightmares; I did not know how much opium the Artist had put into me, but it was enough that I still felt it, even now. And I wanted more. As Rosanna's soft hand stroked my hair, however, I descended into a deep, mercifully dreamless sleep.

It was early evening when I woke, Rosanna still at my side. She led me from the tent into the heart of the bustling gypsy camp. I leaned on her as heavily as was proper, as my legs were leaden and my right side was numb after my operation. With my arm in a sling and an eye-patch over one eye, I must have looked like a real wounded soldier, though I certainly didn't feel like one.

The camp was made up of around twenty gaily painted caravans, and several tents of varying sizes, sheltered on all sides by copses of woodland through which sparse trails wound in all directions. A group of men were gathered around a large fire in the centre, exchanging stories, whilst another man thrummed softly on a mandolin. Half a dozen old women were preparing game and vegetables for a feast, and I felt ravenous at the sight of it. Young girls carried water back from a nearby stream, while the lads of a similar age tended the spotted ponies and sturdy cobs that were kept nearby in a makeshift paddock. Smaller children still ran barefoot around the campsite, playing hide and seek around the caravans and carts, climbing trees and giggling as if they had no cares in the world.

We took our place by the fire, sitting on the fallen bough of an old tree, and Rosanna swayed to the mandolin music. The assembled men greeted us cheerfully, and one offered me a cup of mulled wine from an iron pot near the fire. I was unsure whether alcohol would do me any good, but Rosanna passed it over to me and smiled, and so I took it. A few of the children poked their heads around wagon wheels and out of tent flaps to get a look at the one-eyed stranger, and their playful curiosity made me feel at ease. I joined in the talk around the campfire, which was all of poaching game, drinking wine and travelling faraway lands. I knew plenty on that last topic, and very soon felt less of a stranger than I had expected. Presently, a group of men emerged from the woods—some of them little more than youths, really—carrying bundles of sticks and logs, and Rosanna stood up and waved to them.

'Gregor, Willem!' she called out. She nodded towards me, and two of the men peeled off from the group and came to us. As they drew near, Rosanna said to me: 'John, you will be happy to know these men; they saved your life back in London, and brought you to our camp.'

I certainly was glad to know them, and I rose unsteadily, helped partway by Rosanna, and shook each man by the hand. Gregor was a gruff, dark-bearded man, of the same Romani stock as Rosanna, I guessed. Willem, by contrast, was a slight, mousey-haired fellow, with grey eyes that darted furtively about, and hands that were rough like a labourer's, but slender like a pickpocket's.

'Pleased to make your acquaintance, guv,' said Willem, in an unmistakeable cockney twang. 'Very glad you're still in the land of the living.'

'Not half as glad as I am, Willem. And might I say, you have the sound of a Londoner about you?'

'That's because I am one, sir. Or was. William, is me name, though these folks all call me *Villem*, after the German way, like. I travel with 'em, sir—London got a bit tasty for my liking a few months back, sir, and so's I stay on the road now. Keep me head down, if you see, sir.'

I saw only too well. That he had fallen foul of the law at some point was evident, but nevertheless he had done me a good turn, and could do no real harm out here in the countryside.

'My friend,' said Gregor, in an accent more in keeping with the gypsy camp, 'my heart is glad that you live. Willem and I were about to leave the docks for the last time, and he saw you floating down the river. We thought you were dead for sure, but we felt your heart beat, and took you to a man we know in the East End. He make you well; take out bullet and fix up your eye. This is good. To think—if you had floated by just five minutes later, we would have been gone, and you would surely have drowned. This was meant to be.'

'It was fortunate indeed—but to go to so much trouble… and expense?'

Gregor and William exchanged glances, and then looked at Rosanna, who nodded assent.

'What?' I asked.

'My friend,' said Gregor, 'when we pulled you from the river, we knew that we had to bring you here. Rosanna had…' he tailed off.

'Foreseen it,' Rosanna said, and my blood ran cold.

'What do you mean… foreseen it?' I asked, hardly wanting the answer.

'In my crystal ball, as you would say,' Rosanna shrugged.

'Well, sort of, sir. We was on the lookout for an injured stranger, you see,' William said, 'on account of Rosanna's instruction, like. But injured strangers are ten a penny in London, 'specially down by the docks. Then you come floating by, and we fish you out the Thames, and Gregor and me, we argues a bit about whether you were the one or not. After all, you didn't look as if you'd pull through, pardon me for saying so. I was sure Rosanna wasn't wanting no dead fella bringing back to camp. But while we was arguing, this toff comes walking by—'

'Toff?' I interjected.

'Yessir. Dandy fella 'ee was. And he tells us to take you to a 'pothecary, and gives us ten shillings to cover the bill. So we did, and when the old sawbones says you'd pulled through, we figured you must be the one. So we brought you back with us, see?'

'Not really,' I said. I looked again to Rosanna. '"The one"? Your crystal ball?'

'Gregor, Willem, I'm sure the captain is very grateful. Would you leave us, please?' she said. The two men left at once.

'John Hardwick, there is much to talk about, and much to explain. But trust me when I tell you that you are safe. Please, enjoy the hospitality of the camp, get well, get strong, and I promise I will make everything clear to you, all in good time. Will you trust me?' She held out her hand.

Even the suggestion of prescience and crystal balls or whatever else had put me on my guard. After Sir Arthur's warning, after the Artist in particular, I did not feel able to let myself fall into another circle of prophecy and destiny, from which it seemed there would be no escape. I wondered, too, at the identity of the 'toff' William had mentioned—was he a friend? A fellow agent? Or simply a well-meaning passerby? Part of me knew, deep down. I recalled the look of regret on Ambrose's face as I'd staggered back from the gunshot and fallen into the Thames. If Ambrose Hanlocke had come back for me, out of guilt or sense of misplaced fellowship, then perhaps he was not beyond redemption. But it would take far more than fishing me out of the river to atone for his treachery against the Crown. I hoped it had merely been a stranger who had paid William and Gregor; that would make it all the easier to hate Ambrose Hanlocke.

In the end, I pushed such thoughts aside, and listened to Rosanna, though I barely felt I had a choice. Her voice—her very presence—soothed me, and although I had doubts, they ebbed away as she spoke. Now, it seems almost as if I was enchanted by her. Then, I felt I could trust her wholeheartedly. So I set aside my questions, just for a while, and took her hand.

We strolled through the camp as the sun set. Fires were lit, and every man, woman and child gathered round them to eat and drink, and sing and talk. It seemed a thriving little community, full of people who I would never have so much as looked at had I not fallen into dire straits. And yet their lives, though poor, seemed full, and I felt a pang of sadness that I did not belong anywhere the way these people belonged with each other.

Soon I was eating a hearty game stew with crusty bread out of a tin bowl, and drinking mulled wine and joining in the gypsies' songs, though I did not speak Romani and did not understand the meaning. Every man I spoke to that evening was careful not to ask me how I had come to be floating face down in the Thames, and in fact they did a good job of pretending not to care. The more I talked to them, the more I realised that William was not the only outsider amongst them—they were not all Romani, but were instead from many countries and all walks of life. They were all escaping something, and had found some common bond of fellowship in this itinerant wagon train, where their past lives did not matter. I liked that a great deal, for I did not have to speak of the horrible things that haunted me, nor have to say anything that might compromise my position.

Throughout the evening, Rosanna was never far from my side. When she went away to fetch food, or talk with other groups, I saw her looking back at me, and she smiled when our eyes met. There were other women in the camp, some pretty, some plain, but none as captivating as my nurse. It was William who caught me looking at her lingeringly.

'She's something, ain't she boss?' he said. 'Maybe too good for the likes o' me, but a gentleman like yourself... well, you never know.' I took his words as a reproach, though I doubt he had intended them as such, for I was coveting the girl in a most ungentlemanly fashion.

'What makes you think I'm a gentleman?' I asked.

'It's obvious, sir. Man of breeding, you are. We don't talk about past lives here, sir, but you'll forgive me that I guessed that you was a copper or a soldier, or some such, just as soon as we pulled you out the Thames. Rosanna says you're a captain, so I s'pose I was right. I won't say nothing, sir. But that Rosanna—she's a beauty and no mistake.'

'I suppose she is, William. But why did you say she's too good for you? Surely you're all equals here?'

'Ho! Not quite, sir. For the most part, maybe—we all talk and make merry, and we all have a say about who joins and where we go next, and so on. But someone has to make the decisions—cast the deciding vote, so to speak—and that someone is your Rosanna, sir. Most of the people here are Romanies, and they look to her for leadership.' He took a swig of beer from a bottle; I guessed that mulled wine was too rich for his tastes.

'But she is certainly not the oldest here, and she's a woman to boot. Why would the likes of Gregor take orders from her? I thought gypsies were ruled by the menfolk?'

'That they are, in the main. S'true,' agreed William. 'But the old boss died of consumption a couple o' years back, and Rosanna was his eldest daughter. He never had no sons, just five girls, and all of them with the Sight, so they say, and so they rule the roost. She's a princess in their world, sir, of high birth. That's why she's too good for me; I'm no bloody prince, that's for sure!' He chortled at that, with no bitterness. William was one of those common men who knew his station in life, and perhaps had found a better place with a more equal share amongst the gypsies than he ever could in London.

'You said something about the "Sight"?' I asked. I felt light-headed. Hadn't Sir Arthur's man described his master's 'gift' as such?

'Oh yes, sir. Well, it's not really my thing, I'm sure, but a lot of these folk reckon the Sight is real enough. They say them with the Sight can see the future—read your palm and all that stuff. Fortune-tellers, we'd call 'em. But the Romanies take it more serious, like. They won't move camp unless the signs are right. If they catch a cold they're straight off to the boss' caravan for some herbal remedy or other. A superstitious lot and no mistake.'

William told me of the 'Five Sisters'—Rosanna, Drina, Nadya, Elsbet and Esme—and how they held sway over the camp. I came to the conclusion that half the men—William included—were in love with the girls, and the other half were their blood kin. However, whilst it was easy to see the good in such 'pretty young things', as William put it, I was guarded. For good or ill, clairvoyants, mediums, table-rappers—call them what you like—

had been at the very heart of this whole sorry affair with the Othersiders, and the thought that Rosanna was such a person tore at me. I was not sure whether to be afraid for her, afraid of her, or bitter that even here, amidst an illusory pastoral bliss, my bizarre adventures seemed determined to continue. I was starting to believe that there were no coincidences any more; that everything was linked somehow to the coming of the invaders from the other side. These thoughts swam around my head. I had been given a second chance, that much was certain, and it was my solemn duty to recover my strength and make the best of that opportunity.

'You look like you're sickening again, sir,' said William.

'You may be right,' I said. 'I think perhaps I should retire.' I made to stand, but William put a hand on my arm, and looked about the camp to make sure no one was watching. He reached inside his waistcoat, and pulled out a small brown bottle, the sight of which made my heart lurch. I struggled to retain my composure.

Laudanum.

'Pardon sir, but I have a confession to make. The 'pothecary gave us this, for you, like. But I kept it.' He looked shame-faced. 'I had the habit back in the day, something chronic, and I thought maybe... well, I was wrong. You need it more than me by the looks of you. Please, with my apologies.' He thrust the bottle into my hands, and had I not taken it would have let it fall to the ground. William had turned and gone before I could say anything more. All I could do was stare numbly at the bottle in my hand, and return to my tent.

When I awoke the next morning, Rosanna was already in my tent, wringing out some cloths over a bowl.

'I hope you slept well, my Captain,' she said, without looking up from her chores. 'We shall change your dressing, and then you will be ready to face the day.'

I did not argue. Rosanna cleaned my wounds and applied ointment and fresh bandages. The bullet wound did not look so bad, and I once again counted my lucky stars that I had survived. In fact, I did not feel too bad at all, though I remembered why most suddenly, when Rosanna held up a laudanum bottle, with half its contents gone.

'Where did you get this?' she asked, her smile gone, her eyes cold.

'I... for the pain...' I was too ashamed to explain.

'I have seen these marks, John Hardwick,' she said, grabbing my good arm to indicate the needle-marks, some of which were still fresh from the Artist's torture-room. 'This is the last thing you need, no? Now where did you get it?'

'Willem,' I said, sorrowfully. 'He was doing me a kindness. He did not know.' I hung my head. The moods came over me too easily when I was under the influence of that hateful drug, and I shifted from high spirits to despair in an instant. I already felt wretched, for the crude form of opium that laudanum represents provided only fleeting relief from the weight of the world, bringing in return the emptiness of lucidity and physical hunger more quickly than the pure form of the drug.

I felt a soft hand on my chin, and Rosanna turned my face to within an inch of her own.

'There will be no more, my Captain,' she said softly. 'You are stronger than you think. Stronger than this. Choose to be happy and healthy, here with us—with me—and it will be so. Do you understand?'

'Yes,' I said. She stroked my face and stood, and as she left the tent and I stared after her rare beauty, I believed it.

Less than an hour later, she returned, and we breakfasted on unleavened bread, fried mushrooms and peppery morsels of game. I had no idea what the meat was, and decided it was best not to know—the previous day I was sure I had seen hedgehogs and squirrels amongst the hunters' haul.

That day, I left the tent unaided, and Rosanna walked next to me around the camp rather than acting as my crutch. I had slept late, and there was hardly a soul to be seen. The day was remarkably mild—we were worlds away from the torrential rain of London, it seemed—and the air smelt of charcoal smoke, morning dew and sweet summer meadows. When I asked where everyone was, Rosanna told me that they were at work; the men were cutting wood, or hunting, or labouring on nearby farms. The older women were down by the stream washing clothes or fetching clean water, whilst the younger women walked the long miles into the villages to sell flowers, charms and scents, or look for work further afield in factories. Even the children worked, grooming the horses and tidying the camp. I suspected that a good few were making a nuisance of themselves in the villages, too, though I held my tongue. Everyone had a duty to perform, it seemed, except for me. When I voiced my concern that I was imposing on the Romani hospitality, Rosanna smiled sweetly and said: 'But Captain Hardwick, you are providing work for me. My own days of idleness are over now that I have you to tend to.'

We were interrupted presently by two girls, who greeted Rosanna cheerily. I recognised them from the previous evening.

'John, these are my sisters, Nadya and Elsbet,' Rosanna said, introducing each in turn. There was certainly a family resemblance—Nadya was perhaps twenty years old if that, and Elsbet was barely sixteen I guessed. They were pretty, full of laughter, and they spoke with Rosanna most excitedly. They slipped into some cant of their own language at times, and it was hard for me to follow. Elsbet giggled throughout the exchange like a dizzy schoolgirl, and occasionally looked at me in a strange fashion that I could not interpret. When they had done with their gossip, the two younger sisters went on their way, leaving Rosanna and me to continue our walk.

'Two more of the Five Sisters,' I said. 'They are not quite what I expected.'

'Oh,' Rosanna said, cocking her head. 'What did you expect?'

'I don't know,' I replied. 'Perhaps I thought they'd be more… serious.'

Rosanna laughed long at this. I seemed to make her laugh a

lot, though never intentionally. In fact, I'd never known anyone laugh so much.

'What's so funny?' I enquired.

'You are, John Hardwick. I've never known a man so sombre. Tell me, are all men like this in London?'

I thought on this for a moment, before replying: 'More or less.' That just made her laugh again.

'I am the oldest of the Five Sisters,' she explained. If any of us should be "serious", it is me, because all the responsibility for the family is mine. But none of us here is sorrowful—we have good lives, freedom, fresh air and good companions. And my sisters are in the bloom of youth, unmarried and carefree. What do they have to be serious about?'

'It's just that I... I heard that you fulfil an important role in the camp. I wondered if the responsibility would sit heavily on the shoulders of someone so young.'

'You have been talking to Willem, and Willem talks too much. He is new here, and he does not understand our ways; not yet. Later you will meet my other two sisters, and you will see for yourself how happy they all are. Perhaps they can teach an old soldier how to lighten his heart, no?'

She skipped ahead, glancing playfully over her shoulder at me, enticing me to follow. With that, the subject was changed to lighter topics, and she would brook no more talk of her sisters or her own 'responsibility'. I was far too polite to ask her openly about 'the Sight', not to mention too reluctant to spoil the moment by gleaning answers that I did not want to hear.

When our walk was over, Rosanna made me a cup of nettle tea and left me to sit for a spell in the centre of the camp. A little boy, no older than five (though I've never been good at guessing the age of children) caught my attention. He was hiding underneath a blue-painted caravan, pulling faces at me. I pulled one back, and he squealed in delight and ran away.

It occurred to me that I must look a fright, but the boy didn't seem to mind. In London I doubted very much that my appearance would be so readily accepted as it was here. And that thought led me to wonder what exactly I was doing here at all. It was too easy to stay, to use my scars and wounds as an excuse to shirk my duty. It was equally easy to dismiss my colleagues at the club—especially Hanlocke—as Othersiders. If I could trust no one, not even Sir Toby, who then could I report to? I was anonymous here, and alone. Yes, it was easy to stay, to recuperate, to prepare myself; but at some point I had to face up to my responsibility. And I had to do that before Lazarus, the hateful parody of my father, could achieve his goal.

My woolgathering was soon interrupted, however, by the sound of clattering wagon wheels upon the rough track leading to our clearing. A few gypsies raced towards the newcomers. A brightly coloured caravan trundled into the camp, along with half a dozen horsemen. As I stood to glean a better view of the strangers, I saw a lean man jump down from the caravan, and I watched Rosanna greet him with a hug. He was a handsome man, of a similar age to me, though of a rougher demeanour. I felt a pang of jealousy as he lifted the woman I barely knew from her feet and swung her round as she laughed out loud. I shifted uncomfortably before deciding to walk over and meet the newcomers.

As I drew near to them, it was apparent that Rosanna was telling him about me, and as she spoke to him, her back to me, he fixed me with a most calculating glare from his dark, smouldering eyes. Rosanna must have realised I was approaching, for she turned, still smiling, and took my arm, pulling me over so she could introduce me.

'John, this is Andre—he helps me to run this troupe,' she said. 'Andre has been gone these past two weeks, working in the next county.'

I offered him my hand, but the tall gypsy merely looked me in the eye with callous disregard.

'You want to be careful,' he said, turning back to Rosanna and snubbing me completely. 'This one's trouble.'

'Oh Andre, have you forgotten me so quickly? I can handle him.' Rosanna spoke as though I were not there.

Andre scoffed. I do believe, jealousy aside, that he was the rudest man I'd met since returning to England. Even the Artist had remembered his manners.

'I know you well, Rosanna. Better than anyone.' His dark eyes flicked back to me as he said that. Better than anyone. Did he see that I was flustered? Had I in some small way presented myself like a rival for her affections? 'I'm going to water the horses—we'll talk more later,' he said. And with that, he turned his back on us and went about his business.

Rosanna linked my arm with hers and walked me away from the newcomers.

'Well, of all the…' I began, but she interrupted me.

'Do not worry about Andre. He mistrusts strangers, especially townsmen like you. And he is over-protective. You will come to be great friends, I'm sure.'

I did not think that at all likely. 'Over-protective? Of you?' I asked, fishing for details of their history.

'Yes, but it is only natural. After all, we were betrothed once.'

She said it so matter-of-factly that I don't suppose she even realised the effect her words had on me, nor how my stomach lurched. My reaction surprised even myself. *You barely know the girl*, I told myself again.

'You said "were"… why did you not marry?' I tried to appear nonchalant, but I doubt I was successful. Rosanna rather graciously pretended not to notice.

'Our parents always thought we were a good match, and wanted us to marry. I think we would have, although I always thought of Andre more as a brother than a husband. Then my father died, and my duties to my sisters—and to my people—had to come before marriage.'

'He still has feelings for you, that much is clear.'

'Perhaps. Or maybe it is just habit that makes him watch over me so. Now that my sisters are old enough to take care of themselves—and take husbands of their own—Andre thinks our wedding should go ahead. But we don't love each other; not like that. He clings to the past, when all I see is the future.'

I wondered if I was part of that future, and I wanted to ask her as much, but then I felt foolish again, and instead said nothing, walking with Rosanna in a companionable silence.

'If you want to make yourself useful,' she said after a short while, 'you can help me make a fire. Some of the men will be back from their hunting soon, and they will be hungry.'

I agreed at once—I did not enjoy being treated as an invalid, and any opportunity to earn my keep was welcome. We set to work, gathering the driest twigs and branches from the forest. As we were building the fire, some of the women from the newcomers' caravan came to help, bringing bundles of newspaper to help kindle the fire, fresh vegetables and jars of herbs. Rosanna greeted them warmly and let them help, but I was aghast when I saw that the first newspaper they had begun to tear up was barely a week old. I stopped them from defacing the precious paper any further, attracting some rather queer looks, and Rosanna quelled their annoyance with some Romani words. But this was a rare treasure indeed—news at last from the outside world.

I quickly became absorbed in the tattered 'paper, whilst Rosanna looked on, doubtless disapproving of how easily distracted I was. The paper was dated 16th April, and I scanned every article, looking for any news on the case. When I found it, I fair held my breath as I read.

BODIES OF MURDERED POLICEMEN FOUND

LONDON—The bodies of two of the police officers believed murdered on the Isle of Dogs on Monday have been recovered from the Thames.

Sergeant Samuel Boggis, 37, and Constable Reginald Clegg, 34, were found yesterday evening by a group of mudlarks on the Surrey side of the River. It is believed that they were killed before being thrown into the Thames. Constable Clegg had recently been promoted to Special Branch, your correspondent understands, after distinguishing himself in the pursuit of suspected Fenian anarchists after January's Bond Street bombing.

Scotland Yard has so far refused to confirm or deny reports that two other officers are still missing in action, presumed dead. However, a statement was made this morning by Detective Inspector Melville of Special Branch. He said: 'The loss of any officer in the line of duty is always a great tragedy. For two to be found murdered is an outrage. The good people of London should rest assured that no effort will be spared in bringing the perpetrators of these heinous crimes to justice.'

Not bloody likely, I thought, screwing up the paper in anger. The Artist had sent a dire warning to Scotland Yard, and to Apollo Lycea. He would not have done so were he not confident that he was beyond the law—whatever hold he and his wretched paintings had over the great and the good of England, it was vice-like. Finding myself in a sudden black mood, I stormed off to my tent.

To her credit, Rosanna left me to my own devices for a respectful length of time before following me, newspaper in hand.

'I wondered what had distressed you, Captain Hardwick, and then I saw it. Are you one of the officers in this story?

I nodded. 'I am.'

'Then you should be happy, not angry.'

'Happy! How can you say that?' I snapped. 'The enemies of England run rampant, three good men are dead, and I am here helpless, weak as a kitten and meandering around on woodland walks.'

'Calm yourself, my Captain,' Rosanna said, in such a soothing voice that I was stopped in my tracks. 'It is no good for you to get so excited. I say you should be happy, and indeed you should be. Whether you want to hide from the world or plot your revenge, you can do so at your leisure. After all, everyone who knows you, everyone who hates you or loves you, thinks that you are dead. You are free.'

TWELVE

The festivities began early. It was Elsbet's sixteenth birthday, and, given her station amongst her people, this coming of age was a cause for great celebration. A feast was prepared, and as day turned to gloaming the merrymaking began. There was fiddle music, dancing, roast venison, pork, partridge and pigeon, mulled wine, beer and roaring fires. Children sat around wide-eyed as an old man told them stories of great adventures in far-off lands; toasts were made and folk songs sung; young lovers spun each other around in whirling dances to the frenetic music.

I sat some distance from the revelry, thinking somewhat solemnly about my next move in this intricate game; a game in which I was an unwilling participant. Gregor sat with me for a time, but our stilted conversation was interrupted when Nadya and another of the Five Sisters, introduced to me as Drina, came over to bandy words with him. The big man clearly had a lot of love in his heart for the girls, and let them poke fun at him, before leaping to his feet with a roar and scooping Drina up in his arms and slinging her over his shoulder. Nadya danced away from the two of them, clapping her hands together with glee. When Gregor set Drina down lightly, the two sisters each grabbed one of his large hands and dragged him off to the circle to dance. He looked at me over his shoulder as he went, shrugging his heavy shoulders. I laughed at their antics, and waved Gregor away. As I turned back to my cup, I looked up to see that Rosanna had joined the party. She was away from me, on the other side of the bonfire, and I found myself staring at her absent-mindedly as she moved amongst the assembled travellers. When she got up to dance, I could not take my eyes off her.

It was then that I was caught out. I almost jumped from my seat as I felt hands pinch at my sides, and I turned around with a start to see young Elsbet, giggling at my foolishness.

'I saw you looking at her,' she said. Her accent was much softer than that of her sisters, I noticed—she sounded far more like an English girl than any of the other gypsies, though her dark hair, dusky complexion and large brown eyes marked her instantly as Rosanna's kin. 'You like her, I can tell.' The girl had caught me out eyeing her sister like a silly schoolboy. I searched my faculties for a clever retort, but was found wanting.

'She's... been very good to me. Of course I like her,' I said, coyly. This brought another giggle from the girl.

'She likes you too you know. She told me. She said, "Oh, my handsome stranger has come at last. My wounded soldier."' At this, she clasped her hands together, and took on a wistful air in mockery of Rosanna. I did not believe her charade for an instant, much as I would have liked to.

'It is not kind to make fun of guests at your own party. Nor of your sister,' I chided, light-heartedly. I confess she had confounded me. As much as I may have dreamed of childhood recently, I had completely forgotten how to hold a childish conversation.

At this, Elsbet grinned, stuck out her tongue at me, and ran out of sight. I scoured the darkness for her with my good eye, but saw nothing; the ringing of childish laughter was all I was left with. I smiled to myself, shook my head, and turned, where I met with another surprise. Andre was standing over me. He must have been silent as a cat to have come so close to me without my hearing. I was surprised also to see William standing behind him, looking oddly sheepish, and another man whom

I did not recognise, though I guessed he must have been part of Andre's troupe. There was something untoward about their approach. Andre's lips had a warm smile upon them, but his eyes were saying something else; he was scrutinising me, as though studying an enemy. I got to my feet immediately.

'My friend,' Andre began, 'we got off on the wrong foot earlier. I have come to make amends. Willem here has told me that you are an honest man, and came here not of your own choosing. I cannot bear you a grudge for this.' With that, he offered me his hand—the wrong hand, for my left was in a sling. There was an awkward moment, then his smile broadened and he held out his right hand instead. It was poor etiquette, but was it gypsy ignorance of manners, or a deliberate jape at my expense? I could not be sure, and so I shook his hand.

'Anyway,' Andre said, 'we should drink together, and be merry.' He took two glasses from the surly man behind him, and thrust one into my hand. In it was a clear liquid, which I took for some kind of 'moonshine'. All three of the men wore half-smiles. I looked at William, and he did not betray any malice, and so I clinked my glass to Andre's.

'*Egészségetekre,*' he said.

I was wary, but not wary enough. I took a gulp of the foul liquid, expecting it to be strong, but was ill-prepared for the effect it had. Andre, it is fair to say, took only the most minuscule sip, and I did not notice if he swallowed it, for my throat was instantly afire and my remaining eye streamed. I coughed and spluttered and actually bent double. William slapped me on the shoulder, laughing whilst saying, 'That's the good stuff, eh?' Yet the slap to my wound was surely intentional, and sent a flash of agony down my arm.

I was taken aback for a moment, but knew that the scene could turn ugly depending on my next action. It was no small mercy, then, that the decision was taken from me. Rosanna stepped in just as I had managed to get my fitful coughing under control. She snatched the glass from the laughing Andre's hand,

and gulped down all of the fiery alcohol in one go, without so much as flinching. She held Andre's gaze defiantly, and tossed the glass aside where it smashed against a tree stump. William and the other man shuffled backwards, and Andre's grin evaporated.

'Rosanna can hold her drink better than this old soldier, no?' Andre said sarcastically.

'The captain is my guest, and he is a sick man. To play such jokes on a sick man is not honourable.' She said something more, in the Romani tongue, and it sounded ill.

The surly man and William each intervened, coaxing Andre away from us.

'Come, Andre, the night is young,' the surly man said. 'No need to get drunk so early.'

Andre backed away from us, grinning. 'Another time, maybe,' he said. With that, they went back to join the party, leaving Rosanna and me alone.

'Thank you,' I said. 'What was that?'

'Vodka; strong vodka. My father used to call it "burning water". We make it ourselves; the weaker stuff we drink, and the stronger stuff we use to wash wounds and clean the caravans. This is the strong stuff—you should rub it on your shoulder, not put it in your belly.'

Rosanna linked my good arm.

'Come, Captain—do not let their tricks spoil the evening. It is my sister's birthday; she is a woman today, and we should make merry.'

I followed her into the heart of the camp, and soon the unpleasant episode was all but forgotten. Though I drew the line at dancing, given my ailments, I did my best to join in with the others, to sip slowly at hot mulled wine and tell pink-cheeked children stories of tiger-hunts in India and mountaineering in the Far East. I tried to sing with the bards, though my efforts at grasping both the melody and the language led to peals of laughter all round. An hour or more passed before Rosanna returned to me, clearly pleased with herself for encouraging me into the fold.

'Well, my Captain, what do you think of our little family now?'

'I think you are most hospitable,' I replied, tactfully.

'But…?' she said, putting words in my mouth.

'I'm not so sure about the other half of the "family",' I said, nodding towards a group of men on the fringe of the camp, Andre at their head. 'Black sheep, I think we'd call them back home.'

She smiled at the jest. 'And where do you call "home" these days, John Hardwick?'

'I… I'm not sure I really have a home, as sorry as that sounds.'

'It does not sound "sorry" at all,' she said. 'It sounds as if you are right at home amongst us, for are we not all drifting where the wind takes us? Perhaps you should stay. Follow your feet; indeed, you should follow me.'

For a moment I wanted nothing more than to tell her that I would cast off my old life like a masquerade costume and travel the country with the gypsies. However, I knew in my heart it could not happen, and that I was merely delaying the inevitable by staying with her. My induction into Apollo Lycea had placed a weight upon me even greater than my old captaincy of the Lancers.

'Rosanna, you must know I cannot stay much longer. Now that I am over the worst of it, I must return to London.'

'Why? So you can get yourself killed properly this time?'

'So that I can warn my superiors.'

'Warn them? If they are so "superior", do you not think that they can cope without you whilst you recover? Are you always so headstrong, John?'

I thought about that for a moment. 'I suppose I am, yes,' I replied.

'So am I,' she said. She unlinked my arm, and took a few steps away from the fireside, before turning and holding out her hands. 'Walk with me, Captain John Hardwick.'

I felt a little abashed—I was actually nervous about walking off into the woods with this sultry beauty whom I hardly knew, and I hesitated in taking her hand.

'Are you not a gentleman, Captain?' she asked, her head inclined to one side, and her pout returning. 'Will you let a lady walk the woods alone?'

Put like that, I had no choice. I held her hand—it was cold from the night air—and I rose to my feet in an ungainly fashion. I was still not myself, and I had drunk three cups of wine, which had certainly not been wise, no matter what my hosts said. Rosanna picked up a lantern, and we took our leave, I daresay with certain eyes from within the camp glaring daggers at my back.

We walked along a woodland path, the sounds of merriment from the camp growing softer as we wended our way though the trees. It was dark, and what little speckled light we walked by was provided by a low crescent moon. I had to stop frequently to rest and lean on poor Rosanna, so it was not much of a walk at all, but she did not complain. Finally, we reached another clearing, from where we could see the stars. Rosanna set down her lantern and took both my hands in hers, and faced me.

For a moment I did not know what to do, or what to expect. I felt like a college boy again, bashful and awkward. Not only that, but I was intimidated—she was strong, and apparently a princess, and I was a battered, weak, one-eyed man in borrowed clothes.

'John Hardwick,' she said, firmly. 'You have been talking to Willem, and my sisters, too. Did you talk about me?'

'I… well… that is to say… ' I fumbled.

Rosanna threw back her head and shook out her tousled hair and laughed. I remember thinking that her laugh marked her out from the fine ladies I had known before, in England, India and China. Those ladies barely parted their lips and laughed only softly, being careful to hold themselves with utmost decorum at all times. To think on it, one never sees a lady's teeth. Rosanna was different—she was warm and genuine, and perhaps a little wild.

'What did they say?' she asked, smiling.

'They… Willem said you were royalty. That you are the leader of those people.'

'And?'

I realised where the conversation was heading. I did not know whether to play the game or not. In truth, I wanted the moment with her to last forever, but it is my nature to be blunt, and so I was then, for better or for worse.

'He said that you had a gift. "The Sight" he called it. That you can see things that other people cannot see.' I did not want to dwell on what Sir Arthur Furnival had said: that I would meet others like him, and should be wary of them.

'And do you believe him?' she asked. Her eyes gazed deep into mine. They were like fathomless pools, and regarded me with a curious mixture of kindness and intense scrutiny.

'I believe a good many things these days that perhaps I would have once thought foolish. I cannot discount the possibility.' God! What a prig I sounded. She laughed at me again, and I couldn't blame her.

'I am glad you cannot discount the possibility that I am gifted,' she said.

'My dear lady, that is not what I—'

'I am teasing you, Captain Hardwick,' she said, laughing again. 'And I am no lady.'

'Rosanna, whatever else you may be, I am sure that you are a lady. Not in the truly English sense perhaps, but a lady nonetheless.'

For just a moment she looked at me in earnest, and I think she perhaps regarded me with a fondness too deep for our incredibly short acquaintance. But it was a fleeting moment, and the familiar, carefree smile quickly reappeared.

'Always so serious, Captain. That is why I knew you were the one.'

For a second I thought she spoke of me romantically, in that silly way that girls do, but the cold creep that rose from the base of my spine alerted me before I realised—she was not talking of trysts, but of prophecy, and not for the first time that night I found myself lamenting the absurd descent into the supernatural that my life had taken.

'What do you mean?' I asked, already half-knowing and fearing the answer. Her lovely smile disappeared again, but her eyes remained kind and twinkling. There was no malice in her, I was sure, but I was afraid all the same.

'Your coming here was as the turn of the seasons. It was foreseen,' she said. 'A week ago, my sisters and I saw you in a dream. Not you, exactly, but yet you still. We all awoke with the same premonition—the scarred man with the serious face will come to us, we said. He has died and been reborn; he walks between worlds. He represents danger to us all, but we must not turn him away, for he will need our help if he is to fulfil his destiny. It is foreseen, so shall it come to pass.'

The sudden change in her tone, and the outpouring of information, was much to absorb. As were her words. 'It was foreseen', she kept saying. Hadn't Tsun Pen said those very words to me, when speaking of his own survival of the coming storm?

'Rosanna... I—I mean you no harm. As soon as I am well enough I shall be on my way. I promise you that I will not allow my presence here to be a threat to you.'

'I know, Captain,' she said, somewhat sadly. 'You are not the threat. It is what you carry with you. There is a darkness inside you, and my people believe that darkness attracts darkness. You do not mean us harm, but harm will find us anyway, because of you.'

'I don't know what to say. If you are so certain of this, why help me at all? You are their leader—the others look to you, don't they?'

'Yes, but they know that to follow one such as me will not always be singing, dancing and drinking by the fireside. They know that there is a destiny, which cannot be denied, and they play their part. Perhaps you cannot understand this, coming from a city of rules, and commerce… and lies.'

'I think I understand all too well. You speak of duty, obligation—honour, even. I think we are not so very different in that respect.'

She smiled at me broadly, and shook her head.

'No, my brave Captain, we are nothing alike. I am afraid that you are too bound by rules, and laws and money, and officers in smart uniforms, and battles against enemies that you do not even know. No; my people do not follow out of duty, they follow out of love. And I do not think you understand that at all.' She turned her back to me, doing me the courtesy of sparing my blushes. But if anything her words struck a chord in me, a longing for something more than the life I had. And despite that—or perhaps because of it—I decided to set aside my feelings, and do my duty as a soldier; as an agent of the Crown.

'And they all love you? They would all follow you through dangers untold, if they knew what was in store? Even those who are not truly your people?' I was perhaps more interrogatory than I had intended. She looked over her bare shoulder, and her large dark eyes held mine fixedly.

'You mean men like Willem?' she asked. 'Perhaps. Yes, I believe so, because they owe us more than even the bonds of blood and ancestry can enforce, more even than belief in the Sight can inspire. Do you know of what I speak, John Hardwick?'

I nodded. 'Freedom,' I replied.

She spun around, and placed her hands on my chest tenderly, and looked up at me, her face so close to mine that I felt the flutter of her eyelashes against the stubble on my chin.

'Freedom is the only thing worth living for, Captain. And it is the only thing worth dying for.' For a moment, I thought she was going to kiss me, and I longed for her to do so, but again an instinct within me pulled me away.

'Freedom is a right, which in my country must be earned. Tell me, Rosanna, how many crimes have your followers committed? How many people have they hurt or robbed? And don't pretend as though they are all latter-day Robin Hoods—I have seen men like Willem before, many times. He may be a likeable rogue, but he is a rogue nonetheless, and if he were not here with you, I imagine he would be serving time at Her Majesty's pleasure.' No sooner had I uttered the words than she pulled away from me. I regretted my tone instantly, but I cannot say even now that I did not mean what I had said. However, in the presence of a woman so beautiful, so fierce—perhaps I was a fool not to follow my heart. The moment of tenderness was shattered, and she stepped back from me, her face expressionless, illuminated like a masterwork of Rembrandt in the warm glow of the lantern.

'These are my people, Captain. They come from all walks of life, and yes, it is true, they are not all innocents. They are the poor, the meek and the dispossessed. You may also find amongst them thieves, beggars and even murderers. Does that shock you? But listen to me, Captain John Hardwick, with your fine feeling and parade-ground rules: these people are good, for all of the sins of their pasts, and they deserve a second chance. Your government will not grant them that, nor would your Queen, but I can offer them sanctuary. Here they have *Romanipen*. We survive, my people survive—our way of life survives—by the virtues of the waifs and strays who come to us. They are bound to me as I am to them, and I would not change it for the world. You want the truth? Gregor is wanted for murder. Willem was a pickpocket for all his life. And yet those two men were risking everything just by being in London, because I asked them to work the docks to earn us money. And had I not asked them, they would not have fished you out of the river, and you would be dead. Do you understand?'

'Murder...' I muttered. 'Rosanna, I owe them my life, it is true, but does that compensate for the taking of another?' The tangled web of cause and effect in which I was trapped was beginning to make my head spin. Everything from my liberation in Burma right up to this encounter with Rosanna and her disciples—all of it seemed either startling serendipity or devious design. I was starting to hope that I would not find out where the path would lead, whilst dreading that it was already 'foreseen'.

'And is murder never justified, Captain? Would you not murder the men who did this to you, given the chance?' She flourished her hand up and down, indicated my eye, my bandaged shoulder, the whole broken mess of me.

'I would, and I would expect to face severe questions for it. Penalties, even. There are consequences...'

'Those consequences are very different for an officer, a gentleman, and a poor gypsy from across the sea. You must know this; you are no fool.'

'Rosanna I... I don't know what to say. You know what I am, what I stand for.' I was still struggling to reconcile the fact that Gregor, my saviour, was a murderer. More than that, I was thinking of what Sir Arthur had told me, that I would be betrayed more than once. I was now among criminals, putting my life in their hands. Would Rosanna betray me? Her people? I certainly had little cause to trust them.

'Pah! Find me twelve men in your city as honest as the men in my camp, and I will pluck the very stars from the sky. I tell you this, John Hardwick—you will have to make your decision tonight. Right this instant. If you want to summon the law and throw my family in jail, then go and do so. The nearest town is that way.' She pointed violently, her arm outstretched fully for emphasis. Her eyes were wild with passion, and her cheeks were the colour of fire. 'But if you want my help, then come back to the camp, go to bed, and sleep in the company of those brigands you so despise. If they do not slit your throat in the night, and you wake refreshed in the morning, then we will talk some more.'

I tried to say something to stay her ire, but the words would not come. And then I was taken by surprise as she snatched up the lantern with one hand, grabbed a handful of my hair in the other, and kissed me hard. I dissolved in an instant; there was such fury and passion and life in her that I had neither the will nor the inclination to resist. And then she pulled away once more, and with fire in her eyes she pushed me hard in the chest. The pain flared up in my shoulder, and I fell backwards into a patch of ferns, such that for a moment I was engulfed in a dark green sea. I heard her say, with an air of petulance: 'A kiss, Captain Hardwick, so that perhaps you might remember what it is like to feel.' And with that she was gone.

When I finally clambered out of the undergrowth, I was alone on a dark forest path, with no sign of Rosanna or the lantern, and only the trees and stars as witnesses to the kiss that still lingered on my lips.

The next morning I greeted the day with an aching head and leaden limbs. My shoulder burned with pain and my head spun from the wine. I was in the tent again, and the sound of industry and toil could be heard all around me through the muffling canvas walls. I was half dressed—I recalled stumbling through the woods in pitch darkness, before finding the camp again after God knows how long. I had sneaked to the tent like a thief in the night, shame-faced at my treatment of Rosanna, angry at her treatment of me, and more than a little embarrassed at my moral transgression. My situation was not unlike my time in India; what would I have said to the men under my command if they had fraternised with the locals, and taken romantic evening strolls with the sultry, barefoot girls of that far-off land?

I rubbed at my face in an effort to expunge the grogginess, and with no small effort managed to sit up and pull on my britches. No sooner had I done so than a man appeared at the flap of the tent. It was Gregor. I had not yet given him a thought, but now he was at my door it all came rushing back to me—how on earth could I stay with these people, who harboured such men? And yet I said nothing. Gregor had a broad smile on his face, and a jug of water in his hand.

'My friend, you drank too much last night, eh?'

I managed to nod. My whole perception of Gregor had changed overnight.

'Rosanna said to bring you water and medicine, and make sure you get some rest. You make her mad last night, no?'

'Something like that,' I managed to reply. He handed me the water and two small, pale blue pills. 'What are these?' I asked suspiciously. Gregor shrugged.

'From doctor. Stop you getting sick again.'

The pills did not resemble anything that I knew better to avoid, and so at Gregor's insistence I took them. I drank the water thirstily, cup after cup until it was gone.

'Now,' said Gregor, 'you should rest. Another day, maybe two, and you will be strong again. I bring you food now, then you sleep.'

'Wait,' I said, as he turned to leave. 'I feel well, honestly. What time is it?'

'Almost noon. But you are sick. We will talk more later.' And with that, the burly gypsy was gone again. I was half tempted to leave anyway, but when I tried to stand I felt light-headed. For a horrible moment I thought I really had been drugged, but I quickly reminded myself of my injuries, the volume of river water I must have swallowed recently, and the amount of spiced wine I had consumed the night before. I sat down on the bed again.

There was a chair by the bed, where Rosanna had sat when she'd nursed me. Again I reproached myself, for although she had had another motive for helping me, certainly, she had still done me a great kindness. And if what she had said last night was true, she did so despite the harm it would bring her people, and that showed a strength of character that I admired. I noticed that there was a book on the chair, and I picked it up idly—it was a copy of Dickens' *Great Expectations*, its marbled jacket faded and bent, and its pages well thumbed. There was an inscription on the first folio: *To Rosanna, my guiding star*.

'I see you decided to return.' The voice shocked me, and I dropped the book on the chair, and looked around to see

Rosanna standing at the foot of the cot bed. Her hair was tied back under a braided headscarf, and her dress was white and long. I was too mindful of the previous night's events to make good conversation, and I barely managed to mutter some nonsense to the affirmative.

'It is good that you are back, Captain. I did not know for sure if you would go to the town and bring back an army of policemen. I am glad you did not.'

'Rosanna… I am sorry to have caused you offence,' I said. It was not the best apology, but it was a start.

'Captain Hardwick, I fear I overestimated you. I thought that you were ready, but it was too much, too soon. Perhaps we can try again, when you are well.'

I did not know whether she was talking about my 'foreseen' destiny again, or something else. In either case I was inclined to agree; but before I could answer she moved to where I was sitting and took up the book that I had been looking at.

'*Great Expectations…* not the most cheerful tale, but one that I have read many times. I read it while I watched over you, John Hardwick, and I wondered what kind of a man you would turn out to be when you woke. Perhaps you would be Bentley Drummle, Magwitch, or maybe even Pip. I imagined you as them as you slept.'

I had not read the book for many years, but I recalled the story quite well. I believe she was weighing me up as either the roguish bully who was only outwardly a gentleman; the piteous fugitive who was also the most honest man of the tale; or the young hero, so foolish at first, only claims the woman he loves after causing himself and her great pain. I was not sure it was really fair to compare me to any of them, but I knew which I currently appeared to be, and I tried not to grimace at the thought.

'And which of them am I?' I asked, as optimistically as I could.

'None. You are Joe Gargery, I think. It seems I will be for ever condemned to wait for my Prince Charming.'

She looked at me for a moment, and I was at a loss for words. Did she mean to say that I was unambitious and hen-pecked? Or earthy and kind? Then she laughed, and I felt relieved; it had been just one night, but I had missed her laughter.

'John Hardwick, you are such a serious man. Perhaps Dickens was like you as a boy, which is why many of his stories are so bleak?'

'Who is it from? The book, I mean?'

'My father. He was a clever man—he taught himself to read when he was a youth, and he taught me and my sisters. I read it every year on the anniversary of his death. He was a good man, a good leader of these people.'

'I… I did not realise that it is a sensitive time. I am sorry for your loss.'

'Do not apologise,' she said, perhaps misunderstanding the sentiment. 'I was mourning, yes, but then you came along, my brave soldier, and took my mind off it. I did not have to nurse you myself, but it was better than spending the nights alone with Mr. Charles Dickens.'

She sat beside me on the bed, and I took great care not to look at her askance, or do anything that might suggest impropriety. My adherence to decorum only seemed to encourage her, and she shuffled closer, and took my hand. 'I have asked Gregor to look after you today. It would do you good to talk to him—I mean it, John. Ask of him whatever you need to salve your conscience. And then get some rest, take the air—but no drinking today!'

She stood, and I felt suitably chided. She looked down at me and shook her head.

'What am I to do with you, John Hardwick?' she asked. 'I know—when you are stronger we will go riding. I will show you such countryside as will lighten even your heavy heart. And then we shall see how you feel about our little family, eh?'

'I would like that,' I said. Then, almost as an afterthought I asked: 'You said before there was a town nearby—which is it?'

'Always wanting to get back to your old life,' she chastened me. 'The way you court danger, Captain Hardwick, I think you are more eager to see the next, no?'

'Please,' I said, perhaps too pleadingly. She sighed at me, in her customary way.

'It is called Faversham, I think. We can go there if you like; they are not too disapproving of my kind, if you can stand to be seen with a gypsy woman.'

Faversham! Again I was left befuddled by a string of coincidence.

'Faversham is close to my old home,' I remarked. 'This is... uncanny.'

Rosanna looked as surprised as I sounded.

'John,' she said softly, placing a hand against my cheek, 'perhaps it is time you stopped fighting against the signs. Perhaps it is time to see where they are leading you.'

I put my hand to hers, brushing it gently with my fingertips. My senses were full of her; I could notice nothing but her lavender scent, her warmth. It was somehow comforting, and where my head had been full to bursting with thoughts of destiny and precognition just moments before, I was immediately soothed. What a spell she had cast on me, this dusky witch of the Romani.

She smiled, stepped away from me, and turned to leave. 'Eat, rest, and grow strong,' she said. 'Tomorrow we will talk, and see what lies in store for us.' With those cryptic, mildly encouraging words, she made to leave, but I called her back.

'Rosanna, there is one thing I need, though I don't know if you can help.'

'Name it.'

'I need some good clothes. If we are to go riding, these just won't do,' I laughed.

'My Captain, I think perhaps your heart has not fully left the city. I will see what I can do, no? But in return, you must get some rest.' With that, she left me to my own devices.

I must confess that the idea of lollygagging around for the day seemed somewhat appealing, but instead I dragged myself from my cot a short while later, determined to ignore Rosanna's advice and make myself useful.

The camp was a little busier than it had been on the previous afternoon, but still there were few of the men around to ask for work, except for some of Andre's friends, who I would have spoken to only if they were the last men on Earth. Instead, I reacquainted myself with Drina, who in turn introduced me to another of the Five Sisters, Esme. When I told them I wanted to work to pay my way, they gave me queer looks, and told me that I was ill-suited to heavy work in my condition. However, I persisted, and offered to do anything that would prove useful: fetch water, wash clothes, and so on. Finally they relented, and took me to a group of old women who were on their way to carry out those very tasks at a brook on the eastern side of the woods. Some of my new-found workmates could barely speak English, and poked fun at me relentlessly, grinning at me toothlessly and laughing through wrinkled lips. Still, I went with them, determined that I was good for something.

The day did not pass as quickly as I had hoped, for my industry was painstaking with one arm, and the washer-women were not the greatest conversationalists. Despite the drawbacks, I managed to pick up a few words of the Rom tongue, which I was surprised to discover was not too dissimilar to Rajasthani, a language I had some grasp of. It was not enough to converse, but certainly enough to catch the gist.

When the time came to return to camp, I believe I had earned their acceptance, if not their approval. The same could not be said, however, of the gypsy men. When I returned with the old women and set down my pail of water, I noticed a small group of rough-looking sorts pointing at me and laughing. Standing not far from them, in the shadow of a large elm, was Andre, who glowered at me. With him, again, was William—the two had become thick as thieves. I wanted to go over to the men who mocked me for doing 'women's work', to say something terribly clever to put them in their places. Instead, I held my peace, and when one of the old women tugged at my shirtsleeve and ordered me to carry the pail to the centre of the camp, the little gang of gypsy men burst into laughter at my expense. I reddened, but did not rise to it. I did as I was bid, and when the work was done I returned to my tent in a most irritable mood.

I kept my own counsel for a while, scouring the old newspaper—which I had clung to jealously—for every scrap of news and gossip, and even leafing through Rosanna's copy of *Great Expectations*, though I could not concentrate on the prose. I was too absorbed in my thoughts; whenever I was alone I found myself brooding on Lazarus, on Lillian, on Ambrose, and wondering how on earth I could return to London, or whether I ever could. Even these dark thoughts helped to take my mind from my withdrawal, for the sickening hollow within me was often so strong that I almost stormed to Rosanna's caravan more than once to find the half-bottle of laudanum.

I did not pop my head outside of the tent for several hours. Presently, Gregor entered the tent, returned from a day's work at one of the factories near Faversham.

'Friend John,' he said, 'I have something for you.'

Gregor handed me a package. I tore through the brown paper and found a serviceable suit of clothes, about my size. Finally I had a clean shirt, trousers without holes, and a thick tweed jacket that made me look more like a local landowner than a wandering gypsy. I thanked Gregor profusely, and asked if there was anything I could do in return, but he would not hear of it.

'It is nothing,' he said. 'Tomorrow you go out with Rosanna, and maybe you will impress her in your fine clothes, no? Or maybe you do not understand Romani women at all, eh? We will see.' He grinned at me as he said this. 'It will soon be time to eat,' he said. 'Now you can, how do you say? "Dress for dinner".' With a hearty laugh, he left the tent. Unlike William, whose motives and loyalties I could not fathom, Gregor was an open book, and good-natured. I reminded myself again that he was a murderer on the run, and scowled. I wondered where the clothes had come from—a landowner's washing-line, I had no doubt—but decided it was better not to ask.

When I ventured outside the tent at last, the sky was a deep blood red, and the atmosphere in the camp was subdued after the excesses of the previous night's revelry. I ate a hearty stew, got to know my hosts a trifle better than before, and eventually managed to steal a few moments with Rosanna.

She was in a melancholy mood, reminiscing about her late father, perhaps because I had reminded her of her loss. It was strange to see her that way—the very solemnity that she had accused me of was now surrounding her like a cloak. I sat with her for an hour at least, talking of my own childhood—the happier times—and reminding her that she had many reasons to be thankful. Her sisters loved her, her people respected her, and she had the freedom to roam where she wished and live how she wanted. As we watched the moon rise high in the sky, the mandolin player strummed a sad song, and Rosanna placed her head on my good shoulder. I breathed in the scent of her. I had had no wine that night, and did not need any, for her company was intoxicating.

When I returned to my tent, I felt the oddest mixture of sadness and elation, as if my heart was being pulled in two. I felt so at home amongst the gypsies, and yet so out of place, and thoughts of Rosanna filled my mind as though I were a love-struck youth. When I fell asleep, there were none of the feverish nightmares or fitful awakenings that had so characterised my nights of late. No dragons, no burning cottages, no sinking ships or devilish siblings. Instead I slept soundly, and dreamt of childhood and balmy summer days, of pretty girls in yellow dresses, and of lavender scents.

THIRTEEN

It was good to be back in the saddle again after so long. Rosanna had presented me with a piebald horse—a good-natured, broad-backed animal—and she had been surprised at how quickly I had taken to such a large beast; but in truth it was not much different from riding the tall, muscled hunters of my old regiment. I felt better for my change of attire also. Gregor had done well, presenting me with a set of tweeds and a flat cap, so that I resembled a country squire (albeit one on a rather scruffy mount). Rosanna, as expected, looked radiant and exotic, wearing a loose blouse, beaded waistcoat and baggy silk trousers beneath a skirt made of brightly coloured scarves.

The further we rode from the sheltered camp and into more cultivated land, the more familiar it all seemed. I was so near to my old home—albeit one that I had not seen for almost twenty years—that even my encounter with Lazarus and Agent Lillian Hardwick could not quash the lure of nostalgia that swelled within me. We spent a pleasant morning riding along beaten tracks and field boundaries, along vaguely familiar country lanes and towpaths. Now and then we skirted hop fields and saw plumes of smoke drifting idly from the chimneys of the oast-houses. As we neared Faversham itself we rode along the boundaries to the great cherry orchards, shaded from the sun by trees fifty feet high. The weather was fine, the conversation easy, and I felt more at home than I had at any time since my return to England. There was something special—safe, I suppose—about the pastoral bliss of Kent. It seemed a million miles from the dangerous alleyways of the East End, though it was not far at all: not far enough, leastways.

We passed by the creek to the north of Faversham, and stopped to eat our picnic, lying on a hillside for a while watching the clouds drift by. They were growing dark again, and we knew that the break in the weather would not last long. As we lay there in a companionable silence, Rosanna's hand reached for mine. I thought at first to withdraw, but then told myself that to do so would be folly—how often does such a perfect moment occur in one's life, especially in the life of a man such as I, scarred and broken as I was. I squeezed her hand, and thought how soft it felt in my own. I remember being surprised by the roughness of my own hands—that told its own tale; an artistic life spurned for a decade of war and toil. Was it any wonder, then, that in that moment I rejected the reserve of my upbringing and instead indulged fully in the tenderness of that beautiful woman? If my father could have seen me, lying beside a gypsy girl in a meadow, he would have been incensed. It was then that I had the most curious thought—I did not care a fig! All my life I had tried to please my father—or my father's ghost, at least—and if there was one thing that his dreadful 'reappearance' on the banks of the Thames had taught me, it was that I had spent my life pursuing the wrong goals. Those goals had brought me nought but pain. In my darkest hours these past days I had come to rue the day I'd ever signed my commission, or donned my uniform. I cursed the name of Marcus Hardwick.

I turned my head to look at Rosanna, and found her already looking at me, and I thought that perhaps it was all worth it. Whatever I had been through, whatever destiny or providence or whatever it was might yet visit upon me, there was still this. There was still her.

'I could lie here for ever,' she said, as if reading my thoughts. Perhaps she had been.

I smiled at her simply, for I could not find the words. She seemed to understand. Then a great splotch of rain hit me on the forehead, then another and another, until it was clear that the heavens were opening. We did not move at first, so caught up were we in the moment. Our smiles turned to laughter, and as the April shower grew heavier we leapt to our feet and dashed to the shelter of the nearest tree where the horses were tethered.

'What shall we do now?' Rosanna asked.

In response, I produced my watch-chain, upon which hung an iron key. It had stayed with me even as I'd half-drowned in the Thames, and fate had brought me back to that white farmhouse that harboured so many mixed feelings and memories for me.

'What is that?' she asked.

'A key to the past, I think. I am going to take you home.'

And with barely another word, we mounted our scruffy horses and rode off into the deluge.

The farmhouse was exactly as I'd dreamed it, set back from a narrow lane, hidden by tall hedgerows. The whitewashed walls, the thatched roof, the paint peeling off the front door; nothing had changed in well over a decade. The gravel drive at the front of the house led to a small lawn that, curiously, was neatly trimmed, although it was a different story at the rear of the property: the grass was tall, the little apple orchard had run wild, and the kitchen garden was all bare earth and weeds. The garden gate, so vividly rendered in my dream, was there still, set into the wall leading to the pasture, surrounded by honeysuckle. The nagging sense of dread and apprehension, conjured by the remnant of my nightmares, was exorcised almost in an instant by my sheer joy at seeing the old house again.

Rosanna was sheltering from the rain under the little porch at the front door, waiting somewhat impatiently for me to tether the horses in the small lean-to beside the house. I noticed that the outbuilding, too, had been used fairly recently to house at least one horse. Before I could launch a further examination of my old playgrounds, I was interrupted by Rosanna's call, asking me if I intended to leave her in the rain all day. I returned to my companion, pausing momentarily as I saw the carved stone crest above the porch. I had almost forgotten it.

'John?' Rosanna frowned.

I reached up and traced my fingers over the wet stone. The emblem of the dragon was worn, but still proud, a heraldic sigil left by whomever had built the cottage a hundred years ago. It was doubtless the origin of my fevered dreams, and only now did I remember the fanciful stories that the crest had inspired during my childhood.

I broke from the daydream as Rosanna tugged at my arm. With the rain still tumbling down from a grey sky, I returned to my companion, and we bundled into the house.

For a moment I was overwhelmed by how perfectly my old home had been preserved, like a doll's house that had never been played with. Then I realised that it was for a very simple reason— the house had been used. There was barely a cobweb, nor any speck of dust. The fire grates had been swept, and dry logs were stacked in the inglenook of the living room. Casks of paraffin for the lamps were lined up on the floor of the pantry, and we found tapers and matches in the kitchen drawers. Though there was nothing perishable in the house I was thankful to find a canister of tea, and there were plenty of pots, pans, utensils, tools and crockery. I was surprised to find my father's old shotguns still resting in the gun cabinet, looking as clean and pristine as ever. When I thought of my father, I thought of his armchair by the fire in the living room, and was perplexed to find his favourite book still sitting there on the side table, Stendahl's *Le Rouge et le Noir*. I reached out to touch its worn cloth cover with some trepidation, as if doing so would summon the man himself back into his armchair like a ghastly apparition. But no ghost was forthcoming; I touched the lettering on the cover, and tried to remember my father reading the book to me as a child, in an effort to teach me French.

Rosanna looked around the rest of the house and found that not all of the rooms were so well kept; some were cleared of all signs of human activity, though had the odd packing-box here and there full of old ornaments, bedlinen, scores of books, and children's toys—most of which I recognised as though I had seen them only yesterday. I leafed through a few old volumes of foreign gazetteers and maps of the Empire—they brought a smile to my lips even now. I could not resent those treasured old tomes for starting me on this life of adventure any more than I could resent my own mother for having given birth to me. A man makes his own decisions, and carves his own destiny—though admittedly it had become increasingly difficult to keep telling myself that.

It was most curious to me that the bedchamber, bathroom, living room and kitchen were so homely looking, whilst the rest of the house stood silent and unlived in. If my feelings of nostalgia for the house had not been so strongly rekindled, I would have felt as though I was intruding in someone else's home.

'It looks as though the estate manager has taken a few liberties of late,' I remarked. 'Baxter, I believe his name is. Still, I cannot blame him for staying here occasionally, I suppose, and his endeavours have certainly done us a good turn today. Nevertheless, I shall go to see him tomorrow and inform him that I have returned. Lord only knows when I'll be able to lay my hands on the requisite paperwork to prove my identity, though.'

'He will just have to take your word as a gentleman,' said Rosanna, putting her arms around my neck and looking up at me with her large, dark eyes. 'You are still a gentleman, aren't you?'

As our lips drew close, I realised the irony of her question. Gentlemen do not, I was sure, take wild gypsy women to isolated cottages. Nor do they wear stolen clothes, or fight thugs in the East End. These were things I might expect of the treacherous Ambrose Hanlocke, who had called me the 'last honest man in

London'. But I was not in London, and if there was one thing I had learned in the past weeks, perhaps more so than in all my time fighting abroad, it was that life is full of surprises, and that a man must adapt to them to survive. As I kissed her, it did not feel like 'survival', but it did not feel ungentlemanly either.

'You know,' she said, 'that you are not the only one who has rules to live by, and to break. Being here with you would be considered shameful… if my sisters behaved this way, I would be expected to banish them. But I am the head of the family now, and I decide which rules to live by, and which to break. Is it the same for you, my wounded hero? Do you control your own destiny at last?'

'Let me make up a fire to dry our clothes,' I said, changing the subject rather clumsily, 'and then I must secure the house in case the caretaker tries to gain admittance. If Thomas Baxter braves the weather and calls today, he will find his new employer in attendance.'

It did not take long to get the fire going—I guessed that the chimney had been swept regularly too. Even though it was still afternoon, we were forced to light some oil lamps, as the dun sky cast a grey and gloomy aspect throughout the house. We sat by a crackling fire, huddled in thick blankets and talking of every topic under the sun whilst our clothes dried on the clothes-horse and the rain pattered off the window panes. We ate the remnants of our picnic for dinner, and drank tea when the last of our wine had gone. I asked Rosanna, perhaps too forwardly, if the others would miss her back at camp if she did not return that night. She smiled at me so sweetly, and beheld me so intently, that I fair melted. It was all the answer I required. When it became apparent that we would stay the night in the farmhouse, I waited for a break in the rain—or as good a one as could be hoped for—and dashed outside beneath my woollen blanket to locate some feed for the horses and ensure that the little stable was secure. When I returned to the house, Rosanna was standing by the fire, with no blanket around her, her form silhouetted in the orange glow of the flames. The curtains were closed, and she turned to look at me with the light of the fire dancing in her dark eyes. If this is immodesty, I thought, then perhaps it is not such a bad thing.

As the first peal of thunder of the coming storm rumbled outside the farmhouse, I took her in my arms and kissed her, breathing in the scent of her and revelling in her warmth. She held my hand, and led me upstairs to the bedchamber. Even as I look back on that night, there is nothing that feels wrong—the opposite, in fact. Perhaps society will judge me more harshly for my 'impropriety', but in that moment I loved her like no one before, and I daresay like no one who will come after.

The house was aflame. Somewhere behind me I could hear my mother sobbing. I had tried to get her to leave but she would not; not until Lily had come back. I stood on the kitchen step, feeling the heat of the flames licking at my back, gazing out to the garden gate. The sky was red as blood, and the dragon wheeled and arced far above us, unconcerned with us now. Perhaps it, too, was looking for a loved one.

The gate flew open, and a man in black was framed in the glowing embers of the burning field behind him. It was my father, and he had a bundle in his arms. I ran to him, crying out, but he ignored me and marched past me towards the house. My sister was dead or dying, soaked to the skin and unmoving in his arms. Her knotted hair stretched across her face, which seemed pale and almost blue. Her left arm hung limp, swinging with every step that my father took towards the burning house. The dragon roared, the fire crackled, my mother screamed. Through it all I stared back towards them, as if there was nothing else in the universe, and became transfixed by the swaying of her small hand, with droplets of rainwater running from her wrist to her fingertips, and dripping from her nails. They seemed to splash to the ground with more force than all the distractions around me, as if my senses were heightened to some preternatural degree.

As my father stepped over the threshold, with my sister in his arms, the fires that had threatened to consume the little farmhouse were magically extinguished, and the painted kitchen door slammed shut behind them, leaving me standing agog in the dark kitchen garden, tears streaming down my face. Just like that, all was silence, until I heard it—a whisper that seemed to circumvent my ears and grow like a fully formed idea in my mind.

The sins of the father shall be visited on the son.

It came from behind me, I was sure of it; from the garden gate. I turned slowly, not wanting to see whoever it was that had spoken. Yet no one was there. The gate was closed once more, and I was quite alone. Then it came again, the voice in my mind, yet which I was sure was coming from the gate. I found my courage, and stepped towards it. I could smell the honeysuckle, and feel the wet grass beneath my bare feet.

I reached the door in the high wall: the garden gate that Lily had always called the 'secret door'. I held out my hand—a child's hand, I noticed for the first time—and traced the cracks in the old blue paint with my fingertips. I reached down to the latch tentatively, until my small fingers closed around the cold iron. I swung the gate open towards me, and stared into the abyss that was just moments ago a field of glowing red embers. Except now, behind that gate stood a man, staring back at me with only one eye. An eye-patch covered his right eye—but he looked like me. I put my fingers instinctively to my missing left eye…

…And then I woke with a start, fair jumping out of my skin. In my bleary, half-awake state, it was difficult to take in what was happening. I was outside, by the garden gate. My feet were bare, I was dressed only in long-johns, and I was soaked through as the rain pummelled down at me. I was standing at the garden gate, which was flung wide open. However, instead of looking upon the pasture beyond, I was staring at my own reflection. I could scarce comprehend what was happening—it was as though someone had placed a mirror in the gateway. I was dreaming no longer, of that I was certain.

As I looked closely, I saw that each time a drop of rain hit the 'mirror', a small ripple appeared in its surface, smoothing out again with a fizz. I could hear a strange trilling hum, so quiet as to be almost inaudible, like bees on a summer's day. I stared at my reflection—it was certainly me, and not some imposter from another universe that stood before me; I could see that from the long-johns and eye-patch—but I saw a strange yellow light around the edges of the reflective pane, which periodically crackled with some sort of electrical force.

I rubbed at my face, using the cold rain to revive myself, then I chanced a look back to the farmhouse to ensure that Rosanna was not witness to these strange events. The house was dark, and the curtains were drawn. Satisfied, and feeling somewhat restored to wakefulness, I turned to the portal. I knew that this was a gateway to the other side—I did not need William James to tell me that I stood before one of the wondrous portals that paved the way to the ruination of our great Empire. But what to do? I thought hard, and was struck by a sudden fear—how long exactly had this portal been here? I had not opened the gate when we arrived at the house, so it could have been there all along. The house had been tidy and lived in; I had assumed that the caretaker had stayed on his last visit, but what if it was serving a more nefarious purpose? Lazarus was in London, and London was less than fifty miles away. This house—my home—could well have been used as a safe-house for Otherside agents for goodness knows how long. And in fact… the thought occurred to me so suddenly that my heart raced at the wild ideas passing through my mind. Could it be? Could this portal be the Lazarus Gate? Could Lazarus be using this very doorway, Lily's 'secret door', to pass to and fro between the worlds?

Half-mad with the idea, I put up my hand and reached out to the surface of the shimmering portal. It seemed to hum a little louder the closer my fingers got to it. If this was the Lazarus Gate, then I could pass through it, quite unharmed—the question of where I would end up or what I would do once there was of secondary concern whilst I was in that excited state. If it was not the Lazarus Gate, however, then I would be courting a fate worse than death. I would soon be sporting a hook for a hand at the very least, to complete my transformation into a pirate of old, or else I would be turned inside out like the wretches I had put to death at the Artist's lair. That thought certainly made me pause. I stood there dumbly, with my hand outstretched to the portal, which rippled at my mere proximity as if it were a fishpond and the carp were rising to my hand to feed.

I realised it was folly to try to pass through without further investigation. I clenched my fist and took a step backwards. As I did so, I got the fright of my life—a hand burst from the portal, causing great ripples in its surface that crackled with amber light. The humming sound increased to fever pitch, and another hand appeared, and then an entire man, barrelling into me with some force. I staggered backwards, struggling to keep my feet as a man in black tumbled through the portal, like Alice passing through the looking glass. His forceful entry into our world was heralded by a shower of sparks that danced around his form, and at first I could see nothing of his features amidst the confusion. I wrestled free of his grasp and turned to face my attacker.

'Jim? No...'

Before me stood James Denny, garbed all in black, from bowler hat to shiny shoes, with an arrogant snarl on his lips. The shock I received at seeing a man from the other side emerge from a portal—a man whom I knew—was quickly replaced by fear for my life, as I saw that in his hand Jim now held a pistol. He reached for me, grabbing my wrist in a vice-like grip, and jabbed the gun towards my stomach.

I smacked aside his gun arm with my left hand, stepped

forwards and delivered an almighty head-butt to the bridge of his nose. That shook him all right, and the look of surprise that crossed his face showed that he had not been expecting a dirty fight. But I had not survived so long without soiling my hands. Though he may have been surprised, however, he was also tenacious; to my consternation he kept hold of both my wrist and the revolver. I had to press home my small advantage whilst I could, for a protracted struggle against an armed opponent could only go against me in my wounded state. I planted my feet as the agent raised the pistol again, and braced myself for the pain as I twisted under his arm and flipped him over my right shoulder as I had been taught to do by the native troopers back East. This time my manoeuvre had the desired effect— Jim went over me and hit the mud flat on his back with a loud slap, finally releasing his grip on the gun. I yelped in pain as my wounded shoulder took his weight, but remained focused. As Jim went down he relaxed his grip on my wrist, allowing me to grab his arm and twist it hard. My training came back to me in an instant—I threw myself backwards to the ground, holding his arm out straight and wrapping my lower legs around his neck. I pulled on his arm with all the strength I could muster to keep him prone, whilst choking him with my legs.

Was this my James Denny? Had he been one of them all along, like Ambrose? If so, could I kill him if I had to? I tried to push these thoughts aside; if I could only subdue him, I would have the answers I craved.

I cast a glance down and saw his free hand scrabbling about for the gun. I pulled harder at his arm, but though my technique had proven efficacious, my wounded state had left me too weak to maintain the hold for long, and as I faded he came on again with remarkable tenacity. Pushing himself into a crouching position with his legs, he reached further and further until his fingers grasped the barrel of the pistol. Seeing that my choke-hold had failed, and that Jim was on the verge of arming himself once more, I had no choice but to break off and reengage on more advantageous terms. I untangled myself from him, keeping hold of his hand, and sent a kick with my heel into the side of his head. That caused him to cry out in agony, and I quickly rolled onto my feet and sprang towards the gun. We both had a hand on it, and we rolled and grappled in a deadly wrestling match, each trying to wrest the weapon from the other.

He cast a glance at my shoulder. Partially dressed as I was, the strapping over my wound was visible, and this belied my Achilles heel. He risked letting go of the gun with one hand, and punched my shoulder repeatedly, until the pain was more than I could bear. My instincts betrayed me and I let go of the gun in order to defend myself. With a sneer of triumph he took a proper hold of the gun, and tried to stagger to his feet in order to carry out the execution. I turned flat on my back, and delivered a two-footed kick to his midriff as hard as I could. He scrabbled backwards and, to my utter good fortune, slipped on the mud and fell over once more.

I was sluggish getting to my feet this time, and he was quicker. Again, Jim snatched the gun up from the floor, and he had almost trained it on me when I leapt forwards and delivered a fist to his jaw. A left hand to his stomach took the wind out of him, and I grabbed the gun yet again. His grip was still vice-like, but he had shown me so far that he had not seen much action—my experience was telling despite his superior strength. He clawed at my wounded shoulder desperately, but this time I set myself against the pain, and risked everything on one wild swing of my right arm, ramming my elbow into his nose, which submitted to the impact with a satisfying crack. The gun was mine, and I stumbled forwards, throwing myself away from the man in order to give myself time and space to take aim.

Jim was still on his feet, but doubled over, wiping the blood from his face as the rain poured off him in dark red rivulets. He held his other hand out straight, as if to indicate that he wanted no more.

'How many more?' I shouted above the lashing rain. 'How

many more of you are coming from that portal?'

He gave no answer.

'Answer me, damn you!' I demanded.

Quick as a flash, the man had another gun in his hand—a derringer. He had a mechanism up his sleeve, much like Boggis had when he'd attacked Tsun Pen. But there was no time to reflect on what that coincidence might mean. We each pulled the trigger of our guns at the same time. The pistol, which looked very much like the service revolvers I was used to, did not make a loud report, nor did I feel the recoil that I had braced myself for. Instead, the moment my finger touched the trigger the muzzle glowed as red as hot coals; there was a soft click, followed by a loud fizzing noise and a brilliant flash of blue light. No bullet projected forth from the barrel of the gun, but rather an arc of brilliant electricity, like lightning, which struck Jim Denny square in the chest. In an instant I saw a patch of embers glowing near the agent's heart as his waistcoat caught fire, and his entire body was engulfed in a coruscating filigree of light. He convulsed and then, as the light flickered away, dropped to the sodden earth, seemingly lifeless.

I was so stunned by the sight that I was unaware if I had even been hit or not. He had certainly got his shot away, from a more conventional cartridge pistol. I felt a sharp pain at my right ear, and checked myself instantly, discovering that he had just nicked me. There was barely any blood that I could see—I had been lucky.

The high-pitched drone began almost immediately, emanating quite clearly from the body. That confirmed it to me—he was quite dead, and the Othersiders were reclaiming the body by means of their fell technology. I did not know whether or not to grieve, but I knew that I had to search him whilst I still could. I positioned myself so that I could see the portal, which still rippled and convulsed with power, whilst I crouched down and went through the man's pockets. I availed myself of the spring-loaded derringer and the few cartridges that he had on his person, and found a black leather wallet in his inner jacket pocket. Even as I rifled his other pockets, the droning noise grew louder and his body seemed to fade away before my eyes, becoming a sort of dull amber light which at first shone through his eyes, nostrils and mouth, and then seemed to take hold of him. Each atom of his body began to glow and fade in turn, and as it did so it apparently ceased to exist in our world. James Denny faded away layer by layer, until only nothingness remained.

Dumbfounded, I knelt in the mud as the rain washed away any trace that my mysterious assailant had ever been there at all. I stared intently at the garden gate portal, training my gun on it, terrified that more Othersiders could come through at any moment. I saw my own reflection once more, and wondered if the mirrored surface of the gateway was an indicator of sorts—could it be that one could see through a portal if it was safe to pass through, as William James had done when he had spied that mysterious 'window' into another world? I was on the 'wrong' side of the portal, and thus saw only myself reflected. That is how Jim had surprised me, I speculated—he could see me, but I could not see him. If there were others, then they could see me still.

When the blood stopped pounding in my ears and calm was restored, I realised many minutes must have passed, and I was alone in the garden, with only the sound of the torrential rain hitting the mud-slicked lawn and weed-filled beds for company. I staggered back to my feet, trying to think of my next course of action beyond catching my death. That thought hit me hard—it was how my sister had come by the ailment that had killed her all those years ago. It was through this very gate that my father had carried her after she had wandered off through the meadow. Lily had been ill and feverish for weeks, but we thought she would mend. Then one fateful night something had caused her to sleepwalk out of the house in the driving rain. My father had found her half a mile away, sick with exposure from which she never recovered. I had dreamed it earlier, for the first time since I was a boy.

With a grim aspect coming over me as I remembered those troubled times—memories that I had locked away deep inside for many years—I marched to the gleaming portal and slammed the gate shut upon it, drawing the bolt across. I did not know how to dissipate the energies of the portal, but I remembered Sir Arthur Furnival's theory that a portal must be contained in an actual doorway—I resolved therefore to break down the wall and remove the physical archway altogether as soon as I could locate the means.

It was then that I heard a cry of alarm, and my name being called. At once I snapped back to the here and now, recognising the shout as Rosanna's. With the strange gun and the derringer in my hands, I raced into the house. Rosanna was already hurrying down the narrow staircase, and we near collided with each other. She looked frightened when she saw me in my wild state, but checked herself.

'Rosanna, are you hurt?'

'Hurt?' she replied, confused. 'John… what has happened to you?'

'I heard you cry out,' I persisted. I was gravely aware that the threat might not be over, and that other agents could be nearby.

'I… I had a terrible vision, John, in my dreams. My sisters are in danger, I know it. We must return to them at once.'

'Your sisters…' I parroted, my mind full to bursting.

'John, tell me what happened!' she cried, pulling me back to my senses.

'We are not safe here,' I told her. 'Go and get some clothes for us both, and we will go back to the camp. Now.'

Uncharacteristically, she obeyed without another word, and ran back upstairs. I was shivering, wet through, covered in mud and weary. I struck a match and lit a candle, using the weak light to see by as I opened the wallet that I had found on my attacker's body. There was a good deal of money in it—fifteen guineas in notes in a silver money clip, and a few coins—it looked exactly like our own currency, emblazoned with the head of Victoria, not Albert, probably for infiltration purposes. There was also a neatly folded piece of paper, and half a dozen calling cards. Cards which revealed the man's identity and made a lump form in my throat that I found hard to swallow. They were small ivory cards, with neat copperplate print which read:

CMDR JAMES P. DENNY
The Apollonian Club
Pall Mall, London

I could barely fathom it at first. Could it really be that the club—and thus the Order of Apollo—was active on both sides of the veil? Could it be that the agents I faced were members of an alternate version of Apollo Lycea? Or had they actually infiltrated the Apollonian in our own world and simply bore cards to mask their identity? But then I was struck by a mixture of relief and anxiety. It seemed to me unlikely that this 'Commander Denny' was the man I knew back in London, unless things had moved on most unexpectedly in my absence. But at the same time, the Artist had given me pause to believe that I could trust no one, and indeed I was still unsure whether or not any of members of the order I had met so far could be trusted at all. Ambrose Hanlocke had seen to that. But this... The card I held in my hands was a vital clue; a clue that suggested there was at least one man in London I could trust. If Captain James Denny still served at Horse Guards, then he was the genuine article, for his malevolent doppelgänger was now dead by my own hand. If he did not, then I had lost another friend, and on that I did not wish to dwell.

Still pondering this as I heard Rosanna's footfall on the stairs once more, I unfolded the piece of paper. It was as I had suspected—a list of coordinates next to, presumably, the names of assassination targets, written in Myanmar. It was hard to make out—I was by no means fluent in the written language—but it was not the same as the copy book I had examined previously.

The coordinates were longer, and there were multiple rows of them next to each name. Many of the names were the same, and I recognised one of the written characters from my time in prison in Burma—it was often seen on the doors of cells of unidentified prisoners who were unable or unwilling to reveal their true identities. I reasoned that Rosanna's vision about her sisters provided the key. Though I did not understand every word I was reading, logic dictated that the targets moved around a lot, and the long list of coordinates were known refuges or last known addresses. Also, the names of the targets were not certain; in some cases perhaps only a first name was known to the Otherside agents, in other cases only the sex of the target. It seemed reasonable to assume that they were hunting nomads—they were looking for Rosanna and her sisters, 'witches' and 'seers' all. All of this, however, was speculation; without the other book, which I had used as a cipher and which should now, I hoped, be in the hands of the real Jim Denny, I could not be completely certain.

Rosanna appeared with a towel that she had found, wrapped it around my shoulders, and fussed at me to clean myself up quickly and get ready to go. She was most anxious to return to the camp, and I did not blame her. It was then that we both heard a commotion outside—the sound of bolts being drawn, of whinnying horses and of gravel crunching beneath hooves.

'The horses!' I cried, and raced to the front of the house. Flinging the door open, I watched from the porch as two figures in black disappeared round the hedges at the end of the gravel drive, atop our horses.

'Confound it all!' I shouted, brandishing the gun impotently in the direction they had travelled.

'John—who were they?'

'Soldiers. Assassins. Whichever they purport to be, they are the enemy of us all. Get dressed; I'll explain on the way.'

* * *

The house was little over a mile away from the Ship Inn, which thankfully was still in business after all these years, although as expected it was closed for the night. The walk there in the dark, along winding, pitted lanes and in pouring rain was a challenge, and tested my memory and sense of direction to their limits. I had an old kit-bag from the farmhouse attic slung over my left shoulder, filled with anything useful we could find at the house before departing—I had made it clear that we were heading into danger, and should not do so unprepared, no matter the urgency. We had held a blanket over our heads as we walked, though it did not protect us fully from the elements, and by the time we reached the doors of the inn we were thoroughly soggy and miserable.

I pounded hard on the front door, waited in vain for a response, and then pounded again. It must have been almost three in the morning, and no one was up. However, my persistence paid off—a window slid open above us, and a gruff voice called out.

'What the bloody 'ell's goin' on out there? Who's this calling at this hour?'

I pulled the blanket back and looked up, being careful to leave Rosanna's face obscured so as not to court unfavourable reactions to her race.

'Sir—we are in dire need of horses, and perhaps a gig,' I called up. 'We are on an errand of some urgency, and our horses have been stolen.'

The man was tough-looking, middle-aged, with thinning hair and a furrowed brow. As soon as I said the word 'stolen' he looked suspicious, and must have wondered if we were thieves ourselves, come to rob him in the night.

'Stolen? Round here? I think you ought to clear off. I don't know you, and I don't trust people who come a-calling at such an hour.'

'Please, good sir,' I insisted, and I pulled the blanket away from myself, and removed my hat so that he could see me. 'I am Captain John Hardwick, recently returned from fighting in the East. I own the farmhouse up the road there—Bluebell

Cottage—you might remember my father, Brigadier Hardwick?'

The man squinted. He took the oil lamp from his bedside and held it out of the window to cast a little more light on us.

'Some rogues have come to my house this night and stolen our horses,' I continued. 'I intend to go to town immediately and wake the local constable, but we must have transport. I will pay you double your usual rate if you will do us this kindness.'

The man seemed convinced by my small lie—at least I hoped so, as he closed the window without another word, and the light went out. A few moments later we heard the bolts being drawn back on the heavy pub door. The landlord, whose name we learned was Flint, came out in a mackintosh and heavy work boots, carrying his lamp. He inspected us thoroughly.

'Gypsy girl?' he asked, rudely.

'Indian,' I lied again, mustering a tone of indignation. 'I've been serving abroad for a long time.'

The challenge to the man's values was laid down. It would be improper for him to question me about whether I had taken a foreign wife or a foreign servant, but the implication in either case was that I was his superior, and he had already strayed too close to the line drawn by propriety. Flint merely nodded and turned away, leading us to the stables.

When we stepped inside out of the rain, he indicated a little neck-or-nothing gig and a sturdy pony.

'I can spare this 'un. But it's most irreg'lar—I'll have ten shillings; we'll see about the change if'n you bring it back.'

'Be a good fellow and get her ready, and I'll make it a guinea.' I took out a note from the roll I had taken from the late Commander Denny, and watched as Flint's eyes lit up at the sight of it.

Flint could not work fast enough thereafter, and in ten minutes we were ready to go. With a parting word of thanks to our ungracious saviour, we rattled off down the road back to the camp. Our only hope was that the Othersiders had not pinpointed the location of Rosanna's people—they would have to search the countryside based on their best intelligence, whilst we could go there directly. We had lost over an hour, though, and could only pray we would not be too late.

FOURTEEN

The caravans were burning. Lit in the roaring flames, Rosanna's face would have been hard as stone, were it not for the tears streaming down her cheeks. Men were running to and fro with pails of water, trying to put out the worst blazes, whilst horses bolted terrified into the woods. The rain had eased to a pitiful drizzle just when we needed the elements to do their worst.

I leapt from the gig, pistol in hand. Another arc of lightning flickered out from the black treeline, illuminating the scene of abject panic for a split second before sparks flew from the side of a tent and the canvas went up in flames. I dashed towards the location of the shot, leaping over the remains of the night's cook-fire as I went. A few frightened gypsies recognised me, but were too caught up in their own fearful efforts to intervene. All except one, that is; as I neared the treeline I saw the towering figure of Gregor bellowing orders in the Romani language, pushing fleeing men back towards the fires and using his imposing presence to lead his people. He may have been doing his best to save the camp, but I needed his help more than those painted caravans did. I slapped him on the shoulder—he spun around wide-eyed, and seemed relieved to see me.

'We are under attack!' I cried. 'The enemy is there. Take this and follow me!' I tossed him a shotgun and pointed to the trees. He snatched the weapon out of the air, and followed me without a word, vengeance burning in his eyes.

Dawn was approaching, and the sky was taking on a pale yellowish hue, though the woods were still unsettlingly dark. We separated, scanning the shadows for any sign of movement, but being careful to keep each other in sight at all times. The agents had evidently moved on from their initial vantage point, perhaps unaware that we were on their trail.

Then I saw it—less than twenty yards ahead, beyond some low scrub, a tiny dot of red light, like a glowing cigarette on the draw. It was followed instantly by a flash of blue light, and screams from the gypsy camp. I need say nothing, as Gregor saw it too and sprang forwards through the bushes, shotgun readied. I was several paces behind him. I heard a cry of alarm, followed by the boom of the shotgun. I barrelled through the undergrowth, to see Gregor standing over the prone figure of a man in a black suit. The whining sound began to rise from the agent's body, but there was no time to lose searching the man.

'I am certain there's another. Be alert!' I hissed.

Gregor needed no instruction, until he chanced a look back at the body of the felled man, and saw the corpse dissipate into so many specks of light, before fading into thin air.

'By all that is holy!' he cried. 'What are we fighting? Are these men, or phantoms?'

'Sometimes they are both,' I replied, scanning every shadow in search of my prey. I was glad Gregor was a man of such stern stuff, for a lesser ally would have been frightened out of his wits to see such a thing with no prior warning. 'Gregor, listen—they are here for the girls, the Five Sisters. Don't ask me why, but they wish them harm. Where are they?'

'Why, they are…' he began, but he was cut off by a blood-curdling scream that pierced all of the sounds of commotion at the gypsy camp.

We raced back whence we had come, Gregor leading the way

to the tent of the Five Sisters, for he knew instinctively what was happening. Two girls were fleeing the tent, running towards us, with Rosanna close behind them, pushing them away. As we reached the tent-flap, a Romani man staggered out of it, blood gushing from his throat. Gregor did not check his stride—he brushed past the wounded man and burst into the tent, his bravery and rage driving him forward with equal power. Before I could step inside, there was a flash of brilliant light from within, and I saw several figures silhouetted through the canvas in a tableau of battle. The tent caught fire in an instant, but I dived though the flap and into the fray.

'You! You should be dead!' screamed a woman. I recognised the voice at once. Lillian was before me, pointing a pistol at us, whilst holding a knife to the throat of a Romani girl, whom I recognised as Rosanna's sister, Nadya. Another of the sisters, Elsbet, lay on the floor of the tent, her throat slit from ear to ear and her vitality drained in a great pool, staining her pretty dress crimson. The fire spread all around us, and I could feel the heat at my back.

'Let her go, Lillian,' I said, trying to sound calm.

'Do not call me that!' she snapped. 'Never—not you! I am leaving this rats' nest alive, and you are going to let me, do you understand? Or this girl dies.'

'Is she not one of the witches that you hate so much? You will kill her anyway… we both know that. Let her go and put down the weapons, and you will be spared.' I noticed that there was another tent-flap opposite us, directly behind the agent—she would escape us unless I could think quickly. If only I'd had the time to prime the Derringer device I had acquired, I would have been able to use the element of surprise—but alas, I had no such resource to call upon.

'Do you understand nothing?' she cried. 'What matter my life compared to the lives of a world. Do you think I would barter with you, or allow myself to become your captive? This will not happen. Back away, unless you want us all to burn alive!'

'I understand—but you must also understand that we both fight to save a world. You from forces unknown, and I from you! And I swear to you, I will fight every bit as hard. If you kill this girl, there is no universe in which you can hide!' As I spoke, my rage increased—logic and reason released its sway over me, and I played into my enemy's hands.

'To hell with you!' she snarled. She raised her boot into the small of Nadya's back, and gave the girl a tremendous kick, propelling her across the tent towards me. I caught the girl, whilst Gregor raised his shotgun again to fire at Lillian. The shotgun blast rang out, but Lillian dived backwards, away from the buckshot, and flipped through the tent-flap like an acrobat.

Even before we could react further, a great part of the tent roof peeled away as the flames ate at it, and it collapsed around us. We could stay inside no longer, for the smoke and flames now billowed up towards the rent in the roof, and so I dragged the terrified girl from the tent whilst Gregor snatched up poor murdered Elsbet. Once outside, he bellowed for men to stop Lillian, whose slender form was even then mingling with the shadows of the forest as she sprinted away with prodigious speed. Rosanna had returned with more help. Nadya hugged her sister hard, and all of the girls let out such a mournful wail upon seeing their beloved Elsbet so brutally slain. I had no time to comfort Rosanna, and I stepped away to leave them to their grief, handing Gregor some cartridges as I did so. We ran to the forest, determined to catch the agent before she eluded us once more.

We ran until our legs ached and our lungs almost burst. Branches tore at our faces and ancient roots conspired to trip us with every other step, and it seemed that we could not possibly catch Lillian, so nimble and sure-footed was she. We lost sight of her more than once, and only the fluttering of disturbed birds or the snapping of a branch underfoot kept us on her trail. It was getting lighter now, and even the densest parts of the forest were welcoming the first weak rays of sunlight. With light came our hope of catching our enemy.

Just as we thought we neared her location, we were both surprised as we plunged from the undergrowth at the same time onto a little dirt road, lined with trees on both sides and barely wide enough for even the smallest cart. Neither of us had realised how far we had pursued our quarry, and we looked around in desperation, squinting in the half-light.

'There!' shouted Gregor, and headed off down the road.

I saw at once a shadowy figure, some fifty yards away on the bend of the road, and we gave chase. As soon as we got a clear view of Lillian, Gregor snapped off a shot with both barrels of his sporting gun. It was folly—my father's shotguns were sixteen-bore, and Gregor was far from a crack shot. All he achieved was to send a flock of roosting wood pigeons soaring from the tree-tops. Lillian's pale face turned and fixed us with a glare. It was as though she had been unaware of our presence until the shotgun blast had rung out and echoed through the woods. Her response was to level her pistol at us once more—I was at a loss; I needed her alive to get to the bottom of Lazarus' plans, but it seemed she was intent on murder and destruction.

I barely had time to push Gregor aside as the lightning arced past us, smouldering the humid air and making our hair stand on end as it went, before striking a nearby oak tree with such force that the bough was sundered with an almighty crack. The tree, kindling as it fell, hit the ground between us and the agent, sending us scurrying for safety so as not to be crushed. Gregor's foot was trapped beneath its trunk, but I managed to avoid the felled oak, and scrambled through its branches to see if Lillian was still there. I caught sight of her, and saw why she had stopped on the road. She had been saddling her horse—Rosanna's horse—and was now mounted and ready to flee the scene of the crime. And yet she had paused, waiting to see if I had survived. When she saw me scrambling clumsily through the fallen branches of the oak tree, she cast a devilish smile my way and then, turning away, set the horse off down the road at a canter. She had eluded me again.

* * *

Back at the camp, the last of the fires were dying, and plumes of grey smoke drifted into the pale morning sky with a tranquillity that belied the turmoil below it. The camp was desolate—perhaps half the caravans and tents had been destroyed. Men sat around dumbstruck, children screamed and women sobbed. And at the heart of the camp there was a gathering around the body of Elsbet, with such an outpouring of grief over her loss that I could hardly bear to go near. All through the camp I attracted stares. Some seemed to say 'Why? What have we done to deserve this?' Others seemed more accusing—I was the stranger who was foretold, was I not? Rosanna's message of hope at my arrival had been tempered with a warning that I would bring great danger upon them. I turned my head away in shame, for I knew that I was a herald of great dismay for those poor people.

When I did finally approach the grieving sisters, it was as though they did not even see me. They were locked in their mourning, and had their own ways and traditions to uphold before an outsider such as I could even be acknowledged. So I walked away from them, alone, wracked with remorse for their loss, and with anger at the invaders who had visited such violence on the people who had shown me such kindness.

I walked beyond the boundaries of the camp until I reached a little lane that wound down to a stream. There I sat for a while, staring at the babbling water and thinking about what I must do next. I felt distant—too remote to be of any use to anyone. In taking the opportunity to recover from my ordeals out here in my homeland, I had turned my back on my duty. I knew that I had to return to London, and perhaps should have done so already. But of course, had I done that I would not have held Rosanna in my arms, and she would most likely be dead at the hands of my Otherside sister. I could do no right for doing wrong, it seemed; but would I really have done anything differently, given the chance? Would I allow my sense of duty to guide me back to London, knowing that Rosanna would be lost if I did? Rosanna and her little coven knew the risk they took in helping me, and yet they helped me all the same, and were now paying the price. This was their destiny, just as it was mine.

I was brought back to the present by the arrival of Gregor. The big man sat on a low dry stone wall next to me, and passed me a cigarette.

'I have seen some things, friend John, that I did not think were possible,' he said, pausing to take a draw. 'I had no time to think on these things at the time, but I have time to think now. Who were those people? Who was that woman?'

I did not know how much to tell Gregor, or how much he would understand. Though I had come to think of him as a good man, he was not made for outlandish philosophical theories about mirror universes and magic portals. But he did not deserve a lie, so I told him, as best I could, what he needed to know to understand the threat, if not the cause.

'They are agents; spies,' I said. 'Like me, I suppose, but enemies of the Crown. As far as I know, their mission is to cause anarchy and chaos, until they are strong and we are weak. Then they will strike.'

'Why? To what end?'

'To take over the world.'

Gregor nodded acceptance. I think perhaps he needed to hear that our enemies had a purpose of great import, in order to make sense of the despair and anger he was feeling. I could understand that.

'When we were fighting,' he said, 'you told me that they were here for the Five Sisters. Look, friend John, we are Romani, we are nomads... we are nobody. If someone wants to rule the world, they kill kings and politicians—the leaders of the great nations, not a little gypsy princess. Why did they do this thing? Was it because we helped you?'

He was trying to sound reasoned, but this last question was

delivered with emotion that betrayed him. He had trusted me, and did not want his suspicions to be true.

'No… I don't know,' I answered honestly. 'Until last night they believed me dead, just as my employers back in London must believe me dead. No, I believe they would have come for the sisters, whether I had been here or not.'

Gregor nodded, and sat in silence with me for a while. When Rosanna approached, Gregor made to say something, to console her perhaps, but no words would come. She squeezed his shoulder and gave him some silent word, at which he left us alone. Her eyes were red from crying, but the tears were passed. Her features were set.

'It isn't over, is it?' she asked.

I shook my head. What could I say?

'I brought you here, John,' she said. 'I knew the dangers that we faced, the risk you presented, and yet I took you in anyway. It was… foreseen.' Her voice cracked. 'But I should not have gambled Elsbet's life. If I had known…' Now a tear came, and she blinked it back. 'All of us knew the risk… but not her, John; not her…'

I held her, and saw that she was tensed, fists clenched.

'Rosanna, listen to me,' I said, suddenly struck by an idea: the seed of a plan that began to take root. 'I should have died in London, but I was given another chance. I wish I could have saved Elsbet. I would do anything to make it right, but there is still danger ahead. Those people, our enemies, will be back. Now that they know I'm here, I think they will be more determined still. Rosanna, you say my coming was foreseen? Well, then I am ready to face my destiny. But for that, I need you. I need your sisters. I need the Sight.'

'John, not now, this is not the time!'

'There is no time,' I said. 'Don't you see? Everything that has happened to us has been for a reason. Elsbet's death can't have been in vain. If we are to avenge her, we must act. We must find out what our enemy plans to do next, and we must stop him. Whatever it takes.'

* * *

Rosanna had begged me for one day to perform the proper rituals for Elsbet, and I had relented, on the condition that the camp moved so that the Othersiders could not easily find it. The gypsies spent the rest of the day and much of the evening moving what remained of the camp further east, and this was no easy task. Horses that had fled during the night had to be caught, carts had to be prepared or even constructed from spare parts to provide transportation for the infirm. Some of the men were appointed as scouts and guards, and patrolled the locale ceaselessly for any sign of would-be attackers. Through all of this, the funerary rites for Elsbet were begun. Her body was washed and bound by those camp followers who were not of Romani blood, for a Rom may not touch the body of the deceased. Elsbet's nose and mouth were filled with pearls so that evil spirits could not enter her body. Her favourite possessions were placed alongside her, whilst everything else that she owned was burned, removing all ties that her spirit had with the camp so that she would not be forced to walk the earth for ever after. Half a dozen messengers were sent out from the camp in all directions, to take word of Elsbet's death 'to the ends of the earth'—only when her friends and distant relatives received the news and came to Rosanna's camp could the funeral be held. Until then, Elsbet's name could not be uttered out loud, and her sisters would wear only white or red garments as a symbol of their mourning. I was touched by the intricacy of the preparations, and amazed at how little direction the gypsies required—they all seemed to know what was required of them, and mobilised as if for war, with an efficiency that would pride the greatest industrialist.

I helped where I could, but in the afternoon I took my leave of the camp for a few hours. That night, we would set our plans in motion. Gregor told me where to meet up with them later that evening, a secret location where the Othersiders would surely not find them, and I left him my shotgun, hoping he would not have need of it before my return.

My purpose that day was to visit Faversham, and meet with the caretaker of my old house. It was possible that the man would have some knowledge about the comings and goings of the Othersiders, whether he understood their motives or not. I suspected that he would be ignorant of the details, but I would be on my guard—I could trust no one until the affair was brought to a close.

I rode into Faversham and found a small inn to stable my horse and refresh myself. I asked there about the whereabouts of Thomas Baxter. I was in luck, as it was one of the market days in the town, and thus the main bar was busy with patrons. Amongst the farmers, gamekeepers and ploughmen in the inn, my rather battered tweeds, flat cap and even eye-patch did not attract much undue attention, and I was told that Mr. Baxter could be reached through the offices of Boughton & Sons estate management, off Market Place. With time of the essence, and a sense of grim purpose about me, I set off to the office.

It seemed that Mr. Baxter was under the impression that my father was very much alive. When I identified myself as John Hardwick, owner of Bluebell Cottage, he presumed that Marcus Hardwick had either passed away recently or had signed the deeds to the property over to me personally. His office had received the instruction from the solicitor, Mr. Fairclough, that the house was to be attended to regularly, but then less than six months ago Brigadier Sir Marcus Hardwick had come 'back from the dead', and had informed Boughton & Son's that there had been a terrible mistake; that he had not perished, and that the Ministry of Defence had gotten his papers mixed up. Since then, Mr. Baxter had been employed to keep the place tidy but very little else.

This revelation, that Lazarus could have been so brazen for so long, rather took me by surprise. And what was I to tell poor Mr. Baxter? That the man he took with his own eyes to be Marcus Hardwick was an imposter? Or a ghost? No, I could not raise any alarm. Instead, I thought on my feet and sold Mr. Baxter a lie—lying, it seemed, was becoming second nature to me.

'Don't worry, Mr. Baxter,' I said, 'my father is in rude health. Indeed, you are right enough—he has signed the cottage over to me in the hope that, now I am returned from service abroad, I might settle down and perhaps even find a wife. I see you've done a fine job of looking after the place, as I called in just last night. I expect my father will call in again from time to time—if he does so, do remember me to him. I'm afraid we're rather like ships passing in the night these days.'

That should set the cat amongst the pigeons, I thought. Though I did not have much time to be pleased with myself before Baxter surprised me again.

'And your sister, sir. Miss Lillian—will she be coming back now that you own the place? Lovely girl, she is. Sad, though, I always thought, that she still always dresses in black, in mourning for your dear old ma, God rest her soul.'

I almost lost my composure at this statement, but took a gulp of tea to collect my thoughts before replying.

'I fear the memories in that house are proving more than my sister can bear, the delicate soul that she is. Still, you know Lillian who can tell what she will do next.'

He laughed with me conspiratorially at this jest, though inside I was like ice. In our own world, my gentle sister had died a child, sending our mother into a fatal spiral of melancholia, and leaving me alone to disappoint our father. This harridan from the other side, however, was cruel and dispassionate.

I concluded my business with Baxter as quickly as I could, promising him that the necessary paperwork and deeds of ownership would be with him as soon as I returned to London. In truth, I had no idea then if I would take up residence in Bluebell Cottage when this affair was over, if it was ever over, but I would certainly pay one more visit to pull down that blasted gate!

As I returned to the stables, I remembered to purchase a newspaper from a lad in the high street. When I glanced at the front page the whole world seemed to shrink around me, and I realised that there was no further time for delay. It read:

LONDON SUBJECTED TO REIGN OF TERROR

The city has been plunged into panic, as yesterday London suffered its worst day of anarchy since the Fenian attacks of '85.

With explosions causing mayhem at Gallions Reach, East Ham, Ilford, Hampstead, Crouch End and Islington (in that order), this marked the first time that serious casualties had been inflicted by these dynamiters. Several public buildings were damaged, including a civic hall and library, and more than forty people are believed dead or mortally wounded.

As doctors and fire-men struggled to help the injured and dying, London was subjected to the ugly face of urban society as mass looting took place along evacuated high streets. Late in the evening, fires blazed as the beleaguered city was hit by several arson attacks in Mayfair, Southwark and Battersea.

Assistant Commissioner Bruce of Scotland Yard has sworn today that the perpetrators of these heinous crimes will be brought to justice. He reserved particular disdain for those members of the 'criminal underclass' who brought such shame on the greatest city in the world with their 'despicable and cowardly capitalisation on events of real tragedy, for nothing more than avarice'.

I could read no more. How could it be that I had spent the day in a bustling town, and had heard no one so much as mention this news? The good people of Faversham evidently believed themselves far removed from the affairs of the big smoke; how different their actions would have been if they'd known that the anarchists had struck just last night, a few miles from their homes. Or just how much danger these atrocities posed not just to London, but to the entire globe! I realised then that my consideration for Rosanna's feelings had caused me to delay my plans. I was now more certain than ever that I needed their help to plan my next move, and I had to return to the gypsy camp at once. I purchased an ha'penny map and a storm lantern with the last of my coin, and set off to the agreed meeting place, near a little village on the far side of the expansive Denge Wood. It would be growing dark before I arrived there, and I could not afford to be tardy. And yet, despite my determination, I was reluctant. It was not merely a tearful yet happy reunion with my recently bereaved lover to which I rode; I was on my way to a séance.

FIFTEEN

It was well past midnight. The sisters were clothed all in white, and seated on the floor, huddling together in a conspiratorial circle, with a conspicuous space in their line where the departed Elsbet would have sat. They whispered in a language that was unlike any I had ever heard. The tent was lit only by five candles—one for each of the sisters, living and dead—and the flickering light danced across the silks that lined every inch of the tent walls, throwing a cold and eerie cast upon a scene that by daylight would be cheery and gaily coloured.

A young traveller sat on a stool in the corner opposite me, with a sketching pad in hand. He was not of the blood, but an Irishman, apparently descended from a family of witches. I was told he was a sort of amanuensis, whose role was to interpret the visions of the sisters, and help guide them through the dangerous world of the spirits now that there were only four of them. I was positioned by the tent door, an observer only, and I felt like a complete outsider.

Since returning to the camp, Rosanna had barely spoken a word to me. Gregor had told me that she was unhappy about holding the ritual that night, that her gifts would be clouded by her grief, and that it was bad luck to navigate the afterlife with one so recently deceased. And yet she knew how important it was. She alone of the sisters, as the eldest and wisest, understood that their earlier premonition called for great sacrifice. She was doing it for me, but that did not mean that she could not resent me for asking it of her. I had tried to thank her for her sacrifice, but had been coldly reproached for my efforts, and had thus kept a respectful distance until the hour drew near. Any questions I had about how the séance would proceed were met with cold stares and snapped instructions—and so I sat in my chair, quietly and patiently, until they were ready to begin.

The séance was unlike anything I had expected. There was no table-rapping—nor was there a table to rap upon—no Ouija boards, nor crystal balls either. Instead, the four girls sat facing each other, eyes closed and hands joined together, and muttering all the time in their language. Occasionally the boy in the corner scribbled a note, or seemed to sketch something, though it was difficult to tell what he might usefully be doing in such poor light and with his eyes closed. I was reminded of the Artist, and tried to repress a shudder. A few times one of the girls would speak more loudly, sometimes in Romani, sometimes Spanish and occasionally English. To my surprise, it was Drina who took the lead, not Rosanna—the younger girl was assured and forthright in her statements, directing her sisters and sometimes crying out as if in protest, warning away some dark spirit or other that seemed to be plaguing her.

It was difficult for me to fully embrace what I was witnessing at that point. I had no doubt that the gypsies believed wholeheartedly in their endeavours, but as half an hour and more passed by in the same manner I became increasingly of the opinion that I would learn nothing of use from the sisters. That opinion very soon changed.

I remember growing very tired, and rubbing my eyes to keep sleep at bay whilst all the time the whispering and chanting filled my ears. Then I heard another voice join the throng, as if there was someone new joining in the séance. At this I looked up, and could not believe my own eyes. Elsbet sat in her place with her four sisters, between Rosanna and Nadya, illuminated only by the weak candlelight. Her back was to me, but I knew it was her. She wore the bloodied yellow dress in which she had died, and her form seemed to grow from the very shadows, almost absorbing the wan light from the candles. A chill ran through my veins. I rose to my feet and took a tentative step forward, to convince myself that I was awake and not dreaming, and that the apparition was really in the room with us.

The moment I stepped towards the circle of sisters, an icy gush of air was sucked into the tent through the flap behind me, causing me to stop in my tracks. The candles guttered and went out, one by one, leaving only the glowing wicks and a smell of sulphur on the air. The hairs on the back of my neck stood on end, and I glanced over my shoulder as if expecting another spirit to be looming behind me, and was relieved to find nothing but the flap of the tent rustling in the uncanny breeze. Then I heard a whisper cut the air like a knife, and I slowly turned back to the circle.

'We are one.'

The whisper was so familiar, a phrase from my dreams. And all the sisters spoke it, in unison. They had slipped from the land of the living into a realm of shadow; I had not really believed it possible, but at that moment I was convinced of it. Elsbet was still in their midst, her ghostly hands clasped tight around her sisters. Her body, if the word applies, was almost invisible in the darkness of the tent, but her skin seemed to glow with a translucence that transferred itself to the pure white garments of her sisters, making them shimmer in the gloom as if the girls were all phantoms sent to haunt me.

The Irishman stopped scribbling abruptly, and all was silent. As my eye adjusted to the darkness, I saw my breath misting on the unnaturally cold air. I shivered. And then the sisters began to speak—sometimes together, sometimes in turn. They stared straight ahead, blankly and unblinking, focused on something that no ordinary mortal could see.

'We are one. One against the coming storm.'

'We will all be caught in its wrath. There is no escape. It is as certain as the tides.'

'Unless…' This time one voice rang out. It was Drina. 'Unless the dragon comes.'

'He is afraid,' said Rosanna. 'He cannot do the thing that he knows he must. We will be consumed. All will be flames, and the dragon will burn with the rest.'

No.

I could not see the speaker's lips, but I heard the whisper, as soft and chill as winter's first snow, cutting through the other voices and silencing her sisters. It was Elsbet.

He is afraid. He is a child. He is the son of the dragon. But he can succeed where others have failed. He must join us, for without knowledge he is nothing. With the Sight he is our only hope.

As Elsbet's voice left my mind, I realised that I had been transfixed, staring into space like the gypsy girls before me. I did not know how much time had passed, but I blinked myself back to the present, and realised also that the four living sisters were now looking directly at me. The fifth, the shade, still had her back to me, but now the head turned to look over her shoulder. Her dark hair seemed to float out of the way as she moved inexorably slowly, as if she were lying in a deep pool of water. The side of her face came into view—her skin, once dark, was now pale as ivory. I saw her lips, cracked and blue, parted sensually as if she were still in a trance. And then the eyes opened… good Christ, those eyes; wide and black, like the dead eyes of a shark. They flicked upon me, and I could not suppress a murmur of fear. I was paralysed as the spirit beheld me.

In an instant, my mind was filled with such visions as I could not bear. Fires burned; a pair of dragons wheeled and fought in a red sky; a great city—London, perhaps—was host to a grotesque carnival, with men and women cavorting in painted masks while all around them buildings burned; a monstrous spider rose from a burning river, bringing death to everything it touched with its massive legs. Men fought with rifle and bayonet—men of all nations died in droves. And through it all, at the heart of chaos, was a golden arc of light, a portal of such cyclopean magnitude and brilliance that no living thing could approach it—yet through it came a gibbering horde of monsters that were the bane of men, and harbingers of the end of all things. I closed my eyes tight as I wrestled with the painful succession of images, and opened them only when the visions had stopped.

Elsbet was gone. Rosanna and Nadya held out their hands towards me.

'Come,' said Rosanna. 'Join us and see for yourself.'

I could not have been less inclined to sit beside two such pretty girls if I had tried, but I took my place—Elsbet's place—all the same, and linked hands with them.

The whispering began again. The girls rocked back and forth; the Irishman scribbled. At first, I experienced nothing whatsoever, and felt rather foolish. Had I imagined the manifestation? I was certainly over-tired, and the atmosphere of the tent was frowsty and dreamlike. I very soon felt that my foolishness was not my vision, but my scepticism, as Drina shouted out:

'He comes! He who died and has risen again—he comes to destroy our world by fire!'

She had to be referring to Lazarus. I blurted out: 'When? Where?' and received a hard squeeze of my hand from Rosanna.

'He is the old dragon,' Drina continued, in a voice that did not sound like her own. It was deep and guttural, and did not seem to come from her throat at all. I glanced at her, and saw that her eyelids flickered, and behind them her eyes were rolled back showing only bloodshot whites. 'The old dragon is empty inside. He is the destroyer of worlds and the healer of worlds. He has seen his realm burn, and seeks to burn ours and everyone within it. Only the young dragon can stop him, but he does not have the strength. So we are doomed; it is foreseen.'

'It is foreseen,' the other sisters whispered in unison.

I wanted to ask further questions, but there was something

terrible in the aspect of Drina, and I felt that further interruption might either break the spell or do her harm. I had heard too many tales of mesmerism gone awry, or spiritualist trances broken without a thought for the mental well-being of the medium. Whether I fully believed such reports or not, it seemed wrong to test the theory here.

'Our doom is written,' Drina eventually continued, almost in a whisper. 'It comes on a most auspicious day. As the witch-fires die to embers, the dragon will come through the ancient arches, and set the very river awash with fire and death. Beyond that, there is nothing. Only darkness awaits us.'

I felt my spine tingle. The sisters were staring at me—not fully conscious, I think. Then I realised that they were not actually beholding me at all, but were looking through me, or past me. The hairs on the back of my neck stood on end once more, and I am ashamed to say that I was gripped by fear. I battled the funk as best I could, and turned my head to see what they were all looking at. And then I saw the scene from earlier in reverse. I was staring towards the tent door, and standing there was a tall shadow, blurry and indistinct at first.

Where had previously been an empty tent, cast in darkness, there was now a cascade of shimmering, dancing lights, of red, purple and green. As we watched, a pinprick of brilliant white light appeared in the centre of the display, and began to widen in a circle, eating into the rest of the iridescent lights like a burning hole in a piece of paper. As the circle grew bigger, the brilliant white began to fade, until soon the entire vista was like a large window looking upon another place entirely, blurred at first as though we were gazing upon a scene through ill-matched spectacles, but eventually clearing. I rubbed at my eye, and tried to convince myself that I was hallucinating, but I was not. I stood, disengaging from the circle of gypsy girls, and stepped towards the queer image that now filled the tent, as though it had been cut in twain. The image shimmered occasionally, like a pool of water rippling in a breeze, but otherwise it was quite clear, and I was dismayed.

I peered not into a gypsy tent, or even into the Kentish fields beyond, but into a large hospital ward. Upon thirty or more spindly stretchers lay patients, in great distress. I could not hear them, but I could see that they were crying out, or mouthing words with a look of agony etched on their faces. All of them were strapped down, like lunatics; tubes fed into their arms, and most had a mesh of wires attached to their part-shaven heads, running to strange machinery at their bedsides. Nurses ran this way and that to attend to each patient, while men in long white coats stood next to the machines, making notes based on the sequence of flashing lights and twitching needles that perhaps only they could decipher.

My eyes was drawn through the disturbing scene to the patient nearest to me—so near that I felt I could reach out and touch her, though the thought that this 'window' could be a tear in the veil, such as was experienced by William James, prevented me from doing so. The patient, a young girl, was all too familiar. Though her head was shaven and her features drawn and gaunt, I recognised Elsbet at once. A girl of sixteen, imprisoned and experimented upon, screaming in terror at her tormentors. I knew that feeling; it was all too recent in my mind.

And watching over it all, in the centre of the ward with his back to us all, was a figure quite apart from the others. A man dressed all in black, with flint-grey hair poking from beneath a Derby hat. Lazarus. My breath caught as I realised at once what I was looking upon. This was not a tear in the veil; how could it be? I was seeing not the far side of my present location, but some other place entirely, and those upon whom I spied could neither see me, nor the means of my surveillance. Or so I thought.

It began with the girl. Elsbet quietened abruptly, and though her head was restrained, fixed forward by a harsh metal brace, her eyes flicked towards me. The others followed suit; every one of them—psychics all, I assumed—stopped their screaming and struggling, and stared at the corner of the ward at the invisible spy. The incorporeal mirror through which I watched began to ripple more ardently, and finally I saw, with growing dread, the man in black turned to see what had distracted his subjects so. For a moment, his eyes met mine. Lazarus saw me, or felt my presence, I was sure of it. It was then that a sound began to emanate from the mirror—a high-pitched whine. Lazarus squinted, and scowled, and through some inexplicable means I knew we were undone. Over the noise, something else caught my attention; something worse.

All around the spectral image, the shadows flurried and gathered, tendrils of smoke-like blackness forming all around it. I saw—I think I saw—tiny, clawed hands in their hundreds scrabbling at the edges of the ethereal window; at the very edges of reality. I stepped back in terror, as the mirror began to peel away, and myriad tiny eyes peered at me from the space between. Something was ripping its way into our world from another universe entirely; I could feel it, gnawing inside me, screaming in my mind.

We are one.

The cacophony of demonic howls and screeches mingled with the whining sound of Otherside devices, and I understood at last the forces with which we dabbled. The forces that the Othersiders sought to escape.

I turned at once to the sisters, and took Nadya by the shoulders and shook her, though she would not at first be roused. The noise grew louder, reaching fever pitch. Whether it was the sisters' doing, or the psychics from the other side, I felt that the veil was about to tear, with dire consequences.

'Wake them!' I shouted to the Irishman, who stood gawping at the darkness; he saw something too. 'Do it now, for God's sake!'

He hesitated, not sure whether to flee, to resist me, or obey me. Finally, he moved between the girls, shaking them awake while muttering something in a language I could not fathom. The sisters blinked, half-awake; the whining noise subsided instantly. I breathed a sigh of relief, and turned back to find the shimmering mirror gone.

But in its place, standing in the darkness, was Elsbet. Her face, luminescent and dreadfully pale, seemed to loom from the shadows. Her movements were awkward, jerky, and she started to walk towards us, each step like a snapping motion, as though her limbs were not her own. The wraith drew nearer, and I could not take my eyes off it. My morbid terror held me, petrified. The spirit's eyes, black as night, remained fixed on mine during her advance. Soon she stood over me, and her raven-black garb seemed nought but a cloak of mist and shadow, enveloping me, choking the breath from my body. I began to panic, as I felt caught up in a tumult of cloistering darkness and smoke.

With every effort I could muster I stepped towards the phantom, battling all the while against the spectral mist that filled my lungs and clouded my vision.

'Elsbet... I'm so sorry,' I whispered. I felt it most keenly then, the guilt over the girl's death flooded over me.

No sooner had I uttered the words than the ghost was gone. I blinked, dumbfounded, unsure what was happening to me.

You will burn them. You will bring about their destruction. It is foreseen.

It came from behind me, from the circle, and I wheeled about to face it.

Elsbet's dead face was mere inches from my own. Taller in death than she had been in life, and with a ghastly pallor to her skin, it seemed that there was nothing else in the tent, nothing else in the world beyond that terrible visage and the blackness that surrounded us. Her frightful eyes blinked open, revealing once more the dread black orbs. Her lips seemed to creak apart, and a hoarse, rasping sigh rattled from her. Then her head tilted backwards, ever further, revealing a throat cut across by an assassin's blade. Blood spilled from the sickening wound in a hideous torrent, staining the floor crimson. As the blood splashed onto me, the ghoul began to scream like a banshee. I was overcome. My screams and her screams became one, until I passed out, hitting the floor of the tent quite unconscious.

The next thing I remember was Gregor handing me a tin cup full of strong black tea. I was sitting outside the tent, next to a small, crackling fire, with a woollen shawl draped over my shoulders. My head pounded, and I was shivering, though the night was mild. I looked up at the sky, and saw that it grew pale already. Surely I would not see out another dawn! When I asked Gregor what had happened, he gave a heavy shrug of his broad shoulders.

'They ask me to carry you out here. They say you saw something in a vision. They have been in there talking about it for hours.'

'Hours!' I cried, alarmed. I stood up, quite forgetting the cold and my tiredness. 'I must go back inside.' I set down my cup and started towards the tent, then paused, checking back to see if Gregor would stop me. The big man merely turned back to the fire to light a cheap cheroot. Romani customs and taboos were still a mystery to me, but I was encouraged by Gregor's inaction, and so continued on my way. I stopped briefly at the tent-flap, remembering part of the horrid experience I had had in there, before drawing a deep breath and entering.

To my considerable relief, the tent was more brightly lit than earlier. A lamp was burning, along with more candles. The four sisters and the Irishmen sat in the centre of the space, though all signs of the séance had been cleared away. They looked up at me as I entered—the Irishman wore a strange expression, partly deferential and partly afraid, I thought. Could he have seen what I had seen? The thought of it made me shudder.

'You may go now, Donal,' Rosanna said to the youth. 'We thank you for your efforts.' The Irishman bowed his head and walked past me, casting only the minutest glance at me with his small green eyes before leaving the tent.

'I don't know what happened to me,' I said, 'but I pray it

was not in vain. Did you find what we were seeking?' Even as I spoke I saw a sullenness about the girls, a groaning sadness that pervaded the air. Rosanna got to her feet.

'Dear sisters, would you return to the caravan? I must speak to the captain alone.'

The captain? There was something in Rosanna's manner that was not right. Whatever had passed between us during my short time with her seemed dim and distant since the tragedy of the previous night. Was it just grief, I wondered? Her large, dark eyes were fixed upon me, and did not leave me until the last of the sisters had departed the tent.

'You have endangered us all. I knew this would happen, and I knew we had to help you, but this... I do not know if we can assist you further, John Hardwick. Your destiny is changing all the time. It is a dark path that you tread, and it is not a path that my sisters and I can unravel.'

This statement, delivered without her usual passion, left me reeling.

'Rosanna, I don't understand. What did you see? What does it mean?'

'We saw what you saw, and perhaps more besides. We saw the fate of the world in the balance. Fear, war and bloodshed. We saw death and destruction on a scale unimaginable. And you were at the heart of it all, John. What are you involved in?'

'You have the truth of it, I think. England—the world—is about to be threatened by forces that I can barely fathom. Forces so powerful that they just might succeed and spell the end of us all. An army is coming that wishes to conquer all in its path, and I don't know if I can stop it. I needed your help, Rosanna—and your sisters—because this army is not entirely... conventional. God, how can I explain? Let us just say that they have powers not unlike your own, and they use these powers to hide from us until they are ready to strike.'

'The woman who attacked us at the camp... she was one of these invaders?'

'Yes.'

'And she sought to kill me and my sisters to prevent us from helping you?'

'No... I don't believe so. She did not know I was alive until last night, because she thought she had seen me killed back in London.'

'Ah... she is Lillian?' said Rosanna. My heart lurched at the name. How could she have known? She saw my confusion and said: 'You spoke her name many times during your fever. You asked over and over why she had done this thing to you. Was she a lover?'

'Good Christ, no,' I protested. 'It is... complicated.'

'With you, John, I think it always is, and always will be.'

'Please, Rosanna,' I said, 'you must tell me what you saw. Or at least help me to understand. I must know when and where these invaders will strike.'

She reached past me and opened a book. The scrawls within were almost indecipherable to me, though occasionally there was a crude drawing of some resonant thing—a feverish rendering of a dragon silhouetted against a large moon; a ship passing beneath a bridge; a hideous spider with eight sinister eyes staring at me from the page.

'The attack will follow the night of the burning witches. At first we thought the vision spelled our doom, and our distress was such that our sight was clouded for a time. But then we realised that it was a sign.'

'Burning witches? I have heard this before.' I shuddered. What was it that Lillian had said? *A fitting tribute, the burning of witches at the stake as in days of old.*

'Then you should have listened to the signs,' she said. 'The burning of the witches is an auspicious day, known to our German kin as Walpurgisnacht—you call it May Eve. It will happen before the sun rises on May Day, I am sure. And the invaders will come by ship to these lands. It is clear—they will pass by a great bridge, and sail into the heart of a city, where they will kill everyone they can. And you, John Hardwick; you will be there. There will be men with you—some you can trust, and some that you cannot, though you may not know which are which until the end. Does this make sense to you?'

I was transfixed by the revelations. It all made perfect sense, and I knew from my own hellish dreams and the things I had seen during the séance exactly what I needed to do.

'May Day...' I said, distantly. 'There is so little time to prepare. But at least I know where they will strike. I will stop them.'

'But will you stop them, John?' she asked. 'The vision was quite clear—you will hesitate, and you may well fail. There was an army of men in masks, symbolising treachery; people who are not as they appear. And there is a man, like you, who will stop at nothing to destroy us all. You know him, and for some reason you will find it hard to face him.'

'Lazarus...' I said.

'Ah. He who has risen. Yes, this makes sense now. He will oppose you to the bitter end, and the portents suggest that he will succeed. But the future is not written; you could still win, though the odds are stacked against you. Tell me—if this "Lazarus" is to destroy your Empire, and kill us all in the name of his cause, why would you hesitate to kill him?'

'Because... he is my father.'

It was Rosanna's turn to be shocked. And it was the first time I had said it aloud—the first time I had admitted it to myself, and the suddenness of the proclamation was a surprise even to me. The Artist had told me the terrible secret to break my spirit, but I had convinced myself that it was a lie, even though I knew the truth in my heart. And when Lazarus had stepped out of the shadows with the gun in his hand... there was no doubting it. He was my father, and a traitor to the British Empire. I was his son, and this Otherside Lillian was not his daughter.

'Your father...' Rosanna repeated. 'I understand now. And it was your father then who tried to murder you in London? How could any father treat his child so?'

'We never exactly saw eye-to-eye, though I confess shooting me and leaving me to die in the Thames was a somewhat extreme measure. The other side must have offered him something too good to refuse. He was once a servant of the Crown, like me, but he has forsaken his oaths. And, also like me, everyone in London believes him dead.'

'No amount of varnish can hide the grain of the wood...' she muttered absently. 'So you must first return to London and find your allies, I suppose—and then you will stop your father?'

'I'm afraid I don't know who my allies are. The enemy could be anyone. My father was the most pious man I ever knew—not for God, but for Queen and country. If he could be turned... not to mention those agents and spies who have walked in our midst for goodness knows how long... No, my dear, I am afraid I will be without allies until I can work out who I can trust.'

All of Rosanna's portents had pointed to the fact that I would shy from killing Lazarus, and they were right. Regardless of what he had done, and how he had mistreated me, I knew that if there was any way of ending the madness without killing Marcus Hardwick, I would have to find it.

'In the vision, you and he were the same,' Rosanna said, her eyes fixed on me. 'Two sides of the same coin. The sins of the father shall be visited on the son.'

'We are nothing alike! I... I saw him at work, in there—I saw what he does. He was my father once, but now he is a monster.'

'Tell me, what else did you see?' she asked me, her face grave.

'I... what do you mean?' I faltered. 'Did you not see it too?'

'The visions are often different for all of us. But for you—without the Sight—to see something so terrible that it frightened you so... Even Donal was unnerved. What did you see?' She seemed wary.

I told her everything. The hospital, Elsbet, the strange apparatus... Lazarus. She listened, and when I finished, she nodded sagely.

'John Hardwick, you have seen the source of our power.

Somewhere out there, beyond the veil of life and death, are our other selves. From these spirit guides we draw our strength. All of us, all of my sisters, have seen our guides during our visions. And now you have seen Elsbet. Although my little sister is passed, her spirit lives on, and you are the key to everything, John.'

'The key? I don't understand.'

'You can bring Elsbet back. She is trapped in another world, a mirror realm. You have seen her... you know how to travel there, and will do so before the end. You can bring her back to us.'

'Rosanna... it's not like that. This isn't some mirror world of spirits and fairies—this is another world beyond our own. The Elsbet that I saw is not your sister, not really. Elsbet is gone.'

When the slap came, I was wholly unprepared, and my face stung hot.

'Is this how you repay us?' she snapped. 'She appeared to you so that you would save her, so that you would bring her home. We risked everything for you! Elsbet gave her life for you, and—'

I held her arms as the tears came, but she would not be calmed. She pulled away from me and glared at me.

'Rosanna, please... please do not cry. I swear to you I will do all in my power to stop these invaders. And when it is over I will return to you, and I will never again give you cause to shed tears.'

'Bold words, and a promise you will not keep,' she said.

'Rosanna, I tell you again, the girl I saw was not your sister. Please trust me—I know of what I speak. Is not Lillian from the same world?'

'Lillian does not suffer as Elsbet suffers.' She turned her back to me, and gazed into the flame of a candle. On a small table next to her was the book that Donal had been scribbling in throughout the séance. She traced her fingertips across its cover and sighed.

'I will tell you what you need to know. But I do not help you for your sake, for our sakes, or for your Empire. I help you for Elsbet, for revenge... to repay a debt of blood. My people will assist you as much as they can, if I command it, though you must promise not to put them in harm's way.'

'Of course…'

'Swear it,' she said, firmly.

'I swear it, and I accept your offer most thankfully.'

'Very well,' she said. 'There is something more; something else that I must tell you. The fight that is to come is all we were able to see. Win or lose, we could see nothing beyond it—it seems, John, that our fate rests in your hands, for the future of my people is unwritten… This scares me.'

'Do not be afraid.' I moved to kiss her, but she turned away.

'No, John.'

I understood that she was grieving, and I guessed from our earlier conversations that it was not seemly for a Romani woman to cavort with an outsider so soon after meeting, if at all. I think also that she wanted to distance herself from me in case the worst happened—that I might fall in battle, or perhaps even join my father rather than do what was right. I needed her so badly, which seemed foolish to me even then, as I had known her such a short time. I accepted her resolution with as much grace as I could.

'You are right. We have only a few days, and there is much to do.' I turned to leave, but stopped by the opening of the tent. 'I won't let you down, Rosanna,' I said.

Her reply struck me numb.

'Hear me, John Hardwick. My sister lives still, out there, and she is in pain. It is foreseen. I do not care whether you believe it or not. If you do not return with Elsbet, do not return at all.'

I stepped out of the tent, my head hung low.

With relations strained to breaking between Rosanna and I—though I barely understood how they had become so—I took my leave of the gypsy camp the next morning, and headed back to Bluebell Cottage. Rosanna, true to her word, ordered Gregor and a dozen able-bodied men to accompany me, and stay with me until the time came to return to London.

The cottage would not be safe until we had made it so. We made a thorough search of the house and gardens and, satisfied that we were alone, found as many tools as we could and set about dismantling the wall of the kitchen garden, and the ominous blue-painted garden gate. I was almost surprised to find the portal still active, and the gypsies were loath to go near it at first, crossing themselves and spitting in its direction. I knew trying to explain the science of the thing was useless, and was surprised when Gregor stepped in and stirred the men to action.

'Yes, my friends, this thing is bad magic, a gateway to evil, perhaps to the spirit world itself. But our friend John has told us that our enemies used this very door to travel here, and to attack us. They killed Elsbet.' At this he choked back his emotions. 'If we do not destroy this foul thing, who is to say that our enemies will not return? Would you let them come and kill our princesses, like assassins in the night? We men must take action, or we are not men at all!'

With those words, Gregor overcame his own superstitious fear, raised a hammer and smashed it against the lintel of the gateway. Red bricks fell away from tired masonry, and the energy of the portal seemed to lap around the hole like waves filling a rock-pool. I confess I had no idea what would happen if we tore down the wall. Would the energy merely dissipate? Or would it react violently, inflicting injury on us all? Even worse, would the portal remain in place, floating in thin air? Regardless of the answers to these questions, and the inherent dangers of dabbling with such uncanny forces, we followed Gregor's example. We took the door off its hinges, and attacked the archway with picks and hammers. The honeysuckle and ivy was torn from the walls, the dead wood and the new, bringing down cement in powdery clouds as it reluctantly gave up its purchase. Bricks fell to the ground in heaps as we toiled, and with each new breach made in the wall, the portal ebbed and flowed, and let off a frightening noise as though we were wounding it.

Finally, with a tremendous swing of his hammer, Gregor dealt the blow that sent the archway and a good part of the wall toppling to the ground, rendering it nought but a pile of rubble and a cloud of dust. As he did so, there was a blinding flash of light that made us step quickly away. One of the men cried out in alarm; another cursed. And then there was calm.

The sheet of amber light that had fluctuated and writhed beneath the arch now grew dim, turning a deep, luminescent orange, and seeming almost to solidify before our eyes. Then it began to break up, small holes appearing in its surface at first, then larger ones. And each part of the dead portal that gave way shattered into tiny orange fragments, which drifted upwards, spiralling into the sky and scattering on the breeze like the sparks from a bonfire. Up and up they travelled, until there was nothing left of the portal before us and we saw only a gloomy meadow beyond the wall. But in the sky, something was happening. As the trail of tiny sparks began to fade and dissipate, strange colours rippled above us in the air, shimmering fans of purple and gold appeared to us against the darkening sky, as though some heavenly hand had taken a rainbow and smudged it against the grey clouds. A faint rustling noise could be heard, as of wind blowing through reeds, followed by an indistinct whispering like the hollow chattering of distant ghosts. The noises faded almost as soon as they had begun, and as the wondrous colours in the sky grew dim, I stood next to my silent companions, and I remembered William James' tale about the aurora borealis, and the strange events that he had experienced; strange events that had signalled the coming storm, and had perhaps changed the fate of the world.

That night, we sat in the garden around a bonfire. The men had spent too long on the road to feel comfortable in the cottage, and I for one felt disinclined to return to what was once my home.

We formulated plans and strategies for the coming storm, and prepared as best we could for our return to London. There was still time to prepare before May Day, which was only a small mercy. We would have to arrive in the city in the dead of night so that my band of wanted men would be able to go unnoticed. Any policemen we encountered during the hours of darkness were as likely to be Othersiders as friends, so any sway I held over the Metropolitan Police would be of little use. I needed friends in London if the plan was to succeed—I was expecting to face an invasion force, and needed an army to stop them. But there was only one man I could trust for certain, if he were alive at all. I deliberated on that question long and hard, before finally setting pen to paper and sending a lad off to the nearest telegraph office. I prayed that my missive would reach James Denny, and reach him in time.

PART 3

'I have fought for Queen and Faith like a valiant man and true.
I have only done my duty as a man is bound to do.'

ALFRED, LORD TENNYSON

SIXTEEN

I stood in the doorway of the derelict boathouse, looking out across the black waters of the Thames, which refracted the light from the large moon in its gentle ripples. London Bridge loomed over the river, a wispy fog curling around its noble granite arches. The bank of the Thames opposite was almost invisible in the dark and fog, giving the impression that the bridge went on for ever, spanning an endless black gulf that led to who-knows-where, its gaslamps faint smudges painted on a gloomy canvas. It was May Day, and this was the calm before the storm. I drank down the last dregs of a cup of strong coffee and turned back to the boathouse, where my prisoner had stirred again.

'Look here,' he cried in muffled tones through the hessian sack over his head, 'this is a bloody outrage! Do you know who I am? I'll have your heads for this!'

The gypsies stood around the boathouse, stifling laughter at the prisoner's impotent rage—he was tied to a chair and surrounded by men, and was going nowhere. At a nod from me, Gregor removed Ambrose's hood, and my former friend blinked up at me with a look of disbelief on his face.

'John... what the devil? How?'

'Hello Ambrose. I suppose you're surprised to see me alive. Unless, of course, you've seen Lillian recently.'

Ambrose looked uncertain for a moment, but found his composure remarkably quickly.

'John, have you lost your mind? I'm overjoyed to see you alive and well, but what are you doing? Tsun Pen killed our men— we thought he'd done away with you too—and now William Melville is baying for blood. If Special Branch have their way there'll be a war on the streets, and you're here playing silly beggars! Let me go, and we'll go and report to Sir Toby.'

'War on the streets? That is exactly what he will have, though not against the Chinese underworld or Irish anarchists. I know everything, Ambrose,' I said. 'I've learned all I need to know about the Othersiders, about Lazarus and Lillian, and about you.' Ambrose looked more agitated again.

'What are you saying? You believe James' fairy stories? And you think I'm part of it? Listen to yourself, John; it's insane.'

'It does sound that way, doesn't it,' I agreed. 'Your treachery was unexpected, Ambrose. But now everything is clear to me.' I leaned towards Ambrose, revealing my eyepatch to the light. 'The loss of an eye has, if anything, helped me see more clearly than ever.'

'What have they done to you? John...'

'Are you honestly pretending that it wasn't you I encountered on the Embankment, Ambrose? That you didn't assist Lazarus in my attempted murder?'

'I don't know what you're talking about!' he said, desperation gripping him. You've suffered terribly, that is clear, and you've had some great mental strain. But the Artist... the torture, the opium—it's taken its toll on you old chap.'

'I never mentioned torture, or opium, and I doubt it made the papers,' I said, calmly. 'You gave yourself away that night, Ambrose. I tried to persuade myself at first that it wasn't you, that it was your double, but that's impossible.'

'What are you babbling on about?' he snapped. 'It must have been my double. Yes, maybe James was right all along. There's another me in London... What's he done, John?'

'Gregor,' I said, turning to the big gypsy who stood waiting for my orders, 'is this the toff who paid you to take me out of the city?'

Gregor nodded. 'Aye, that's him. Oily fellow.'

'A witness places you at the scene, Ambrose. Hard evidence.'

'But... why would I save you if I was trying to kill you?'

'Guilty conscience, I shouldn't wonder. Perhaps you started to believe that we really were friends. I don't care.'

'John, you can't condemn a chap on the word of a bloody gypsy!'

I turned and picked up Ambrose's cane, unsheathing the concealed blade in front of him, ensuring that the threat was not lost on him.

'In the Artist's lair, Lillian told me some interesting things. She told me how the Othersiders always kill their doubles on our side as a rite of passage, before assuming their identity. You must have killed Ambrose Hanlocke what... six years ago? Seven? That's a long time to keep up such an act. It's made you soft.'

'What poppycock!' Ambrose snorted.

'Captain Denny over here has been busy these last few days. Busy digging into your affairs. It's interesting, don't you think, that you were a go-between for the government and a group of Chinese drug-traffickers on the Isle of Dogs? Jim tells me that you have used your network of Chinese criminals as informants from the underworld ever since. I know you had those thugs assault me after my first night at the club, so that you could "rescue" me and earn my trust. I now know that you left me deliberately in that flat on Commercial Road, probably hoping I'd die in the blast.'

'John... you can't honestly believe that!' he protested, rather half-heartedly, I felt.

'Honestly? An interesting choice of words. Remember when you mocked me, and called me the "last honest man in London"? An unusual jest, and one that I heard again shortly afterwards. Lillian used those exact words when she tortured me and ordered me killed. And judging by your reaction so far, the last you saw of her was when she told you I'd been dumped in the Thames; correct?'

'John, listen; you have it all wrong.'

'You still haven't asked me who Lillian is,' I said. 'But that's because you already know full well.'

'An imaginary friend, for all I know!' he retorted. 'You're not in a fit state for this, John. You're twisting the facts to suit your hypothesis. Let me go... we can go back to the club and sort all of this out like gentlemen. I won't hold it against you, after what you've been through.'

'And I think you know exactly what I've been through. There is one other detail that you got wrong, Ambrose. One little slip... I don't believe you meant it, but I also don't think you expected me to live long enough to press you on the matter. You told me you had met my father, and whether you joined the club four years ago, or six, or seven, it matters not: my father apparently died ten years ago.'

'It was before...' he began to say, desperation finally creeping into his voice.

'No, Ambrose. You and Marcus Hardwick would never have moved in the same circles. And you spoke about my father in rather disparaging terms... if you'd known him before his "demise", you would not have done so. He was a hero.'

'Look, let's say all this is true, why would I do it? Why would I try to destroy the world—a world that lets me live a good life? A normal life.'

I drew the sword fully from its lacquered black sheath, and held its point to Ambrose's chest.

'To save your people from extinction. To claim our world for your own because yours is in a sorry state. And the greatest reason of them all: survival. I don't know if the real Ambrose Hanlocke was as callous and carefree as you, the kind of man who would leave his supposed friend to die in an explosion, or let him meet his doom in an opium den. If he was such a man, then I suppose you play your part well.'

There was silence for a moment. Ambrose's shoulders sagged, and he seemed to grow weary all of a sudden. He looked up at me with a gravity that I had never before seen in him.

'He was worse,' Ambrose said, sounding unlike his usual self. 'He was the greatest cad in England, and I had no qualms about strangling the life out of him and taking everything that was his. I was twice the man he was, and he didn't deserve to be so privileged whilst I was living in a world of nightmares. That's what you want to hear, isn't it? There; you have your bloody confession. Now do what you will—kill me if you must—just end this tedious game.'

'Not just yet, Ambrose,' I said, coldly, sheathing the thin blade again. 'I know that you've been stalling for time; that you're only confessing now because you know it's near dawn, and the war is about to start. But unfortunately for you, I do have some use for you still, and unless you want to look like me when this is done, you'd better start toeing the line... "old chap".'

Darkness crossed Ambrose's features.

'You're a bloody fool!' he snarled. 'When Lazarus comes, this river is going to run red with the blood of the fine people of London, and what are you doing? You're skulking in this rat-hole with a bunch of stinking gypsies. There's a fleet on the other side of the veil, couching at the door like the very hounds of hell, and there's sod all you can do to stop them!'

'There's the Ambrose I've come to know—showing your true colours at last. But I wouldn't be sure about any of that. What do you think, Captain Denny?' I turned towards the open doors of the boathouse as I said this, and Jim stepped into view, cutting a lean figure amidst the wispy morning mist.

'I think that in less than half an hour I'll have twenty naval guns on the north bank, and a hundred marines ready to board any vessel that puts out in this river. Sir.' He addressed me as his superior, purely for Ambrose's benefit.

'This is beyond the pale!' snapped Ambrose. 'Have you

learned nothing, John? Why, even I don't know all of the agents infiltrating this city. If he's gone out of his way to earn your trust, he's probably as crooked as they come. Why trust him and not me?'

I did not wish to play my hand completely; I wanted Ambrose to squirm. And so I did not mention that I had already killed Jim's double. Instead, I leaned close to Ambrose, face to face with my betrayer, and I set my features as hard as stone. 'If for no other reason than because he's a captain in Her Majesty's Army, Mr. Hanlocke. Service before country; country before Queen; Queen before God.'

Ambrose looked at me with incredulity. 'You really are the greatest fool I've ever met. Do you think your dear father gave a monkey's about the army when he came over to our side? When he abandoned you? Do you think he'll hesitate when he has to kill you? Because I'm bloody certain you won't have it in you to kill him.'

'My father,' I yelled in Ambrose's face, 'is a traitor, and I'm damned if I'll follow his example. I know full well that he is the key to this invasion. I want to see him stand trial for what he's done; and I'll gladly see him hang.'

'Oh, I'm afraid you'll have to do better than that,' he said, sardonically. 'While Lazarus lives, we have hope. The power required to open the Lazarus Gate is immense—enough to shut down all of London twice over, I'd wager—but they won't stop trying just so you can put their most valuable asset on trial. The best scientists of my world have transformed London Bridge into the greatest electrical conductor ever devised. His Majesty has assembled a fleet of shallow-draught vessels from all over the world, capable of bringing your London to its knees in a matter of hours. It took years to persuade Lazarus to defect, and to build these devices. These are not the actions of despots and conquerors; these are the actions of desperate people whose world is about to crumble. This is our final throw of the dice, and Lazarus is the key. They can keep the portal going as long as his heart beats, and they will stop at nothing to escape into this world.'

'Escape?' Jim interjected. 'You make them sound like refugees, and yet they act like warmongers.'

'We *are* refugees! Have you any idea of what's happening on the other side, right now? The gates of hell are open. Demons cavort in the streets; blood rains from the skies, and the dead do not rest easy in their graves. Entire cities have seceded from the Empire, ruled by degenerates who feast on human blood. People die in their thousands every day, and every resource we have is geared towards holding the devil at bay. At least, it was until your father turned. Now we've let fire and blood wash the streets of every city in the civilised world while we prepare to make this one our new home.'

'You speak of this act as though it is understandable— forgivable even!' I replied. 'And yet you plan nothing short of genocide. Did none of your kind try to find a peaceful solution? Or did you not stop to think that a people who could fall so far deserve to be damned?'

Ambrose looked stung by this reproach, and hung his head.

'There is no peaceful solution. How could there be? Could millions of wretches really cross over to this world seeking asylum, especially as they are all doubles of people already here, living or dead? No, John—the powers that be have long since set their minds to this course of action, and today it all comes to fruition.'

'Unless I kill my father. Why? Why does he have to die, Ambrose?'

He looked at me forlornly, and I wondered then if this trickster could have some genuine feelings of comradeship for me.

'You know of the devices that we all carry within our bodies— the devices that return our mortal remains posthumously to our own world? Well, they are located near our hearts. I said that we still have hope whilst Lazarus' heart beats, and I meant it quite literally. The device that he carries is… unique. It helps to form the bridge between our worlds, making it a more stable passage that can support travel in both directions. In fact, it has allowed even our normal gateways to remain open for longer periods than ever before—perhaps even indefinitely. When he dies, the gates that have sustained our presence in this universe for so long will close. We have to pray that, at the very least, the invasion is successful before we lose him.'

'If he is so vital to your plans, why place him on the front line? My father should know better than that.'

'He has no choice, John. He has to be with the first wave in order to give the gate the best chance of working. Just as he has had to return here regularly over the past few years.'

'I don't understand,' I said.

'Nor do I,' Jim echoed. The blank looks on the faces of the gypsies indicated that they hadn't understood anything at all that had been said so far.

'Look,' said Ambrose, with a defeatist air, 'I am no scientist. I've been here so long that my knowledge may not even be up to date. But it was explained to me thus: every living thing has a resonance, a pitch, like a tuning fork. You can't hear it—no one can—but it's there all the same. Things on this side resonate differently from things in my universe, and the two have a hard time coexisting. It's as though the universe recognises invaders, and tries to push them out—only if it succeeds in doing so, the results are rather messy for the traveller. Short visits are fairly easy, but longer trips, well... they need a locus, something to stabilise the frequency. Do you follow at all?'

'Partly,' I said. It was outlandish, and I began to realise the genius of the Othersiders. After all, if Ambrose Hanlocke could grasp such recondite theories, then everyone on their side must be at least as devilishly clever. But of course, I was forgetting that the Ambrose I thought I knew was merely the part of an accomplished actor. 'Please go on... at least humour me.'

'Very well. When your father defected to our side, he was implanted with a device similar to the one that all of us carry.

The devices ease our passing and prolong our stay by tuning our frequencies partway towards yours, and for Marcus Hardwick it was essential in order for him to remain in our universe. However, your father is different. Our scientists discovered that the longer he spent in this universe with his new implant, the longer all of our gates remained stable. This was the discovery that ultimately led to the Lazarus Gate. Perhaps he is unique—he's the only true defector from your side ever to cross the veil, so we'll never know. But in any case, he has somehow helped to disguise our presence in this world from the natural forces that seek to expel us. This universe treated us as foreign bodies—a virus, I suppose—but no longer. Lazarus is our Trojan horse, and today is the time of our *coup de grâce*.'

I turned to Jim, who had taken out his pocket-watch. He nodded to me.

'And the time is imminent, it would seem,' I said.

Ambrose glared at me.

'Don't look so surprised, Ambrose, it's not only your kind who can be one step ahead. As soon as I discovered the date and place, and that the invasion would be a naval one, it was obvious that it would have to begin at low tide. London Bridge was not designed with large vessels in mind. So, I believe 3 a.m. is the optimum time for Lazarus to strike.'

'Very clever, John,' Ambrose said. 'But you don't seem terribly well prepared. I suppose there aren't many people you can trust. I wonder if any of Captain Denny's soldiers are actually agents from my side? Even I wouldn't know for sure. That is the gift that your father has given us—the ability to infiltrate your world with impunity.'

'Those men are hand-picked,' snapped Jim.

'So was I,' sneered Hanlocke. 'By Sir Toby Fitzwilliam, no less. We can all be poor judges of character—I mean, look at the company John is keeping these days.'

'Please Ambrose, be civil,' I said. 'Gregor needs little enough invitation to snap your neck, after what your fellows did to his people. Your friend Lillian killed a gypsy princess in front of us both—it has given us common cause.'

He thought about that for a second before replying: 'Lillian Hardwick is hardly my friend. I barely know the girl, save that she is Lazarus' right hand. She came from nowhere, promoted by virtue of being the daughter that Lazarus thought he'd lost, all those years ago.'

'If my sister had survived in this world, I would have recognised her sooner, when I first laid eyes on her at Commercial Road.'

'Good Lord...' he said. 'I didn't even know she was the one. God's own truth, John—I received the order to flee the building. I caught only the briefest glimpse of the agents.'

'They seem to keep you in the dark quite a bit, Ambrose. Perhaps you aren't so important to their plans after all,' I said, hoping to rile him.

'I never was, John. I am one of many agents sent to live among you. My reports are doubtless useful, but my fate is inconsequential to the greater mission. Information is one-way; no one tells me anything in case...' He paused.

'In case you find yourself too deep in the mire? In case you start to feel at home on this side of the veil, and decide that you'd like a cosier life, away from the dangers of "hell"? Is that it?' I prompted him.

'Something like that,' he replied, quietly. He looked down, ruefully. Perhaps I had hit the nail on the head.

'Ambrose... you have been surprisingly forthcoming with information. I thought I'd need to be more... persuasive. I hope you haven't been feeding us more lies.'

'Believe what you will, John,' Ambrose said, wearily. 'Truth be told I'm tired of it all. I knew the time of the invasion was near, but didn't know when exactly until you dragged me down here. I felt relief—I've been too long living this lie; living like him. Would you believe that I was nothing like the Ambrose Hanlocke from your world before I took on this role and now... now I cannot work out where he ends and I begin. I promise you, John, I haven't lied to you. It's just that your efforts will be in vain—there's no point pretending otherwise. I wish it wasn't so; there are good people in this world who are about to die. If there was another way I would take it. But the decision does not rest with me; it never has. I can change nothing. Why don't you run along and try to save the world, and leave me be.'

'Ambrose, I... Look, why don't you help us? You can still be of consequence, and you can save millions of lives.'

'No, John, I can't. Nor can you. You're merely trying to postpone the inevitable.'

'John, we need to get moving,' said Jim. 'Not long to go.'

I instructed Gregor to pick one of his men to stand guard over Ambrose, and the rest of us went outside and began to make our way to the bridge. In the early hours of the morning, even the great metropolis was calm and still, and it was hard to imagine what chaos was to come into the world, as if from nowhere. Even as I reflected on that, a low tolling bell could be heard sounding off in the distance, marking the hour.

'Three o'clock,' said Jim. 'If your theory is right, all hell should be breaking loose right about now.'

We made our way to the water's edge, in the shadow of the great bridge, where a skiff was waiting for us. Six armed men crewed the boat, and I eyed them warily—Ambrose had given me enough suspicion of my fellow man to last me a lifetime. However, if I could not trust these men then what hope was there? We were few in number and the danger was great indeed. I instructed Gregor to take the other gypsies up the wide stone stair of London Bridge and position themselves above us in the many parapets of the bridge's piers. They had been given rifles, and I thought it best that they fight at a distance; I had promised Rosanna, after all, that I would take no unnecessary risks with their lives. A band of armed gypsies was not easily concealed in London, so Jim had taken precautions. The local beat bobbies had been paid to keep their distance, and soldiers stood on every street corner nearby, disguised as civilians, ready to turn back anyone who tried to access the bridge. There were not enough of us to fight a war, but there were enough to board the first vessel to appear, and hopefully to end the battle before it even began. I wondered if Sir Toby had heard of the operation yet, and what he would think of my actions in circumventing Apollo Lycea in favour of the army. I imagined he would take a dim view, and I did not relish my next meeting with him, should I survive the night.

We stepped into the boat, and the oarsmen took up positions, ready to push off. Before that moment, the very idea that the Lazarus Gate would open and a force of invading soldiers from another world would appear before us seemed unreal—an impossible fantasy that had somehow taken root in my mind and driven me to delusion. But if I had any doubts as to the very real danger posed by the Othersiders, they were instantly obliterated, for no sooner had we taken up our positions than a series of strange phenomena began to manifest, heralding the start of the battle. We found that our sense of hearing was dulled, and an unbearable pressure rose in our ears, causing each man to put his hands to his ears and exercise his jaw. Some of the men nearby groaned as the pressure caused their heads to ache. All around us, the darkness seemed cloying as the very air appeared to thicken. The inky black water beneath our little boat that had previously seemed so gentle now appeared as a ponderous swell, as though the entire river was composed of glutinous oil.

Just as the atmosphere became unbearable, the fearful high-pitched humming began. It had been there all along, I think, almost inaudible, but now it rose in pitch and intensity, signalling some great rent in the fabric of our universe. With my hands over my ears, I turned to look at the shadow-shrouded archways of London Bridge. Fine lines of crackling energy were cascading from the apex of each arch, following the curve of the brickwork and fizzling out in the water, like sparkling dynamite fuses. More and more trails of sparks crawled down the masonry, until the underside of each arch was illuminated by their radiance. The trilling noise intensified further, and I heard men cry out along the riverbanks, and on the parapets above us, as the pain in their heads began to overcome them. And then it happened.

A flash of brilliant light made us all turn our heads away from the bridge. When the light faded, the noise and pain had stopped, and there was a moment of utter calm. The moment that had seemed to last an age had finally passed, and the splashing sound of river water around our boat was once again natural. I turned back to the bridge, and was struck with awe and wonder. Each of the five arches was now filled with a sheet of soft light, like huge windows of amber-glass. Where the light touched the surface of the river, the water steamed and the otherwise smooth veil of light rippled at its touch. A soft yellow glow reflected off the waves of the Thames, like the delicate light of an autumn moon. The last time I had seen a portal to the other world, it had been like a mirror, reflecting our own world back at me. This one, however, was translucent; shadows flitted and darted behind it. It was as though we were peering through yellowed gossamer into a long-forgotten and mysterious realm beyond. The sense of wonder from everyone assembled was palpable— but that wonder very quickly turned to dread.

A great shadow, darker than the rest, appeared at the central arch, the largest of the five. A part of the shadow made contact with the portal from the other side, causing a bright, coruscating light to flare around the foreign object. It was the bowsprit of a vessel, which was slowly pushing its way through to our world in a blasphemous birth. It took some moments before the prow of the ship loomed into view—part thrust into our world, and the rest in shadow. Energy crackled and raged around every inch of the ship; this was a vessel of war, born unto violence, and I saw that it was not alone as the shadows behind the other arches grew darker and loomed larger. The time for action had come.

Our boat had barely carried us into position near the central arch when the gunfire began. At least twelve yards of prow had pushed into our world, and the gypsies up on the bridge had caught sight of the first enemy sailors to come through with it. The Othersiders were at their most vulnerable, for they could not make a ship battle-ready until it was all the way through the portal and they had a true sight of their targets. Jim had instructed his men on the banks of the river not to fire upon the first ship that came through, for that was the vessel we intended to board. However, the gypsies and the few soldiers on the parapets above were there to clear the decks so that we could climb aboard and find Lazarus. Only then would this nightmare be at an end.

As the reports of the rifles grew more infrequent, we asserted that the advance guard must have ducked for cover or retreated back though the portal, leaving us clear to send up our grapples and begin the climb to the deck. I had not thought through the difficulties of such a climb with a wounded shoulder, and I was by far the slowest man up the ropes. Thankfully, the need to answer the call to action was greater than my frailties, and I soldiered on, finally heaving myself over the gunwale in time to see Jim and his men taking up firing positions on our portion of the deck. The prow of the ship was bereft of hatches as far as I could see, so we knew we would have to fight our way along the length of the vessel to get to my father. The ship was a flush-decker, and there was little cover, so we hunkered down behind the anchor machinery in the centre of the deck. Through the amber portal we could see indistinct shapes running to-and-fro, and I was certain that the Othersiders could see us as similar shades. They had numbers on their side, and we could not tarry long before they plucked up the courage to come at us again. I said as much to Jim, who nodded grimly and snapped orders to his men. The ship was creeping further and further into our world, and the central structure, which was probably the command bridge, was looming closer. We could see the indistinct figures of men assembling in the walkways on either side. Would Lazarus be amongst them?

Would he have made it so easy for us?

Four of Jim's men fanned out, making for opposite sides of the ship so as to guard against attacks from either of the walkways. Two large howitzers, one positioned on either side of the foredeck, were slowly revealed as the ironclad ship groaned and creaked into existence. The crews of the guns scurried back to their own side of the veil as soon as they were met with gunfire from above and afore, and the guns provided our men with invaluable steel-plated cover. The other two men remained at the anchor crank, ready to cover our advance. As soon as the command bridge came into view, Jim and I planned to run to it whilst the men on either flank took care of the enemy. Before long, the crackling energy that signalled the emergence of some foreign object began to dance around the great block of dark iron, and the armour-plated frontage of the ship's control tower loomed over us, its tiny windows too high to reach, and with no signs of ingress. Despite the rather daunting appearance of the vessel, Jim and I stuck to the plan, and raced to the foot of the iron wall. No sooner had we reached it than the first wave of enemy marines came through the portal—hard-bitten men brandishing rifles. The first man from each side of the ship fell instantly, and only one marine managed to return fire rather ineffectively before the marksmen on the parapets of London Bridge fired down upon them. The crossfire was brutal, and the marines fell over each other to scramble back beyond the portal. I was just beginning to wonder if it was even possible to fire a weapon though the shimmering gateway when my question was answered—a bullet ripped through the veil and slammed home against the arm of one of Jim's men. There had been no gunshot, only a flare of white light as the gateway resisted the projectile for but the briefest moment.

This action sparked the most terrifying engagement, as the men on both sides, both buoyed and panicked by the fact that the veil offered no real protection, began to fire wildly at the obscure shadows beyond. The deck of the ship was lit by dazzling flashes of light as bullets ripped through the air, ricocheting off iron rails, embedding themselves in wooden decking, and only occasionally drawing blood from a combatant. The orderly conduct of our men was soon dashed, and it became every man for himself. We realised that we could not hold our position, and Jim was first to react, barking orders at some men to cover the port side, whilst ordering all of the others to fix bayonets and prepare to enter melee on the starboard. The prospect was not a thrilling one, but I drew my pistol, gritted my teeth, and prepared to charge.

'Are you sure this is safe?' yelled Jim.

'As sure as I can be,' I replied.

'Then let's go. For Queen and country and all that!'

And just like that, we threw ourselves through the portal.

It was the strangest sensation I have ever felt. Rather than pass through a veil of energy in the blink of an eye as I had expected, we had to push our way through the membranous portal, which took on the consistency of treacle. Time itself seemed to flow slowly, and for a horrible moment we were trapped like flies in amber. I remember panicking that perhaps we weren't meant to cross; I could not see Jim even though he had been right next to me, and I could hear nothing but strange, muffled echoes, and the sound of my own blood rushing in my ears. Just as I thought that it was the end of the road, that perhaps I would die trapped between the worlds, or be turned inside out when we reached the other side, we emerged in a flash of light, gasping for air and plunged into a fight for our lives.

A bullet zipped past me, tearing my coat and rippling into the portal, causing me to discharge my pistol instinctively into the group of enemy sailors who faced us. I put down one of them for certain, and put the fear of God into several others before they fell upon us with rifle butts and bill-hooks. I fell to the ground, and fired again, catching an assailant in the chest. The buck-toothed man gasped his last breath and fell on top of me, pinning me to the ground. I looked around in desperation, feeling warm blood ooze onto me and hoping that it was not my own. Jim had been hit in the arm by the opening volley, and had dropped to one knee, battling manfully with his sabre against three men who were pressing towards him. The ship was no larger than a frigate, and the gangway that faced us was only a few yards wide, which prevented our enemies from outnumbering us too severely—and yet they were proving equal to the task of overcoming our rather weak assault, so shaken as we were by the passage between the worlds.

Just as I thought we were done for, two of Jim's men found their courage and charged through the portal. One of them, a big, broken-nosed man, held his rifle across himself and pushed over two Otherside sailors like ninepins; the other man, a wiry sort with a large, puckered scar on his right cheek, skewered an adversary with his bayonet. In the confusion, I managed to heave the dead man off me and stagger to my feet, hauling Jim up too. Our men took up firing positions near a bulkhead and cleared our path with expert precision, and in the brief respite we took stock of our surroundings. We were in the shadow of the central arch of London Bridge. The ceiling of the bridge above us was covered in pipes and bundles of cables, which sparked periodically as they conducted huge amounts of electricity between the arches. It seemed that the whole structure had been transformed into some gigantic, diabolical science experiment. The masts and spars of the ship, though not as tall as one would find on a conventional Navy vessel, almost scraped the inner archway, and tiny streaks of lightning darted betwixt spar and cable. It had been the old waterman, Grimes, who had mentioned the Thames tides to me, and by my reckoning the tide was now at its lowest; even so, the shallow-draught warship could only just scrape under the bridge. Looking along the length of the vessel, the walkway opened out onto a long, flush deck, with compact smokestacks dotted along its centre line. Howitzers lined the ship's deck—I counted eight on each side of the vessel—and amidst the smoke and steam we could discern dozens more sailors running to and fro.

Without a word from us, the smaller of the two marines opened the bulkhead door beside him, and before we could stop him he had lit a stick of dynamite, thrown it inside and closed the door behind it. There was a loud *bang*, followed by muffled cries.

'What are you doing?' I yelled. 'We're here to find their commander!'

The man shrugged. 'Orders is to kill him,' he said, by way of explanation.

I shot a glance at Jim, who likewise shrugged, and I realised that he was right. By fair means or foul, we were there to assassinate Lazarus.

'Well then,' I said, 'just you be careful with that dynamite; it's not known for its stability.'

'Best not ask where he got it,' Jim interjected, with a wry smile.

Jim issued orders to his men to secure the aft portion of the walkway, and defend it against the marines who would surely join the fight any second. We moved along the walkway behind them, forced somewhat by the portal, which crept up behind us inch by inch as the ironclad continued its slow progress. The bulkhead was soon half-swallowed up by coruscating light, but that was no longer our prime concern. A few yards ahead was a stair rail, leading up to the bridge. Jim and I would have to brave it whilst the sailors below covered our ascent.

Jim went first up the steep steel-shod steps, while I struggled up behind him. He had given me no time to volunteer to go ahead, even though his injury meant he'd had to sheathe his sabre in order to make the climb. The first I knew that there were enemy marines in our path was when one came flying over the rail above, almost knocking me down the stairs. Jim had virtually run into the fellow as he reached the upper platform, and had heaved the man over his shoulder and sent him crashing to the deck below. I gritted my teeth, wincing at the thought of having to fight on with my own injuries, and raced up the stairway as fast as I was able. At the top was a platform, and a doorway to the bridge, but there was no further time to assess the situation. Jim was even then engaged in a brawl with another marine, whilst a second was racing at him with a naval axe at the ready. I drew my pistol and snapped off a round, taking the man in the side and sending him spinning away. Jim had by then bested his man, and kicked him down the stairway opposite, where he collided with his onrushing accomplices.

Jim indicated the door next to him, and we did not pause before flinging it open and rushing inside. Most of the bridge section had now passed further towards the portal, and as we entered the room we saw a sheet of shimmering light bisecting it; the glowing amber window between worlds seemingly could not be obstructed even by walls of iron. The ship's captain stood by the wheel, wrestling with it as the portal enveloped him. Flanking him were two midshipmen, who turned with a start as Jim and I made our presence known. One tried to stop us, but Jim hit the man full in the stomach and shoved him aside, before drawing his sabre and pointing it at the second sailor, who threw up his arms in surrender. Jim threw the man from the room and fastened the door tight shut. By then the captain had sunk into the portal, with just a man-shaped outline of tiny dancing sparks to account for his whereabouts. I girded myself and leapt through after him, hoping upon hope that the gate would allow me to cross back and forth an unlimited number of times.

Again, I was plunged into that strange half-world, and my arms drove forwards with great difficulty against the sheer 'thickness' of the air around me, until I caught hold of the captain's shoulders. In a trice we were both on the other side of the veil, and the captain cried out in alarm—he was clearly new to the sensation of traversing between the worlds and was now as disorientated as I had been; added to that, I was dragging him from the ship's wheel, and he must have thought that the very hounds of hell were pulling him back to where he belonged. I wrested him from the wheel and threw him across the bridge. He clattered into a metal desk, sending charts and ledgers scattering across the floor. I pulled out my revolver and held it to the man's head.

'Lazarus,' I snarled. 'Where is Lazarus?'

'Who are you? What are you doing?' he said, pathetically. He looked a man of experience rather than a green sailor, but I doubted he had ever seen real fighting, man-to-man.

Before I could say more, Jim appeared behind me, through the portal.

'The ship's picking up a bit of speed,' he said. 'No time to waste; best kill this wretch and move on.'

Taking Jim's cue, I cocked the revolver and nodded grimly. The ruse was enough; the captain, whose brow was soaked in nervous sweat, broke down.

'Please, no! I'll tell you what you need to know—but it won't do you any good. Lazarus is in his cabin, aft. But you'll never get past the marines.'

'Thank you, you've been most cooperative,' I said, pistol-whipping the man unconscious. I imagined at worst he'd wake up with a headache, though what fate would await him in his own world should we succeed was anyone's guess.

'He may be right,' said Jim. 'We've managed to gain ground, but the ship is under propulsion and is coming through whether we like it or not. And if Lazarus is well guarded… this could be suicide, John.'

'True, but duty calls,' I said, determinedly. 'And besides, I think we can create a little distraction whilst we're here.'

I took hold of the ship's wheel, and with all my might turned it as far as it would go to port, and then grappled with it as it spun back, and took it all the way to starboard. Jim cried out protestations, but was too late—the ship swayed to the left and we heard a terrible scraping sound as the ironclad hull met the solid stone buttresses of the bridge; then the whole vessel lurched violently, heeling to starboard.

We steadied ourselves and looked out of the fore windows. The sky in our London had turned a pale orange colour, making the cityscape a series of smudged, black silhouettes as the lingering fog slowly relinquished its grip on the capital. It was a second of serenity, quickly shattered by the sound of cannonades. The naval guns on the shore had opened fire at Lazarus' flagship, and as the first shell hit the prow the entire ship trembled. I had a feeling that the armoured behemoth was designed to take a pounding, but it still made me feel better knowing that the guns were there.

'What the devil are they doing?' asked Jim, incredulously. 'They have orders not to fire until the second ship is sighted.'

'I imagine they're panicking,' I replied. 'And who can blame them? Come on, Jim—let's not stay here to get blasted apart by your guns. We have work to do.'

And with that, we plunged once more into the breach, emerging back on the other side in the control room that was shrinking in size, inch by inch, as the ship crept through the portal. We paused, realising that the only way out was through the door that Jim had barred, and that there were probably armed enemies on the other side of it. Our fears were quelled, however, by the sounds of pounding on the bulkhead door, followed by a cry of: 'Sir! It's Vickers, sir. We've secured the bridge, and the reinforcements have arrived.'

We flung open the door, and saw Vickers, the big soldier, standing before us in the shadow of the bridge. The sounds of battle were all around us, and Jim complained to his man that the reinforcements had come too early.

'We're showing all of our hand,' he said, 'and the enemy will make us pay for it. Who gave them the order?'

'Dunno sir. Sorry sir,' Vickers replied.

'Don't look a gift horse in the mouth,' I interjected, and jollied Captain Denny along. Lazarus had to be found quickly if we were to put a stop to the madness. If the other enemy vessels broke through, we would not have enough men on alert to stop the invasion.

We rushed down the stairs onto the main deck, where men were engaged in vicious firefights and hand-to-hand combat. Some of Jim's soldiers were hunkered behind the gunwales, exchanging fire with sailors from the other ships off to either side. Their efforts were ineffective given the range, but I admired their enthusiasm, and it seemed as though we were winning the fight for the deck.

Seeing an opportunity, I raced towards the centre of the deck, pistol drawn, finally escaping the clutches of London Bridge's dark shadow and emerging into the red light of dawn. But as I glanced about me, I saw that it was not dawn that greeted me, but a vision of such dizzying terror that I can barely put it into words even now.

For the first time I saw daylight on the other side, but it was no natural atmosphere. In the other world, the sky was afire, a swirling tumult of liquid flame that hung in the air in place of clouds. The Thames stretched out beneath it, reflecting orange fire in every ripple, and much wider than in our own world. Beyond the bounds of Southwark, it seemed that acres of city had fallen away as if eroded by the river, or perhaps spirited away into some other realm, some other hellish universe that craved the desolation of the Othersiders' world. In that widening stretch of scarlet waterway, the invasion fleet was assembled—not one ship for each of the arches of London Bridge, but a flotilla of a size not seen since the Armada. Hundreds of ships, boats and skiffs filled the Thames, flying the colours of a dozen great nations. They waited like a pack of hounds for the orders of their huntmaster: the herald of our doom that Lazarus represented. The city itself was dark and satanic, with towering spires and structures dwarfing even the familiar features of St Pauls, and gigantic chimneys pouring thick smoke into the burning sky. Other black shapes flitted and floated in the air above those forbidding structures, like swarms of huge flies buzzing over a midden heap that, even here, had surely once been the jewel in the Empire's crown. Some of those airborne specks were familiar—

dirigibles and balloons, or else clearly of human design—and yet others seemed alien, jerking about the sky spouting jets of steam and fire. Even those dire creations of men paled in comparison, however, to the flying Things that swooped and soared upon the flaming thermals on great membranous wings. That sight, observed in but an instant, was dizzying and terrible, but I could have coped with the madness of it all had I not then seen the abomination that presided over it all. Above the horizon was a cyclopean black form, cast against the roiling tempest of fire like an obscene shadow-play of unimaginable scale. It seemed at first like a huge, clawed hand, flexing towards the pale, muted sun, but it was nothing so... human. It was an indistinct form, sometimes solid and black as night, sometimes as intangible as smoke; a tangle of writhing tentacles and claws that scraped at the heavens, holding all of this Other London in its thrall. I do not know what it was, nor what force had unleashed it upon the Othersiders' world; all I know is that I was struck most horribly by the fearful sight of it, stricken momentarily mad at the thought of such powers in the universe. The longer my gaze lingered upon it, the more I convinced myself that I could hear it—or, rather, feel it—whispering and scratching; scratching in my mind. I closed my eye tight, but that only seemed to make the hideous noise louder, as if inhuman fingers were probing within my skull.

A heavy shove brought me to my senses. Vickers had pushed me to the deck, and as I looked up I saw him punch an Otherside marine square on the jaw, knocking the man over with one terrific blow. Vickers extended his hand, and I took it gratefully and let him heave me to my feet.

'That fella nearly done for you, sir. You'd do well to keep your good eye open, if you don't mind me saying.'

'Not at all, Vickers, thank you,' I said, dusting myself down. I looked around, averting my gaze from the terrible sights of the city beyond, though I knew they were there still from the cold creep at the back of my neck. 'Where is Captain Denny?' I asked.

Vickers gave a shrug. 'Went on ahead, I s'pose.'

'Then there's not a second to lose. Come on, man!'

And with that we raced towards the cabins at the rear of the vessel, dodging clumsy attacks and swirling melees as bullets whipped past us. We passed the next smokestack, and were momentarily obstructed by an enemy marine who was as surprised to see us bearing down on him as we were to see him. Vickers did not stop, but instead shoulder-barged the man, flattening him on the lime-washed deck. We did not pause—judging by the number of friendly soldiers who had already forced their way this far along the ship, the man would have enough on his plate without pursuing us. The fighting raged around the chimneys, around the howitzers and winches. Our numbers were fewer, but the Othersiders were not expecting to fight on board their own vessel, and I imagined that the troop transports were elsewhere in the flotilla. The other ships in the invasion fleet had stayed their course, and were not advancing through the portals; I could only assume that they had to be certain of Lazarus' presence on the other side before they dared cross in numbers. Likewise, I had to be sure that he never set foot on our side of the veil again. But something gnawed at me. Jim had been dismayed that his men had disobeyed his orders, even though their actions had benefitted us, and now he was missing. What had Ambrose said? 'Even I don't know all of the agents infiltrating this city. Why trust him and not me?' Could he be one of them? I shuddered at the thought, and prayed it would not turn out so.

As Vickers and I reached the door to the officers' quarters, the ship heeled again, lolling to starboard. A tremendous clanging noise resonated across the metal hull of the ship. I looked out across the river, thinking at first that the Othersiders were firing upon their own ship, but they were not, of course.

'Them's our guns, sir,' said Vickers. 'Reckon they'll sink this tub soon enough.'

It certainly seemed as if the big man was right. However, I

also saw with dismay that the ship to our port side had begun to load its launches with marines, undoubtedly to send across and liberate the ship we were on. I did not know if the sound of guns in my own London would have brought further reinforcements, but if it did not then we certainly had insufficient men for the task of holding the ironclad. With this as motivation, I flung open the door to the officers' quarters and went inside, with Vickers in tow.

We found ourselves in a cramped corridor, with wide-open bulkhead doors off to left and right, and another at the end. Through each of the side doors were flights of steel-shod stairs, and the faint thrum of machinery suggested that they led to the engine rooms and, most likely, the crew quarters. I had spent a long time aboard various ships, and knew the ship's mess and captain's cabin would be straight on. I made for the door ahead of us, but was distracted by Vickers as he made a pained 'Oomph!' I spun around in time to see that a marine had clubbed Vickers across the shoulders with a rifle, though the big man miraculously kept his feet. Vickers turned with surprising speed, and began to wrestle the gun from the grasp of his attacker. He spared a moment to look over his shoulder and shout to me: 'You go on, sir; I'll handle this.' As Vickers proceeded to push his assailant back out of the door, I made yet again for the bulkhead door at the end of the corridor, which was invitingly ajar.

With my gun drawn, I pushed the door open slowly, but was betrayed by its horrendous creaking. The room within was gloomy and quiet, and the sounds of combat outside were so muffled that they might as well have been a mile away. I stepped cautiously into the room, which ran almost the width of the ship, with a dining table taking up most of its length. The drapes on either side were drawn. I was about to dismiss the mess as empty and continue across to the captain's cabin when a voice made me freeze.

'It's about time—I thought I would be waiting until hell froze over for you to arrive... brother.'

I turned on my heels to face the threat. There was no mistaking

Lillian's voice; so cold, cruel and mocking, but still melodic and wanton. There she was, sitting at the head of the mess table, her feet up on the boards showing her long legs and stiletto-heeled boots. How I had not seen her when I first scanned the room I could not fathom, for her white face shone in the gloom like moonlight shining on porcelain.

'Where is your father?' I growled.

'You mean *our* father, John. He's through that door,' she replied, nodding her head towards the bulkhead door on the other side of the table. 'But of course, you won't get an audience with the great man this time. You'll just have to settle for me.'

I kept my pistol trained on her.

'You make a poor substitute, I'm afraid. Both for him, and for Lillian.'

Her eyes narrowed and her face lost its mocking smirk. Her eyes were strange—almost shining in the darkness.

'John, you wound me so,' she said, but this time with malice dripping from her words. 'To compare me so unfavourably to a sickly, simpering, dead thing like her... How cruel boys can be.'

I swallowed my anger, and began to edge around the table, taking the route furthest away from her and keeping my pistol trained on her at all times.

'The eye-patch is so dashing,' Lillian said. 'Such a clever affectation; but then, you always were one for appearances. A nice suit, money in your pocket, a dusky maiden on your arm. Did you even know your gypsy whore's name? Or are you as shallow as you as look?'

'Enough!' I snapped. I had reached the door, and had one hand on the lever to unlock it. 'I should have killed you back in Kent, but be assured I will not hesitate out of feelings for my real sister, nor because you are a woman. I am here to find Lazarus, and you will not stop me.'

'It's funny, John,' she giggled. 'That's almost exactly what he said.'

She looked to her right, and I followed her gaze to a dark

shape on the floor. James Denny lay in the corner, a few feet from Lillian's chair, in a puddle of dark liquid that crept slowly along the chequered tiles.

'Damn you!' I cursed, but as I turned back, thrusting the gun towards her with murderous intent, Lillian had already darted from her seat. My shot rang out, striking the back of the oaken chair where Lillian had been.

She moved with cat-like grace and uncanny speed, and I fired twice more at shadows before she vaulted across the table and kicked the gun from my hand. Her boots were capped and studded, and pain shot along my arm. She was supremely confident in her own speed and agility, so much so that she was willing to pit them against my bullets, and rightly so, it appeared. She struck out at me with bare hands, again and again, in much the same way that those Chinese soldiers had taught me back in Hong Kong. I took satisfaction from the look of surprise on her unblemished face when I blocked her strikes once, twice, three times, before striking back and forcing her on the defensive. She was incredibly fast, but she struggled to turn aside my blows, instead using her agility to dance away from me as well as she could in such a confined space. Lillian hopped backwards, seating herself on the tabletop almost daintily, before sending a kick my way that struck me hard on the side of the face. I reeled backwards, and then she was at me again, this time kicking out at me with those wickedly heeled boots. I had not realised what a detriment one eye could be until that moment; her feet seemed to slide out of view before reappearing again so quickly that I could barely move in time. The metal points scratched at my cheek; ever backwards she drove me, until I almost tripped over the prone body of Jim Denny. As I stumbled, I was driven insensible with rage at the sight of my stricken friend, and when the next kick hurtled through the gloom, this time aimed at my good eye, I caught it in my right hand and twisted Lillian's ankle with all my might, before throwing her off balance into the wall.

We both paused, panting for breath. Lillian wiped a trickle

of blood from her mouth with dainty gloved fingers, and looked at it with distaste. She was dressed outlandishly, as always, but I realised then that her attire was practical rather than immodest. She was a fighter, not a lady, and her tight-fitting britches and severely tailored bodice were designed to afford her freer movement, and probably also to distract any male opponents who challenged her. But not me; I was her brother, in spite of it all, and how I hated her.

She screamed like a banshee and hurled herself at me. I caught sight of a flash of steel in her hand, though where it had come from I knew not. She slashed across at me in a feint, before spinning at me with a vicious heel-kick which I struggled to avoid. My rudimentary knowledge of the Eastern arts had given me the edge in my fight on the docks, but against this trained killer I was a novice, and I was tiring. I stumbled to the chair where Lillian had been sitting, where I stooped and feigned fatigue; predictably, she did not stop, but arced another kick at me, intending to crash her foot down upon the back of my head. I twisted aside, pushing the chair towards her. Her leg crashed onto the headrest and she grunted in pain as her ankle hit the sturdy wood. I ploughed forwards, putting my weight behind a punch, which connected with her jaw and crumpled the harridan to the ground beside Jim. It was the most unnatural thing in the world for me to strike a woman, but in that moment all I could picture was her mocking smile as she stood next to Tsun Pen in his torture chamber, and how she had snarled as she stood over the body of poor Elsbet.

I caught sight of my revolver near the wainscoted wall and picked it up, cocking the hammer and aiming it at Lillian as I stepped over her. It was then that Vickers entered the room, looking worse for wear but still fighting fit. He sealed the hatch behind him and moved around the table towards us.

'You been fighting a girl, sir?' he asked, almost laughing, but then he stopped short. 'Blimey, is that Captain Denny?'

'It is,' I said, my eyes still fixed on Lillian. 'Vickers, this business is almost over. I want you to stay here and watch this woman like a hawk until I return. She is a killer, and undoubtedly has more concealed weapons on her person. Do you have a weapon?'

'That I do,' he replied, and my stomach lurched as I felt the cold steel of a blade at my throat, and a powerful arm wrenching at my injured shoulder. 'Drop the gun, guv.'

Lillian's eyes gleamed, almost violet in the gloom, and her callous smile returned. Now I knew what those eyes reminded me of: a snake, cold and calculating, devoid of human empathy.

She stood up, almost slipping in Jim's blood as she did so. Her face was no longer unblemished; a single ringlet of dark hair had come unpinned, and was hanging loose over her smooth, milk-white forehead.

'Hold him, Mr. Vickers; I want to end this my way,' she said. She stood poised, ready to kick out at me. I struggled against the big man's strength, but it was folly—he was as strong as Gregor. 'These boots are of my own design,' Lillian continued. 'One kick is as much a surety of death as a bullet wound, and just as quick. I will make it quick, brother—I owe you that much at least.'

She put one hand on the table to steady herself, and raised her long, slender leg from the floor, aiming the spike at my forehead with consummate grace and a morbid sense of theatrics. But what happened next took us all by surprise. Her eyes widened as she lost her balance, and I saw that Jim was not dead. He had grasped Lillian's standing leg and yanked at her ankle with the last of his strength. Again, she found herself toppling to the floor, no longer the balletic assassin. Vickers loosened his grip for a moment in surprise, and I half managed to pull free, driving my elbow into his gut to complete the job, before turning around to kick him hard in the groin. The big man went down easily enough after that, and I spun back to Lillian, stooping to pick up the gun once more, but it was not there. I looked up to see Lillian already on her feet, and heard Jim groan in agony. She had impaled his hand upon the floor, the tiles cracking and the blood pooling beneath her heel. She had my gun in her hands, and was pointing it at me. I held my hands out towards her.

'Do not bother to plead for your life, John. We both know it's gone beyond that. Just know this: when you are dead, every man, woman and child from this world will cross through the Lazarus Gate, and everyone you ever knew or cared about will be replaced by their superiors. Take that with you to the gr—'

I did not let her finish speaking. With a flick of my wrist, the Derringer concealed up my coat-sleeve was in my hand, and I pulled the trigger. The small-calibre bullet was enough for the task, and struck her high, between her ivory throat and the lace ruffs of her bodice. Blood oozed from the small wound, like a ruby pendant, and her reptilian eyes rolled back into her head as she dropped to the floor for the third and final time.

I saw Jim's hand as Lillian's stiletto tore out of it, but then he succumbed again to unconsciousness. I had no time to check on him with Vickers nearby, and indeed the big soldier had already heaved himself to his feet. I did not pause, but used every ounce of strength to pick up a chair from my side of the table and smash it over Vickers' head.

I turned to retrieve my gun yet again, staring into Lillian's cold, dead eyes as I did so. I felt something strange in that moment—remorse perhaps—for the girl she could have been rather than the woman she had been. Whatever fleeting emotion it was, it soon gave way to anger; I was in no mood for mercy or for niceties. I marched over to Vickers, who was dragging himself towards the exit, blood trickling from his ear down his neck. I pressed the cold barrel of the gun up against his head and pulled back the hammer. He flinched at the click.

'When did you turn?' I demanded. 'Or are you one of them?'

He looked at me defiantly. 'I'm not one o' them. I'm Hardwick's man—your pa's, like—always have been. I figured if this was what he wanted, then it must be right. Said he'd look out for me and mine when the revolution come. I volunteered for this duty on the Brigadier's orders, like. Proper gentleman he is. I'd follow the Brigadier to hell and back, and you should too, if you're any kind of son.'

'Sorry to disappoint you,' I growled, and struck the man hard on the temple. He crumpled to the floor, just as the ship's captain had.

I made sure that the door was secure, then checked on Jim. He had a nasty gash to the back of his head, and a gouge in his hand, but he was still breathing. Satisfied, I turned to the door to the captain's cabin. I muttered an oath under my breath to come back for Captain Denny, pressed the metal lever, and stepped through the bulkhead door.

The spacious cabin was empty, as devoid of furnishing and finery as it was of people. The affectations of imperialist quarters—plush fabrics, shelves of books, leather chairs and comfortable beds seen in most of the warships I had travelled on—were here eschewed in favour of a desk, stowage trunk and simple hammock. Marcus Hardwick had never been a man for home comforts.

In the endmost wall was a row of small, circular windows, crusted with sea-salt and grime. I peered through one, and saw movement outside on the 'captain's walk', a rather outdated balcony, more suited to a pirate galleon than a modern warship. There were two dark figures outside, but I could not make out who they were. I reloaded my pistol, took a deep breath, and stepped out onto the platform.

A cold breeze hit me as I stepped outside, and I had to squint to save being dazzled by the orange light from the burning sky above King Albert's England. A star-spangled American flag fluttered overhead, casting a snaking shadow across the walkway. I was standing on the captain's walk—a platform barely two yards wide—and above me a system of winches and pulleys jutted out over the stern of the ship. These held a small steam launch, which hung over the water next to the platform's railing. My father was no more than six feet away from me, operating the winch that was lowering the launch to the river.

On the launch itself, struggling with the pulleys, was Hanlocke. Ambrose saw me first, and did not seem terribly surprised. I pointed my gun first at him, then at Lazarus.

'You really do have the lives of a cat Ambrose,' I said. 'How the devil did you get here?'

'Same way as you, old chap,' he replied with an air of nonchalance, 'though with more style, naturally. Did you really leave me with a single guard? And one who could be easily bought? Tut tut.'

Lazarus had seen me, and was already reaching into his coat.

'That's enough. It's over, Lazarus,' I said, trying hard not to sound as weary as I felt. Lazarus stopped and glared at me.

'Can you not call me father? You know the truth of it now, surely.' His voice brought back a host of memories, of childlike fears and longings, and of standing by a grave at a rain-sodden churchyard where I swore an oath to do my father proud. I steadied myself with the simple thought that this man was so far removed from the Marcus Hardwick I remembered that he may as well be an Othersider by birth. 'I'm surprised your sister didn't stop you,' he continued. 'What have you done with her?'

'She was not my sister. She was a crazed animal—a murderess—and I did the only thing that could be done with such a creature.' I surprised myself with the venom in my words, and it certainly seemed to move Lazarus.

'Was? So, you have killed her. You really are a wretched boy, to have taken from me all that I have worked to regain. And I suppose you think you have it in you to kill me, too? Do you think you can slay your own father?'

'The Marcus Hardwick I knew would never turn his back on his country; whatever you are, you are not my father!'

'My country? What do I owe a world that took my daughter from me? That drove my wife into an early grave, and left me with a weakling poet for a son? You are half the man I ever was. I was fighting in India when Dora hanged herself; and I was fighting for a cause that was unjust and petty. Can you understand what it is to lose everything dear to you, for nothing?'

'Bastard!' I roared, his words stinging me and driving me into a rage. 'She was my mother! You left us to fend for ourselves after Lillian died; you left me to pick up the pieces alone. I never stopped thinking you were a great man; I joined the army for you. When I was tortured, the only thing that got me through it was thinking about what the great Brigadier Hardwick would have done.'

'You were captured because you were a poor soldier,' Lazarus retorted. 'Never promoted above captain, at your age? You're a disgrace. I heard you'd been assigned to a security detail in Burma? To get you out of the way, most like. If you'd had the courage of your convictions, rather than following in my shadow, you could have been a man. Instead, you stand before me like a savage before Caesar. You cannot stop me, and when I have delivered these people—this entire world—to safety, I will retire home and be with my darling wife, my Dora. She has lost both her children now, but this time I'll be there for her. The knowledge of their bravery and sacrifice will give her strength. We will live in a world united rather than one divided by petty squabbling and warring.'

'You plan to kill untold millions of people, and claim it is for love? Is that what you tell yourself?'

'I tell myself that this world had everything I desired. Everything! My dear wife, alive and well; a daughter beautiful and fierce; a son who was strong and courageous, killed for trying to save the world…'

'His world! Not yours.'

'He did his duty! I respect that more than your pitiful attempts to earn redemption.'

'Don't lecture me about duty!' I snapped. 'You abandoned your own quickly enough; to your country, your regiment, and your family. I never thought I would see the day when the great Marcus Hardwick would be revealed as a traitor. You say you're ashamed of me? Then we make a pretty pair.'

'This is a charming family reunion, but unless you really are planning to kill your father, I'm afraid we must get on.' It was Ambrose, making light of a dire situation as always. I turned the gun on him again.

At this, Lazarus took a step towards me, and I swung the gun back onto him. I knew I should have just pulled the trigger, but I felt I was waiting for… something; some sign to affirm my actions perhaps.

'Not another step, Lazarus. You will not set foot through that gateway, even if it means consigning you to hell.'

'We're already in hell, John,' Lazarus replied. 'Have you not looked up at the sky? There are worse things than death, as I'm sure you now realise. So here's what is going to happen: I am going to board this launch, and pass through the gate unnoticed whilst your pathetic little soldiers swarm all over this ship. You'll probably go down with the ship, but that will prove no great loss, and as you drown in the Thames for a second time, you will see our glorious fleet sailing up the river. Once I'm safely on the other side, the passage will be much smoother for our comrades.'

He turned his back on me, utterly certain of himself, and started to climb aboard the launch. Even then, he was overconfident, overbearing and cantankerous, and as I realised that his plan was to simply ignore me, my anger boiled over. I pulled the trigger: the bullet hit his shoulder. He fell to the deck, trying to grab at the rail to steady himself.

'I'm sorry, Father,' I said, coolly. 'I can't allow that.'

I took one pace forward, but quick as a flash Ambrose made a move, pulling a lever on the pulley system. I did not see exactly what he was doing, and snapped off a shot, only hitting the launch's steam-funnel. Too late, I realised what Ambrose had done. A bundle of chains with a large iron hook on the end came loose behind me, and swung at me with some force. I was alerted by the rattling of the chains, and ducked instinctively, though the heavy hook caught my injured shoulder. As the pain coursed through me, Lazarus turned over, still on the walkway, but now with a gun in his hand. I leapt back as he fired, and was half-blinded by the flash of blue light that burst from the gun. The arc of lightning fizzed, hitting the bundle of chains and lighting them up with crackling energy and showers of sparks. The energised mass of metal swung back towards me, and I backed away as far as I could go, firing off another shot blindly to keep Lazarus pinned down. But by then Ambrose had leapt from the boat, and he struck down at me with the weighted silver handle of his cane, driving the metal knob down onto my weak shoulder. I cried out in pain and was forced to drop to one knee. As I raised the gun to shoot at him, he struck me again, this time on the right wrist, and I dropped the revolver. Ambrose kicked it along the deck towards Lazarus.

I flailed at Ambrose wildly and fought to my feet, leaning against the rail at the end of the captain's walk, but the game was up. I had not taken my chance; I had tried to find answers to the questions I had been asking ever since I had learned of my father's involvement, and that delay had cost me, and the whole world. As the chains stopped swinging and the electricity within them died away, Lazarus and Ambrose stood side by side. My father pointed his lightning gun at me.

'Agent Hanlocke,' he said to Ambrose, 'this man is of my own blood, for all of his faults. Please be kind enough to finish him quickly, and then get the launch ready. We're wasting time.'

Ambrose said nothing, only drew his cane-sword and pressed the point to my chest. I held my breath—I had no more tricks up my sleeve, only an inexorable wait for my end to come. And then Ambrose lowered his sword, and stepped back behind my father, shaking his head.

'I'm terribly sorry, sir,' he said, 'but I'm afraid I've become rather fond of John during our time together. I just can't do it. Perhaps I should just get the boat ready?'

Lazarus gave him such a look of disgust—the look long reserved for disobedient servants and his disappointing son—that I half expected Ambrose to wither away under the gaze.

Lazarus then turned his gun onto me again, and with a complete lack of emotion in his voice said: 'Don't worry about the weapon; it's surprisingly humane. Your heart will stop long before you burn to death… goodbye John.'

But he did not pull the trigger. Instead he let out a small whine, and his eyes widened so far I thought they would pop out of his skull. A long, red spike pushed its way from his chest towards me, like the probing tongue of a snake, before withdrawing again just as rapidly. Lazarus dropped his gun and staggered to the railing, looking every bit as bewildered as I did. Ambrose took out a handkerchief and casually wiped the blood from his sword.

'What…?' I could not form any more words, so surprising was this latest lucky escape from certain death.

'Couldn't let him kill you, old chap,' said Ambrose. 'Just like I couldn't let you kill your old dad, no matter how much of a tyrant he was. Now you can go home without that hanging over you.'

I stepped towards him, flabbergasted.

'Ambrose…'

'Bet you wish you'd stayed in the country now, eh?' he said. 'Told that bloody gypsy to keep you there, come what may. Willem, wasn't it? Paid him up front, too.'

'But what about you? What happens now?' I asked, still too stunned to take in what he was saying.

'Oh, I suppose I'll be—' But that was all he managed. A shot rang out, and Ambrose clutched at his ribs as his shirt became a red rag. Lazarus clutched a derringer of his own, which he'd concealed the whole time—he'd had the better of me all along, but hadn't needed to show his hand. He gurgled blood from his throat, laughing even in his final moments.

As Ambrose stumbled to the wall and slid down it onto the planked walkway, I stepped towards Lazarus, but could not reach him in time.

'Goodbye, son,' he whispered, hoarsely, and pushed himself over the rail with the last of his strength. I rushed to the edge of the captain's walk and looked over, just in time to see an arm vanishing beneath the choppy water. He was gone.

I turned back to Ambrose, who was slumped in a heap by the cabin door.

'I don't understand,' I said.

'You never do, you silly sod,' gasped Ambrose, grunting in pain and holding his wound. 'But Lazarus is dead, or as good as. Look, the gate won't hold for long now; you have to go, old chap.'

'Come with me. Whatever happened before, your actions have set it right. Even Sir Toby wouldn't hang you!'

'He bloody might! And prison certainly doesn't suit me. Besides, this thing in my ticker won't let me leave,' he said, tapping his chest. 'Most of the portals were closed to power this one. The gate will close soon, and when it does we'll all be summoned back, dead or alive; dragged back to hell.'

'I... I don't know what to say.'

'You were right,' he said, his voice breaking, 'I was too deep in the mire. We... we had no right.' Ambrose fumbled around on the floor and took up his cane. 'Take this... call it a parting gift. I've got five more back home anyway. My real home, that is. It's saved your life twice already; maybe the third time will be the charm.'

I took the cane-sword from him, and noticed for the first time that its silver knob was engraved with an elegant, swirling 'H'. *For Hanlocke, or for Hardwick... fate, again*, I thought. I stood up, but felt bitterly sad at leaving Ambrose behind. For all he had done, I thought that perhaps he had been my friend, at least for a short time. He pushed at my leg feebly, and I saw that the blood was gushing from him. I could do nothing; Ambrose Hanlocke's sudden turn of heroism had been his final act.

'Now go!' he said. 'You don't want to be stuck here, believe me.'

I opened the door to the captain's cabin, and turned back once more—looking first to Ambrose, then to the hellish skyline behind us—before taking my leave.

* * *

Gunfire sounded all around us and the entire ship shook and rolled as it began to sink into the blood-red Thames. Jim was a dead weight, and no one was in any state to help me carry him. Men from both sides ran for their lives as the five amber portals began to gutter like dying candles. The enemy sailors had launched their lifeboats and were even leaping overboard in panic. In desperation, or perhaps one last fit of defiance, the other ships waiting to launch their invasion had turned their broadsides on Lazarus' vessel, determined to at least take down the soldiers who had foiled their plans. Either that, or the tenuous pacts that had held all those foreign powers together had died with my father. The ship burned beneath a scarlet sky, as in my dreams.

With every step we took, the Lazarus Gate seemed to grow dimmer, flickering in and out of existence. Sometimes Jim managed a few steps, whilst at others I was dragging him along, leaving a trail of slick crimson behind us. My shoulder burned, and I thought perhaps it would be easier just to stay there, on the wrong side of the gate, and accept whatever punishment the Otherside forces threw at me. But then I remembered the shadowy Thing at my back, and the horror of it spurred me onwards.

At least half the ship had pushed through the gate, and it was still moving forwards, inertia carrying it. The thick cables lining the arches of London Bridge were damaged; burning, and showering the deck with great cascades of orange sparks. The ship had scraped the side of the bridge, and dragged across the cables, grinding the infernal machinery and causing untold damage to my father's masterwork.

We were close—maybe ten yards from the gate—when the boat heeled abruptly. The deck rose up to meet us as we tumbled over, and we almost fell into one of the raging deck-fires, but somehow I managed to roll us away from it. I looked up and saw the gateway begin to close in on itself. The edges of the portal grew dark, roiling and undulating like thick black smoke, before shrinking inwards inch by inch towards the centre, leaving shimmering, hot air in its wake.

The amber window grew smaller by the second, as did our chance of escape. I dragged Jim to his feet once more and began to move towards salvation. When I looked up again, I could see the rest of the Othersiders' world beyond the portal rather than our own—an endless red sky above a dark, hopeless city. The portal began to close around the ship's hull, and as it did so there rose up the most awful metallic groan, as if the ironclad would be crushed by some gigantic, unseen hand. At this terrible sound, I roared my defiance, and lifted Jim fully onto my shoulders. The wound burned, and my legs almost gave way, but some inner strength drove me on, one step at a time. Even as we were wreathed in coruscating light from the portal, I could not be sure we would make it. Ahead, I could see first the strange, gelatinous amber mass of the portal, then it seemed to flicker for an instant to reveal that fell red sky, then again to reveal the pale sky of home. Then I saw other things, too—London in ruins, then a city of towering steel and glass palaces, then a humid jungle with the Thames twisting through its verdant heart, followed by a world submerged beneath the ocean, with London a floating city. Other, even more indescribable and fantastic places came and went in swift succession, shimmering into focus for brief moments before dissipating, snatched away like the vestige of a dream. It was maddening, dizzying, but I knew then I was seeing the places between worlds—the infinite possibilities of William James' multiverse, finally brought into focus by the energies of the Lazarus Gate. Other worlds, other times, perhaps, any of which could have provided safe haven for the Othersiders, had they eyes to see.

But such wonders were secondary to the fear I felt at being left in an even more alien world. I was almost grateful, then, when I found myself wading through the thick, amber air once more, with its muffled whispers and strange, predatory shadows that seemed to stalk us on the periphery of my vision. And how sweet the air was when finally I forced my way through the portal, and both Jim and I fell onto the foredeck, looking up at a sky where the last of the stars were blinking out of sight as the morning light chased them from the heavens.

I do not recall how Jim and I came to be on the north bank of the Thames. I was told later that we had been spotted leaving the portal by the rearguard of our soldiers, and one of them had recognised Captain Denny and bundled us onto a launch. All I remember is sitting on the river wall with a blanket over my shoulders, watching as the front half of Lazarus' ship upended and began to sink into the river. When the portal had closed, it had cut the ship clean in two, and the exposed decks jutted almost vertically from the water like ribs sawn in a cross-section by a butcher's hand. It burned like a beacon while its prow thrust into the silt bed of the Thames.

There was chaos all about us, of course. Dozens of Otherside sailors, common men with no strange devices implanted into their hearts, swam to the banks or clung to wreckage, perhaps stranded for ever in a foreign land, if nature itself did not reject them first; who knew? I supposed that even prison in our world would be preferable to liberty in their own. The soldiers Jim had hired had blocked the streets and the bridge, not even letting the police through until we were sure that every Otherside agent who may have been lurking in our midst had been dragged back whence they had come via their implants. If any still remained after that, only time would tell what would become of them. When the police finally did arrive, they in turn had to contend with crowds of onlookers who had started to gather when the first howitzers had sounded. Even the Metropolitan Police, however, had not been able to stop the mudlarks from scurrying through the blockades to the riverbanks. Ruddy-faced children began to pick through the mud for any valuables they could find in the wreckage; it was their living. How else could they and their families survive? If there was any important evidence amongst the debris, it would likely never be found.

A crowd had gathered on the bridge, unperturbed by the efforts of the policemen to hold them back. At their arrival, the gypsies slipped away, abandoning their rifles and vanishing into the throng which now looked down on the burning ship with morbid curiosity. I wondered how on earth anyone could explain these events to the public.

I clambered to my feet, and checked back on Jim. The ambulance had arrived, and he was being loaded aboard it.

'Take care of him,' I said. 'He's a war hero.'

I looked back at the sinking ship one last time as it turned onto its side and came to a final rest on the bottom of the river. As it did so, the ship's name flashed up towards the rising sun, and I stood open-mouthed as I read it. It was the ship from my dreams.

It was the *USS Helen B. Jackson.*

SEVENTEEN

The weeks that followed were all a blur. I spent a period of time in hospital, and was subjected to the most thorough and tiresome series of interviews and 'debriefs' from Home Office officials, Her Majesty's Army and, of course, Apollo Lycea. Occasionally I would see Jim wheeling along the hospital corridors in his invalid chair, though we were rarely permitted to speak to each other whilst the official reports of the Lazarus affair were being drawn up. When I was discharged from hospital, I spent a few days in barracks at Horse Guards, voluntarily; the offer had been extended by the major who had been sent to question me, and I felt as though a bit of military routine would help to discipline my mind before I returned to the more chaotic civilian life. My body healed quickly enough, to be sure, but I did not feel myself in my mind, and feared I never would after what I'd seen. In truth, I wanted nothing more than to get my affairs in order, pack up my things from Mrs. Whitinger's house, and set off to find Rosanna, hoping that she would welcome me even though I had destroyed all hope of a reunion with Elsbet. I knew that her ultimatum had been delivered out of grief, and was certain that my absence would have sweetened her disposition.

On the morning of 28th May, Jim paid me a visit. This was not in itself unusual, for we had spent much time together since the battle on the *Helen B. Jackson*, but on this day he was uncommonly serious, and I knew that duty called.

'It's time,' Jim said, simply.

I nodded. 'Let me change into a suit,' I said. 'I doubt Sir Toby would appreciate seeing his agents in army uniform.'

Half an hour later, we were in a cab, heading towards the river.

The address that Jim had been given was on St Katharine Docks, opposite the Royal Mint. After walking fruitlessly back and forth along the crowded street, we finally noticed a narrow doorway sandwiched between two Port Authority buildings, anonymous but for a small stone cameo of Apollo above its lintel. I rapped on the door, showed my card to the porter, and we were led down a long flight of stairs, at once transported to a world of espionage away from the hustle and bustle of London's streets.

The size of the facility was impressive, spanning far beneath the water level, with large corridors and service tunnels feeding storerooms directly from the docks. It was into one of these secure storerooms that we were led, although the description perhaps does not do it justice. A large, vaulted cellar stretched before us, with whitewashed walls and electric light illuminating the space. Smartly dressed scientists and their assistants marched along aisles between massive tables and rows of lockers, carrying out tests on bizarre-looking machinery and cataloguing recovered artefacts from the wreck of the *Helen B. Jackson*. Overseeing all of this were Sir Toby and Sir Arthur Furnival, and another man, who was introduced to me as Lord Cherleten. At last, we met.

His lordship was a lean man, with a stern face and a weak, clean-shaven chin. His unruly crop of red hair was fading to grey, and he held himself with such rigid and haughty bearing that he appeared always to tower over us, although he was little taller than Jim and me. He said little, merely nodding to me when we were introduced. Sir Arthur, on the other hand, shook my hand warmly, for we had not seen each other since that fateful meeting with William James, which seemed like a lifetime ago.

'Here you have it,' Sir Toby said. 'This facility houses the salvage from the Lazarus Gate incident.' The word 'incident' barely seemed to do the ordeal justice, but I said nothing. 'There is more out there, we're sure,' Sir Toby continued, 'but where it is now is anyone's guess. We'll be trawling the Thames for months to come, and we have agents sweeping every warehouse and fencing operation in London and beyond.'

'What will be done with it all?' I asked.

'If there's anything that our scientists deem safe to use, then it will be signed over to the armoury under Lord Cherleten's care,' Sir Toby replied gruffly. Anything else will either be destroyed, if possible, or else locked away in our most secure vaults and never spoken of again.'

Even now, Sir Toby was stressing that secrecy was the order of the day; as if that were lost on any of us.

'And the Othersiders' weapons?' I asked. Sir Toby raised an eyebrow. 'Those lightning guns would come in handy in a tight spot.'

I made a wry smile, and was surprised to see it returned by Lord Cherleten.

'His Lordship is of a similar opinion,' said Sir Toby. 'However, it seems there are certain... side effects... to their use, which we have yet to fully investigate. Until then, they will be kept down here for further tests.'

'Side effects?' Jim asked.

'It's what—ahem—Sir Arthur here calls "psychic resonance",' said Sir Toby. 'Perhaps you could explain it?' he asked the other baronet.

'I only wish I could do so satisfactorily,' said Sir Arthur. 'It seems that our scientists are struggling to ascertain quite how these weapons work. The construction is brilliant, but straightforward enough, and can be replicated... except that our versions do not function well, if at all. By all rights, the Othersiders' weapons should not work, and yet they do. And this, I believe, is to do with the unique resonance of the other universe.'

'A frequency,' I said. 'Like a tuning fork pitched to an off-key.'

Sir Arthur looked at me with surprise. 'Precisely, my dear fellow. On the other side, this "frequency" allows psychic phenomena to flourish, often with deadly results, and appears to permit the creation of outlandish weaponry. Whatever... entities, shall we say... prey on the Othersiders, I believe they do so because they are attracted to this frequency.'

'Like a beacon in the darkness,' I muttered, feeling a coldness sweep over me.

Sir Arthur nodded gravely. 'Each time our men have used the weapons, I have felt a strange sensation, as of a presence in the room, trying to enter our world. But this is only the half of it.'

'Oh?'

'Captain Hardwick, Captain Denny,' Sir Toby interjected, 'I think perhaps you had better accompany us.'

We left the room and walked along another broad corridor, stopping at the door of another large chamber. Sir Toby opened the door, and we peered inside. What I saw within gave me pause. Laid out on mortuary slabs, covered with white shrouds, were bodies. Dozens of them.

'What... who are they?' I asked.

'Othersiders,' said Sir Toby. 'Forty-two of them. Drowned in the Thames, or killed in battle.'

'And not dragged back to their own side?'

'No. As we suspected, the common soldiery were not fitted with the devices that were afforded their best agents. In death, they are stuck here. Our medical staff wishes to study them before they are... disposed of.'

'Disposed of?' Jim asked. 'Will they be given a Christian burial? Whatever their nature, they are still men and women of England, are they not?'

'Their nature is not entirely understood,' said Sir Toby. 'They still resonate with the other side; what will become of them over time is anyone's guess. And… they are not entirely alone in there.'

'I don't understand,' I said.

'These bodies are a danger to us all, Captain,' said Sir Arthur, as if the words pained him. 'Something… terrible… hungers after these poor souls, and the longer their remains are here, the stronger the force becomes. Whether the sensation will fade over time now that the Lazarus Gate is closed, or whether we have irrevocably brought some threat into our world, only time will tell. What we will do with the survivors is anyone's guess.'

I knew there were survivors from the wreck, but did not know what had become of them.

'How many?' I asked.

'Scores of them, that we know of,' Sir Toby said. 'Probably more out there, fleeing justice. And who knows what weapons they carry, or what powers they wield.'

'You think some of their psychics crossed over?' I asked.

'We are certain of it. We have two of them here.' Sir Toby and Lord Cherleten were stony-faced. Jim looked at me in disbelief. 'Come,' said Sir Toby. 'Come and meet them.'

We stood in what resembled a small hospital ward. Two patients—an old man and a young girl—were strapped down to metal-framed beds, much as I had seen in my vision of the other side. They were heavily sedated, and it was plain to see the red marks on their foreheads where the Othersiders had clamped them in cruel apparatus. I could not look at them. I trembled, and struggled to control myself as Sir Toby explained things to us, lest he see my agitation.

'There is something strange happening to those of a… "psychic" persuasion across the city,' said Sir Toby. 'Many of them have been reporting strange dreams and visions, something to do with a storm. They say the Thames will flow red with blood, and fire will rain from the skies. Sir Arthur has experienced this for himself.'

'Where did you find them?' I asked. I was beginning to feel faint.

'We believe they were aboard the ship,' said Sir Toby. 'They were found floating down the river, attached to a piece of wreckage, half drowned. Their fellows were not so lucky.'

'There were thirteen in all,' said Lord Cherleten. This was the first time he had spoken, and it startled me. His voice was thin and cut-glass. 'All of them secured to the very workings of the Othersiders' ship—like a living engine, designed to ease the passing of the vessel through the portal. Ingenious, really.'

'Cutting them free seemed to cause them great distress,' Sir Arthur interjected. 'And when they become distressed… strange things happen.'

'Such as?' I asked, although I knew the answer already.

'Lights flicker on and off; objects fly about of their own accord. The policemen who disentangled them were incapacitated by sudden headaches that caused them to lose control of their own limbs. And apparently they saw… things.'

'Wh… what things?'

Sir Arthur looked at me with trepidation in his eyes. 'Monsters, Captain. They saw monsters.'

'We keep them sedated at all times now, until we can determine the cause. Or until we can send them back.' Sir Toby broke the fraught moment that Sir Arthur and I shared, and I was almost glad of it.

'If their own universe does not somehow claim them,' Lord Cherleten mused absently, 'they may yet have a part to play in the ongoing struggle.'

'Ongoing, my lord?' I asked.

Cherleten looked askance at me as though appalled that I had addressed him directly.

'We cannot be sure the conflict is over,' he said with distaste. 'We must prepare ourselves as if for war; to do otherwise would be foolish.'

'You have struck a great blow for our side,' said Sir Toby,

reassuringly. 'If the intelligence you provided is correct, then it is highly unlikely that the Othersiders could attempt another invasion. But there are certain... complications; other threats that we must consider.'

Jim spoke up. 'Sir Toby, do you mean to say it is not over?'

'I mean to say we don't know, my boy. If some of those sailors that came through the gate were left stranded here rather than being returned to their own side, it stands to reason that there may have been other... refugees... who took their chance to flee their world. William James thinks that their presence here may be causing some kind of temporary upset. Sir Arthur here says the number of sightings of ghostly apparitions in London has more than trebled this last week alone. We are hearing reports of haunted houses, demonic possession, strange lights in the sky... it's happening across the country. We are keeping this to ourselves for now, for there is no need to cause widespread panic over what are, thankfully, isolated cases. But we here must all face facts—what happened on the other side could happen here, unless we are vigilant.'

I could think of nothing but the shadow on the sky, of clouds of fire and swarming things swooping over a shattered city. I remembered, too, the scrabbling claws that I had seen during Rosanna's séance, and the recollection struck me dumb.

'Isn't it rather dangerous to keep such volatile prisoners and materiel together?' asked Jim.

'There's a reason this place is built beneath the docks,' said Lord Cherleten. 'Should our... assets... become too unstable, or should our enemies attempt to liberate them. Well...'

'You flood it,' Jim said. Lord Cherleten nodded.

'Come,' Sir Toby said. 'We have seen enough here. We should return to the Apollonian. I believe Lord Cherleten has an assignment for Captain Denny, while I would speak to you further, Captain Hardwick.'

I nodded, and allowed the others to leave the room before me. As I joined them, I took one last look back at the sleeping girl covered in bruises and needle-marks; the psychic Othersider whose presence had so unnerved me, and who might yet spell calamity for us all.

It was Elsbet.

I stood in Sir Toby's dark, wainscoted office for what seemed like an eternity as he flicked through papers, making the occasional note in the margins. The ticking of the large carriage clock on the mantel seemed to grow steadily louder, until my thoughts were crowded from my own mind and all I could concentrate on was the rhythmic *tick-tick-tick*. Finally, Sir Toby rose from his leather chair and strolled over to the window of the office, indicating for me to follow him. We talked whilst looking out of the second-floor window of the Apollonian, across St James's Square.

'Your report was most thorough, Captain Hardwick. I understand that you've been through quite the ordeal, and I must congratulate you on a job well done.'

Whilst his words provided some small comfort, I had indeed been through 'quite the ordeal', and I could barely think of appropriate words for the situation. I shuffled my feet and merely thanked him. There was an awkward silence, and I seized the moment.

'Sir Toby, I... I feel I must ask something of you,' I said.

'My dear fellow, for you, anything.'

'It's not a favour, as such. More a question to fill in the blanks, if you get my meaning.'

'Information is intelligence, my boy. And the imparting of intelligence, in this line of work, usually does constitute a favour. But you've earned more than one, so go ahead.' He smiled. I think I may have warmed to him slightly then, to his comradely manner concealed beneath a veneer of refinement. But I still did not truly trust him.

'One thing that confused me all along, was the question of why. Why did you really invite me into the Apollonian? Why was I picked for this... this mission? I know what you told me at the start: that my experiences in Burma—and beyond—proved my credentials. But then there was the Artist, and the things he said made me doubt...' I checked myself. I did not want to say that I doubted Sir Toby's word. He did not look away from the window.

'Go on,' he prompted, sensing my reticence.

'Very well,' I said. 'It seems to me that it's simply too much of a coincidence that you requested me personally to work this case. You must have had reason to believe that I had some connection... I must ask how, if only to close the door on the matter.'

Sir Toby nodded. With barely a mutter he walked over to a pastoral painting on the wall, next to a crowded bookcase. I remembered the first time I had been summoned to his office and seen him gazing at the painting... but that was a different painting, something darker and more surreal, and I held my tongue as I fought back the memories of the foreboding canvases in the Artist's lair. To my surprise, Sir Toby moved the frame, revealing a small safe behind it. I heard the quiet click of the combination, and after a moment at the open safe, Sir Toby swung the door-painting shut, and turned to me, clutching in his hand a cracked leather wallet.

'The agent we told you about, the one from the other side, who died at Marble Arch... it was not just a pocketbook that we retrieved from him. He had this with him too; the only things that identified him at all.' Sir Toby opened the wallet and pulled out a charred card, which he offered to me. 'Captain, I have known for a long time that you were coming. That this day was coming. After Marble Arch... well, let us just say that I moved heaven and earth to find you, to free you.'

I stared at Sir Toby, and then looked to the card, almost not daring to turn it over in my hand. It was tattered and scorched. But turn it over I did, and squinted at the faded writing. I think I knew what I was about to read even before I had made out the inscription.

It left me reeling, but Sir Toby was not done with me yet. He handed me the wallet, and went back to his desk. There was little else of interest, save one thing. A photograph, small, creased and scorched, but unmistakeable. It was a portrait of my mother. She was older than I remembered—so much so that it could not possibly be the Dora Hardwick whom I knew to be dead, but it was her all the same.

When I looked back to Sir Toby, blinking back a tear, I saw that he had placed on the desk between us a larger photograph.

'The final piece of the puzzle, John,' he said softly. 'I am afraid this leaves us in no doubt. Do you recall James' slideshow, when he first explained to you what we were dealing with? Well, he… we… chose not to include this picture. It was taken by the police photographer, and is the face of the agent that Melville shot dead at Marble Arch. Imagine that the hair around the temples was not flecked with white. Imagine that the scar on the right cheek was gone, and that the chin was clean-shaven rather than adorned with that rather fetching beard. Does he remind you of anyone?'

I do not know how long my moment of confusion lasted, but when I came to my senses I saw that Sir Toby was still looking at me, pale-faced and grave. The man in the picture, lying on the slabs by the Marble Arch, was me; there was no question. It was a picture of me at Marble Arch, taken on the very day—almost the very hour—that I had been released from a filthy prison on the far side of the world. And I was dead.

'Considering that Melville is one of the finest detectives in the land,' said Sir Toby, in a lighter tone, 'I am somewhat surprised that he did not see the resemblance immediately. I had almost hoped that he would—he would have thought you were a ghost, perhaps. When I explained it to him later…'

'That's why he looked at me so strangely later in the meeting room, after you had called the recess,' I said. 'But you knew. And if you saw the resemblance, then you must have at least been curious about the other Marcus Hardwick.' I spoke out of turn, but Sir Toby let it pass.

'Will you have a glass of Scotch?' he asked, and I thought for a second he was being evasive. However, as he poured the glasses he went on: 'I knew about Lazarus, and I wondered if we had finally discovered what had become of Brigadier Sir Marcus Hardwick.'

I took the whisky as it was offered, and stared at Sir Toby.

'You… you knew he wasn't dead?' I asked, almost in a whisper.

'I'm afraid so. Or, the army suspected as much, and I was one of the few outside their ranks entrusted with the information. I am sorry, John, for your loss—of your father and… of what came afterwards—but you must understand that the possible capture or defection of one of the best commanders in the British Army could never become common knowledge. We had no way of knowing what happened to Marcus. After his disappearance we unearthed intelligence that he was meeting quite regularly with suspicious characters, whom we took to be foreign agents. I suppose that wasn't far from the truth. And later… well, we began to see his handiwork turned against us in the years to follow, and our darkest fear was realised. Marcus Hardwick was a traitor.' Sir Toby took a deep swig of his Scotch.

'Do you remember the painting that used to hang there?' he said, indicating the safe on the wall. I nodded; it had played on my mind several times. 'It was a painting of the retreat through Caboul,' he said. I dreaded what was to come, for I knew my father had served in Afghanistan twice, once when he was a young man at Caboul, one of the British Army's greatest defeats. 'I was there,' Sir Toby went on. 'It was where your father saved my life in the face of terrifying odds, and where we sealed our friendship. I was wounded, trapped on a bridge spanning a mountain pass, with Ghilzais attacking from one side, and too few of our men on the other. Marcus Hardwick dashed across the bridge and carried me to safety; he took a bullet for his trouble. That action earned me an honourable discharge, and won your father a medal and a captaincy. Tsun Pen sold that painting to me. It showed a very different turn of events; it depicted a man in white, stricken on a bridge—me, I suppose—and a soldier turning his back and leaving him for dead. Leaving him and walking towards the enemy on the other side of the pass. The inscription on the back read: "Keep your friends close, and your enemies closer". It was a long time before I even suspected the significance—before I gave Tsun Pen's reputed powers any credit whatsoever. But later... I looked at that painting every day, and knew the truth of it. On May Day, I burned it.'

'You knew my father was behind the bombings... you used me,' I said, shocked.

'This is the secret service, Captain; we do what we must for the good of the Empire. At first, yes, you could say that I used you. I did not know the nature of Marcus' plans—how could anyone guess?—and I thought perhaps his son could bring him in without any... undue unpleasantness. But later, you proved yourself a capable agent; I was bloody glad to have you on the case at the end. When we started to piece together the plot, and realised the significance of your double, we started to wonder if Marcus Hardwick was behind it at all, or whether this Lazarus fellow that we'd heard about in whispers was his double. Perhaps he'd taken Marcus' identity years earlier, and had infiltrated us. We did not know the truth of it until you uncovered it. You should be proud.'

My hands were trembling, and I set down the glass so as not to slop whisky over Sir Toby's plush carpets. 'You must have known, in the end, what would happen. He was my father!' I snapped. Sir Toby's cold eyes flared.

'And he was my friend! He betrayed us both, and now we

must count the cost. But do not doubt, John, for one second, that my attachment to your family name will earn you special consideration. You are a spy; you may not think it, but that is exactly what you are. You receive the information that you need to know to get the job done, as do I; you are owed no more and no less than that.' He glanced down, and I saw that he had not meant to be so harsh. If he had been my father's friend, and had once cared for my family, then perhaps this affair had been hard on him too. But I felt betrayed; as if I was grieving the loss of my parents again.

'I should have liked to know, sir, that I was burying an empty coffin ten years ago. I should have liked to know that I was marching to war in the name of a traitor rather than a hero.'

'And then, perhaps, you would never have become involved in this sorry affair. Would that have been better, John? Do you think the bombs would have stopped falling had you never gone to India? Do you think the invasion would have been foiled regardless? By whom? You needed a shove out of the door, for the good of us all. By God, if there's one thing you should have learned from all this, it's that everything happens for a reason. Perhaps you were put on this earth to save it... take some solace from that, eh.'

I nodded, and I saw the sense in his words. 'Perhaps you're right,' I said. 'Though there is much I wish I had done differently, or not done at all.'

'I am sorry for the subterfuge, John, really I am. I knew in my heart that you could overcome the sins of your father and bring this case to a close; but I never meant for you to suffer unnecessarily. That business with the Artist... that is my only real regret. He will be dealt with.' There was menace in Sir Toby's voice. If what Tsun Pen had said to me in his studio was true, then he was far beyond the reach of the law, and far above petty revenge, and yet Sir Toby Fitzwilliam was not a man to be trifled with.

'With all due respect, Sir Toby,' I said, 'I got the distinct impression that the Artist had inveigled his way into some powerful cliques. Is there anything to be done about him?'

'My dear boy, our order may be a den of spies, and subterfuge may often be our modus operandi, but we pride ourselves on the heritage of Apollo. That statue outside the club symbolises courage and honour; we take difficult decisions—sometimes unpalatable ones—but we do the right thing, for Queen and country. At one time, Tsun Pen may have been allowed to live and work in his own particular élan, but that time has passed. The seal of Apollo Lycea carries weight still, and can do good in this world; that is something your father came to doubt. That seed of doubt ultimately made him ripe for corruption, and open to the idea of treachery.'

Talk of my father's great betrayal did not sit well with me. I finished my whisky, and tried to change the subject. 'So… what happens next?' I asked.

'Next? I think you should take some time to yourself. Perhaps repair to the country, get back to your old self. You've earned it—not only have you averted a threat of incalculable import, but you uncovered a traitor in our very midst, and brought a new recruit in Captain Denny.'

I was uncertain how I felt about Jim's recruitment. I still had no experience of working for Apollo Lycea beyond the case of the Lazarus Gate, and if all assignments were so trying, I would not wish them on my worst enemy, let alone my friend.

'Will the army let him join us permanently?' I asked, hesitantly.

'On the condition that he first completes his tour in India. Those far-off lands seem to make formidable proving grounds, do they not? Besides, why would they object? They let us have you, did they not?'

It had not occurred to me that Sir Toby would have talked to the army about my recruitment, but now it seemed obvious. I had convinced myself that I had escaped the military life, and had engaged with the order of my own free will; how blind I had been. With such high stakes, how could my part in the game have ever been left to chance?

'Besides,' Sir Toby continued, 'we have some gaps in the ranks now, so to speak. Hanlocke an infiltrator, and I'm afraid to say not the only one… We have only thirteen operatives remaining, if I may still include you among their ranks… But this is not your concern. Like I said, you should take some leave; disappear.' Sir Toby held out his hand to me. 'You've done well, John,' he said, as I shook it. 'You should take that rest. Think about getting away for a bit; to Wales, or Cumberland, perhaps.'

I nodded, thanked Sir Toby for the drink, and turned to leave. But it would not prove so easy.

'Oh, John,' he said, as if absent-mindedly. 'There is one more thing, if I could impose on your time a moment longer.'

I turned back with some reluctance, with an awful feeling that Sir Toby had saved the worst till last.

'I'm afraid there were some… discrepancies… in your report,' he said. 'I'm sure you understand that we have to clear them up, for due diligence and all that.' I nodded, and it began to dawn on me where the conversation might be headed. Sir Toby was back at his desk, and the folio he had been reading when I arrived was open once more. 'You say that after you escaped the Artist and were shot by Lazarus, you were pulled out of the Thames by a passer-by, and later made for your old home in Kent to plan your next move. The thing is, John, the army surgeon says that your shoulder wound was grievous, and that you must have been treated by a professional. That being the case, it is strange that the identity of the man who saved you, not to mention this surgeon, are missing from your report. It is the least detailed section of your account, and it seems to me that you were most careful not to mention who helped you. It seems rather remiss, don't you think?'

I had half expected the question to come, but was still unprepared for Sir Toby's withering gaze. I hesitated too long before giving my rehearsed response. 'The men who helped me were not strictly operating on the right side of the law at the time. In return for their help, I swore on my honour as an officer and a gentleman that I would not mention their names in my report. As such, I had hoped that I would not be pressed on the matter.' I said it as confidently as I could, each word chosen to evade further questioning; but Sir Toby was more determined than most, and infinitely more well-informed.

'I would not dream of compromising your honour, John, unless I felt it was gravely important. The report of Captain Denny, not to mention the sworn statements of two Metropolitan police constables and six soldiers, make mention of a gang of armed gypsies seemingly under your command, running around London during the attempted invasion. One of those gypsies was recognised by a policeman as a suspect in an unsolved murder inquiry. Tell me, John; were these gypsies the men who saved your life? Is it them you are trying to protect?'

I considered my answer carefully, and decided that the closer I could make my statement to the truth, the better it would go. 'It is, Sir Toby. The men who helped me were gypsies, yes, working illegally on the docks when they found me face down in the Thames. I do not believe any of them capable of murder, and they showed enormous courage and self-sacrifice to assist me against the Othersiders.'

'John, whether you believe they are murderers or not, the fact remains that we have a number of fugitives loose in England who bore witness to the May Day battle. We have taken great pains to cover up all knowledge of the Othersiders—not an easy task, with half a burning ship floating down the river, I'm sure you'll agree—and we can't now have loose ends. We need to bring these men in, if only to debrief them. I presume you know where they're camped?'

As it happened, I knew exactly where they were camped, as they were probably still awaiting the gathering of Romani from across the Channel in order to conduct Elsbet's funeral, but I did not want Sir Toby to know that. 'Roughly,' I said, 'but you know what gypsies are like. Always on the move, you see.'

'Quite, quite. Regardless, though, we will have to conduct a thorough search of the area and bring them in for questioning. I imagine you'll be wanting to get back to Kent anyway, won't you, to see your Indian bride?' He looked up at me from beneath his bushy eyebrows, his pale eyes piercing my soul. I did not know what to say to that, and even as I began my protestations, he cut me off. 'John, you were not exactly discreet whilst you were in Kent, and although it took us a while to find out all about your movements, intelligence did eventually reach us. I have not yet pieced together every part of your lost weeks, but a picture is becoming clearer. That you became involved with a gypsy girl is no concern of mine; spies do all sorts of things in the line of duty, and are only human after all. That you would seek to hide all mention of these gypsies from me, however, is troubling. And then of course, there is this.' Sir Toby produced a battered pocket-book from his desk drawer, and my heart sank when I saw that it was the one I had entrusted to Mrs. Whitinger to send to Jim.

'Do not worry, John,' said Sir Toby. 'Under the circumstances, it was quite prudent that you should send this to Captain Denny, but all intelligence wends its way back here in the end. I've had our boys take a look at this again. There are gypsies named on these lists, and I wondered if they might be the self-same group.'

'I'm sure I do not know,' I said. But I suspected that they were—the Othersiders only concerned themselves with proven mediums, and I had met none so powerful or accomplished as the Five Sisters.

'Are you trustworthy, John?'

'Of course!' I was outraged by the question, and blindsided by Sir Toby's mounting evidence. I struggled to keep my feelings in check. 'Haven't I proved that?'

'You have, John, yes. But when a man harbours secrets from us, it is like that they will grow into hidden agendas. When that happens... well, you don't have to look far to see the results, do you?'

'I am not my father,' was all I could say.

'Thank goodness for that,' said Sir Toby. 'But you have the same background, the same motivations... and by your own admission you had contact with this "Lillian Hardwick" whilst in Kent. When faced with your sister, seemingly returned from the grave, you may well have had the same feelings that your father had upon meeting her. No, John, I am not saying you are a traitor, but I am saying that you are a man, and that sometimes men can be weak.'

'Not I, not this time. I did my duty.'

'And you did it very well; exceptionally so. You never did say how exactly you came by your intelligence about the date of the invasion. I understand that you discerned the location from the Artist's paintings, but beyond that... it seems quite a stretch for you to be in the right place at the right time, with Hanlocke captured and a dozen gypsy gunmen in tow.'

'I did not glean any information from Otherside informants, if that is what you mean, Sir Toby.'

'No, I don't believe you did. Sir Arthur Furnival believes that you must have had help of an even more... esoteric kind; a pretty young gypsy fortune-teller, perhaps?'

I flushed, and this must have given me away. 'Again... even if that is true, then it matters not. We achieved the right result; the Empire is saved. I would rather let these gypsies go on their way in peace—it is the least we can offer them in return for their help.'

'Damn it, man!' Sir Toby snapped at me. 'Have you any idea of the forces you're toying with? Were you not paying attention at the docks? Your own observations proved the truth of the Othersiders' claims: that their world is a living hell, being somehow consumed by powers beyond their ken. That was caused by psychics, and witches, and all these other lunatics who claim to see the future, or conduct occult rituals in their mansions at the weekend. Just because the Lazarus Gate is closed does not necessarily mean we are safe; if what Sir Arthur says is true, then the psychics of this world are experiencing something hitherto unheard of, some kind of mass vision. Perhaps they're heralding the same disaster that claimed the other side. Do you see now? If you encountered a genuine psychic on your travels, then you had best come clean about it now, because at best they will know more than we would like them to, and at worst they could be a short fuse connected to a very large bomb.' I stared at him in disbelief, but his glowering eyes were unreadable.

'Perhaps I can sweeten the pot,' he said at last, his tone softening. 'It is not our custom to leave our best agents unrewarded for a job well done. You were willing to walk out of here empty-handed, and I respect your humility, though I do not think it would have been very fair. I have already had the paperwork drawn up and signed; it is up to you whether or not you're ready to earn it.' He may as well have been speaking in riddles, but he took two pieces of paper from his desk drawer and passed them to me. One was signed by Lieutenant-General Sir George Byng Harman, the Military Secretary, and the other by Sir Henry Ponsonby. I scanned the words and my head began to swim.

'What does this mean?'

'It means, John, that if you step out of your father's shadow and do your duty, then the card I handed you earlier will cease to be the lot of your double on the other side, and instead become your own. How does "Colonel Sir John Hardwick" sound?'

'Sir?'

'I have called Apollo Lycea an order many times, have I not? A knightly order, John; as ancient and proud as the Templars. The Order of Apollo answers to the Crown, and the Crown rewards its soldiers well.'

'But to earn my promotion, I must break my word and betray my honour?'

'No. You must choose not to betray your country, and lead us to the people you so evidently care about, for their own good.'

I thought of Elsbet's double lying in the order's secret facility. I thought of the things I had seen at the gypsy camp. The Five

Sisters had, through their ritual, torn a hole in the fabric of reality, or so it had appeared to me. If Sir Arthur's babbling about 'psychic resonance' was to be believed, their powers would now only be increased. I remembered Rosanna's angry words to me. 'If you do not return with Elsbet, do not return at all.' I shuddered at the thought of reuniting this Elsbet with her kin; at the thought of that great shadow on the sky appearing over my London.

'Sir Toby, can you promise me that they will be treated fairly?' I asked, heart-sick for even contemplating it. 'Without them I could not have completed the assignment, and I shudder to think what would have happened.'

'You have my word, John. Now, complete your report.' He turned his writing slope around to face me, and my report was upon it, his own handwritten notes filling the margins. He placed a supplementary statement sheet within the folio, and slid the whole lot to me across the desk. I took up a pen and stared at the blank sheet of paper. I had no idea whether or not Rosanna would understand my reasons, but I hated to think of her in distress because of those terrible visions. She would be brought into custody for her own protection, I was sure, and I would use my powers as an agent of Apollo Lycea to bring us together again. As for the others... Sir Toby promised fairness, and I had no reason to doubt the old man. And so, knowing that I would change the fate of those gypsies who had so laudably helped me, I amended my report and handed it back to Sir Toby.

What I did was not to secure a promotion. I would gladly have handed in my commission there and then would it have done any good. In part I did it to protect Rosanna and her sisters from the terrible fate that the Othersiders had suffered; a fate that I had seen with my own eyes, and that haunted me every moment of every day. But I knew in my heart of hearts that my real reason was to prove that I was not my father's son; that Apollo Lycea could always rely on me to do what was needed.

That the Hardwick name could be relied upon to do the right thing, for Queen and country.

As I left the Apollonian that night, I felt wretched.

That, I suppose, should have been the end of my tale. But of course, there was the matter of Rosanna and her people. I am sure that Sir Toby had told the truth—those gypsies with a price on their heads were rounded up and given a fair trial—but 'fair' does not necessarily mean 'just'. I discovered only recently that Gregor was found guilty of murder, and is to hang; for all my influence now there is nothing I can do to stop it. Many of the Romani were apprehended and treated roughly—some of the children were taken away from their parents, who were adjudged incapable of looking after them, and they were promptly sent to the workhouse, where I can only imagine they endure a harsher life than any they could experience on the road. A young woman matching the description of her sister, Nadya, was arrested. I did not know—and had never bothered to ask—if Rosanna's sisters had ever been involved in criminal activity. Nadya had briefly worked in service to a family in Dorset, and when she left to return to her people, her mistress had informed the constabulary that several valuable pieces of jewellery had gone missing. I had no way of knowing if the accusations were true or not, but Nadya was sent to a women's prison nonetheless, on the word of a rich old woman who could have been senile or bigoted or both. Of Rosanna, there has been no word. As far as I know, she has not been found, and remains high on the order's list of targets.

The very incident that caused me to set down this adventure on paper happened four weeks ago. I had returned to my lodgings after a night at the Army & Navy Club—the 'Rag', as Ambrose would have called it—which I now frequent in lieu of the Apollonian. Unlike the irrepressible Mr. Hanlocke, I could not bring myself to treat my place of employment as a club after everything that had happened. As I staggered upstairs to my room, perhaps a little worse for wear after one too many glasses of Tokay, Mrs. Whitinger had called to me. This was most unusual, as the hour was late and she was normally early to bed. She had for me a letter, in an envelope that was unaddressed save for a name—'Hardwick'. She informed me that the letter was hand-delivered by an impudent boy. 'If I didn't know better,' she'd told me, 'I'd have sworn he was a little gypsy boy, the rascal.'

Those words made my heart beat harder in my chest. I thanked Mrs. Whitinger, and bade her goodnight. In my room, I sat staring at the envelope, almost not daring to open it. It smelt faintly of lavender perfume, and I realised that I had a tear in my eye.

Cursing myself for a fool, I tore open the envelope. Inside I found a card—my card, dirty and dog-eared. The very card, I believed, that had taken a swim with me in the Thames, and had been used by Gregor and William to identify me. On the back of it, inscribed in a small, neat hand, were the following words:

I was wrong. You are Compeyson, and I am Miss Havisham. I should have left you in the river to meet with the fate that was written. I curse the day we met.

The writing was smudged, and I fancied it was by her tears, shed with passion as she wrote. I could not shake the image from my mind, that the tears of joy that I would perhaps have once inspired were now ones of bitterness, sorrow and hatred. I had made her cry, after I had sworn that I would never in my life do as much.

Stung by the words on the card, I let the note fall from my hands, and opened the drawer of my writing desk almost automatically. The familiar, small wooden box lay within; a box that I had not opened even in the darkest days following the closure of the Lazarus Gate. How many times in the past had I resisted by telling myself that my father would not have been so easily tempted? Those temptations proved too much for me that night, and I allowed myself some release from the self-pity that consumed me. The next day, I was so shamed by my weakness that I disposed of the hypodermics and their dreadful solution, and burned the wooden box on my sitting-room fire. That night, as my craving for sweet release began again, I instead took out my journal, and began to write this document. Perhaps in doing so I will make some sense of what happened to me. Perhaps I will earn some forgiveness, should anyone ever read my story.

I think on my decision every day, and I am always reminded of the immortal line from Dickens: 'I was too cowardly to do what I knew to be right, as I had been too cowardly to avoid doing what I knew to be wrong.' Before setting down this tale, I have neither spoken nor written of Rosanna, yet the thought of what her fate must have been after my betrayal has ever preyed on my mind and haunts my dreams.

I can picture a day, far in my future when I am old and grey and someone asks me if I have any regrets in life. I believe I shall answer: 'Just one.'

Just one.

ADDENDUM

26th June, 1891

I have felt compelled to add one last chapter to my testimony; the only such note that I am willing—indeed, that I am able by oath and duty—to record. Since the destruction of the Lazarus Gate, I have become much changed. It is only by reading the notes of barely a year ago that I realise how much. There is, of course, no going back; the old John Hardwick is dead.

On the evening of 13th June 1891, I undertook an assignment for the Order of Apollo, one that I had been anticipating for a long time, and one that I accepted without hesitation, despite the risks, despite all I knew. It was not a mission of diplomacy, nor an act of war—it was revenge, pure and simple. On that night, accompanied by a small group of soldiers of my own choosing, plucked from the ranks of my old regiment, I returned at last to the Isle of Dogs.

The Artist had been working feverishly for hours. In the darkness of his studio, his four arms scratched and scrubbed at a large canvas, working in perfect unison like the many legs of a spider spinning an intricate silken thread. The room was dark, save for the pale stream of light from a lonely gaslight outside that shone through the grime-smeared windows of the apartment and threw into stark relief the tall, slender figure of a man possessed, and yet dispossessed—a man without a world. Despite the gloom, every brushstroke, placed as it was at break-neck speed, was daubed in its proper place, with the style and confidence of an accomplished master. Tsun Pen needed no eyes to see; the inspiration flowed through him from an unseen source, his arms working automatically to render his latest masterpiece. He believed himself the weaver of the very strands of fate, the architect of the destinies of lesser men. But he was not; he was a criminal, a murderer, a blackmailer. He was my enemy. And for all his powers of prescience, he had no idea that we stood in the shadows, watching his every move.

Some small sound distracted the Artist for a second, perhaps made by one of my men being uncharacteristically careless. As one Tsun Pen's arms stopped their creative flurry, and he stood in the moonlight, head inclined to listen, motionless as a statue of some many-limbed Eastern deity.

'Hu? You know better than to disturb me when I am working.'

There was no reply, but the Artist seemed to sense at once that he was not alone. I imagined that no one had ever managed to take him by surprise before; leastways not since the fateful night when Lazarus had taken his revenge upon the House of Zhengming, the night when Tsun Pen had become something... other.

'I know you are there,' he said. 'I do not know how you got in here, but it does not matter. You are a fly, and you have flown into the wrong web.'

'Even spiders have their predators,' I said, and took a step forward, this time allowing the boards to creak beneath my boot. The Artist spun instantly in the direction of my voice.

'How, pray tell, did you evade my men? And why did my monkeys not screech at your presence?' The Artist's voice was calm and steady. His business had resumed in the wake of the Othersiders' failed invasion, and once more he operated in the belief that no one would dare do him harm. To Tsun Pen, we were insects, come to frighten and threaten, and we would be found as wanting as the last men who had tried.

'I have my ways,' I said, 'as you have yours.' At an unspoken command, one of my men moved slowly from his position, unfurling himself from the rafters where he had lain for an hour, and allowing himself to make but a small noise as he dropped to the floor—a telltale scuff that would betray the presence of another enemy. Tsun Pen did not turn towards it as we had calculated, instead remaining stock still, facing me, ready to spring into action when the intruders thought him unprepared.

'And why are you here?' the Artist said, warily. 'Surely Scotland Yard has not sent you—they would not be so bold a second time, I think.'

'It does not matter who sent me,' I said, and I sensed Tsun Pen's confusion as my voice came from his right. I had learned much in the intervening year since my torture; if I wished, I could walk unseen and unheard. Even by one such as the Artist. 'All that matters is that your time has come, Tsun Pen.' I unwrapped an object that I had been carrying, and threw it to the floor next to the Artist's feet. It landed with a metallic clang. By the look on Tsun Pen's face, I gathered he knew what it was instantly.

'Poor Hu,' he said, reaching down and picking up the metal hook. 'Loyal to the end.'

'He was.' I was behind him now. Tsun Pen swallowed hard. Was he finally afraid? Was that perspiration on his brow?

He seemed to gather his courage when he spoke. 'Your little games have provided some distraction, and the loss of Hu is most regrettable, but it is time to end the charade and spell out your terms. We both know that not even the police commissioner would dare arrest me, and no judge in the land would convict me. I own them all. So spit it out; what do you want?'

'Take him,' I said. Tsun Pen, with astonishment, realised that the instruction was not aimed at him, but at my men—there were three others in the room, and he had sensed only one, and only then because we had allowed it. The three soldiers rushed at him, but the Artist was slippery as an eel. In an instant he had dropped his brushes and pulled a blade from behind the easel, and his flailing arms moved with uncanny speed against his attackers. One man fell as he was slashed with the razor-sharp knife, another fell to a pummelling fist from the unnatural giant. They battled in the moonlight, thrust and parry, attack and riposte, until I stepped from the shadows myself, silent as a cat, and sliced across the back of the Artist's calf with a slender blade. Tsun Pen went down on one knee, crying out in pain, and the other men pounced upon him like hyenas. He struggled hard against the combined strength of the men who restrained him, but it was to no avail. These predators had the better of him.

With the last of the Artist's struggles over, I stepped towards him, my footfall heavy, measured. He would feel fear this night, this monster, this killer. I walked around to face my enemy. Even on his knees, the Artist was almost as tall as a normal man, and so I leaned forward, so that the Artist could feel my breath on his cheek.

'An eye for an eye,' I said. And the Artist's expression changed, as finally he knew me.

'Captain Hardwick?' said Tsun Pen, and he tried to stifle a mocking laugh. 'So, you have come back twice the man. And it is not the Queen's justice you seek, but vengeance, am I right?'

'These days, they are one and the same thing.' My voice was a growl of barely restrained hatred. The Artist tensed as he felt something cold and sharp scratch against his chest. If he had not been blind, he would have seen the moonlight reflect for a second off the thin fencing blade, and glint off the silver pommel engraved with the monogrammed 'H'.

'You would kill me in cold blood? Unarmed, and restrained? Can you really do this thing, Captain Hardwick?'

'It's Colonel Hardwick now,' I said.

'Pah! Have you finally put to rest the ghost of your father then, and become the dragon of my nightmares? I very much doubt it. You are weak, too weak for the task that has been assigned you.'

My blade plunged into the Artist's chest, as straight and true as an arrow. His breath rattled, and blood bubbled up from his punctured lung to spill out over his robes. I pulled away the sword, and the soldiers let go of the Artist's arms. Tsun Pen dropped to the floor, holding himself up with the last of his strength, trying to form his dying words, though it pained him to do so. Finally, he looked up at me as though he were not blind at all, with that familiar, hateful sneer on his lips.

'Like... father... like son,' he gurgled through his own blood, before dropping to the floor dead.

Only then did I swing a lantern towards the canvas on which the Artist had been working so feverishly. What I saw made me swallow hard, and set my jaw so that no trace of emotion would be displayed to my men.

In the ruins of a great gothic castle, beset with thick cobwebs, a gigantic spider lay in its death throes, its bloated abdomen sliced in twain by the sweeping claws of an enormous red dragon. From the spider's wound, a hundred of its tiny offspring fled, pouring from their grotesque parent like grain from a sack, before climbing towards—and onto—a third figure. A radiant woman with dark eyes, wearing a yellow dress now swarming with arachnids, with a veil of webs draped upon her. I reached out my hand, almost not daring to touch the canvas, but finally put my fingers to Rosanna's face. The wet oil paint smudged at my touch, and I withdrew my hand at once, mortified at the dark stain I had created upon her.

I stepped back from the Artist's body, away from the easel, as the blood slicked across the floorboards towards me. I wiped my blade clean, and left the room.

* * *

We left the Artist's apartments by the back stair, making our way through the twisted innards of the House of Zhengming, a warren of passages and apartments, until eventually we reached a dead end, a passageway terminating at a brick wall where I was certain the inner door to the opium den should have been. To our left was a small set of steps leading to a damp, brick cellar lit by green paper lanterns. The last time I had seen that room, the niches beneath its low vaulted arches had been occupied by the half-dead opium fiends whose entire lives had been given over to chasing the dragon. Now it was cold and empty, and not where it should have been. The dead end should have been the exit to the opium den, I was sure of it. In fact, the back stair should not have led us here at all… Was this a different cellar? It was possible, but it looked so familiar. In the centre of the flagstoned floor was a sad, flat cushion, where the old Chinese man with the rheumy eyes had sat, grinning at me with his gummy mouth.

'We must have got turned around, sir,' said Sergeant Whittock. 'Should have turned left a ways back.' Whittock was a practical man, and a loyal one, which was why I had requested him and the two others be assigned to my command whilst they were on leave from India. Along with Lieutenant Bertrand and Corporal Beechworth, we made up a group of four assassins who had achieved what Special Branch could not.

'Perhaps,' I said, absently. I stepped down into the cellar. The room was twisted, the ceiling and floor uneven—improbably so, I thought, even if it had been under the effects of subsidence for many years. At the far end was a wooden door, which I had not seen before. Stepping towards it, I felt the familiar cold creep up my spine, that strange prescient feeling that had warned me so often of supernatural dangers. Yet the Lazarus Gate was closed, so what was this? I held out a hand and placed it on the rough wood of the little cellar door. The wood did not resist, but instead submitted to my touch, bending as if it were made of rubber. There was a low humming sound coming from behind it, and I knew then that I did not need to open the door. I remembered what the Artist had told me: 'My humble opium den, though unchanged from an outside perspective, has increased in size considerably. Some of the rooms, however, are quite inaccessible, due to the unstable effect of sharing space and time with another universe entirely.' The House of Zhengming was not in this world or the next, but a contorted labyrinth bestriding two universes; at least, I hoped that it was only two. The closure of the Lazarus Gate had not changed the peculiar nature of the Artist's noisome den, and who knew how many doors led to worlds beyond the veil, or what might one day venture through them? I couldn't help but think of the hideous Thing that I had seen in the sky on the other side, the tentacled monster that still haunted my nightmares, scratching inside my mind every time I tried to sleep. I shuddered. I thought of Larry Ecclestone, whose body had never been recovered. Could it be that he had been pushed through one of these doors? And if so, what hell was he now trapped in?

'There is no escape from the house of the dead,' I muttered under my breath.

'What was that, sir?' Lieutenant Bertrand had entered the cellar, wondering what had got into his commander. I turned to him.

'I said we should burn this place. Burn it to the ground.'

ACKNOWLEDGEMENTS

My heartfelt thanks are extended to my friend George Mann, for learnin' me a thing or two and offering much support. Thanks also to former partner in crime Mat Ward, whose advice and patience have been invaluable. A secret handshake goes out to my very own clandestine club, the Diogenes (a.k.a. Andy, Dom, Gav, Adam, Max, and Sarah) for providing a wellspring of inspiration.

As this is a debut novel, it would be remiss not to thank my editor, Ali Nightingale, and my agent, Jamie Cowen, for taking a punt on me. Clearly two people of unimpeachable character, fortitude and astonishing good taste, I'm sure everyone can agree.

The greatest thanks, of course, are reserved for my lovely wife, Alison, not just for believing in *The Lazarus Gate*, but for putting up with my eccentric dildrams and whiff-whaff for so long and with such grace, even in the knowledge that it shall continue for the foreseeable. Or at least until I earn enough shillings to mend the time machine.

ABOUT THE AUTHOR

Mark A. Latham is a writer, editor, history nerd, frustrated grunge singer and amateur baker from Staffordshire, UK. A recent immigrant to rural Nottinghamshire, he lives in a very old house (sadly not haunted), and is still regarded in the village as a foreigner.

Formerly the editor of Games Workshop's *White Dwarf* magazine, Mark dabbled in tabletop games design before becoming a full-time author of strange, fantastical and macabre tales, mostly set in the nineteenth century, a period for which his obsession knows no bounds.

Follow Mark on Twitter: @aLostVictorian